BEST STORIES OF
WALTER DE LA MARE

Best Stories of
WALTER
DE LA MARE

faber and faber
LONDON · BOSTON

First published in 1942
by Faber and Faber Limited
3 Queen Square London WC1N 3AU
Second impression September 1942
Third impression August 1943
Fourth impression April 1945
Fifth impression December 1945
Sixth impression June 1947
Seventh impression February 1957
First published in Faber Paperbacks in 1983
Reprinted 1984

Printed in Great Britain by
Whitstable Litho Ltd., Whitstable, Kent
All rights reserved

British Library Cataloguing in Publication Data

De la Mare, Walter
Best Stories of Walter de la Mare.
I. Title
823'.914(F)   PR6007.E3
ISBN 0-571-13076-3

CONTENTS

*

AUTHOR'S NOTE

*

The stories contained in this volume have been selected from four collections entitled *The Riddle*, *The Connoisseur*, *On the Edge*, and *The Wind Blows Over*. Their arrangement is not in order of date of publication. Needless to say, the 'best' in the title of this volume merely implies a personal preference. No tale from the collections entitled *Broomsticks*, *Told Again*, and *The Lord Fish*, which are intended for children, has been included.

W. DE LA M.

1941

THE ALMOND TREE

*

My old friend, 'the Count' as we used to call him, made
very strange acquaintances at times. Let but a man have
plausibility, a point of view, a crotchet, an enthusiasm, he
would find in him an eager and exhilarating listener. And
though he was often deceived and disappointed in his finds,
the Count had a heart proof against lasting disillusionment.
I confess, however, that these planetary cronies of his were
rather disconcerting at times. And I own that meeting him
one afternoon in the busy High Street, with a companion on
his arm even more than usually voluble and odd—I own I
crossed the road to avoid meeting the pair.

But the Count's eyes had been too sharp for me. He twitted
me unmercifully with my snobbishness. 'I am afraid we must
have appeared to avoid you to-day,' he said; and received my
protestations with contemptuous indifference.

But the next afternoon we took a walk together over the
heath; and perhaps the sunshine, something in the first freshness of the May weather, reminded him of bygone days.

'You remember that rather out-of-the-world friend of mine
yesterday that so shocked your spruce proprieties, Richard?
Well, I'll tell you a story.'

As closely as I can recall this story of the Count's childhood
I have related it. I wish, though, I had my old friend's

gift for such things; then, perhaps, his story might retain something of the charm in the reading which he gave to it in the telling. Perhaps that charm lies wholly in the memory of his voice, his companionship, his friendship. To revive these, what task would be a burden? . . .

'The house of my first remembrance, the house that to my last hour on earth will seem home to me, stood in a small green hollow on the verge of a wide heath. Its five upper windows faced far eastwards towards the weather-cocked tower of a village which rambled down the steep inclination of a hill. And, walking in its green old garden—ah, Richard, the crocuses, the wallflowers, the violets!—you could see in the evening the standing fields of corn, and the dark furrows where the evening star was stationed; and a little to the south, upon a crest, a rambling wood of fir-trees and bracken.

'The house, the garden, the deep quiet orchard, all had been a wedding gift to my mother from a great-aunt, a very old lady in a kind of turban, whose shrewd eyes used to watch me out of her picture sitting in my high cane chair at meal-times— with not a little keenness; sometimes, I fancied, with a faint derision. Here passed by, to the singing of the lark, and the lamentation of autumn wind and rain, the first long nine of all these heaped-up inextricable years. Even now, my heart leaps up with longing to see again with those untutored eyes the lofty clouds of evening; to hear again as then I heard it the two small notes of the yellow-hammer piping from his green spray. I remember every room of the old house, the steep stairs, the cool apple-scented pantry; I remember the cobbles by the scullery, the well, my old dead raven, the bleak and whistling elms; but best of all I remember the unmeasured splendour of the heath, with its gorse, and its deep canopy of sunny air, the haven of every wild bird of the morning.

'Martha Rodd was a mere prim snippet of a maid then, pale and grave, with large contemplative, Puritan eyes. Mrs. Ryder, in her stiff blue martial print and twisted gold brooch, was cook. And besides these, there was only old Thomas the gardener (as out-of-doors, and as distantly seen a creature as a dryad); my mother; and that busy-minded little boy, agog in wits and stomach and spirit—myself. For my father seemed but a familiar guest in the house, a guest ever eagerly desired and welcome, but none too eager to remain. He was a dark man with grey eyes and a long chin; a face unusually impassive, unusually mobile. Just as his capricious mood suggested, our little household was dejected or wildly gay. I never shall forget the spirit of delight he could conjure up at a whim, when my mother would go singing up and down stairs, and in her tiny parlour; and Martha in perfect content would prattle endlessly on to the cook, basting the twirling sirloin, while I watched in the firelight. And the long summer evenings too, when my father would find a secret, a magic, a mystery in everything; and we would sit together in the orchard while he told me tales, with the small green apples overhead, and beyond contorted branches, the first golden twilight of the moon.

'It's an old picture now, Richard, but true to the time.

'My father's will, his word, his caprice, his frown, these were the tables of the law in that small household. To my mother he was the very meaning of her life. Only that little boy was in some wise independent, busy, inquisitive, docile, sedate; though urged to a bitterness of secret rebellion at times. In his childhood he experienced such hours of distress as the years do not in mercy bring again to a heart that may analyse as well as remember. Yet there also sank to rest the fountain of life's happiness. In among the gorse bushes were the green mansions of the fairies; along the furrows before his adventurous eyes stumbled crooked gnomes, hopped bewitched robins. Ariel trebled in the sunbeams and glanced from the dewdrops; and he heard the echo of distant and magic waters in the falling of the rain.

'But my father was never long at peace in the house. Nothing satisfied him; he must needs be at an extreme. And if he was compelled to conceal his discontent, there was something so bitter and imperious in his silence, so scornful a sarcasm in his speech, that we could scarcely bear it. And the knowledge of the influence he had over us served only at such times to sharpen his contempt.

'I remember one summer's evening we had been gathering strawberries. I carried a little wicker basket, and went rummaging under the aromatic leaves, calling ever and again my mother to see the "tremenjous" berry I had found. Martha was busy beside me, vexed that her two hands could not serve her master quick enough. And in a wild race with my mother my father helped us pick. At every ripest one he took her in his arms to force it between her lips; and of those pecked by the birds he made a rhymed offering to Pan. And when the sun had descended behind the hill, and the clamour of the rooks had begun to wane in the elm-tops, he took my mother on his arm, and we trooped all together up the long straggling path, and across the grass, carrying our spoil of fruit into the cool dusky corridor. As we passed into the gloaming I saw my mother stoop impulsively and kiss his arm. He brushed off her hand impatiently, and went into his study. I heard the door shut. A moment afterwards he called for candles. And, looking on those two other faces in the twilight, I knew with the intuition of childhood that he was suddenly sick to death of us all; and I knew that my mother shared my intuition. She sat down, and I beside her, in her little parlour, and took up her sewing. But her face had lost again all its girlishness as she bent her head over the white linen.

'I think she was happier when my father was away; for then, free from anxiety to be for ever pleasing his variable moods, she could entertain herself with hopes and preparations for his return. There was a little summer-house, or arbour, in the garden, where she would sit alone, while the swallows coursed in the evening air. Sometimes, too, she would take me for a long walk, listening distantly to my chatter, only, I think, that she might entertain the pleasure of supposing that my father might have returned home unforeseen, and be even now waiting to greet us. But these fancies would forsake her. She would speak harshly and coldly to me, and scold Martha for her owlishness, and find nothing but vanity and mockery in all that but a little while since had been her daydream.

'I think she rarely knew where my father stayed in his long absences from home. He would remain with us for a week, and neglect us for a month. She was too proud, and when he was himself, too happy and hopeful to question him, and he seemed to delight in keeping his affairs secret from her. Indeed, he sometimes appeared to pretend a mystery where none was, and to endeavour in all things to make his character and conduct appear quixotic and inexplicable.

'So time went on. Yet, it seemed, as each month passed by, the house was not so merry and happy as before; something was fading and vanishing that would not return; estrangement had pierced a little deeper. I think care at last put out of my mother's mind even the semblance of her former gaiety. She sealed up her heart lest love should break forth anew into the bleakness.

'On Guy Fawkes' Day Martha told me at bedtime that a new household had moved into the village on the other side of the heath. After that my father stayed away from us but seldom.

'At first my mother showed her pleasure in a thousand ways, with dainties of her own fancy and cooking, with ribbons in her dark hair, with new songs (though she had but a small thin voice). She read to please him; and tired my legs out in useless errands in his service. And a word of praise sufficed her for many hours of difficulty. But by and by, when evening after evening was spent by my father away from home, she began to be uneasy and depressed; and though she made no complaint, her anxious face, the incessant interrogation of her eyes vexed and irritated him beyond measure.

' "Where does my father go after dinner?" I asked Martha one night, when my mother was in my bedroom, folding my clothes.

' "How dare you ask such a question?" said my mother, "and how dare you talk to the child about your master's comings and goings?"

' "But where does he?" I repeated to Martha, when my mother was gone out of the room.

' "Ssh now, Master Nicholas," she answered, "didn't you hear what your mamma said? She's vexed, poor lady, at master's never spending a whole day at home, but nothing but them cards, cards, cards, every night at Mr. Grey's. Why, often it's twelve and one in the morning when I've heard his foot on the gravel beneath the window. But there, I'll be bound, she doesn't *mean* to speak unkindly. It's a terrible scourge is jealousy, Master Nicholas; and not generous or manly to give it cause. Mrs. Ryder was kept a widow all along of jealousy, and but a week before her wedding with her second."

' "But why is mother jealous of my father playing cards?" 'Martha slipped my nightgown over my head. "Ssh, Master Nicholas, little boys mustn't ask so many questions. And I hope when you are grown up to be a man, my dear, you will be a comfort to your mother. She needs it, poor soul, and sakes alive, just now of all times!" I looked inquisitively into Martha's face; but she screened my eyes with her hand; and instead of further questions, I said my prayers to her.

'A few days after this I was sitting with my mother in her parlour, holding her grey worsted for her to wind, when my father entered the room and bade me put on my hat and muffler. "He is going to pay a call with me," he explained curtly. As I went out of the room, I heard my mother's question, "To your friends at the Grange, I suppose?"

' "You may suppose whatever you please," he answered. I heard my mother rise to leave the room, but he called her back and the door was shut. . . .

'The room in which the card-players sat was very low-ceiled. A piano stood near the window, a rosewood table with a fine dark crimson work-basket upon it by the fireside, and some little distance away, a green card-table with candles burning. Mr. Grey was a slim, elegant man, with a high, narrow forehead and long fingers. Major Aubrey was a short, red-faced, rather taciturn man. There was also a younger man with fair hair. They seemed to be on the best of terms together; and I helped to pack the cards and to pile the silver coins, sipping a glass of sherry with Mr. Grey. My father said little, paying me no attention, but playing gravely with a very slight frown.

'After some little while the door opened, and a lady appeared. This was Mr. Grey's sister, Jane, I learned. She seated herself at her work-table, and drew me to her side.

' "Well, so this is Nicholas!" she said. "Or is it Nick?"

' "Nicholas," I said.

' "Of course," she said, smiling, "and I like that too, much the best. How very kind of you to come to see me! It was to keep *me* company, you know, because I am very stupid at games, but I love talking. Do you?"

'I looked into her eyes, and knew we were friends. She smiled again, with open lips, and touched my mouth with her thimble. "Now, let me see, business first, and—me afterwards. You see I have three different kinds of cake, because, I thought, I cannot in the least tell which kind he'll like best. Could I now? Come, you shall choose."

'She rose and opened the long door of a narrow cupboard, looking towards the card-players as she stooped. I remember the cakes to this day; little oval shortbreads stamped with a beehive, custards and mince-pies; and a great glass jar of goodies which I carried in both arms round the little square table. I took a mince-pie, and sat down on a footstool near by Miss Grey, and she talked to me while she worked with slender hands at her lace embroidery. I told her how old I was; about my great-aunt and her three cats. I told her my dreams, and that I was very fond of Yorkshire pudding, "from under the meat, you know". And I told her I thought my father the handsomest man I had ever seen.

' "What, handsomer than Mr. Spencer?" she said laughing, looking along her needle.

'I answered that I did not very much like clergymen.

' "And why?" she said gravely.

' "Because they do not talk like real," I said.

'She laughed very gaily. "Do men ever?" she said.

'And her voice was so quiet and so musical, her neck so graceful, I thought her a very beautiful lady, admiring especially her dark eyes when she smiled brightly and yet half sadly at me; I promised, moreover, that if she would meet me on the heath, I would show her the rabbit warren and the "Miller's Pool".

' "Well, Jane, and what do you think of my son?" said my father when we were about to leave.

'She bent over me and squeezed a lucky fourpenny-piece into my hand. "I love fourpence, pretty little fourpence, I love fourpence better than my life," she whispered into my ear. "But that's a secret," she added, glancing up over her shoulder. She kissed lightly the top of my head. I was looking at my father while she was caressing me, and I fancied a faint sneer passed over his face. But when we had come out of the village on to the heath, in the bare keen night, as we walked along the path together between the gorse-bushes, now on turf, and now on stony ground, never before had he seemed so wonderful a companion. He told me little stories; he began a hundred, and finished none; yet with the stars above us, they seemed a string of beads all of bright colours. We stood still in the vast darkness, while he whistled that strangest of all old songs—"the Song the Sirens sang". He pilfered my wits and talked like my double. But when—how much too quickly, I thought with sinking heart—we were come to the house-gates, he suddenly fell silent, turned an instant, and stared far away over the windy heath.

' "How weary, flat, stale——" he began, and broke off between uneasy laughter and a sigh. "Listen to me, Nicholas," he said, lifting my face to the starlight, "you must grow up a man—a Man, you understand; no vapourings, no posings, no caprices; and above all, no sham. No sham. It's your one and only chance in this unfaltering Scheme." He scanned my face long and closely. "You have your mother's eyes," he said musingly. "And that," he added under his breath, "*that's* no joke." He pushed open the squealing gate and we went in.

'My mother was sitting in a low chair before a dying and cheerless fire.

' "Well, Nick," she said very suavely, "and how have you enjoyed your evening?"

'I stared at her without answer. "Did you play cards with the gentlemen; or did you turn over the music?"

' "I talked to Miss Grey," I said.

' "Really," said my mother, raising her eyebrows, "and who then is Miss Grey?" My father was smiling at us with sparkling eyes.

' "Mr. Grey's sister," I answered in a low voice.

' "Not his wife, then?" said my mother, glancing furtively at the fire. I looked towards my father in doubt but could lift my eyes no higher than his knees.

' "You little fool!" he said to my mother with a laugh, "what a sharpshooter! Never mind, Sir Nick; there, run off to bed, my man."

'My mother caught me roughly by the sleeve as I was passing her chair. "Aren't you going to kiss me good night, then," she said furiously, her narrow under-lip quivering, "you tool!" I kissed her cheek. "That's right, my dear," she said scornfully, "that's how little fishes kiss." She rose and drew back her skirts. "I refuse to stay in the room," she said haughtily, and with a sob she hurried out.

'My father continued to smile, but only a smile it seemed gravity had forgotten to smooth away. He stood very still, so still that I grew afraid he must certainly hear me thinking. Then with a kind of sigh he sat down at my mother's writing table, and scribbled a few words with his pencil on a slip of paper.

' "There, Nicholas, just tap at your mother's door with that. Good night, old fellow," he took my hand and smiled down into my eyes with a kind of generous dark appeal that called me straight to his side. I hastened conceitedly upstairs, and delivered my message. My mother was crying when she opened the door.

' "Well?" she said in a low, trembling voice.

'But presently afterwards, while I was still lingering in the dark corridor, I heard her run down quickly, and in a while my father and mother came upstairs together, arm in arm, and by her light talk and laughter you might suppose she had no knowledge of care or trouble at all.

'Never afterwards did I see so much gaiety and youthfulness in my mother's face as when she sat next morning with us at breakfast. The honeycomb, the small bronze chrysanthemums, her yellow gown seemed dainty as a miniature. With every word her eyes would glance covertly at my father; her smile, as it were, hesitating between her lashes. She was so light and girlish and so versatile I should scarcely have recognized the weary and sallow face of the night before. My father seemed to find as much pleasure, or relief, in her good spirits as I did; and to delight in exercising his ingenuity to quicken her humour.

'It was but a transient morning of sunshine, however, and as the brief and sombre day waned, its gloom pervaded the house. In the evening my father left us to our solitude as usual. And that night was very misty over the heath, with a small, warm rain falling.

'So it happened that I began to be left more and more to my own devices, and grew so inured at last to my own narrow company and small thoughts and cares, that I began to look on my mother's unhappiness almost with indifference, and learned to criticize almost before I had learned to pity. And so I do not think I enjoyed Christmas very much the less, although my father was away from home and all our little festivities were dispirited. I had plenty of good things to eat, and presents, and a picture-book from Martha. I had a new rocking-horse—how changeless and impassive its mottled battered face looks out at me across the years! It was brisk, clear weather, and on St. Stephen's Day I went to see if there was any ice yet on the Miller's Pool.

'I was stooping down at the extreme edge of the pool, snapping the brittle splinters of the ice with my finger, when I heard a voice calling me in the still air. It was Jane Grey, walking on the heath with my father, who had called me having seen me from a distance stooping beside the water.

' "So you see I have kept my promise," she said, taking my hand.

' "But you promised to come by yourself," I said.

' "Well, so I will then," she answered, nodding her head. "Good-bye," she added, turning to my father. "It's three's none, you see. Nicholas shall take me home to tea, and you can call for him in the evening, if you will; that is, if you are coming."

' "Are you asking me to come?" he said moodily, "do you care whether I come or not?"

'She lifted her face and spoke gravely. "You are my friend," she said, "of course I care whether you are with me or not." He scrutinized her through half-closed lids. His face was haggard, gloomy with *ennui*. "How you harp on the word, you punctilious Jane. Do you suppose I am still in my teens?

Twenty years ago, now—— It amuses me to hear you women talk. It's little you ever really feel."

' "I don't think I am quite without feeling," she replied, "you are a little difficult, you know."

' "Difficult," he echoed in derision. He checked himself and shrugged his shoulders. "You see, Jane, it's all on the surface; I boast of my indifference. It's the one rag of philosophy age denies no one. It is so easy to be mock-heroic—debonair, iron-grey, rhetorical, dramatic—you know it only too well, perhaps? But after all, life's comedy, when one stops smiling, is only the tepidest farce. Or the gilt wears off and the pinchbeck tragedy shows through. And so, as I say, we talk on, being past feeling. One by one our hopes come home to roost, our delusions find themselves out, and the mystery proves to be nothing but sleight-of-hand. It's age, my dear Jane—age; it turns one to stone. With you young people life's a dream; ask Nicholas here!" He shrugged his shoulders, adding under his breath, "But one wakes on a devilish hard pallet."

' "Of course," said Jane slowly, "you are only talking cleverly, and then it does not matter whether it's true or not, I suppose. I can't say. I don't think you mean it, and so it comes to nothing. I can't and won't believe you feel so little —I can't." She continued to smile, yet, I fancied, with the brightness of tears in her eyes. "It's all mockery and make-believe; we are not the miserable slaves of time you try to fancy. There must be some way to win through." She turned away, then added slowly, "You ask me to be fearless, sincere, to speak my heart; I wonder, do you?"

'My father did not look at her, appeared not to have seen the hand she had half held out to him, and as swiftly withdrawn. "The truth is, Jane," he said slowly, "I am past sincerity now. And as for *heart* it is a quite discredited organ at forty. Life, thought, selfishness, egotism, call it what you will; they have all done their worst with me; and I really haven't the sentiment to pretend that they haven't. And when bright

youth and sentiment are gone; why, go too, dear lady!
Existence proves nothing but brazen inanity afterwards. But
there's always that turning left to the dullest and dustiest road
—oblivion." He remained silent a moment. Silence deep and
strange lay all around us. The air was still, the wintry sky
unutterably calm. And again that low dispassionate voice continued: "It's only when right seems too easy a thing, too
trivial, and not worth the doing; and wrong a foolish thing—
too dull. . . . There, take care of her, Nicholas; take care of
her, 'snips and snails,' you know. *Au revoir*, 'pon my word, I
almost wish it was good-bye."

'Jane Grey regarded him attentively. "So then do I," she
replied in a low voice, "for I shall never understand you;
perhaps I should hate to understand you."

'My father turned with an affected laugh, and left us.

'Miss Grey and I walked slowly along beside the frosty
bulrushes until we came to the wood. The bracken and heather
were faded. The earth was dark and rich with autumnal rains.
Fir-cones lay on the moss beneath the dark green branches. It
was all now utterly silent in the wintry afternoon. Far away
rose tardily, and alighted, the hoarse rooks upon the ploughed
earth; high in the pale sky passed a few on ragged wing.

' "What does my father mean by wishing it was good-bye?"
I said.

'But my companion did not answer me in words. She
clasped my hand; she seemed very slim and gracious walking
by my side on the hardened ground. My mother was small
now and awkward beside her in my imagination. I questioned
her about the ice, about the red sky, and if there was any
mistletoe in the woods. Sometimes she, in turn, asked me
questions too, and when I answered them we would look at
each other and smile, and it seemed it was with her as it was
with me—of the pure gladness I found in her company. In the
middle of our walk to the Thorns she bent down in the cold
twilight, and putting her hands on my shoulders, "My dear,

dear Nicholas," she said, "you must be a good son to your mother—brave and kind; will you?"

' "He hardly ever speaks to mother now," I answered instinctively.

'She pressed her lips to my cheek, and her cheek was cold against mine, and she clasped her arms about me. "Kiss me," she said, "We must do our best, mustn't we?" she pleaded, still holding me. I looked mournfully into the gathering darkness. "That's easy when you're grown up," I said. She laughed and kissed me again, and then we took hands and ran till we were out of breath, towards the distant lights of the Thorns. . . .

'I had been some time in bed, lying awake in the warmth, when my mother came softly through the darkness into my room. She sat down at the bedside, breathing hurriedly. "Where have you been all the evening?" she said.

' "Miss Grey asked me to stay to tea," I answered.

' "Did I give you permission to go to tea with Miss Grey?"

'I made no answer.

' "If you go to that house again, I shall beat you. You hear me, Nicholas? Alone, or with your father, if you go there again, without my permission, I shall beat you. You have not been whipped for a long time, have you?" I could not see her face, but her head was bent towards me in the dark, as she sat—almost crouched—on my bedside.

'I made no answer. But when my mother had gone, without kissing me, I cried noiselessly on in to my pillow. Something had suddenly flown out of memory, never to sing again. Life had become a little colder and stranger. I had always been my own chief company; now another sentimental barrier had arisen between the world and me, past its heedlessness, past my understanding to break down.

'Hardly a week passed now without some bitter quarrel. I seemed to be perpetually stealing out of sound of angry voices; fearful of being made the butt of my father's serene taunts, of my mother's passions and desperate remorse. He disdained to defend himself against her, never reasoned with her; he merely shrugged his shoulders, denied her charges, ignored her anger; coldly endeavouring only to show his indifference, to conceal by every means in his power his own inward weariness and vexation. I saw this, of course, only vaguely, yet with all a child's certainty of insight, though I rarely knew the cause of my misery; and I continued to love them both in my selfish fashion, not a whit the less.

'At last, on St. Valentine's Day, things came to a worse pass than ever. It had always been my father's custom to hang my mother a valentine on the handle of her little parlour door, a string of pearls, a fan, a book of poetry, whatever it might be. She came down early this morning, and sat in the window-seat, looking out at the falling snow. She said nothing at breakfast, only feigned to eat, lifting her eyes at intervals to glance at my father with a strange intensity, as if of hatred, tapping her foot on the floor. He took no notice of her, sat quiet and moody with his own thoughts. I think he had not really forgotten the day, for I found long afterwards in his old bureau a bracelet purchased but a week before with her name written on a scrap of paper, inside the case. Yet it seemed to be the absence of this little gift that had driven my mother beyond reason.

'Towards evening, tired of the house, tired of being alone, I went out and played for a while listlessly in the snow. At night-fall I went in; and in the dark heard angry voices. My father came out of the dining-room and looked at me in silence, standing in the gloom of the wintry dusk. My mother followed him. I can see her now, leaning in the doorway, white with rage, her eyes ringed and darkened with continuous trouble, her hand trembling.

' "It shall learn to hate you," she cried in a low, dull voice. "I will teach it every moment to hate and despise you as I—— Oh, *I* hate and despise you."

'My father looked at her calmly and profoundly before replying. He took up a cloth hat and brushed it with his hand. "Very well then, you have chosen," he said coldly. "It has always lain with you. You have exaggerated, you have raved, and now you have said what can never be recalled or forgotten. Here's Nicholas. Pray do not imagine, however, that I am defending myself. I have nothing to defend. I think of no one but myself—no one. Endeavour to understand me, no one. Perhaps, indeed, you yourself—no more than—— But words again—the dull old round!" He made a peculiar gesture with his hand. "Well, life is . . . ach! I have done. So be it." He stood looking out of the door. "You see, it's snowing," he said, as if to himself.

'All the long night before and all day long, snow had been falling continuously. The air was wintry and cold. I could discern nothing beyond the porch but a gloomy accumulation of cloud in the twilight air, now darkened with the labyrinthine motion of the snow. My father glanced back for an instant into the house, and, as I fancy, regarded me with a kind of strange, close earnestness. But he went out and his footsteps were instantly silenced.

'My mother peered at me in a dreadful perplexity, her eyes wide with terror and remorse. "What? What?" she said. I stared at her stupidly. Three snowflakes swiftly and airily floated together into the dim hall from the gloom without. She clasped her hand over her mouth. Overburdened her fingers seemed to be, so slender were they, with her many rings.

' "Nicholas, Nicholas, tell me; what was I saying? What was I saying?" She stumbled hastily to the door. "Arthur, Arthur," she cried from the porch, "it's St. Valentine's Day. That was all I meant; come back, come back!" But perhaps my father was already out of hearing; I do not think he made any reply.

'My mother came in doubtfully, resting her hand on the wall. And she walked very slowly and laboriously upstairs.

While I was standing at the foot of the staircase, looking out across the hall into the evening, Martha climbed primly up from the kitchen with her lighted taper, shut-to the door and lit the hall lamp. Already the good smell of the feast cooking floated up from the kitchen, and gladdened my spirits. "Will he come back?" Martha said, looking very scared in the light of her taper. "It's such a fall of snow, already it's a hand's breadth on the window-sill. Oh, Master Nicholas, it's a hard world for us women." She followed my mother upstairs, carrying light to all the gloomy upper rooms.

'I sat down in the window-seat of the dining-room, and read in my picture-book as well as I could by the flame-light. By and by, Martha returned to lay the table.

'As far back as brief memory carried me, it had been our custom to make a Valentine's feast on the Saint's day. This was my father's mother's birthday also. When she was alive I well remember her visiting us with her companion, Miss Schreiner, who talked in such good-humoured English to me. This same anniversary had last year brought about a tender reconciliation between my father and mother, after a quarrel that meant how little then. And I remember on this day to have seen the first fast-sealed buds upon the almond tree. We would have a great spangled cake in the middle of the table, with marzipan and comfits, just as at Christmas-time. And when Mrs. Merry lived in the village, her little fair daughters used to come in a big carriage to spend the evening with us and to share my Valentine's feast.

'But all this was changed now. My wits were sharper, but I was none the less only the duller for that; my hopes and dreams had a little fallen and faded. I looked idly at my picture-book, vaguely conscious that its colours pleased me less than once upon a time; that I was rather tired of seeing them, and they just as tired of seeing me. And yet I had nothing else to do, so I must go on with a hard face, turning listlessly the pictured pages.

'About seven o'clock my mother sent for me. I found her sitting in her bedroom. Candles were burning before the looking-glass. She was already dressed in her handsome black silk gown, and wearing her pearl necklace. She began to brush my hair, curling its longer ends with her fingers, which she moistened in the pink bowl that was one of the first things I had set eyes on in this world. She put me on a clean blouse and my buckle shoes, talking to me the while, almost as if she were telling me a story. Then she looked at herself long and earnestly in the glass; throwing up her chin with a smile, as was a habit of hers in talk. I wandered about the room, fingering the little toilet-boxes and nick-nacks on the table. By mischance I upset one of these, a scent-bottle that held rose-water. The water ran out and filled the warm air with its fragrance. "You foolish, clumsy boy!" said my mother, and slapped my hand. More out of vexation and tiredness than because of the pain, I began to cry. And then, with infinite tenderness, she leaned her head on my shoulder. "Mother can't think very well just now," she said; and cried so bitterly in silence that I was only too ready to extricate myself and run away when her hold on me relaxed.

'I climbed slowly upstairs to Martha's bedroom, and kneeling on a cane chair looked out of the window. The flakes had ceased to fall now, although the snowy heath was encompassed in mist. Above the snow the clouds had parted, drifting from beneath the stars, and these in their constellations were trembling very brightly, and here and there burned one of them in solitude, larger and wilder in its radiance than the rest. But though I did not tire of looking out of the window, my knees began to ache; and the little room was very cold and still so near the roof. So I went down to the dining-room, with all its seven candlesticks kindled, seeming to my unaccustomed eyes a very splendid blaze out of the dark. My mother was kneeling on the rug by the fireside. She looked very small, even dwarfish, I thought. She was gazing into the flames; one shoe curved beneath the hem of her gown, her chin resting on her hand.

'I surveyed the table with its jellies and sweetmeats and glasses and fruit, and began to be very hungry, so savoury was the smell of the turkey roasting downstairs. Martha knocked at the door when the clock had struck eight.

' "Dinner is ready, ma'am."

'My mother glanced fleetingly at the clock. "Just a little, only a very little while longer, tell Mrs. Ryder; your master will be home in a minute." She rose and placed the claret in the hearth at some distance from the fire.

' "Is it nicer warm, Mother?" I said. She looked at me with startled eyes and nodded. "Did you hear anything, Nicholas? Run to the door and listen; was that a sound of footsteps?"

'I opened the outer door and peered into the darkness; but it seemed the world ended here with the warmth and the light: beyond could extend only winter and silence, a region that, familiar though it was to me, seemed now to terrify me like an enormous sea.

' "It's stopped snowing," I said, "but there isn't anybody there; nobody at all, Mother."

'The hours passed heavily from quarter on to quarter. The turkey, I grieved to hear, was to be taken out of the oven, and put away to cool in the pantry. I was bidden help myself to what I pleased of the trembling jellies, and delicious pink blanc-mange. Already midnight would be the next hour to be chimed. I felt sick, yet was still hungry and very tired. The candles began to burn low. "Leave me a little light here, then," my mother said at last to Martha, "and go to bed. Perhaps your master has missed his way home in the snow." But Mrs. Ryder had followed Martha into the room.

' "You must pardon my interference, ma'am, but it isn't right, it isn't really right of you to sit up longer. Master will not come back, maybe, before morning. And I shouldn't be doing my bounden duty, ma'am, except I spoke my mind. Just now too, of all times."

' "Thank you very much, Mrs. Ryder," my mother answered simply "but I would prefer not to go to bed yet. It's very lonely on the heath at night. But I shall not want anything else, thank you."

' "Well, ma'am, I've had my say, and done my conscience's bidding. And I have brought you up this tumbler of mulled wine; else you'll be sinking away or something with the fatigue."

'My mother took the wine, sipped of it with a wan smile at Mrs. Ryder over the brim; and Mrs. Ryder retired with Martha. I don't think they had noticed me sitting close in the shadow on my stool beside the table. But all through that long night, I fancy, these good souls took it in turn to creep down stealthily and look in on us; and in the small hours of the morning, when the fire had fallen low they must have wrapped us both warm in shawls. They left me then, I think, to be my mother's company. Indeed, I remember we spoke in the darkness, and she took my hand.

'My mother and I shared the steaming wine together when they were gone; our shadows looming faintly huge upon the ceiling. We said very little, but I looked softly into her grey childish eyes, and we kissed one another kneeling there together before the fire. And afterwards, I jigged softly round the table, pilfering whatever sweet or savoury mouthful took my fancy. But by and by in the silent house—a silence broken only by the fluttering of the flames, and the odd far-away stir of the frost, drowsiness vanquished me; I sat down by the fireside, leaning my head on a chair. And sitting thus, vaguely eyeing firelight and wavering shadow, I began to nod, and very soon dream stalked in, mingling with reality.

'It was early morning when I awoke, dazed and cold and miserable in my uncomfortable resting-place. The rare odour of frost was on the air. The ashes of the fire lay iron-grey upon the cold hearth. An intensely clear white ray of light leaned up through a cranny of the shutters to the cornice of the ceiling. I got up with difficulty. My mother was still asleep, breathing heavily, and as I stooped, regarding her curiously, I could almost watch her transient dreams fleeting over her face; and now she smiled faintly; and now she raised her eyebrows as if in some playful and happy talk with my father; then again utterly still darkness would descend on brow and lid and lip.

'I touched her sleeve, suddenly conscious of my loneliness in the large house. Her face clouded instantly, she sighed profoundly: "What?" she said, "nothing—nothing?" She stretched out her hand towards me; the lids drew back from eyes still blind from sleep. But gradually time regained its influence over her. She moistened her lips and turned to me, and suddenly, in a gush of agony, remembrance of the night returned to her. She hid her face in her hands, rocking her body gently to and fro; then rose and smoothed back her hair at the looking-glass. I was surprised to see no trace of tears on her cheeks. Her lips moved, as if unconsciously a heart worn out with grief addressed that pale reflection of her sorrow in the glass. I took hold of the hand that hung down listlessly on her silk skirt, and fondled it, kissing punctiliously each loose ring in turn.

'But I do not think she heeded my kisses. So I returned to the table on which was still set out the mockery of our Valentine feast, strangely disenchanted in the chill dusk of daybreak. I put a handful of wine biscuits and a broken piece of cake in my pocket; for a determination had taken me to go out on to the heath. My heart beat thick and fast in imagination of the solitary snow and of myself wandering in loneliness across its untrampled surface. A project also was forming in my mind of walking over to the Thorns; for somehow I knew my mother would not scold or punish me that day. Perhaps, I thought, my father would be there. And I would tell Miss Grey all about my adventure of the night spent down in the dining-room. So moving very stealthily, and betraying no eagerness, lest I should be forbidden to go, I stole at length unnoticed from the room, and leaving the great hall door ajar, ran out joyously into the wintry morning.

'Already dawn was clear and high in the sky, already the first breezes were moving in the mists; and breathed chill, as if it were the lingering darkness itself on my cheeks. The air was cold, yet with a fresh faint sweetness. The snow lay crisp across its perfect surface, mounded softly over the gorse-bushes, though here and there a spray of parched blossom yet protruded from its cowl. Flaky particles of ice floated invisible in the air. I called out with pleasure to see the little ponds where the snow had been blown away from the black ice. I saw on the bushes too the webs of spiders stretched from thorn to thorn, and festooned with crystals of hoar-frost. I turned and counted as far as I could my footsteps leading back to the house, which lay roofed in gloomy pallor, dim and obscured in the darkened west.

'A waning moon that had risen late in the night shone, it seemed, very near to the earth. But every moment light swept invincibly in, pouring its crystal like a river; and darkness sullenly withdrew into the north. And when at last the sun appeared, glittering along the rosy snow, I turned in an ecstasy and with my finger pointed him out, as if the house I had left behind me might view him with my own delight. Indeed, I saw its windows transmuted, and heard afar a thrush pealing in the bare branches of a pear-tree; and a robin startled me, so suddenly shrill and sweet he broke into song from a snowy tuft of gorse.

'I was now come to the beginning of a gradual incline, from the summit of which I should presently descry in the distance the avenue of lindens that led towards the village from the margin of the heath. As I went on my way, munching my biscuits, looking gaily about me, I brooded deliciously on the breakfast which Miss Grey would doubtless sit me down to;

and almost forgot the occasion of my errand, and the troubled house I had left behind me. At length I climbed to the top of the smooth ridge and looked down. At a little distance from me grew a crimson hawthorn-tree that often in past Aprils I had used for a green tent from the showers; but now it was closely hooded, darkening with its faint shadow the long expanse of unshadowed whiteness. Not very far from this bush I perceived a figure lying stretched along the snow and knew instinctively that this was my father lying here.

'The sight did not then surprise or dismay me. It seemed only the lucid sequel to that long heavy night-watch, to all the troubles and perplexities of the past. I felt no sorrow, but stood beside the body, regarding it only with deep wonder and a kind of earnest curiosity, yet perhaps with a remote pity too, that he could not see me in the beautiful morning. His grey hand lay arched in the snow, his darkened face, on which showed a smear of dried blood, was turned away a little as if out of the oblique sunshine. I understood that he was dead, and had already begun speculating on what changes it would make; how I should spend my time; what would happen in the house now that he was gone, his influence, his authority, his discord. I remembered too that I was alone, was master of this immense secret, that I must go home sedately, as if it were a Sunday, and in a low voice tell my mother, concealing any exultation I might feel in the office. I imagined the questions that would be asked me, and was considering the proper answers to make to them, when my morbid dreams were suddenly broken in on by Martha Rodd. She stood in my footsteps, looking down on me from the ridge from which I had but just now descended. She hastened towards me, stooping a little as if she were carrying a heavy bundle, her mouth ajar, her forehead wrinkled beneath its wispy light brown hair.

' "Look, Martha, look," I cried, "I found him in the snow; he's dead." And suddenly a bond seemed to snap in my heart. The beauty and solitude of the morning, the perfect whiteness of the snow—it was all an uncouth mockery against me—a subtle and quiet treachery. The tears gushed into my eyes and in my fear and affliction I clung to the poor girl, sobbing bitterly, protesting my grief, hiding my eyes in terror from that still, inscrutable shape. She smoothed my hair with her hand again and again, her eyes fixed; and then at last, venturing cautiously nearer, she stooped over my father. "O Master Nicholas," she said, "his poor dark hair! What will we do now? What will your poor mamma do now, and him gone?" She hid her face in her hands, and our tears gushed out anew.

'But my grief was speedily forgotten. The novelty of being left entirely alone, my own master; to go where I would; to do as I pleased; the experience of being pitied most when I least needed it, and then—when misery and solitariness came over me like a cloud—of being utterly ignored, turned my thoughts gradually away. My father's body was brought home and laid in my mother's little parlour that looked out on to the garden and the snowy orchard. The house was darkened. I took a secret pleasure in peeping in on the sunless rooms, and stealing from door to door through corridors screened from the daylight. My mother was ill; and for some inexplicable reason I connected her illness with the bevy of gentlemen dressed in black who came one morning to the house and walked away together over the heath. Finally Mrs. Marshall drove up one afternoon from Islington, and by the bundles she had brought with her and her grained box with the iron handles I knew that she was come, as once before in my experience, to stay.

'I was playing on the morrow in the hall with my leaden soldiers when there came into my mind vaguely the voices of Mrs. Ryder and of Mrs. Marshall gossiping together on their tedious way upstairs from the kitchen.

'"No, Mrs. Marshall, nothing," I heard Mrs. Ryder saying, "not one word, not one word. And now the poor dear lady left quite alone, and only the doctor to gainsay that fatherless mite from facing the idle inquisitive questions of all them strangers. It's neither for me nor you, Mrs. Marshall, to speak out just what comes into our heads here and now. The ways of the Almighty are past understanding—but a kinder at *heart* never trod this earth."

' "Ah," said Mrs. Marshall.

' "I knew to my sorrow," continued Mrs. Ryder, "there was words in the house; but there, wheresoever you be there's that. Human beings ain't angels, married or single, and in every——"

' "Wasn't there talk of some——?" insinuated Mrs. Marshall discreetly.

' "Talk, Mrs. Marshall," said Mrs. Ryder, coming to a standstill, "I scorn the word! A pinch of truth in a hogshead of falsehood. I don't gainsay it even. I just shut my ears—there—with the dead." Mrs. Marshall had opened her mouth to reply when I was discovered, crouched as small as possible at the foot of the stairs.

' "Well, here's pitchers!" said Mrs. Marshall pleasantly. "And this is the poor fatherless manikin, I suppose. It's hard on the innocent, Mrs. Ryder, and him grown such a sturdy child too, as I said from the first. Well, now, and don't you remember me, little man, don't you remember Mrs. Marshall? He ought to, now!"

' "He's a very good boy in general," said Mrs. Ryder, "and I'm sure I hope and pray he'll grow up to be a comfort to his poor widowed mother, if so be——" They glanced earnestly at one another, and Mrs. Marshall stooped with a sigh of effort and drew a big leather purse from a big loose pocket under her skirt, and selected a bright ha'penny-piece from among its silver and copper.

' "I make no doubt he will, poor mite," she said cheerfully; I took the ha'penny in silence and the two women passed slowly upstairs.

'In the afternoon, in order to be beyond call of Martha, I went out on to the heath with a shovel, intent on building a great tomb in the snow. Yet more snow had fallen during the night; it now lay so deep as to cover my socks above my shoes. I laboured very busily, shovelling, beating, moulding, stamping. So intent was I that I did not see Miss Grey until she was close beside me. I looked up from the snow and was surprised to find the sun already set and the low mists of evening approaching. Miss Grey was veiled and dressed in furs to the throat. She drew her ungloved hand from her muff.

' "Nicholas," she said in a low voice.

'I stood for some reason confused and ashamed without answering her. She sat down on my shapeless mound of snow, and took me by the hand. Then she drew up her veil, and I saw her face pale and darkened, and her clear dark eyes gravely gazing into mine.

' "My poor, poor Nicholas," she said, and continued to gaze at me with her warm hand clasping mine. "What can I say? What can I do? Isn't it very, very lonely out here in the snow?"

' "I didn't feel lonely much," I answered, "I was making a—I was playing at building."

' "And I am sitting on your beautiful snow-house, then?" she said, smiling sadly, her hand trembling upon mine.

' "It isn't a house," I answered, turning away.

'She pressed my hand on the furs at her throat.

' "Poor cold, blue hands," she said. "Do you like playing alone?"

' "I like you being here," I answered. "I wish you would come always, or at least sometimes."

'She drew me close to her, smiling, and bent and kissed my head.

' "There," she said, "I am here now."

' "Mother's ill," I said.

'She drew back and looked out over the heath towards the house.

' "They have put my father in the little parlour, in his coffin,

32

of course; you know he's dead, and Mrs. Marshall's come; she gave me a ha'penny this morning. Dr. Graham gave me a whole crown, though." I took it out of my breeches pocket and showed it her.

' "That's very, very nice," she said. "What lots of nice things you can buy with it! And, look, I am going to give you a little keepsake too, between just you and me."

'It was a small silver box that she drew out of her muff, and embossed in the silver of the lid was a crucifix. "I thought, perhaps, I should see you to-day, you know," she continued softly. "Now, who's given you this?" she said, putting the box into my hand.

' "You," I answered softly.

' "And who am I?"

' "Miss Grey," I said.

' "Your friend, Jane Grey," she repeated, as if she were fascinated by the sound of her own name. "Say it now—Always my friend, Jane Grey."

'I repeated it after her.

' "And now," she continued, "tell me which room is—is the little parlour. Is it that small window at the corner under the ivy?"

'I shook my head.

' "Which?" she said in a whisper, after a long pause.

'I twisted my shovel in the snow. "Would you like to see my father?" I asked her. "I am sure, you know, Martha would not mind; and mother's in bed." She started, her dark eyes dwelling strangely on mine. "But Nicholas, you poor lamb; where?" she said, without stirring.

' "It's at the back, a little window that comes out—if you were to come this evening, I would be playing in the hall; I always play in the hall, after tea, if I can; and now, always. Nobody would see you at all, you know."

'She sighed. "O what are you saying?" she said, and stood up, drawing down her veil.

' "But would you like to?" I repeated. She stooped suddenly, pressing her veiled face to mine. "I'll come, I'll come," she said, her face utterly changed so close to my eyes. "We can both still—still be loyal to him, can't we, Nicholas?"

'She walked away quickly, towards the pool and the little darkened wood. I looked after her and knew that she would be waiting there alone till evening. I looked at my silver box with great satisfaction, and after opening it, put it into my pocket with my crown piece and my ha'penny, and continued my building for awhile.

'But now zest for it was gone; and I began to feel cold, the frost closing in keenly as darkness gathered. So I went home.

'My silence and suspicious avoidance of scrutiny and question passed unnoticed. Indeed, I ate my tea in solitude, except that now and again one or other of the women would come bustling in on some brief errand. A peculiar suppressed stir was in the house. I wondered what could be the cause of it; and began suddenly to be afraid of my project being discovered.

'None the less I was playing in the evening, as I had promised, close to the door, alert to catch the faintest sign of the coming of my visitor.

' "Run down to the kitchen, dearie," said Martha. Her cheeks were flushed. She was carrying a big can of steaming water. "You must keep very, *very* quiet this evening and go to bed like a good boy, and perhaps to-morrow morning I'll tell you a great, great secret." She kissed me with hasty rapture. I was not especially inquisitive of her secret just then, and eagerly promised to be quite quiet if I might continue to play where I was.

' "Well, very, *very* quiet then, and you mustn't let Mrs. Marshall," she began, but hurried hastily away in answer to a peremptory summons from upstairs.

'Almost as soon as she was gone I heard a light rap on

the door. It seemed that Jane Grey had brought in with her the cold and freshness of the woods. I led the way on tiptoe down the narrow corridor and into the small, silent room. The candles burned pure and steadfastly in their brightness. The air was still and languid with the perfume of flowers. Overhead passed light, heedful footsteps; but they seemed not a disturbing sound, only a rumour beyond the bounds of silence.

' "I am very sorry," I said, "but they have nailed it down. Martha says the men came this afternoon."

'Miss Grey took a little bunch of snowdrops from her bosom, and hid them in among the clustered wreaths of flowers; and she knelt down on the floor, with a little silver cross which she sometimes wore pressed tight to her lips. I felt ill at ease to see her praying, and wished I could go back to my soldiers. But while I watched her, seeing in marvellous brilliancy everything in the little room, and remembering dimly the snow lying beneath the stars in the darkness of the garden, I listened also to the quiet footsteps passing to and fro in the room above. Suddenly, the silence was broken by a small, continuous, angry crying.

'Miss Grey looked up. Her eyes were very clear and wonderful in the candlelight.

' "What was that?" she said faintly, listening.

'I stared at her. The cry welled up anew, piteously; as if of a small remote and helpless indignation.

' "Why it sounds just like a—little baby," I said.

'She crossed herself hastily and arose. "Nicholas!" she said in a strange, quiet, bewildered voice—yet her face was most curiously bright. She looked at me lovingly and yet so strangely I wished I had not let her come in.

'She went out as she had entered. I did not so much as peep into the darkness after her, but busy with a hundred thoughts returned to my play.

'Long past my usual bedtime, as I sat sipping a mug of hot

milk before the glowing cinders of the kitchen fire, Martha told me her secret. . . .

'So my impossible companion in the High Street yesterday was own, and only brother to your crazy old friend, Richard,' said the Count. 'His only brother,' he added, in a muse.

MISS DUVEEN

I seldom had the company of children in my grandmother's house beside the river Wandle. The house was old and ugly. But its river was lovely and youthful even although it had flowed on for ever, it seemed, between its green banks of osier and alder. So it was no great misfortune perhaps that I heard more talking of its waters than of any human tongue. For my grandmother found no particular pleasure in my company. How should she? My father and mother had married (and died) against her will, and there was nothing in me of those charms which, in fiction at any rate, swiftly soften a super-annuated heart.

Nor did I pine for her company either. I kept out of it as much as possible.

It so happened that she was accustomed to sit with her back to the window of the room which she usually occupied, her grey old indifferent face looking inwards. Whenever necessary, I would steal close up under it, and if I could see there her large faded amethyst velvet cap I knew I was safe from interruption. Sometimes I would take a slice or two of currant bread or (if I could get it) a jam tart or a cheese cake, and eat it under a twisted old damson tree or beside the running water. And if I conversed with anybody, it would be with myself or with my small victims of the chase.

Not that I was an exceptionally cruel boy; though if I had

lived on for many years in this primitive and companionless fashion, I should surely have become an idiot. As a matter of fact, I was unaware even that I was ridiculously old-fashioned —manners, clothes, notions, everything. My grandmother never troubled to tell me so, nor did she care. And the servants were a race apart. So I was left pretty much to my own devices. What wonder, then, if I at first accepted with genuine avidity the acquaintanceship of our remarkable neighbour, Miss Duveen?

It had been, indeed, quite an advent in our uneventful routine when that somewhat dubious household moved into Willowlea, a brown brick edifice, even uglier than our own, which had been long vacant, and whose sloping garden confronted ours across the Wandle. My grandmother, on her part, at once discovered that any kind of intimacy with its inmates was not much to be desired. While I, on mine, was compelled to resign myself to the loss of the Willowlea garden as a kind of no-man's-land or Tom Tiddler's ground.

I got to know Miss Duveen by sight long before we actually became friends. I used frequently to watch her wandering in her long garden. And even then I noticed how odd were her methods of gardening. She would dig up a root or carry off a potted plant from one to another overgrown bed with an almost animal-like resolution; and a few minutes afterwards I would see her restoring it to the place from which it had come. Now and again she would stand perfectly still, like a scarecrow, as if she had completely forgotten what she was at.

Miss Coppin, too, I descried sometimes. But I never more than glanced at her, for fear that even at that distance the too fixed attention of my eyes might bring hers to bear upon me. She was a smallish woman, inclined to be fat, and with a peculiar waddling gait. She invariably appeared to be angry with Miss Duveen, and would talk to her as one might talk to a post. I did not know, indeed, until one day Miss Duveen waved her handkerchief in my direction that I had been observed from Willowlea at all. Once or twice after that, I fancied, she called me; at least her lips moved; but I could not distinguish what she said. And I was naturally a little backward in making new friends. Still I grew accustomed to looking out for her and remember distinctly how first we met.

It was raining, the raindrops falling softly into the unrippled water, making their great circles, and tapping on the motionless leaves above my head where I sat in shelter on the bank. But the sun was shining whitely from behind a thin fleece of cloud, when Miss Duveen suddenly peeped in at me out of the greenery, the thin silver light upon her face, and eyed me sitting there, for all the world as if she were a blackbird and I a snail. I scrambled up hastily with the intention of retreating into my own domain, but the peculiar grimace she made at me fixed me where I was.

'Ah,' she said, with a little masculine laugh. 'So this is the young gentleman, the bold, gallant young gentleman. And what might be his name?'

I replied rather distantly that my name was Arthur.

'Arthur, to be sure!' she repeated, with extraordinary geniality, and again, 'Arthur,' as if in the strictest confidence. 'I know you, Arthur, very well indeed. I have looked, I have watched; and now, please God, we need never be estranged.' And she tapped her brow and breast, making the Sign of the Cross with her lean, bluish forefinger.

'What is a little brawling brook', she went on, 'to friends like you and me?' She gathered up her tiny countenance once more into an incredible grimace of friendliness; and I smiled as amicably as I could in return. There was a pause in this one-sided conversation. She seemed to be listening, and her lips moved, though I caught no sound. In my uneasiness I was just about to turn stealthily away, when she poked forward again.

'Yes, yes, I know you quite intimately, Arthur. We have met *here*.' She tapped her rounded forehead. 'You might not suppose it, too; but I have eyes like a lynx. It is no exaggeration, I assure you—I assure everybody. And now what friends we will be! At times,' she stepped out of her hiding-place and stood in curious dignity beside the water, her hands folded in front of her on her black pleated silk apron—'at times, dear child, I long for company—earthly company.' She glanced furtively about her. 'But I must restrain my longings; and you will, of course, understand that I do not complain. *He* knows best. And my dear cousin, Miss Coppin—she too knows best. She does not consider too much companionship expedient for me.' She glanced in some perplexity into the smoothly swirling water.

'I, you know,' she said suddenly, raising her little piercing eyes to mine, 'I am Miss Duveen, that's not, they say, quite the thing here.' She tapped her small forehead again beneath its sleek curves of greying hair, and made a long narrow mouth at me. 'Though, of course,' she added, 'we do not tell *her* so. No!'

And I, too, nodded my head in instinctive and absorbed imitation. Miss Duveen laughed gaily. 'He understands, he understands!' she cried, as if to many listeners. 'Oh, what a joy it is in this world, Arthur, to be understood. Now tell me,' she continued with immense nicety, 'tell me, how's your dear mamma?'

I shook my head.

'Ah,' she cried, 'I see, I see; Arthur has no mamma. We will not refer to it. No father, either?'

I shook my head again and, standing perfectly still, stared at my new acquaintance with vacuous curiosity. She gazed at me with equal concentration, as if she were endeavouring to keep the very thought of my presence in her mind.

'It is sad to have no father,' she continued rapidly, half closing her eyes; 'no head, no guide, no stay, no stronghold; but we have, O yes, we have another father, dear child, another father—eh? . . . Where. . . . Where?'

She very softly raised her finger. 'On high,' she whispered, with extraordinary intensity.

'But just now', she added cheerfully, hugging her mittened hands together. 'we are not talking of Him; we are talking of ourselves, just you and me, *so* cosy; so *secret*! And it's a grandmother? I thought so, I thought so, a grandmother! O yes, I can peep between the curtains, though they do lock the door. A grandmother—I thought so; that very droll old lady! *Such* fine clothes! Such a presence, oh yes! A grandmother.' She poked out her chin and laughed confidentially.

'And the long, bony creature, all rub and double'—she jogged briskly with her elbows, 'who's that?'

'Mrs. Pridgett,' I said.

'There, there,' she whispered breathlessly, gazing widely about her. 'Think of that! *He* knows; *He* understands. How firm, how manly, how undaunted! ... *One* t?'

I shook my head dubiously.

'Why should he?' she cried scornfully. 'But between ourselves, Arthur, that is a thing we *must* learn, and never mind the headache. We cannot, of course, know everything. Even Miss Coppin does not know everything'—she leaned forward with intense earnestness—'though I don't tell her so. We must try to learn all we can; and at once. One thing, dear child, you may be astonished to hear, I learned only yesterday, and that is how exceedingly *sad* life is.'

She leaned her chin upon her narrow bosom pursing her lips. 'And yet you know they say very little about it. ... They don't *mention* it. Every moment, every hour, every day, every year—one, two, three, four, five, seven, ten,' she paused, frowned, 'and so on. Sadder and sadder. Why? why? It's strange, but oh, so true. You really can have no notion, child, how very sad I am myself at times. In the evening, when they all gather together, in their white raiment, up and up and up, I sit on the garden seat, on Miss Coppin's garden seat, and precisely in the middle (you'll be kind enough to remember that?) and my *thoughts* make me sad.' She narrowed her eyes and shoulders. 'Yes and frightened, my child! Why must I be so guarded? One angel—the greatest *fool* could see the wisdom of that. But billions!—with their fixed eyes shining, so very boldly on me. I never prayed for so many, dear friend. And we pray for a good many odd things, you and I, I'll be bound. But there, you see, poor Miss Duveen's on her theology again —scamper, scamper, scamper. In the congregations of the wicked we must be cautious! . . . Mrs. Partridge and grandmamma, so nice, *so* nice; but even that, too, a *little* sad, eh?' She leaned her head questioningly, like a starving bird in the snow.

I smiled, not knowing what else she expected of me; and her face became instantly grave and set.

'He's right; perfectly right. We must speak evil of *no*-one. *No*-one. We must shut our mouths. We——' She stopped suddenly and, taking a step leaned over the water towards me, with eyebrows raised high above her tiny face. 'S—sh!' she whispered, laying a long forefinger on her lips. 'Eavesdroppers!' she smoothed her skirts, straightened her cap, and left me; only a moment after to poke out her head at me again from between the leafy bushes. 'An assignation, no!' she said firmly, then gathered her poor, cheerful, forlorn, crooked, lovable face into a most wonderful contraction at me, that assuredly meant—'But, *yes*!'

Indeed it was an assignation, the first of how many, and how few. Sometimes Miss Duveen would sit beside me, apparently so lost in thought that I was clean forgotten. And yet I half fancied it was often nothing but feigning. Once she stared me blankly out of countenance when I ventured to take the initiative and to call out good morning to her across the water. On this occasion she completed my consternation with a sudden, angry grimace—contempt, jealousy, outrage.

But often we met like old friends and talked. It was a novel but not always welcome diversion for me in the long shady garden that was my privy universe. Where our alders met, mingling their branches across the flowing water, and the kingfisher might be seen—there was our usual tryst. But, occasionally, at her invitation, I would venture across the stepping-stones into her demesne; and occasionally, but very seldom indeed, she would venture into mine. How plainly I see her, tip-toeing from stone to stone, in an extraordinary concentration of mind—her mulberry petticoats, her white stockings, her loose spring-side boots. And when at last she stood beside me, her mittened hand on her breast, she would laugh on in a kind of paroxysm until the tears stood in her eyes, and she grew faint with breathlessness.

'In all danger,' she told me once, 'I hold my breath and shut my eyes. And if I could tell you of every danger, I think, perhaps, you would understand—dear Miss Coppin. . . .' I did not, and yet, perhaps, very vaguely I did see the connection in this rambling statement.

Like most children, I liked best to hear Miss Duveen talk about her own childhood. I contrived somehow to discover that if we sat near flowers or under boughs in blossom, her talk would generally steal round to that. Then she would chatter on and on: of the white sunny rambling house, some-where, nowhere—it saddened and confused her if I asked where—in which she had spent her first happy years; where her father used to ride on a black horse; and her mother to walk with her in the garden in a crinolined gown and a locket with the painted miniature of a 'divine' nobleman inside it. How very far away these pictures seemed!

It was as if she herself had shrunken back into this distant past, and was babbling on like a child again, already a little isolated by her tiny infirmity.

'That was before——' she would begin to explain precisely, and then a criss-cross many-wrinkled frown would net her rounded forehead, and cloud her eyes. Time might baffle her, but then, time often baffled me too. Any talk about her mother usually reminded her of an elder sister, Caroline. 'My sister, Caroline,' she would repeat as if by rote, 'you may not be aware, Arthur, was afterwards Mrs. Bute. *So* charming, *so* exquisite, *so* accomplished. And Colonel Bute—an officer and a gentleman, I grant. And yet. . . . But no! My dear sister was *not* happy. And so it was no doubt a blessing in disguise that by an unfortunate accident she was found *drowned*. In a lake, you will understand, not a mere shallow noisy brook. This is one of my private sorrows, which, of course, your grand-mamma would be horrified to hear—horrified; and which, of course, Partridge has not the privilege of birth even to be informed of—*our* secret, dear child—with all her beautiful hair, and her elegant feet, and her eyes no more ajar than this; but blue, blue as the forget-me-not. When the time comes, Miss Coppin will close my own eyes, I hope and trust. Death, dear, dear child, I know they *say* is only sleeping. Yet I hope and trust *that*. To be sleeping wide awake; oh no!' she abruptly turned her small untidy head away.

'But didn't they shut *hers*?' I enquired.

Miss Duveen ignored the question. 'I am not uttering one word of blame,' she went on rapidly; 'I am perfectly aware that such things confuse me. Miss Coppin tells me not to think. She tells me that I can have no opinions worth the mention. She says, "Shut up your mouth". I must keep silence then. All that I am merely trying to express to you, Arthur, knowing you will regard it as sacred between us—all I am expressing is that my dear sister, Caroline, was a gifted and beautiful creature with not a shadow or vestige or tinge or taint of confusion in her mind. *Nothing*. And yet, when they dragged her out of the water and laid her there on the bank, looking——' She stooped herself double in a sudden dreadful fit of gasping, and I feared for an instant she was about to die.

'No, no, no,' she cried, rocking herself to and fro, 'you shall *not* paint such a picture in his young, innocent mind. You *shall* not.'

I sat on my stone, watching her, feeling excessively uncomfortable. 'But what *did* she look like, Miss Duveen?' I pressed forward to ask at last.

'No, no, no,' she cried again. 'Cast him out, cast him out. *Retro Sathanas!* We must not even *ask* to understand. My father and my dear mother, I do not doubt, have spoken for Caroline. Even I, if I must be called on, will strive to collect my thoughts. And that is precisely where a friend, you, Arthur, would be so precious; to know that you too, in your innocence, will be helping me to collect my thoughts on that day, to save our dear Caroline from Everlasting Anger. That, that! Oh dear: oh dear!' She turned on me a face I should scarcely have recognized, lifted herself trembling to her feet, and hurried away.

Sometimes it was not Miss Duveen that was a child again, but I that had grown up. 'Had now you been your handsome father—and I see him, O, so plainly, dear child—had you been your father, then I must, of course, have kept to the house. . . . I must have; it is a rule of conduct, and everything depends on them. Where would Society be *else?*' she cried, with an unanswerable blaze of intelligence. 'I find, too, dear Arthur, that they increase—the rules increase. I try to remember them. My dear cousin, Miss Coppin, knows them all. But I—I think sometimes one's *memory* is a little treacherous. And then it must vex people.'

She gazed penetratingly at me for an answer that did not come. Mute as a fish though I might be, I suppose it was something of a comfort to her to talk to me.

And to suppose that is *my* one small crumb of comfort when I reflect on the kind of friendship I managed to bestow.

I actually met Miss Coppin once; but we did not speak. I had, in fact, gone to tea with Miss Duveen. The project had been discussed as 'quite, quite impossible, dear child' for weeks. 'You must never mention it again.' As a matter of fact I had never mentioned it at all. But one day—possibly when their charge had been less difficult and exacting, one day Miss Coppin and her gaunt maid-servant and companion really did go out together, leaving Miss Duveen alone in Willowlea. It was the crowning opportunity of our friendship. The moment I espied her issuing from the house, I guessed her errand. She came hastening down to the waterside, attired in clothes of a colour and fashion I had never seen her wearing before, her dark eyes shining in her head, her hands trembling with excitement.

It was a still, warm afternoon, with sweet-williams and linden and stocks scenting the air, when, with some little trepidation, I must confess, I followed her in formal dignity up the unfamiliar path towards the house. I know not which of our hearts beat the quicker, whose eyes cast the most furtive glances about us. My friend's cheeks were brightest mauve. She wore a large silver locket on a ribbon; and I followed her up the faded green stairs, beneath the dark pictures, to her small, stuffy bedroom under the roof. We humans, they say, are enveloped in a kind of aura; to which the vast majority of us are certainly entirely insensitive. Nevertheless, there was an air, an atmosphere as of the smell of pears in this small attic room—well, every bird, I suppose, haunts with its presence its customary cage.

'This,' she said, acknowledging the bed, the looking-glass, the deal washstand, 'this, dear child, you will pardon; in fact, you will not see. How could we sit, friends as we are, in the congregation of strangers?'

I hardly know why, but that favourite word of Miss Duveen's, 'congregation' brought up before me with extreme aversion all the hostile hardness and suspicion concentrated in Miss Coppin and Ann. I stared at the queer tea things in a vain effort not to be aware of the rest of Miss Duveen's private belongings.

Somehow or other she had managed to procure for me a bun—a saffron bun. There was a dish of a grey pudding and a plate of raspberries that I could not help suspecting (and, I am ashamed to say, with aggrieved astonishment), she must have herself gathered that morning from my grandmother's canes. We did not talk very much. Her heart gave her pain. And her face showed how hot and absorbed and dismayed she was over her foolhardy entertainment. But I sipped my milk and water, sitting on a black bandbox, and she on an old cane chair. And we were almost formal and distant to one another, with little smiles and curtseys over our cups, and polished agreement about the weather.

'And you'll strive not to be sick, dear child,' she implored me suddenly, while I was nibbling my way slowly through the bun. But it was not until rumours of the tremendous fact of Miss Coppin's early and unforeseen return had been borne in on us that Miss Duveen lost all presence of mind. She burst into tears; seized and kissed repeatedly my sticky hands; implored me to be discreet; implored me to be gone; implored me to retain her in my affections, 'as you love your poor dear mother, Arthur,' and I left her on her knees, her locket pressed to her bosom.

Miss Coppin was, I think, unusually astonished to see a small strange boy walk softly past her bedroom door, within which she sat, with purple face, her hat strings dangling, taking off her boots. Ann, I am thankful to say, I did not encounter. But when I was safely out in the garden in the afternoon sunshine, the boldness and the romance of this sally completely deserted me. I ran like a hare down the alien path, leapt from stone to stone across the river; nor paused in my flight until I was safe in my own bedroom, and had—how odd is childhood!—washed my face and entirely changed my clothes.

My grandmother, when I appeared at her tea-table, glanced at me now and again rather profoundly and inquisitively, but the actual question hovering in her mind remained unuttered.

It was many days before we met again, my friend and I. She

had, I gathered from many mysterious nods and shrugs, been more or less confined to her bedroom ever since our escapade, and looked dulled and anxious; her small face was even a little more vacant in repose than usual. Even this meeting, too, was full of alarms; for in the midst of our talk, by mere chance or caprice, my grandmother took a walk in the garden that afternoon, and discovered us under our damson tree. She bowed in her dignified, aged way. And Miss Duveen, with her cheeks and forehead the colour of her petticoat, elaborately curtseyed.

'Beautiful, very beautiful weather,' said my grandmother.

'It is indeed,' said my friend, fixedly.

'I trust you are keeping pretty well?'

'As far, ma'am, as God and a little weakness of the heart permit,' said Miss Duveen. 'He knows all,' she added, firmly.

My grandmother stood silent a moment.

'Indeed He does,' she replied politely.

'And that's the difficulty,' ventured Miss Duveen, in her odd, furtive, friendly fashion.

My grandmother opened her eyes, smiled pleasantly, paused, glanced remotely at me, and, with another exchange of courtesies, Miss Duveen and I were left alone once more. But it was a grave and saddened friend I now sat beside.

'You see, Arthur, all bad things, we know, are best for us. Motives included. That comforts me. But my heart is sadly fluttered. Not that I fear or would shun society; but perhaps your grandmother. . . . I never had the power to treat my fellow-creatures as if they were stocks and stones. And the effort not to notice it distresses me. A little hartshorn might relieve the *palpitation*, of course; but Miss Coppin keeps all keys. It is this shouting that makes civility such a task.'

'This shouting'—very faintly then I caught her meaning, but I was in no mood to sympathize. My grandmother's one round-eyed expressionless glance at me had been singularly disconcerting. And it was only apprehension of her questions that kept me from beating a retreat. So we sat on, Miss Duveen and I, in the shade, the day drawing towards evening, and presently we walked down to the water-side, and under the colours of sunset I flung in my crumbs to the minnows, as she talked ceaselessly on.

'And yet,' she concluded, after how involved a monologue, 'and yet, Arthur, I feel it is for your forgiveness I should be pleading. So much to do; such an arch of beautiful things might have been my gift to you. It is here,' she said, touching her forehead. 'I do not think, perhaps, that all I might say would be for your good. I must be silent and discreet about much. I must not provoke'—she lifted her mittened finger, and raised her eyes—'Them,' she said gravely. 'I am tempted, terrified, persecuted. Whispering, wrangling, shouting: the flesh is a grievous burden, Arthur; I long for peace. Only to flee away and be at rest! But,' she nodded, and glanced over her shoulder, 'about much—great trials, sad entanglements, about much the Others say, I must keep silence. It would only alarm your innocence. And that I will never, *never* do. Your father, a noble, gallant gentleman of the world, would have understood my difficulties. But he is dead. . . . Whatever that may mean. I have repeated it so often when Miss Coppin thought that I was not—dead, dead, dead, dead. But I don't think that even now I grasp the meaning of the word. Of you, dear child, I will never say it. You have been life itself to me.'

How generously, how tenderly she smiled on me from her perplexed, sorrowful eyes.

'You have all the world before you, all the world. How splendid it is to be a Man. For my part I have sometimes thought, though they do not of course intend to injure me, yet I fancy, sometimes, they have grudged me *my* part in it a little. Though God forbid but Heaven's best.'

She raised that peering, dark, remote gaze to my face, and her head was trembling again. 'They are saying now to one another—'*Where is she? where is she? It's nearly dark, m'm, where is she?*'' O, Arthur, but there shall be no night *there*. We must believe it, we must—in spite, dear friend, of a weak horror of glare. My cousin, Miss Coppin, does not approve of my wishes. Gas, gas, gas, all over the house, and when it is not singing, it roars. You would suppose I might be trusted with but just my own one bracket. But no—Ann, I think—indeed I fear, sometimes, has no——' She started violently and shook her tiny head. 'When I am gone,' she continued disjointedly, 'you will be prudent, cautious, dear child? Consult only your heart about me. Older you must be. . . . Yes, certainly, he must be older,' she repeated vaguely. 'Everything goes on and on—and round!' She seemed astonished, as if at a sudden radiance cast on an old and protracted perplexity.

'About your soul, dear child,' she said to me once, touching my hand, 'I have never spoken. Perhaps it was one of my first duties to keep on speaking to you about your soul. I mention it now in case they should rebuke me when I make my appearance there. It is a burden; and I have so many burdens, as well as pain. And at times I cannot think very far. I *see* the thought; but it won't alter. It comes back, just like a sheep—"*Ba-aa-ah*", like that!' She burst out laughing, twisting her head to look at me the while. 'Miss Coppin, of course, has no difficulty; gentlemen have no difficulty. And this shall be the occasion of another of our little confidences. We are discreet?' She bent her head and scanned my face. 'Here,' she tapped her bosom, 'I bear his image. My only dear one's. And if you would kindly turn your head, dear child, perhaps I could pull him out.'

It was the miniature of a young, languid, fastidious-looking officer which she showed me—threaded on dingy tape, in its tarnished locket.

'Miss Coppin, in great generosity, has left me this,' she said, polishing the glass on her knee, 'though I am forbidden to wear it. For you see, Arthur, it is a duty not to brood on the past, and even perhaps, indelicate. Some day, it may be, you, too, will love a gentle girl. I beseech you, keep your heart pure and true. This one could not. Not a single word of blame escapes me. I own to my Maker, *never* to anyone else, it has not eased my little difficulty. But it is not for us to judge. Whose office is that, eh?' And again, that lean small forefinger, beneath an indescribable grimace, pointed gently, deliberately, from her lap upward. 'Pray, pray,' she added, very violently, 'pray, till the blood streams down your face! Pray, but rebuke not. They all whisper about it. Among themselves,' she added, peering out beneath and between the interlacing branches. 'But I simulate inattention, I simulate. . . .' The very phrase seemed to have hopelessly confused her. Again, as so often now, that glassy fear came into her eyes; her foot tapped on the gravel.

'Arthur,' she cried suddenly, taking my hand tightly in her lap, 'you have been my refuge in a time of trouble. You will never know it, child. My refuge, and my peace. We shall seldom meet now. All are opposed. They repeat it in their looks. The autumn will divide us; and then, winter; but, I think, no spring. It is so, Arthur, there is a stir; and then they will hunt me out.' Her eyes gleamed again, far and small and black in the dusky pallor of her face.

It was indeed already autumn; the air golden and still. The leaves were beginning to fall. The late fruits were well-nigh over. Robins and tits seemed our only birds now. Rain came in floods. The Wandle took sound and volume, sweeping deep above our stepping stones. Very seldom after this I even so much as saw our neighbour. But I chanced on her again one still afternoon, standing fixedly by the brawling stream, in a rusty-looking old-fashioned cloak, her scanty hair pushed high up on her forehead.

She stared at me for a moment or two, and then, with a scared look over her shoulder, threw me a little letter, shaped like a cock-hat, and weighted with a pebble stone, across the stream. She whispered earnestly and rapidly at me over the water. But I could not catch a single word she said, and failed to decipher her close spidery handwriting. No doubt I was too shy, of too ashamed, or in a vague fashion too loyal, to show it to my grandmother. It is not now a flattering keepsake. I called out loudly I must go in; and still see her gazing after me, with a puzzled, mournful expression on the face peering out of the cloak.

Even after that we sometimes waved to one another across the water, but never if by hiding myself I could evade her in time. The distance seemed to confuse her, and quite silenced me. I began to see we were ridiculous friends, especially as she came now in ever dingier and absurder clothes. She even looked hungry, and not quite clean, as well as ill; and she talked more to her phantoms than to me when once we met.

The first ice was in the garden. The trees stood bare beneath a pale blue sunny sky, and I was standing at the window, looking out at the hoar-frost, when my grandmother told me that it was unlikely that I should ever see our neighbour again.

I stood where I was, without turning round, gazing out of the window at the motionless ghostly trees, and the few birds in forlorn unease.

'Is she dead, then?' I enquired.

'I am told,' was the reply, 'that her friends have been compelled to have her put away. No doubt, it was the proper course. It should have been done earlier. But it is not our affair, you are to understand. And, poor creature, perhaps death would have been a happier, a more merciful release. She was sadly afflicted.'

I said nothing, and continued to stare out of the window.

But I know now that the news, in spite of a vague sorrow, greatly relieved me. I should be at ease in the garden again, came the thought—no longer fear to look ridiculous and grow hot when our neighbour was mentioned, or be saddled with her company beside the stream.

AN IDEAL CRAFTSMAN

*

Away into secrecy frisked a pampered mouse. A scuffling of bedclothes, the squeak of a dry castor followed, and then suddenly the boy sat up and set to piecing together reality with scraps of terrifying but half-forgotten dreams.

It was his ears had summoned him, they were still ringing with an obscure message, a faint *Qui vive?* But as he sat blinking and listening in the empty dark he could not satisfy himself what sound it was that had actually wakened him. Was it only a dying howl from out of one of his usual nightmares, or had some actual noise or cry sounded up from the vacancy of the house beneath? It was this uncertainty—as if his brain were a piece of mechanism wound up by sleep—that set working a vivid panorama of memories in the little theatre of his mind— cloaked men huddled together in some dark corner of the night, scoundrels plotting in the wind, the pause between rifle-click and the loose fall, finally to culminate in the adventure of glorious memory—raiding Jacobs.

He groped under his pillow for the treasures he had concealed there before blowing out his candle—a box of matches, a crumbling slice of pie-crust, and a dingy volume of the Newgate Calendar. The last usually lay behind the draughty chimney of his fireplace, because Jacobs had the habits of a ferret and nothing was safe from his nosings. He struck a match soundlessly on the edge of his mattress. Its flare lit up his lank-haired head, his sharp face and dazzled eyes. Then the flame drooped, went out. But he had had time to find the broad glossy belt he had cut out of a strip of mottled American cloth and the old sheathed poniard which he had months ago abstracted from his father's study. He buckled on the belt round his body in the dark over his night-shirt and dangled the rusty blood- (or water-) stained poniard coldly on his hip. He pulled on his stockings, tilted an old yachting cap over his eyes, and was fully equipped.

In this feverish haste he had had little time to ponder strategy. But now he sat down again on the edge of his bed, and though he was pretending to think, his brows wrinkled in a frown, he was actually listening. Even the stairs had ceased to creak. And the star that from a wraith of cloud glittered coldly in the night-sky beyond the rift between his curtains made no sound. He drew open his door, inch by inch, still intent, then stepped out on to the landing.

The first danger to be encountered on the staircase below was his father's bedroom. Its door gaped half-open, but was it empty? It was here on this very spot, he remembered with a qualm, that Jacobs had once leapt out on him. He saw in memory that agile shape stepping hastily and oddly in the dusk, furious at sight of the eavesdropper. And in an instant the tiny blue bead of gas on the landing had expanded into a white fan-shaped glare. Not so to-night. With a gasp and an oblique glance at the dusky bed and the spectral pendent clothes within, he slid by in safety on his stockinged feet, and so past yet another door—but this one tight shut, with its flower-painted panels—the door of his mother's gay little sitting-room, his real mother's, not the powdery eyebrowed stepmother who a few hours before had set out with his father, on pleasure bent.

A few paces beyond he trod even more cautiously, for here was a loose board. At the last loop of the staircase Jacobs'

customary humming should issue up out of the gloom beneath
—the faint tune which he rasped on and on and on, faint and
shrill between his teeth, superciliously, ironically, in greasy
good-humour or sly facetiousness—he would hum it in his
coffin perhaps. But no, not a sound. The raider hesitated.
What next? Where now? He listened in vain.

And then, he suddenly remembered that this was 'silver'
night. And doubtless—cook and housemaid long since snoring in their attic—a white glittering array of forks and spoons,
soup ladles, and candlesticks were at this very moment spread
out in bedaubed splendour before the aproned tyrant. For
Jacobs was not only queer in his habits and nocturnal by
nature but a glutton for work. But if it was silver night, why
this prodigious hush? No clang of fork ringing against its
neighbour; not a single rattle of whitening brush on metal
reached his ears.

Slim as a ferret himself, he hung over the loop in the staircase as he might have hung over the Valley of Death; but still
all was strangely quiet. And so, with a pang of disappointment, and at the same moment with a crow of relief, the boy
came to the conclusion that Jacobs was out. And not for the
first time either. He must have had a visitor—the woman in
the black bonnet, with the silver locket dangling on her front,
perhaps. As likely as not, they had gone off gallivanting together, and would re-appear about eleven o'clock, Jacobs
either swearing and quarrelsome or amiably garrulous.

But the boy was no fool. In spite of this sinister hush in the
house—as if its walls were draped with the very darkness of
night—Jacobs *might* perhaps be busy over his silver. Shammy,
however hard you rub with it, makes little sound. And if he
were, then too much confidence would mean not only a sudden pursuit, a heart-daunting scuttle up the stairs, and Jacobs
with his cane cutting at his legs from behind, but the failure
of his raid altogether. Nothing then but a bit of stale pie-crust
for his midnight feast. So he trod on velvet down the stairs,

his damp palm shunning the banister (*that* squeak would wake an army!), his lips dry and his tongue rolling in luxury of anticipation. And soon he was in the hall, with all the empty rooms of the house above his head, and minified in his own imagination to a mere atom of whiteness in the dusk, a mouse within smell of the cat. His rusty poniard clutched tight between his fingers, his stomach full of fear and his heart noisy as a cock-crow, he pushed on.

The staircase ran widely and shallowly into the hall; there was more light here, a thin faint glow of gas-light, turned low. He could distinguish the dark shapes of the heavy furniture, as he stalked on through this luminous twilight. But the back passage to the kitchen quarters was hidden from elegant visitors by a muffled door with a spring, which Jacobs, when it suited him, kept propped wide open. This passage, if followed to the end, turned abruptly at right angles; and at the inner angle near the fusty entry to the cellars he paused to breathe and then to listen again. Once round the corner, along the passage in front of him the kitchen door would come into view, ajar or wide open, on the right; and the larder itself a few paces further on, and exactly opposite the raider. But before reaching it, the boot cupboard, sour den of long-legged spiders and worse abominations, must be passed, and the window with the panes of coloured glass, looking out on a monstrous red, yellow, or blue garden of trees and stars.

The boy's lean dark face had in his progress become paler and leaner. His legs were now the skinny playthings of autumnal draughts, and at this moment a sound *had* actually reached his ears—the sound as of a lion panting over a meal. A sort of persistent half-choked snuffling. This was odd. This was surprising. Even when, with sleeves turned up and sharp elbows bared, Jacobs was engrossed in any job, he never breathed like that. In general, indeed, he scarcely seemed to be breathing at all; when for example, he stooped down close handing a dish of cabbage or blanc-mange at the Sunday dinner table of a taciturn father. *This* breathing was husky and unequal, almost like a snore through nostrils and mouth. Jacobs must be drunk, then; and that would mean either a sort of morose good-humour, or a sullen drowsy malice, as dangerous as it was sly. The adventure was losing its edge. Even the hunger for romance in the boy's Scots-French blood died down within him at recollection of the dull, dull-lidded eyes of Jacobs half drunk.

There came a sudden *crkkk* and the squeak as of a boot. The boy bit hard on his lip. Yet another slow sliding step forward; the kitchen door *was* ajar. A spear of yellow light warned the intruder. But light—spear or no spear—was as vitalizing as a sip of wine. Red-capped, pock-marked faces, all sorts and conditions of criminals, buccaneers and highwaymen, gore and glory, flocked back again into the boy's fancy. An icy delicious shiver ran down his spine, for now Jacobs, tied with a tape round the middle, in his green baize apron, must be sitting at not much more than arm's-length from the door. Or if not, who?

Inch by inch, courage restored, he slid on soundlessly, his stockinged foot first pushing forward into the light, then the white edge of his night-shirt. He pressed skin-close to the further side of the passage, and was actually half past the door ajar, when through a narrow chink he glanced into the kitchen, and so—suddenly found himself squinting full into the eyes of the fat woman in the black bonnet. Crouching a little, stiff and motionless, her eyes bolting out of her face, she stood there full in the light of the gas jet over her head, the faded brown hair that showed beneath her bonnet wreathing it as if with a nimbus. The boy stood frozen.

Not for an instant did he imagine he could be invisible to such a stare as that, to eyes which, though they were small and dark showed as round and shining as the silver locket that rose and fell jerkily upon her chest. His mouth opened—mute as a fish; every sinew in his body stiffened in readiness for flight.

But the woman never so much as stirred. Every fibre and muscle in *her* body was at stretch to aid her ears. It looked as if she might be able to hear even his thoughts moving. So would a she-wolf stand at gaze under a white moon, with those unstirring eyes; famished and gaunt. And yet, what in the world was there for *her* to be afraid of? If anybody else was there she would have spoken. She was alone, then? His fingers suddenly relaxed, the scabbard of his poniard rattled against the wall behind him, and there slipped off his tongue the most unlikely question that would ever else have come into his mind. 'I say; where's Jacobs?'

The lids over the little black eyes fluttered and the woman's lips opened in a squawk. Her two rough red hands were suddenly clapped on either side of her mouth. For a moment he thought she was going to scream again, and was thankful when only a shuddering sob followed. 'Oh, sir, how you did startle me. Mr. Jacobs, sir, why just as you was coming—he's gone, sir; he's gone.'

The boy pushed open the door and stood on the threshold. He had supposed it impossible that so stout a woman could speak in so small a voice. Sheer curiosity had banished all alarm. Besides, if Jacobs was out, there was no immediate danger. He looked about him, conscious that he was being closely watched from between those square red fingers, and that the forehead above them was deeply wrinkled almost as if the woman were helpless with laughter.

'Why, lor,' she was muttering as if to herself, 'it's only the little boy. My! I thought he was his pa, I did; God bless him. He's come down for a drink of water. That's what he wants. And all in his pretty night-gown too.'

Tears were now gushing down her round cheeks and gurgling in her voice. She walked in angles to a chair and sat there rocking her body to and fro and smiling at him—an odd contorted smile of blandishment and stupidity sicklied over with fear. He blushed, and stared back at her as hot and angry as when in days gone by bent-up wrinkled old ladies used to stop his nurse in the street to ask questions about him, and had even openly kissed him.

This end to his adventure, which seemed to be leading him into difficulties he had never dreamed of, was a bitter disappointment. A drink of water! He resented the presence of this fat woman in the kitchen. He resented even more his own embarrassment. He wriggled under his night-shirt, and was profoundly relieved when those flabby florid cheeks suddenly faded to a mottled mauve, the rocking ceased, and two heavy eyelids slowly descended upon the small black terrified eyes. Even if she *were* going to faint, she would at any rate have to stop staring.

But his troubles were only begun; ugly grunts were proceeding from that open mouth, and the woman's head was twitching oddly. Still, he had had experiences of this kind before. He knew what was to be done, and a scientific callousness gave his remedy zest. On the kitchen table beside some empty bottles of beer and a decanter stood a tumbler half full of water. This he liberally sprinkled on the woman's face and trickled a few drops, not without waste, between her teeth. Grunts expostulated, and the silver locket almost danced. She was coming to. Success stimulated him to fresh efforts; he snatched a scrap of brown paper from among the spoons and climbing up on to a chair lit it at the gas, and thrust it under her nose. It was enough. Such a smother would have stupefied an apiary.

But though the cure was now complete, and worthy of being proudly recorded, one pretty keepsake had been degraded for ever—the memory of his mother, lying on a sofa, and two blue eyes like dawn shining up amid the dewdrops sprinkling her fair cheeks. This fat stranger's petticoat was of coarse red dingy flannel. She was clammy and stupid and ridiculous. Nevertheless, the absurd fear of him or whatever it might be that had brought her to this pass seemed for the moment to be clean forgotten. For when her dazed eyes rolled down from under their lids again and looked out at him, precisely the same expression had come into her face as he had seen on it when he had watched her smiling mawkishly at Jacobs himself.

'Are you better now?' he asked coldly, flourishing the smouldering paper.

The woman smiled again, and nodded.

'I'm afraid I may have burnt you. But there's no other way, you see, though the smell's pretty beastly.' The woman went on vacantly smiling. Not that this stupid wrinkling up of her mouth and cheeks seemed to mean anything. She might have been made of wax. Further parleying, he decided, would be wasted.

'You needn't mention it to Jacobs, you know,' he began. '*I* shan't say anything. You see, I just happened to notice you through the door. I think I'll be going back now. Jacobs is a bit of a. . . .' Nothing very conciliatory could come after that 'bit'. At all events he decided to keep back the word that had so nearly slipped out. The silver locket began to jolt again, and clumsy fingers fumbled at it. The smile was beginning to crystallize into the familiar wrinkled stare.

'You *look* better, *much* better,' said the boy uneasily, edging towards the door. 'I remember once my mother . . .' but his tongue refused for shame to say what he remembered. Also he found it difficult to turn his back on the woman, though when at last he reached the door he whipped round quickly.

'Little boy,' called the woman in a fulsome voice, 'come back! I say!—little *boy*!'

He frowned. Her eyes were now searching his face intently and suspiciously. She had begun to think again. And at sight of their hostility his own underlip drooped into a sullen obstinacy. He didn't mind *her*. If she decided to sneak to Jacobs, that was her look out; meanwhile he could easily manage her alone.

'What?' he said.

'I was took ill, wasn't I? The heat's something awful. *Phh!* But there isn't any need to stare, little boy. I shan't eat you.' Cunning peeped out of the unctuous face, and he merely waited for the trap. 'Not me; and what a pretty belt he's got on,' she continued, rolling her dingy handkerchief into a ball; 'and ain't he got a nice new dagger!'

But even such flatteries as these produced no response. The dagger wasn't new, and the belt was not meant to be pretty. 'I must be going now, thank you,' he repeated. 'Besides, I suppose he'll be back in a minute?'

Her hands stayed motionless, her head had suddenly jerked a little sideways like a thrush's intent on the stirrings of a worm.

'Going,' she repeated, 'why, of course, he must be going, poor lamb: he'll get his death of cold. And wasn't he *good* to me; *good* to me he was. And that clever! You'd have thought he was a doctor!'

Her glance meanwhile was roving in confusion into every corner of the room as though she were looking for something, and was afraid of what she might find. He could hardly keep his own from following them. 'That kind and gentle he was! Just like a doctor he was!' And again a menacing silence swallowed up her words. The boy's face reflected a distrust deepening into hostility. Was the whole thing a cheat then? Was Jacobs as usual playing the sneak? Would he suddenly leap out on him? In any case he knew he was only being cajoled, if not ridiculed.

'There, now!' she suddenly broke out, 'if he isn't *thinking* again. That's what he's doing. He's thinking about what I was saying to meself when that funny dream came over me. That's what he's doing. And why not, I should like to know. Eh?' She shot him a searching, ogling glance.

'I didn't notice,' he answered. 'Your *eyes* looked rather queer, with the whites gone up, and your skin twitched just as if the water burnt it. But *I* didn't mind.'

61

'How long was you there, then? Tell me that?' Her nails were now gripped uncomfortably sharp on his arm. 'You stand there frowning and sulking, my young soldier. And by what rights, may I ask? Just you tell me how long you was there!' Her face had grown hard and dangerous, but he shut his mouth tight and returned sullenly stare for stare. 'So help me,' she half whispered, releasing him, 'now I've been and frightened him again. That's it. He thinks I'm angry with him. Lord love you, my precious, I didn't mean anything like that. Not me. P'raps you just came down for a bit of fun, eh?'

She fixed her eyes on the dagger, and shuddered. 'What was I saying? Ah, yes. How long—*how long* was—you—there?' She stamped her foot. 'That's right, saucer-eyes, stare, stare! Didn't I *say* I'm old and ugly! Ain't *he* said it too? Oh, oh, oh! What shall I do, what shall I do?' She hid her face in her hands and her tears gushed out anew.

The boy stood stiffly at her side. This unexpected capitulation unnerved him, and his heart began to heave menacingly.

'I'm sorry; but I must go now,' he repeated, trying with as little obvious aversion as possible to drag his hand from her hot wet cheek. 'And I don't see what good crying will do.' As if by magic the snuffling ceased.

'Good! Who said, what "good"? It's *me* who must be going, my young man, and don't you make any mistake about *that*!' She shook out her skirts, and searched in vain for the bonnet on her head. He nearly laughed out, so absurd was the attempt —for the bunched-up old thing was dangling by its strings, behind her back. But this retrieved, she drew it on, pushing under it stragglings of her iron-grey hair. Then she opened a fat leather purse, stuffed with keys and dirty crumpled papers.

'Now what have I got here?' she began wheedlingly, as she pushed about with her finger and took out a sixpence. 'What have I got here? Why, a silver sixpence. And who's that for? Why, for any nice little boy what won't spy and pry. That's what that's for.' She stooped nearly double, holding it out to him with bolting eyes in her purpled face. 'What? He won't take it? Shakes his head? Too proud to take it. Oh, very well, very well.'

She opened her purse again and with shaking fingers pushed the sixpence back. She was not crying now, but her face had gone a deathly grey, and a blank, dreadful misery had crept into it. This woman was a very strange woman. He had never met anyone who behaved in such a queer way. He watched her as she went waddling off out of the kitchen and over the stone floor into the darkness beyond. Her footsteps ceased to sound. She was gone, then? And she must have left the garden door open behind her; the wind was bellying in his night-shirt and icy under his arms. Here was the cat come in, too, rolling in its sodden fur on the oilcloth at his feet. 'Puss, Puss,' he said. Where had *he* been to get in such a state. The boy stood dismayed and discomfited, while the cat rubbed its body and its purring jaws against his stockinged legs.

A stark unstirring silence had spread into the kitchen, though the gas was faintly singing—high and from very far away. And, as if to attract his attention, a wisp of hair was patting his forehead under his ridiculous cap-brim. The silence entangled his thoughts in a medley of absurd misgivings productive only of chicken-skin and perplexity. Something had gone wrong—the house was changed; and he didn't know how or why. He glanced up at the clock, which thereupon at once began to tick. His eyes dodged from side to side of the familiar kitchen and then it was as if a stealthy warning finger had been laid upon his thoughts, and chaos became unity.

His roving glance had fallen on the cupboard door. For there in the crack at the bottom of it, shut in and moving softly in the wind, showed a corner of green baize. Jacobs was there, then; bunched up there, then; smiling to himself and waiting, and listening in there, then? The boy stood appalled, his bright black eyes fixed on this flapping scrap of green baize apron. The whole thing *was* a trap. And yet, as he tried hard to keep his wits, he had known instantly there was something wrong—something he couldn't understand. That was just like one of Jacobs's jokes!—jokes that usually had so violent and humourless an ending. And yet. . . . Suddenly the hinges of the outer door had whinnied; he jerked round his head in alarm. It was the woman again. She had come back. Bead-bright raindrops glittered on the black of her jacket, on her bonnet, in her hair. That rigid awful stare of horror had come back into her face. He could move neither hand nor foot; could only stare at her.

'Eh, eh, now!' she was choking out at him. 'So you've *seen* now, my fine young gentleman, have you? That's what you've done. Then what do *I* say; *me*! Keep a civil tongue in your head, that's what *I* say. And tell me this——' The face thrust so close down to his had grown enormous and unspeakably dreadful. Her hot breath enveloped him. 'Where's the gate? Where's the gate, I say? I got lost there among them bushes. I can't get out. D'ye see? I've lost the gate. It's dark. It's come on raining. Where's the *gate*?'

Tiny beads of blood stood on her skin—she must have stumbled into the holly hedge at the foot of the garden by the cucumber frames. She smelt not only of her old clothes but of the night and the rain. And still he made no answer. He had been driven back by that awful and congealed look on her face—beyond fear. He was merely waiting—to find *his* way: this mystery, this horror.

'Eh, now'; she had turned away, her heavy head crooked down over one shoulder, and was speaking this time to herself: 'quiet and silly, that's what *he* is. Nothing much anybody could get out of *him*. But see you here!' She had twisted round. 'It's no good you playing the young innocent with me. You've seen and you know. That's what you've done. And you just tell me this. How *could* I have done it? how *should* I have done it? That's what I'm asking. Just you tell me that. Haven't I come of honest people? And didn't he promise me and promise me? And nothing but lies. And then, "You ain't the first," he says. And me as I am! "You ain't the first," he says. Ay, and meant it. "What, what!" I says. And then he hit me—here, with his clenched-up fist, *here*. "I shan't leave you," I said, "and you can't make me." And all I wanted was just to keep body and soul together. "And you can't make me," that's what I said. "That's all," I said. And then he laughed. "You ain't the first," he says, laughing. And me as I am! . . . Oh, my God, he *won't* understand. Listen, little boy. I didn't know what I was doing; everything went black and I couldn't see. And I put out my hands—to push him off, and my fingers went stiff and a smudge of red came over my eyes, and next thing he fell down like a bundle and wouldn't speak, wouldn't speak. Mind you, I say *this*, if I hadn't drunk the beer, if I hadn't drunk the beer, if I hadn't—done—that. . . .' She faltered, her face went blank as she swayed.

Her listener was struggling hard to understand. These broken words told him little that was clear and definite, and yet were brimming over with sinister incomprehensible meanings. He frowned at the contorted, dark-red moving face and loose lips. One fact and one fact alone was plain. He had nothing to fear from Jacobs. Jacobs was not going to pounce out on him. Simply because Jacobs was gone. Then why. . . ? He twisted about, and kneeling down on the floor by the cupboard beside the cooling kitchen range—with scarcely a glint of drowsy red now in its ashy coals—he struggled with the metal tongue that held back the door. Usually loose, it now turned stiffly and hurt his fingers. Then suddenly it gave way.

And the boy's first quick thought was: Why, he's quite a little man! And the next was one of supreme relief that all this wild meaningless talk was now over. He leaned forward and peered into the puckered-up clay-coloured face, with its blackened lips and leaden-lidded eyes. The chin was dinted in with the claw pin in the cravat. A gallipot stood near—a trap for crickets—touching one limp hand, still smeared with pink plate powder. The door-tongue was stiff, the boy supposed, because the corner of the baize apron had got stuck to the varnish of the frame. You'd have hardly thought, though, there'd be room in the cupboard. But the important thing, the illuminating, inspiring, and yet startlingly familiar thing was the gallipot!

It had touched a spring, it had released a shutter in his mind and set his thoughts winging back to a sooty, draughty chimney where only a few minutes ago—minutes as vast and dark and empty as the sea—he had hidden a book with a wedge of pie-crust on top of it. In that book he had read of just such a gallipot as this—not as a trap for crickets—but a gallipot with a handful of spade guineas in it, which had belonged to an old man who had been brutally strangled in the small hours by his two nephews. They had never been caught either; nobody had even suspected them. They had planned a means of escape—so vile and fantastic that even to watch them at it had made his skin deliciously creep upon him and his hair stir on his head. But it had succeeded, it had *worked*. To the dead old man's four-poster bed they had strung up the body of their victim, and until one of them, on his death-bed, had made confession, the old man's bones had lain beneath the tramplings of the cross-roads. For everybody, even his own relatives, believed that he had hanged himself. This evilly romantic picture had flamed up with an ominous glow in the boy's imagination as he stood there contemplating his quiet enemy. The woman had become utterly unimportant. She was standing by the table, twisting, now up, now down, her dark-green bonnet-strings.

'How did you do it?' said the boy, looking up and leaning back, with a shuddering sigh, upon his heels. 'How on earth? Did he struggle? He couldn't have struggled *much*, I suppose. He's so small. He *looks* so small.'

The questions were unanswered and were unrepeated. He was merely drinking the scene in. That mole upon the bluish close-shaven cheek was certainly grown blacker than it had been in life, more conspicuous.

'But you aren't of course going to leave him like this?' he broke out sharply. 'You can't, you know; you simply can't.' But the woman was paying him no attention. 'Don't you *see*? They'd find it out in no time,' he added petulantly.

Yet even in the midst of this callous analysis, the woman's childlike attitude attracted his sympathy. At sight of the mute huddled contents of the cupboard, she seemed to have forgotten the danger she was in. A vacant immeasurable mournfulness quietened her face. She was crying. 'I'm sorry, but it's no good crying,' he went on, still kneeling on the cold oilcloth. '*That* won't be of any help; and I'd be awfully pleased to help you all I *can*. As a matter of fact I didn't much care for old Jacobs myself. But then, he's dead now. He *is* dead?'

The woman smothered his momentary fear with an eyeshot of horror. 'Well, if he is, I can't see why you shouldn't say so.' She remained motionless. 'Oh, dear,' he muttered impatiently, 'don't you under*stand*? We *must* do *some*thing.' A heavy frown had settled under the streak of dark hair on his forehead. 'You wouldn't stand the ghost of a chance as it is. They'd catch you easy.'

The woman nodded. 'I don't care; I hope they will. I don't care *what* happens now—because I can't think.'

'That's all rot,' said the boy stoutly. 'You've got to.'

The woman was irritating and paradoxical in this mood, and more than ever like a senseless wax model, which, with diabolical tremors, moves its glazed eyes and turns a glossy head. He peered again into the cupboard. Only once before had he seen Jacobs asleep—stretched out on a sofa in the dining-room one sultry afternoon in the streaming sunshine —gaping, sonorous. Then he had gone out as he had come in, on tiptoe. Now he stooped a little closer towards the cupboard, examining what was in it, stretching out even an experimental finger towards the small pallid hand.

He compared the woman's face and this other face, and found a fancy strangely contradictory of the facts. Jacobs was really and truly the man of blood; Jacobs was just the kind of person you'd expect to be a murderer. Not this woman, so fat and stupid. Nobody would be surprised to find *her* body in any cupboard. But Jacobs, small and ferrety, softly rasping his tune between his teeth, on and on. And now Jacobs was dead. So that's what *that* was like. He jerked his head aside, and his eyes became fixed once more on the gallipot. *That* was the real and eloquent thing. His mind had completed its circuit. He stood up convinced.

'It's no good going on like this,' he explained lucidly, almost cheerfully. 'This would be the very first place they would look into. I should look in here myself. But don't you see, you needn't be caught at all if you do what I tell you. It's something I read in a book of mine.'

The woman lifted a mechanical head and looked at him; and as if for the first time. She saw—a meagre boy with linnet legs and narrow shoulders, a lean clean-cut face of a rather bilious brown, and straight dark brown hair beneath a yachting cap; a boy in black stockings, a night-shirt and a shiny belt; his dark eyes, narrowed and intent, set steep in his head. This boy frightened her. She pushed on her bonnet and loosened her dress about her throat.

Manifestly she was preparing to go. He spoke more decisively. 'You don't *see*. That's all,' he said. 'Really, on my word of honour, it would be all right. I'm not just saying so. A baby could do it.'

The woman knelt down beside him in a posture not unlike the inmate's of the cupboard, and solemnly stared into his face. 'Tell me, tell me quick, you silly lamb. *What* did you say? A *baby* could do it?'

'Why, yes,' said the boy, outwardly cool, but inwardly ardent. 'it's as easy as A.B.C. You get a rope and make a noose, and you put it over his head and round his neck, you know, just as if he was going to be hanged. And then you hang him up on a nail or something. He mustn't touch the ground, of course. You throttled him, didn't you? You see there's no blood. They'll say he hanged himself, don't you see? They'd find old Jacobs strung up in the kitchen here and they'll say he's hanged himself. Don't you *see?*' he repeated.

'Oh, I couldn't do it,' she whimpered, 'not for worlds. I couldn't. I'd sooner stay here beside him till they come.' She began to sob in a stupid vacant fashion and then suddenly hiccuped.

'You *could*, I tell you. A baby could do it. You're afraid. That's what it is! I'm going to, I tell you: whether you like it or not.' He stamped his stockinged foot. 'Mind you, I'm not doing it for myself. It's nothing to do with me. You aren't taking the least trouble to understand.' He looked at her as if he couldn't believe any human being could by any possibility be so dense. 'It's just stupid,' he added over his shoulder, as he sallied out to the boot cupboard to fetch a rope.

Once more the tide of consciousness flowed in the woman's stolid, flattened brain. Two or three words of this young hero had at last fallen on good ground. And with consciousness, fear had come back. She came waddling after the boy. The vagrant crawling inmates of the cupboard had been swept carelessly from the corner, and now he was trailing a rope behind him as he went on into the larder for brandy. His match died down meanwhile, scorching his fingers, and he stayed on in the dark, the woman close behind him, rummaging gingerly among the bottles and dishes. And soon his finger-tips touched the sharp-cut stopper. He returned triumphant, flipping from them the custard they had encountered in their search. The woman followed close behind him, stumbling ever and again upon his trailing rope, and thereby adding to her fears and docility. She was coming alive again. Brandy set her tongue gabbling faster. It gave the boy the strength and zeal of a stage villain.

He skipped hither and thither, now on to, now off the kitchen chair he had pushed nearer; then—having swept back the array of pink-smeared silver candlesticks and snuffers that were in his way, he scrambled up on to the table, and presently, after a few lasso-like flings of it, he had run the rope and made it fast over one of a few large hooks that curved down from the ceiling, hooks once used, as Jacobs had told him, to hang up hams on. His mouth was set, his face intent; his soldier grandfather's lower lip drawn in under the upper. The more active he was the more completely he became master of the ceremonies, the woman only an insignificant accomplice, as stupid as she was irresponsible. Even while she helped him drag out the body from the cupboard on to the flat arena of oilcloth, she continued to cry and snivel, as if *that* would be of any help. But a keen impassive will compelled her obedience. She followed the boy's every nod.

And presently she almost forgot the horror of the task, and found a partial oblivion in the intensity of it, though the boy was displeased by her maunderings. They were merely a doleful refrain to his troublesome grisly work. But he uttered no open reproof—not even when she buried her face in the baize apron and embraced the knees of the dead man. Only once she made any complaint against the limp heedless hung-up creature. 'If only,' she assured her young accomplice, 'if only he hadn't gone and *said* as how I wasn't the first. I ask you! As if I didn't know it.' But to this he paid no attention.

And now, at last, he drew back to view his handiwork. This he did with an inscrutable face, a face flattered at his own extraordinary ingenuity, a young face, almost angelic in its rapt gaslit look and yet one, maybe, of unsophisticated infamy. The dwarfish body seemed to be dangling naturally enough from its hook in the ceiling, its heels just free of the chair. And it did to some extent resemble the half-sinister, half-jocular cut that adorned his *Calendar*. Yet somehow he wasn't perfectly satisfied. Somehow the consummation was as

70

yet incomplete. Some one thing was wanting, some blemish spoiled the effect and robbed it of unity. What? He stood hunting for it without success.

He followed the woman into the passage. She walked unsteadily, swaying bulkily to and fro, now and again violently colliding with the wall. 'Oh, it was crule, crule,' she was muttering.

After her stalked the boy, deep in thought. When she stopped, he stopped; when once more she set forward, as patiently he too set forward with her. Which of them was led, and which leader, it would be difficult to say. This dogged search after the one thing wanting continued to perplex and evade him. He decided that it was no good trying. It must be looked to when the woman was gone; when he was alone.

'I think you had better go now,' he said. 'He'll be coming home soon—my father, I mean, and. . . . It's just ten to twelve by Jacobs's clock.' The words conjured up in his mind a vision of his handsome dressed-up stepmother, standing there in the kitchen doorway half-hysterical before her swaying manservant. It faintly, and even a little sadly, tickled his fancy.

He opened the front door. It was still raining, and the smell of the damp earth and ivy leaves came washing into the house. The woman squatted down on the doorstep. 'Where shall I go?' she said. 'Where shall I go? What's the use? There ain't *no*where.' The boy scowled at the dripping trees. The house was surrounded by night—empty and silent but for the smothering soft small whisper of the rain, and the flat *drip, drip* of the drops from the porch.

'What's the use? There ain't *no*where,' again wailed his poor bedraggled confederate. He scrutinized her scornfully from under his tilted yachting cap. 'Wait a minute,' he said. He raced at full speed up the three dark flights of stairs to his bedroom. The book, the mouse-nibbled pie-crust were tossed on to the hearthrug and a florin was dug out of the gritty soot. Down he came again pell-mell.

Like a cat venturing into a busy street, the woman now stood peering out from the last of the three shallow crescent-shaped stone steps under the porch. 'I've brought you this,' he said superciliously.

'Thank you, sir,' said the woman.

She paused yet again, looking at him, in an attitude now familiar to the boy—the fingers of her knuckled left hand, with its thick brassy wedding-ring, pressed closely against mouth and cheek. He wondered for a moment what she was thinking about, and he was still wondering when she stepped finally off out into the rain.

A shrill shout followed her. 'I say! Mind that ditch there in the road!' But the only result of this was to bring the woman back again; she knelt and clasped him tightly to her bosom.

'I don't know why or anything. Oh, my lamb, my lamb, I didn't mean to do it and now I haven't got anywhere to go.' She bent low and hid her distorted miserable face on his shoulder. 'Oh, oh, I miss him so. The Lord God keep you safe! You've been very kind to me. But. . . .'

She released him, and waddled out once more under the flat-spread branches of the cedar tree, while the boy rubbed the smarting tears from his neck. He shut the door indignantly. This tame reaction was mawkish and silly. Then he paused, uncertain what to do next. And suddenly memory rendered up the one thing wanting—the master-touch.

Why, of course, of course! Jacobs must have kicked a chair down. You couldn't hang yourself like that without a drop. It was impossible. The boy's valour, after all, was only a little shaken by the embrace. Into the kitchen he walked victorious. The gas was still singing, as it had sung all the evening, shedding its dismal flaring light on wall and clock and blind and ceiling and wide array of glossy crockery. The puckered clay-coloured face looked stupidly at him with bolting, dull, dull-lidded eyes. What was now to be done must be done quickly. He ducked sharply and upset the chair—a little too sharply, for a light spring-side boot had tapped him on the cheek. He leapt back, hot and panting. The effect was masterly. It was a triumph. And yet. . . . He stared, with clenched fists, and whispered over his shoulder to a now absent accomplice. But no, he was alone! Only Jacobs was there—with that drowsy slit of eye—tremulously dangling. And as if, even for him, as if even for *his* clear bold young spirit, this last repulsive spectacle, that last minute assault of a helpless enemy, overwhelming some secret stronghold in his mind, had suddenly proved intolerable, his energy, enterprise, courage wilted within him. The whisper in the dark outside of the uncertain wind, the soft bubbling whistle of the gas, the thousand and one minute dumb things around him in the familiar kitchen —nothing had changed. Yet *now* every object had become suddenly real, stark, menacing, and hostile. Panic seized him. He ran out to the front door and bawled into the dark after the woman.

No answer came. The rain was falling softly on the sodden turf; and here, beneath the porch, in large ponderous drops. The widespread palms of the cedar tree under the clouded midnight lay prone and motionless. The whole world was gone out—black. Nothing, nothing; he was alone.

He ran back again into the house—as if he had been awakened out of a dream—leaving the door agape behind him, and whimpering 'Mother!' Then louder—louder. And all the blind things of the house took wooden voices. So up and down this white-shirted raider ran, his clumsy poniard clapping against sudden corners, his tongue calling in vain, and at last—as he went scuttling upstairs at sound of cab-horse and wheels upon the sodden gravel—falling dumb for very terror of its own noise.

SEATON'S AUNT

*

I had heard rumours of Seaton's aunt long before I
actually encountered her. Seaton, in the hush of confidence,
or at any little show of toleration on our part, would remark,
'My aunt', or 'My old aunt, you know', as if his relative might
be a kind of cement to an *entente cordiale*.

He had an unusual quantity of pocket-money; or, at any
rate, it was bestowed on him in unusually large amounts; and
he spent it freely, though none of us would have described
him as an 'awfully generous chap'. 'Hullo, Seaton,' we would
say, 'the old Begum?' At the beginning of term, too, he used
to bring back surprising and exotic dainties in a box with a
trick padlock that accompanied him from his first appearance
at Gummidge's in a billycock hat to the rather abrupt conclusion of his schooldays.

From a boy's point of view he looked distastefully foreign
with his yellowish skin, slow chocolate-coloured eyes, and
lean weak figure. Merely for his looks he was treated by most
of us true-blue Englishmen with condescension, hostility, or
contempt. We used to call him 'Pongo', but without any much
better excuse for the nickname than his skin. He was, that is,
in one sense of the term what he assuredly was not in the other
sense, a sport.

Seaton and I, as I may say, were never in any sense intimate at school; our orbits only intersected in class. I kept deliberately aloof from him. I felt vaguely he was a sneak, and remained quite unmollified by advances on his side, which, in a boy's barbarous fashion, unless it suited me to be magnanimous, I haughtily ignored.

We were both of us quick-footed, and at Prisoner's Base used occasionally to hide together. And so I best remember Seaton—his narrow watchful face in the dusk of a summer evening; his peculiar crouch, and his inarticulate whisperings and mumblings. Otherwise he played all games slackly and limply; used to stand and feed at his locker with a crony or two until his 'tuck' gave out; or waste his money on some outlandish fancy or other. He bought, for instance, a silver bangle, which he wore above his left elbow, until some of the fellows showed their masterly contempt of the practice by dropping it nearly red-hot down his neck.

It needed, therefore, a rather peculiar taste, and a rather rare kind of schoolboy courage and indifference to criticism, to be much associated with him. And I had neither the taste nor, probably, the courage. None the less, he did make advances, and on one memorable occasion went to the length of bestowing on me a whole pot of some outlandish mulberry-coloured jelly that had been duplicated in his term's supplies. In the exuberance of my gratitude I promised to spend the next half-term holiday with him at his aunt's house.

I had clean forgotten my promise when, two or three days before the holiday, he came up and triumphantly reminded me of it.

'Well, to tell you the honest truth, Seaton, old chap——' I began graciously: but he cut me short.

'My aunt expects you,' he said; 'she is very glad you are coming. She's sure to be quite decent to *you*, Withers.'

I looked at him in sheer astonishment; the emphasis was so uncalled for. It seemed to suggest an aunt not hitherto hinted at, and a friendly feeling on Seaton's side that was far more disconcerting than welcome.

We reached his aunt's house partly by train, partly by a lift in an empty farm-cart, and partly by walking. It was a whole-day holiday, and we were to sleep the night; he lent me extraordinary night-gear, I remember. The village street was unusually wide, and was fed from a green by two converging roads, with an inn, and a high green sign at the corner. About a hundred yards down the street was a chemist's shop—a Mr. Tanner's. We descended the two steps into his dusky and odorous interior to buy, I remember, some rat poison. A little beyond the chemist's was the forge. You then walked along a very narrow path, under a fairly high wall, nodding here and there with weeds and tufts of grass, and so came to the iron garden-gates, and saw the high flat house behind its huge sycamore. A coach-house stood on the left of the house, and on the right a gate led into a kind of rambling orchard. The lawn lay away over to the left again, and at the bottom (for the whole garden sloped gently to a sluggish and rushy pond-like stream) was a meadow.

We arrived at noon, and entered the gates out of the hot dust beneath the glitter of the dark-curtained windows. Seaton led me at once through the little garden-gate to show me his tadpole pond, swarming with what (being myself not in the least interested in low life) seemed to me the most horrible creatures—of all shapes, consistencies, and sizes, but with which Seaton was obviously on the most intimate of terms. I can see his absorbed face now as, squatting on his heels he fished the slimy things out in his sallow palms. Wearying at last of these pets, we loitered about awhile in an aimless fashion. Seaton seemed to be listening, or at any rate waiting, for something to happen or for someone to come. But nothing did happen and no one came.

That was just like Seaton. Anyhow, the first view I got of

his aunt was when, at the summons of a distant gong, we turned from the garden, very hungry and thirsty, to go into luncheon. We were approaching the house, when Seaton suddenly came to a standstill. Indeed, I have always had the impression that he plucked at my sleeve. Something, at least, seemed to catch me back, as it were, as he cried, 'Look out, there she is!'

She was standing at an upper window which opened wide on a hinge, and at first sight she looked an excessively tall and overwhelming figure. This, however, was mainly because the window reached all but to the floor of her bedroom. She was in reality rather an undersized woman, in spite of her long face and big head. She must have stood, I think, unusually still, with eyes fixed on us, though this impression may be due to Seaton's sudden warning and to my consciousness of the cautious and subdued air that had fallen on him at sight of her. I know that without the least reason in the world I felt a kind of guiltiness, as if I had been 'caught'. There was a silvery star pattern sprinkled on her black silk dress, and even from the ground I could see the immense coils of her hair and the rings on her left hand which was held fingering the small jet buttons of her bodice. She watched our united advance without stirring, until, imperceptibly, her eyes raised and lost themselves in the distance, so that it was out of an assumed reverie that she appeared suddenly to awaken to our presence beneath her when we drew close to the house.

'So this is your friend, Mr. Smithers, I suppose?' she said, bobbing to me.

'Withers, aunt,' said Seaton.

'It's much the same,' she said, with eyes fixed on me. 'Come in, Mr. Withers, and bring him along with you.'

She continued to gaze at me—at least, I think she did so. I know that the fixity of her scrutiny and her ironical 'Mr.' made me feel peculiarly uncomfortable. None the less she was extremely kind and attentive to me, though, no doubt, her kindness and attention showed up more vividly against her complete neglect of Seaton. Only one remark that I have any recollection of she made to him: 'When I look on my nephew, Mr. Smithers, I realize that dust we are, and dust shall become. You are hot, dirty, and incorrigible, Arthur.'

She sat at the head of the table, Seaton at the foot, and I, before a wide waste of damask tablecloth, between them. It was an old and rather close dining-room, with windows thrown wide to the green garden and a wonderful cascade of fading roses. Miss Seaton's great chair faced this window, so that its rose-reflected light shone full on her yellowish face, and on just such chocolate eyes as my schoolfellow's, except that hers were more than half-covered by unusually long and heavy lids.

There she sat, steadily eating, with those sluggish eyes fixed for the most part on my face; above them stood the deep-lined fork between her eyebrows; and above that the wide expanse of a remarkable brow beneath its strange steep bank of hair. The lunch was copious, and consisted, I remember, of all such dishes as are generally considered too rich and too good for the schoolboy digestion—lobster mayonnaise, cold game sausages, an immense veal and ham pie farced with eggs, truffles, and numberless delicious flavours; besides kickshaws, creams and sweetmeats. We even had a wine, a half-glass of old darkish sherry each.

Miss Seaton enjoyed and indulged an enormous appetite. Her example and a natural schoolboy voracity soon overcame my nervousness of her, even to the extent of allowing me to enjoy to the best of my bent so rare a spread. Seaton was singularly modest; the greater part of his meal consisted of almonds and raisins, which he nibbled surreptitiously and as if he found difficulty in swallowing them.

I don't mean that Miss Seaton 'conversed' with me. She merely scattered trenchant remarks and now and then twinkled a baited question over my head. But her face was like a dense and involved accompaniment to her talk. She presently dropped the 'Mr.', to my intense relief, and called me now Withers, or Wither, now Smithers, and even once towards the close of the meal distinctly Johnson, though how on earth my name suggested it, or whose face mine had reanimated in memory, I cannot conceive.

'And is Arthur a good boy at school, Mr. Wither?' was one of her many questions. 'Does he please his masters? Is he first in his class? What does the reverend Dr. Gummidge think of him, eh?'

I knew she was jeering at him, but her face was adamant against the least flicker of sarcasm or facetiousness. I gazed fixedly at a blushing crescent of lobster.

'I think you're eighth, aren't you, Seaton?'

Seaton moved his small pupils towards his aunt. But she continued to gaze with a kind of concentrated detachment at me.

'Arthur will never make a brilliant scholar, I fear,' she said, lifting a dexterously burdened fork to her wide mouth. . . .

After luncheon she preceded me up to my bedroom. It was a jolly little bedroom, with a brass fender and rugs and a polished floor, on which it was possible, I afterwards found, to play 'snow-shoes'. Over the washstand was a little black-framed water-colour drawing, depicting a large eye with an extremely fishlike intensity in the spark of light on the dark pupil; and in 'illuminated' lettering beneath was printed very minutely, 'Thou God Seest ME', followed by a long looped monogram, 'S.S.', in the corner. The other pictures were all of the sea: brigs on blue water; a schooner overtopping chalk cliffs; a rocky island of prodigious steepness, with two tiny sailors dragging a monstrous boat up a shelf of beach.

'This is the room, Withers, my poor dear brother William died in when a boy. Admire the view!'

I looked out of the window across the tree-tops. It was a day hot with sunshine over the green fields, and the cattle were standing swishing their tails in the shallow water. But the view at the moment was no doubt made more vividly impressive by the apprehension that she would presently enquire after my luggage, and I had brought not even a toothbrush. I need have had no fear. Hers was not that highly civilized type of mind that is stuffed with sharp, material details. Nor could her ample presence be described as in the least motherly.

'I would never consent to question a schoolfellow behind my nephew's back,' she said, standing in the middle of the room, 'but tell me, Smithers, why is Arthur so unpopular? You, I understand, are his only close friend.' She stood in a dazzle of sun, and out of it her eyes regarded me with such leaden penetration beneath their thick lids that I doubt if my face concealed the least thought from her. 'But there, there,' she added very suavely, stooping her head a little, 'don't trouble to answer me. I never extort an answer. Boys are queer fish. Brains might perhaps have suggested his washing his hands before luncheon; but—not my choice, Smithers. God forbid! And now, perhaps, you would like to go into the garden again. I cannot actually see from here, but I should not be surprised if Arthur is now skulking behind that hedge.'

He was. I saw his head come out and take a rapid glance at the windows.

'Join him, Mr. Smithers; we shall meet again, I hope, at the tea-table. The afternoon I spend in retirement.'

Whether or not, Seaton and I had not been long engaged with the aid of two green switches in riding round and round a lumbering old grey horse we found in the meadow, before a rather bunched-up figure appeared, walking along the field-path on the other side of the water, with a magenta parasol studiously lowered in our direction throughout her slow progress, as if that were the magnetic needle and we the fixed Pole. Seaton at once lost all nerve and interest. At the next lurch of the old mare's heels he toppled over into the grass, and I slid off the sleek broad back to join him where he stood, rubbing his shoulder and sourly watching the rather pompous figure till it was out of sight.

'Was that your aunt, Seaton?' I enquired; but not till then.

'He nodded.

'Why didn't she take any notice of us, then?'

'She never does.'

'Why not?'

'Oh, she knows all right, without; that's the dam awful part of it.' Seaton was one of the very few fellows at Gummidge's who had the ostentation to use bad language. He had suffered for it too. But it wasn't, I think, bravado. I believe he really felt certain things more intensely than most of the other fellows, and they were generally things that fortunate and average people do not feel at all—the peculiar quality, for instance, of the British schoolboy's imagination.

'I tell you, Withers,' he went on moodily, slinking across the meadow with his hands covered up in his pockets, 'she sees everything. And what she doesn't see she knows without.'

'But how?' I said, not because I was much interested, but because the afternoon was so hot and tiresome and purposeless, and it seemed more of a bore to remain silent. Seaton turned gloomily and spoke in a very low voice.

'Don't appear to be talking of her, if you wouldn't mind. It's—because she's in league with the Devil.' He nodded his head and stooped to pick up a round flat pebble. 'I tell you,' he said, still stooping, 'you fellows don't realize what it is. I know I'm a bit close and all that. But so would you be if you had that old hag listening to every thought you think.'

I looked at him, then turned and surveyed one by one the windows of the house.

'Where's your *pater*?' I said awkwardly.

'Dead, ages and ages ago, and my mother too. She's not my aunt even by rights.'

'What is she, then?'

'I mean she's not my mother's sister, because my grandmother married twice; and she's one of the first lot. I don't know what you call her, but anyhow she's not my real aunt.'

'She gives you plenty of pocket-money.'

Seaton looked steadfastly at me out of his flat eyes. 'She can't give me what's mine. When I come of age half of the whole lot will be mine; and what's more'—he turned his back on the house—'I'll make her hand over every blessed shilling of it.'

I put my hands in my pockets and stared at Seaton; 'Is it much?'

He nodded.

'Who told you?' He got suddenly very angry; a darkish red came into his cheeks, his eyes glistened, but he made no answer, and we loitered listlessly about the garden until it was time for tea. . . .

Seaton's aunt was wearing an extraordinary kind of lace jacket when we sidled sheepishly into the drawing-room together. She greeted me with a heavy and protracted smile, and bade me bring a chair close to the little table.

'I hope Arthur has made you feel at home,' she said as she handed me my cup in her crooked hand. 'He don't talk much to me; but then I'm an old woman. You must come again, Wither, and draw him out of his shell. You old snail!' She wagged her head at Seaton, who sat munching cake and watching her intently.

'And we must correspond, perhaps.' She nearly shut her eyes at me. 'You must write and tell me everything behind the creature's back.' I confess I found her rather disquieting company. The evening drew on. Lamps were brought in by a man with a nondescript face and very quiet footsteps. Seaton was told to bring out the chess-men. And we played a game, she and I, with her big chin thrust over the board at every move as she gloated over the pieces and occasionally croaked 'Check!'—after which she would sit back inscrutably staring at me. But the game was never finished. She simply hemmed me in with a gathering cloud of pieces that held me impotent, and yet one and all refused to administer to my poor flustered old king a merciful *coup de grâce*.

'There,' she said, as the clock struck ten—'a drawn game, Withers. We are very evenly matched. A very creditable defence, Withers. You know your room. There's supper on a tray in the dining-room. Don't let the creature over-eat himself. The gong will sound three-quarters of an hour *before* a punctual breakfast.' She held out her cheek to Seaton, and he kissed it with obvious perfunctoriness. With me she shook hands.

'An excellent game,' she said cordially, 'but my memory is poor, and'—she swept the pieces helter-skelter into the box—'the result will never be known.' She raised her great head far back. 'Eh?'

It was a kind of challenge, and I could only murmur: 'Oh I was absolutely in a hole, you know!' when she burst out laughing and waved us both out of the room.

Seaton and I stood and ate our supper, with one candlestick to light us, in a corner of the dining-room. 'Well, and how would you like it?' he said very softly, after cautiously poking his head round the doorway.

'Like what?'

'Being spied on—every blessed thing you do and think?'

'I shouldn't like it at all,' I said, 'if she does.'

'And yet you let her smash you up at chess!'

'I didn't let her!' I said indignantly.

'Well, you funked it, then.'

'And I didn't funk it either,' I said; 'she's so jolly clever with her knights.' Seaton stared at the candle. 'Knights,' he said slowly. 'You wait, that's all.' And we went upstairs to bed.

I had not been long in bed, I think, when I was cautiously awakened by a touch on my shoulder. And there was Seaton's face in the candlelight—and his eyes looking into mine.

'What's up?' I said, lurching on to my elbow.

'*Ssh!* Don't scurry,' he whispered. 'She'll hear. I'm sorry for waking you, but I didn't think you'd be asleep so soon.'

'Why, what's the time, then?' Seaton wore, what was then rather unusual, a night-suit, and he hauled his big silver watch out of the pocket in his jacket.

'It's a quarter to twelve. I never get to sleep before twelve —not here.'

'What do you do, then?'

'Oh, I read: and listen.'

'Listen?'

Seaton stared into his candle-flame as if he were listening even then. 'You can't guess what it is. All you read in ghost stories, that's all rot. You can't see much, Withers, but you know all the same.'

'Know what?'

'Why, that they're there.'

'Who's there?' I asked fretfully, glancing at the door.

'Why, in the house. It swarms with 'em. Just you stand still and listen outside my bedroom door in the middle of the night. I have, dozens of times; they're all over the place.'

'Look here, Seaton,' I said, 'you asked me to come here, and I didn't mind chucking up a leave just to oblige you and because I'd promised; but don't get talking a lot of rot, that's all, or you'll know the difference when we get back.'

'Don't fret,' he said coldly, turning away. 'I shan't be at school long. And what's more, you're here now, and there isn't anybody else to talk to. I'll chance the other.'

'Look here, Seaton,' I said, 'you may think you're going to scare me with a lot of stuff about voices and all that. But I'll just thank you to clear out; and you may please yourself about pottering about all night.'

He made no answer; he was standing by the dressing-table looking across his candle into the looking-glass; he turned and stared slowly round the walls.

'Even this room's nothing more than a coffin. I suppose she

told you—"It's all exactly the same as when my brother William died"—trust her for that! And good luck to him, say I. Look at that.' He raised his candle close to the little water-colour I have mentioned. 'There's hundreds of eyes like that in this house; and even if God does see you, He takes precious good care you don't see Him. And it's just the same with them. I tell you what, Withers, I'm getting sick of all this. I shan't stand it much longer.'

The house was silent within and without, and even in the yellowish radiance of the candle a faint silver showed through the open window on my blind. I slipped off the bedclothes, wide awake, and sat irresolute on the bedside.

'I know you're only guying me,' I said angrily, 'but why is the house full of—what you say? Why do you hear—what you *do* hear? Tell me that, you silly fool!'

Seaton sat down on a chair and rested his candlestick on his knee. He blinked at me calmly. 'She brings them,' he said, with lifted eyebrows.

'Who? Your aunt?'

He nodded.

'How?'

'I told you,' he answered pettishly. 'She's in league. You don't know. She as good as killed my mother; I know that. But it's not only her by a long chalk. She just sucks you dry. I know. And that's what she'll do for me; because I'm like her —like my mother, I mean. She simply hates to see me alive. I wouldn't be like that old she-wolf for a million pounds. And so'—he broke off, with a comprehensive wave of his candle-stick—'they're always here. Ah, my boy, wait till she's dead! She'll hear something then, I can tell you. It's all very well now, but wait till then! I wouldn't be in her shoes when she has to clear out—for something. Don't you go and believe I care for ghosts, or whatever you like to call them. We're all in the same box. We're all under her thumb.'

He was looking almost nonchalantly at the ceiling at the

moment, when I saw his face change, saw his eyes suddenly drop like shot birds and fix themselves on the cranny of the door he had left just ajar. Even from where I sat I could see his cheek change colour; it went greenish. He crouched without stirring, like an animal. And I, scarcely daring to breathe, sat with creeping skin, sourly watching him. His hands relaxed, and he gave a kind of sigh.

'Was *that* one?' I whispered, with a timid show of jauntiness. He looked round, opened his mouth, and nodded. 'What?' I said. He jerked his thumb with meaningful eyes, and I knew that he meant that his aunt had been there listening at our door cranny.

'Look here, Seaton,' I said once more, wriggling to my feet. 'You may think I'm a jolly noodle; just as you please. But your aunt has been civil to me and all that, and I don't believe a word you say about her, that's all, and never did. Every fellow's a bit off his pluck at night, and you may think it a fine sport to try your rubbish on me. I heard your aunt come upstairs before I fell asleep. And I'll bet you a level tanner she's in bed now. What's more, you can keep your blessed ghosts to yourself. It's a guilty conscience, I should think.'

Seaton looked at me intently, without answering for a moment. 'I'm not a liar, Withers; but I'm not going to quarrel either. You're the only chap I care a button for; or, at any rate, you're the only chap that's ever come here; and it's something to tell a fellow what you feel. I don't care a fig for fifty thousand ghosts, although I swear on my solemn oath that I know they're here. But she'—he turned deliberately—'you laid a tanner she's in bed, Withers; well, I know different. She's never in bed much of the night, and I'll prove it, too, just to show you I'm not such a nolly as you think I am. Come on!'

'Come on where?'

'Why, to see.'

I hesitated. He opened a large cupboard and took out a

small dark dressing-gown and a kind of shawl-jacket. He threw the jacket on the bed and put on the gown. His dusky face was colourless, and I could see by the way he fumbled at the sleeves he was shivering. But it was no good showing the white feather now. So I threw the tasselled shawl over my shoulders and, leaving our candle brightly burning on the chair, we went out together and stood in the corridor.

'Now then, listen!' Seaton whispered.

We stood leaning over the staircase. It was like leaning over a well, so still and chill the air was all around us. But presently, as I suppose happens in most old houses, began to echo and answer in my ears a medley of infinite small stirrings and whisperings. Now out of the distance an old timber would relax its fibres, or a scurry die away behind the perishing wainscot. But amid and behind such sounds as these I seemed to begin to be conscious, as it were, of the lightest of footfalls, sounds as faint as the vanishing remembrance of voices in a dream. Seaton was all in obscurity except his face; out of that his eyes gleamed darkly, watching me.

'You'd hear, too, in time, my fine soldier,' he muttered. 'Come on!'

He descended the stairs, slipping his lean fingers lightly along the balusters. He turned to the right at the loop, and I followed him barefooted along a thickly carpeted corridor. At the end stood a door ajar. And from here we very stealthily and in complete blackness ascended five narrow stairs. Seaton, with immense caution, slowly pushed open a door, and we stood together, looking into a great pool of duskiness, out of which, lit by the feeble clearness of a night-light, rose a vast bed. A heap of clothes lay on the floor; beside them two slippers dozed, with noses each to each, a foot or two apart. Somewhere a little clock ticked huskily. There was a close smell; lavender and eau de Cologne, mingled with the fragrance of ancient sachets, soap, and drugs. Yet it was a scent even more peculiarly compounded than that.

And the bed! I stared warily in; it was mounded gigantically, and it was empty.

Seaton turned a vague pale face, all shadows: 'What did I say?' he muttered. 'Who's—who's the fool now, I say? How are we going to get back without meeting her, I say? Answer me that! Oh, I wish to God you hadn't come here, Withers.'

He stood audibly shivering in his skimpy gown, and could hardly speak for his teeth chattering. And very distinctly, in the hush that followed his whisper, I heard approaching a faint unhurried voluminous rustle. Seaton clutched my arm, dragged me to the right across the room to a large cupboard, and drew the door close to on us. And, presently, as with bursting lungs I peeped out into the long, low, curtained bedroom, waddled in that wonderful great head and body. I can see her now, all patched and lined with shadow, her tied-up hair (she must have had enormous quantities of it for so old a woman), her heavy lids above those flat, slow, vigilant eyes. She just passed across my ken in the vague dusk; but the bed was out of sight.

We waited on and on, listening to the clock's muffled ticking. Not the ghost of a sound rose up from the great bed. Either she lay archly listening or slept a sleep serener than an infant's. And when, it seemed, we had been hours in hiding and were cramped, chilled, and half suffocated, we crept out on all fours, with terror knocking at our ribs, and so down the five narrow stairs and back to the little candle-lit blue-and-gold bedroom.

Once there, Seaton gave in. He sat livid on a chair with closed eyes.

'Here,' I said, shaking his arm, 'I'm going to bed; I've had enough of this foolery; I'm going to bed.' His lips quivered, but he made no answer. I poured out some water into my basin and, with that cold pictured azure eye fixed on us, bespattered Seaton's sallow face and forehead and dabbled his hair. He presently sighed and opened fish-like eyes.

'Come on!' I said. 'Don't get shamming, there's a good chap. Get on my back, if you like, and I'll carry you into your bedroom.'

He waved me away and stood up. So, with my candle in one hand, I took him under the arm and walked him along according to his direction down the corridor. His was a much dingier room than mine, and littered with boxes, paper, cages, and clothes. I huddled him into bed and turned to go. And suddenly, I can hardly explain it now, a kind of cold and deadly terror swept over me. I almost ran out of the room, with eyes fixed rigidly in front of me, blew out my candle, and buried my head under the bedclothes.

When I awoke, roused not by a gong, but by a long-continued tapping at my door, sunlight was raying in on cornice and bedpost, and birds were singing in the garden. I got up, ashamed of the night's folly, dressed quickly, and went downstairs. The breakfast room was sweet with flowers and fruit and honey. Seaton's aunt was standing in the garden beside the open french window, feeding a great flutter of birds. I watched her for a moment, unseen. Her face was set in a deep reverie beneath the shadow of a big loose sun-hat. It was deeply lined, crooked, and, in a way I can't describe, fixedly vacant and strange. I coughed politely, and she turned with a prodigious smiling grimace to ask how I had slept. And in that mysterious fashion by which we learn each other's secret thoughts without a syllable said, I knew that she had followed every word and movement of the night before, and was triumphing over my affected innocence and ridiculing my friendly and too easy advances.

We returned to school, Seaton and I, lavishly laden, and by rail all the way. I made no reference to the obscure talk we had had, and resolutely refused to meet his eyes or to take up the hints he let fall. I was relieved—and yet I was sorry—to be going back, and strode on as fast as I could from the station, with Seaton almost trotting at my heels. But he insisted on buying more fruit and sweets—my share of which I accepted with a very bad grace. It was uncomfortably like a bribe; and, after all, I had no quarrel with his rum old aunt, and hadn't really believed half the stuff he had told me.

I saw as little of him as I could after that. He never referred to our visit or resumed his confidences, though in class I would sometimes catch his eye fixed on mine, full of a mute understanding, which I easily affected not to understand. He left Gummidge's, as I have said, rather abruptly, though I never heard of anything to his discredit. And I did not see him or have any news of him again till by chance we met one summer afternoon in the Strand.

He was dressed rather oddly in a coat too large for him and a bright silky tie. But we instantly recognized one another under the awning of a cheap jeweller's shop. He immediately attached himself to me and dragged me off, not too cheerfully, to lunch with him at an Italian restaurant near by. He chattered about our old school, which he remembered only with dislike and disgust; told me cold-bloodedly of the disastrous fate of one or two of the older fellows who had been among his chief tormentors; insisted on an expensive wine and the whole gamut of the foreign menu; and finally informed me, with a good deal of niggling, that he had come up to town to buy an engagement-ring.

And of course: 'How is your aunt?' I enquired at last.

He seemed to have been awaiting the question. It fell like a stone into a deep pool, so many expressions flitted across his long, sad, sallow, un-English face.

'She's aged a good deal,' he said softly, and broke off.

'She's been very decent,' he continued presently after, and paused again. 'In a way.' He eyed me fleetingly. 'I dare say you heard that—she—that is, that we—had lost a good deal of money.'

'No,' I said.

'Oh, yes!' said Seaton, and paused again.

And somehow, poor fellow, I knew in the clink and clatter of glass and voices that he had lied to me; that he did not possess, and never had possessed, a penny beyond what his aunt had squandered on his too ample allowance of pocket-money.

'And the ghosts?' I enquired quizzically.

He grew instantly solemn, and, though it may have been my fancy, slightly yellowed. But 'You are making game of me, Withers,' was all he said.

He asked for my address, and I rather reluctantly gave him my card.

'Look here, Withers,' he said, as we stood together in the sunlight on the kerb, saying good-bye, 'here I am, and—and it's all very well. I'm not perhaps as fanciful as I was. But you are practically the only friend I have on earth—except Alice. ... And there—to make a clean breast of it, I'm not sure that my aunt cares much about my getting married. She doesn't say so, of course. You know her well enough for that.' He looked sidelong at the rattling gaudy traffic.

'What I was going to say is this: Would you mind coming down? You needn't stay the night unless you please, though, of course, you know you would be awfully welcome. But I should like you to meet my—to meet Alice; and then, perhaps, you might tell me your honest opinion of—of the other too.'

I vaguely demurred. He pressed me. And we parted with a half promise that I would come. He waved his ball-topped cane at me and ran off in his long jacket after a bus.

A letter arrived soon after, in his small weak handwriting, giving me full particulars regarding route and trains. And without the least curiosity, even perhaps with some little annoyance that chance should have thrown us together again, I accepted his invitation and arrived one hazy midday at his out-of-the-way station to find him sitting on a low seat under a clump of 'double' hollyhocks, awaiting me.

He looked preoccupied and singularly listless; but seemed, none the less, to be pleased to see me.

We walked up the village street, past the little dingy apothecary's and the empty forge, and, as on my first visit, skirted the house together, and, instead of entering by the front door, made our way down the green path into the garden at the back. A pale haze of cloud muffled the sun; the garden lay in a grey shimmer—its old trees, its snap-dragoned faintly glittering walls. But now there was an air of slovenliness where before all had been neat and methodical. In a patch of shallowly dug soil stood a worn-down spade leaning against a tree. There was an old decayed wheelbarrow. The roses had run to leaf and briar; the fruit-trees were unpruned. The goddess of neglect had made it her secret resort.

'You ain't much of a gardener, Seaton,' I said at last, with a sigh of relief.

'I think, do you know, I like it best like this,' said Seaton. 'We haven't any man now, of course. Can't afford it.' He stood staring at his little dark oblong of freshly turned earth. 'And it always seems to me,' he went on ruminatingly, 'that, after all, we are all nothing better than interlopers on the earth, disfiguring and staining wherever we go. It may sound shocking blasphemy to say so; but then it's different here, you see. We are further away.'

'To tell you the truth, Seaton, I *don't* quite see,' I said; 'but it isn't a new philosophy, is it? Anyhow, it's a precious beastly one.'

'It's only what I think,' he replied, with all his odd old stubborn meekness. 'And one thinks as one *is*.'

We wandered on together, talking little, and still with that expression of uneasy vigilance on Seaton's face. He pulled out his watch as we stood gazing idly over the green meadows and the dark motionless bulrushes.

'I think, perhaps, it's nearly time for lunch,' he said. 'Would you like to come in?'

We turned and walked slowly towards the house, across whose windows I confess my own eyes, too, went restlessly meandering in search of its rather disconcerting inmate. There was a pathetic look of bedraggledness, of want of means and care, rust and overgrowth and faded paint. Seaton's aunt, a little to my relief, did not share our meal. So he carved the cold meat, and dispatched a heaped-up plate by an elderly servant for his aunt's private consumption. We talked little and in half-suppressed tones, and sipped some Madeira which Seaton after listening for a moment or two fetched out of the great mahogany sideboard.

I played him a dull and effortless game of chess, yawning between the moves he himself made almost at haphazard, and with attention elsewhere engaged. Towards five o'clock came the sound of a distant ring, and Seaton jumped up, overturning the board, and so ended a game that else might have fatuously continued to this day. He effusively excused himself, and after some little while returned with a slim, dark, pale-faced girl of about nineteen, in a white gown and hat, to whom I was presented with some little nervousness as his 'dear old friend and schoolfellow'.

We talked on in the golden afternoon light, still, as it seemed to me, and even in spite of our efforts to be lively and gay, in a half-suppressed, lack-lustre fashion. We all seemed, if it were not my fancy, to be expectant, to be almost anxiously awaiting an arrival, the appearance of someone whose image filled our collective consciousness. Seaton talked least of all, and in a restless interjectory way, as he continually fidgeted from chair to chair. At last he proposed a stroll in the garden before the sun should have quite gone down.

Alice walked between us. Her hair and eyes were conspicuously dark against the whiteness of her gown. She carried herself not ungracefully, and yet with peculiarly little movement of her arms and body, and answered us both without turning her head. There was a curious provocative reserve in that impassive melancholy face. It seemed to be haunted by some tragic influence of which she herself was unaware.

And yet somehow I knew—I believe we all knew—that this walk, this discussion of their future plans was a futility. I had nothing to base such scepticism on, except only a vague sense of oppression, a foreboding consciousness of some inert invincible power in the background, to whom optimistic plans and love-making and youth are as chaff and thistledown. We came back, silent, in the last light. Seaton's aunt was there—under an old brass lamp. Her hair was as barbarously massed and curled as ever. Her eyelids, I think, hung even a little heavier in age over their slow-moving inscrutable pupils. We filed in softly out of the evening, and I made my bow.

'In this short interval, Mr. Withers,' she remarked amiably, 'you have put off youth, put on the man. Dear me, how sad it is to see the young days vanishing! Sit down. My nephew tells me you met by chance—or act of Providence, shall we call it? —and in my beloved Strand! You, I understand, are to be best man—yes, best man! Or am I divulging secrets?' She surveyed Arthur and Alice with overwhelming graciousness. They sat apart on two low chairs and smiled in return.

'And Arthur—how do you think Arthur is looking?'

'I think he looks very much in need of a change,' I said.

'A change! Indeed?' She all but shut her eyes at me and with an exaggerated sentimentality shook her head. 'My dear Mr. Withers! Are we not *all* in need of a change in this fleeting, fleeting world?' She mused over the remark like a connoisseur. 'And you,' she continued, turning abruptly to Alice, 'I hope you pointed out to Mr. Withers all my pretty bits?'

'We only walked round the garden,' the girl replied; then, glancing at Seaton, added almost inaudibly, 'it's a very beautiful evening.'

'*Is* it?' said the old lady, starting up violently. 'Then on this very beautiful evening we will go in to supper. Mr. Withers, your arm; Arthur, bring your bride.'

94

We were a queer quartet, I thought to myself, as I solemnly led the way into the faded, chilly dining-room, with this indefinable old creature leaning wooingly on my arm—the large flat bracelet on the yellow-laced wrist. She fumed a little, breathing heavily, but as if with an effort of the mind rather than of the body; for she had grown much stouter and yet little more proportionate. And to talk into that great white face, so close to mine, was a queer experience in the dim light of the corridor, and even in the twinkling crystal of the candles. She was naïve—appallingly naïve; she was crafty and challenging; she was even arch; and all these in the brief, rather puffy passage from one room to the other, with these two tongue-tied children bringing up the rear. The meal was tremendous. I have never seen such a monstrous salad. But the dishes were greasy and over-spiced, and were indifferently cooked. One thing only was quite unchanged—my hostess's appetite was as Gargantuan as ever. The heavy silver candelabra that lighted us stood before her high-backed chair. Seaton sat a little removed, his plate almost in darkness.

And throughout this prodigious meal his aunt talked, mainly to me, mainly *at* him, but with an occasional satirical sally at Alice and muttered explosions of reprimand to the servant. She had aged, and yet, if it be not nonsense to say so, seemed no older. I suppose to the Pyramids a decade is but as the rustling down of a handful of dust. And she reminded me of some such unshakable prehistoricism. She certainly was an amazing talker—rapid, egregious, with a delivery that was perfectly overwhelming. As for Seaton—her flashes of silence were for him. On her enormous volubility would suddenly fall a hush: acid sarcasm would be left implied; and she would sit softly moving her great head, with eyes fixed full in a dreamy smile; but with her whole attention, one could see, slowly, joyously absorbing his mute discomfiture.

She confided in us her views on a theme vaguely occupying at the moment, I suppose, all our minds. 'We have barbarous institutions, and so must put up, I suppose, with a never-ending procession of fools—of fools *ad infinitum*. Marriage, Mr. Withers, was instituted in the privacy of a garden; *sub rosa*, as it were. Civilization flaunts it in the glare of day. The dull marry the poor; the rich the effete; and so our New Jerusalem is peopled with naturals, plain and coloured, at either end. I detest folly; I detest still more (if I must be frank, dear Arthur) mere cleverness. Mankind has simply become a tailless host of uninstinctive animals. We should never have taken to Evolution, Mr. Withers. "Natural Selection!"—little gods and fishes! —the deaf for the dumb. We should have used our brains— intellectual pride, the ecclesiastics call it. And by brains I mean —what do I mean, Alice?—I mean, my dear child,' and she laid two gross fingers on Alice's narrow sleeve, 'I mean courage. Consider it, Arthur. I read that the scientific world is once more beginning to be afraid of spiritual agencies. Spiritual agencies that tap, and actually float, bless their hearts! I think just one more of those mulberries—thank you.

'They talk about "blind Love",' she ran on derisively as she helped herself, her eyes roving over the dish, 'but why blind? I think, Mr. Withers, from weeping over its rickets. After all, it is we plain women that triumph, is it not so— beyond the mockery of time. Alice, now! Fleeting, fleeting is youth, my child. What's that you were confiding to your plate, Arthur? Satirical boy. He laughs at his old aunt: nay, but thou didst laugh. He detests all sentiment. He whispers the most acid asides. Come, my love, we will leave these cynics; we will go and commiserate with each other on our sex. The choice of two evils, Mr. Smithers!' I opened the door, and she swept out as if borne on a torrent of unintelligible indignation; and Arthur and I were left in the clear four-flamed light alone.

For a while we sat in silence. He shook his head at my cigarette-case, and I lit a cigarette. Presently he fidgeted in his chair and poked his head forward into the light. He paused to rise, and shut again the shut door.

'How long will you be?' he asked me.

I laughed.

'Oh, it's not that!' he said, in some confusion. 'Of course, I like to be with her. But it's not that. The truth is, Withers, I don't care about leaving her too long with my aunt.'

I hesitated. He looked at me questioningly.

'Look here, Seaton,' I said, 'you know well enough that I don't want to interfere in your affairs, or to offer advice where it is not wanted. But don't you think perhaps you may not treat your aunt quite in the right way? As one gets old, you know, a little give and take. I have an old godmother, or something of the kind. She's a bit queer, too. . . . A little allowance; it does no harm. But hang it all, I'm no preacher.'

He sat down with his hands in his pockets and still with his eyes fixed almost incredulously on mine. 'How?' he said.

'Well, my dear fellow, if I'm any judge—mind, I don't say that I am—but I can't help thinking she thinks you don't care for her; and perhaps takes your silence for—for bad temper. She has been very decent to you, hasn't she?'

' "Decent"? My God!' said Seaton.

I smoked on in silence; but he continued to look at me with that peculiar concentration I remembered of old.

'I don't think, perhaps, Withers,' he began presently, 'I don't think you quite understand. Perhaps you are not quite our kind. You always did, just like the other fellows, guy me at school. You laughed at me that night you came to stay here —about the voices and all that. But I don't mind being laughed at—because I know.'

'Know what?' It was the same old system of dull question and evasive answer.

'I mean I know that what we see and hear is only the smallest fraction of what is. I know she lives quite out of this. She *talks* to you; but it's all make-believe. It's all a "parlour game". She's not really with you; only pitting her outside wits against yours and enjoying the fooling. She's living on inside

97

on what you're rotten without. That's what it is—a cannibal feast. She's a spider. It doesn't much matter what you call it. It means the same kind of thing. I tell you, Withers, she hates me; and you can scarcely dream what that hatred means. I used to think I had an inkling of the reason. It's oceans deeper than that. It just lies behind: herself against myself. Why, after all, how much do we really understand of anything? We don't even know our own histories, and not a tenth, not a tenth of the reasons. What has life been to me?—nothing but a trap. And when one sets oneself free for a while, it only begins again. I thought you might understand; but you are on a different level: that's all.'

'What on earth are you talking about?' I said contemptuously, in spite of myself.

'I mean what I say,' he said gutturally. 'All this outside's only make-believe—but there! what's the good of talking? So far as this is concerned I'm as good as done. You wait.'

Seaton blew out three of the candles and, leaving the vacant room in semi-darkness, we groped our way along the corridor to the drawing-room. There a full moon stood shining in at the long garden windows. Alice sat stooping at the door, with her hands clasped in her lap, looking out, alone.

'Where is she?' Seaton asked in a low tone.

She looked up; and their eyes met in a glance of instantaneous understanding, and the door immediately afterwards opened behind us.

'*Such* a moon!' said a voice, that once heard, remained unforgettably on the ear. 'A night for lovers, Mr. Withers, if ever there was one. Get a shawl, my dear Arthur, and take Alice for a little promenade. I dare say we old cronies will manage to keep awake. Hasten, hasten, Romeo! My poor, poor Alice, how laggard a lover!'

Seaton returned with a shawl. They drifted out into the moonlight. My companion gazed after them till they were out of hearing, turned to me gravely, and suddenly twisted her white face into such a convulsion of contemptuous amusement that I could only stare blankly in reply.

'Dear innocent children!' she said, with inimitable unctuousness. 'Well, well, Mr. Withers, we poor seasoned old creatures must move with the times. Do you sing?'

I scouted the idea.

'Then you must listen to my playing. Chess'—she clasped her forehead with both cramped hands—'chess is now completely beyond my poor wits.'

She sat down at the piano and ran her fingers in a flourish over the keys. 'What shall it be? How shall we capture them, those passionate hearts? That first fine careless rapture? Poetry itself.' She gazed softly into the garden a moment, and presently, with a shake of her body, began to play the opening bars of Beethoven's 'Moonlight' Sonata. The piano was old and woolly. She played without music. The lamplight was rather dim. The moonbeams from the window lay across the keys. Her head was in shadow. And whether it was simply due to her personality or to some really occult skill in her playing I cannot say; I only know that she gravely and deliberately set herself to satirize the beautiful music. It brooded on the air, disillusioned, charged with mockery and bitterness. I stood at the window; far down the path I could see the white figure glimmering in that pool of colourless light. A few faint stars shone, and still that amazing woman behind me dragged out of the unwilling keys her wonderful grotesquerie of youth and love and beauty. It came to an end. I knew the player was watching me. 'Please, please, go on!' I murmured, without turning. '*Please* go on playing, Miss Seaton.'

No answer was returned to this honeyed sarcasm, but I realized in some vague fashion that I was being acutely scrutinized, when suddenly there followed a procession of quiet, plaintive chords which broke at last softly into the hymn, *A Few More Years Shall Roll.*

I confess it held me spellbound. There is a wistful, strained plangent pathos in the tune; but beneath those masterly old hands it cried softly and bitterly the solitude and desperate estrangement of the world. Arthur and his lady-love vanished from my thoughts. No one could put into so hackneyed an old hymn tune such an appeal who had never known the meaning of the words. Their meaning, anyhow, isn't commonplace.

I turned a fraction of an inch to glance at the musician. She was leaning forward a little over the keys, so that at the approach of my silent scrutiny she had but to turn her face into the thin flood of moonlight for every feature to become distinctly visible. And so, with the tune abruptly terminated, we steadfastly regarded one another; and she broke into a prolonged chuckle of laughter.

'Not quite so seasoned as I supposed, Mr. Withers. I see you are a real lover of music. To me it is too painful. It evokes too much thought. . . .'

I could scarcely see her little glittering eyes under their penthouse lids.

'And now,' she broke off crisply, 'tell me, as a man of the world, what do you think of my new niece?'

I was not a man of the world, nor was I much flattered in my stiff and dullish way of looking at things by being called one; and I could answer her without the least hesitation.

'I don't think, Miss Seaton, I'm much of a judge of character. She's very charming.'

'A brunette?'

'I think I prefer dark women.'

'And why? Consider, Mr. Withers; dark hair, dark eyes, dark cloud, dark night, dark vision, dark death, dark grave, dark DARK!'

Perhaps the climax would have rather thrilled Seaton, but I was too thick-skinned. 'I don't know much about all that,' I answered rather pompously. 'Broad daylight's difficult enough for most of us.'

'Ah,' she said, with a sly inward burst of satirical laughter.

'And I suppose,' I went on, perhaps a little nettled, 'it isn't the actual darkness one admires, it's the contrast of the skin, and the colour of the eyes, and—and their shining. Just as,' I went blundering on, too late to turn back, 'just as you only see the stars in the dark. It would be a long day without any evening. As for death and the grave, I don't suppose we shall much notice that.' Arthur and his sweetheart were slowly returning along the dewy path. 'I believe in making the best of things.'

'How very interesting!' came the smooth answer. 'I see you are a philosopher, Mr. Withers. H'm! "As for death and the grave, I don't suppose we shall much notice that." Very interesting. . . . And I'm sure,' she added in a particularly suave voice, 'I profoundly hope so.' She rose slowly from her stool. 'You will take pity on me again, I hope. You and I would get on famously—kindred spirits—elective affinities. And, of course, now that my nephew's going to leave me, now that his affections are centred on another, I shall be a very lonely old woman. . . . Shall I not, Arthur?'

Seaton blinked stupidly. 'I didn't hear what you said, Aunt.'

'I was telling our old friend, Arthur, that when you are gone I shall be a very lonely old woman.'

'Oh, I don't think so;' he said in a strange voice.

'He means, Mr. Withers, he means, my dear child,' she said, sweeping her eyes over Alice, 'he means that I shall have memory for company—heavenly memory—the ghosts of other days. Sentimental boy! And did you enjoy our music, Alice? Did I really stir that youthful heart? . . . O, O, O,' continued the horrible old creature, 'you billers and cooers, I have been listening to such flatteries, such confessions! Beware, beware, Arthur, there's many a slip.' She rolled her little eyes at me, she shrugged her shoulders at Alice, and gazed an instant stonily into her nephew's face.

I held out my hand. 'Good night, good night!' she cried. 'He that fights and runs away. Ah, good night, Mr. Withers; come again soon!' She thrust out her cheek at Alice, and we all three filed slowly out of the room.

Black shadow darkened the porch and half the spreading sycamore. We walked without speaking up the dusty village street. Here and there a crimson window glowed. At the fork of the high-road I said good-bye. But I had taken hardly more than a dozen paces when a sudden impulse seized me.

'Seaton!' I called.

He turned in the cool stealth of the moonlight.

'You have my address; if by any chance, you know, you should care to spend a week or two in town between this and the—the Day, we should be delighted to see you.'

'Thank you, Withers, thank you,' he said in a low voice.

'I dare say'—I waved my stick gallantly at Alice—'I dare say you will be doing some shopping; we could all meet,' I added, laughing.

'Thank you, thank you, Withers—immensely,' he repeated. And so we parted.

But they were out of the jog-trot of my prosaic life. And being of a stolid and incurious nature, I left Seaton and his marriage, and even his aunt, to themselves in my memory, and scarcely gave a thought to them until one day I was walking up the Strand again, and passed the flashing gloaming of the second-rate jeweller's shop where I had accidentally encountered my old schoolfellow in the summer. It was one of those stagnant autumnal days after a night of rain. I cannot say why, but a vivid recollection returned to my mind of our meeting and of how suppressed Seaton had seemed, and of how vainly he had endeavoured to appear assured and eager. He must be married by now, and had doubtless returned from his honeymoon. And I had clean forgotten my manners, had sent not a word of congratulation, nor—as I might very well have done and as I knew he would have been pleased at my doing—even the ghost of a wedding present. It was just as of old.

On the other hand, I pleaded with myself, I had had no invitation. I paused at the corner of Trafalgar Square, and at the bidding of one of those caprices that seize occasionally on even an unimaginative mind, I found myself pelting after a green bus, and actually bound on a visit I had not in the least intended or foreseen.

The colours of autumn were over the village when I arrived. A beautiful late afternoon sunlight bathed thatch and meadow. But it was close and hot. A child, two dogs, a very old woman with a heavy basket I encountered. One or two incurious tradesmen looked idly up as I passed by. It was all so rural and remote, my whimsical impulse had so much flagged, that for a while I hesitated to venture under the shadow of the sycamore-tree to enquire after the happy pair. Indeed I first passed by the faint-blue gates and continued my walk under the high, green and tufted wall. Hollyhocks had attained their topmost bud and seeded in the little cottage gardens beyond; the Michaelmas daisies were in flower; a sweet warm aromatic smell of fading leaves was in the air. Beyond the cottages lay a field where cattle were grazing, and beyond that I came to a little churchyard. Then the road wound on, pathless and houseless, among gorse and bracken. I turned impatiently and walked quickly back to the house and rang the bell.

The rather colourless elderly woman who answered my enquiry informed me that Miss Seaton was at home, as if only taciturnity forbade her adding, 'But she doesn't want to see *you*.'

'Might I, do you think, have Mr. Arthur's address?' I said.

She looked at me with quiet astonishment, as if waiting for an explanation. Not the faintest of smiles came into her thin face.

'I will tell Miss Seaton,' she said after a pause. 'Please walk in.'

She showed me into the dingy undusted drawing-room, filled with evening sunshine and with the green-dyed light that penetrated the leaves overhanging the long french windows. I sat down and waited on and on, occasionally aware of a creaking footfall overhead. At last the door opened a little, and the great face I had once known peered round at me. For it was enormously changed; mainly, I think, because the aged eyes had rather suddenly failed, and so a kind of stillness and darkness lay over its calm and wrinkled pallor.

'Who is it?' she asked.

I explained myself and told her the occasion of my visit.

She came in, shut the door carefully after her, and, though the fumbling was scarcely perceptible, groped her way to a chair. She had on an old dressing-gown, like a cassock, of a patterned cinnamon colour.

'What is it you want?' she said, seating herself and lifting her blank face to mine.

'Might I just have Arthur's address?' I said deferentially. 'I am so sorry to have disturbed you.'

'H'm. You have come to see my nephew?'

'Not necessarily to see him, only to hear how he is, and, of course, Mrs. Seaton, too. I am afraid my silence must have appeared. . . .'

'He hasn't noticed your silence,' croaked the old voice out of the great mask; 'besides, there isn't any Mrs. Seaton.'

'Ah, then,' I answered, after a momentary pause, 'I have not seemed so black as I painted myself! And how is Miss Outram?'

'She's gone into Yorkshire,' answered Seaton's aunt.

'And Arthur too?'

She did not reply, but simply sat blinking at me with lifted chin, as if listening, but certainly not for what I might have to say. I began to feel rather at a loss.

'You were no close friend of my nephew's, Mr. Smithers?' she said presently.

'No,' I answered, welcoming the cue, 'and yet, do you know, Miss Seaton, he is one of the very few of my old schoolfellows I have come across in the last few years, and I suppose as one gets older one begins to value old associations. . . .' My voice seemed to trail off into a vacuum. 'I thought Miss Outram', I hastily began again, 'a particularly charming girl. I hope they are both quite well.'

Still the old face solemnly blinked at me in silence.

'You must find it very lonely, Miss Seaton, with Arthur away?'

'I was never lonely in my life,' she said sourly. 'I don't look to flesh and blood for my company. When you've got to be my age, Mr. Smithers (which God forbid), you'll find life a very different affair from what you seem to think it is now. You won't seek company then, I'll be bound. It's thrust on you.' Her face edged round into the clear green light, and her eyes groped, as it were, over my vacant, disconcerted face. 'I dare say, now,' she said, composing her mouth, 'I dare say my nephew told you a good many tarradiddles in his time. Oh, yes, a good many, eh? He was always a liar. What, now, did he say of me? Tell me, now.' She leant forward as far as she could, trembling, with an ingratiating smile.

'I think he is rather superstitious,' I said coldly, 'but, honestly, I have a very poor memory, Miss Seaton.'

'Why?' she said. '*I* haven't.'

'The engagement hasn't been broken off, I hope.'

'Well, between you and me,' she said, shrinking up and with an immensely confidential grimace, 'it has.'

'I'm sure I'm very sorry to hear it. And where is Arthur?'

'Eh?'

'Where is Arthur?'

We faced each other mutely among the dead old bygone furniture. Past all my analysis was that large, flat, grey, cryptic countenance. And then, suddenly, our eyes for the first time really met. In some indescribable way out of that thick-lidded obscurity a far small something stooped and looked out at me for a mere instant of time that seemed of almost intolerable protraction. Involuntarily I blinked and shook my head. She muttered something with great rapidity, but quite inarticulately; rose and hobbled to the door. I thought I heard, mingled in broken mutterings, something about tea.

'Please, please, don't trouble,' I began, but could say no more, for the door was already shut between us. I stood and looked out on the long-neglected garden. I could just see the bright weedy greenness of Seaton's tadpole pond. I wandered about the room. Dusk began to gather, the last birds in that dense shadowiness of trees had ceased to sing. And not a sound was to be heard in the house. I waited on and on, vainly speculating. I even attempted to ring the bell; but the wire was broken, and only jangled loosely at my efforts.

I hesitated, unwilling to call or to venture out, and yet more unwilling to linger on, waiting for a tea that promised to be an exceedingly comfortless supper. And as darkness drew down, a feeling of the utmost unease and disquietude came over me. All my talks with Seaton returned on me with a suddenly enriched meaning. I recalled again his face as we had stood hanging over the staircase, listening in the small hours to the inexplicable stirrings of the night. There were no candles in the room; every minute the autumnal darkness deepened. I cautiously opened the door and listened, and with some little dismay withdrew, for I was uncertain of my way out. I even tried the garden, but was confronted under a veritable thicket of foliage by a padlocked gate. It would be a little too ignominious to be caught scaling a friend's garden fence.

Cautiously returning into the still and musty drawing-room, I took out my watch, and gave the incredible old woman ten minutes in which to reappear. And when that tedious ten minutes had ticked by I could scarcely distinguish its hands. I determined to wait no longer, drew open the door and, trusting to my sense of direction, groped my way through the corridor that I vaguely remembered led to the front of the house.

I mounted three or four stairs and, lifting a heavy curtain, found myself facing the starry fanlight of the porch. From here I glanced into the gloom of the dining-room. My fingers were on the latch of the outer door when I heard a faint stirring in the darkness above the hall. I looked up and became conscious of, rather than saw, the huddled old figure looking down on me.

There was an immense hushed pause. Then, 'Arthur, Arthur,' whispered an inexpressibly peevish rasping voice, 'is that you? Is that you, Arthur?'

I can scarcely say why, but the question horribly startled me. No conceivable answer occurred to me. With head craned back, hand clenched on my umbrella, I continued to stare up into the gloom, in this fatuous confrontation.

'Oh, oh,' the voice croaked. 'It is *you*, is it? *That* disgusting man! . . . Go away out. Go away out.'

At this dismissal, I wrenched open the door and, rudely slamming it behind me, ran out into the garden, under the gigantic old sycamore, and so out at the open gate.

I found myself half up the village street before I stopped running. The local butcher was sitting in his shop reading a piece of newspaper by the light of a small oil-lamp. I crossed the road and enquired the way to the station. And after he had with minute and needless care directed me, I asked casually if Mr. Arthur Seaton still lived with his aunt at the big house just beyond the village. He poked his head in at the little parlour door.

'Here's a gentleman enquiring after young Mr. Seaton, Millie,' he said. 'He's dead, ain't he?'

'Why, yes, bless you,' replied a cheerful voice from within. 'Dead and buried these three months or more—young Mr. Seaton. And just before he was to be married, don't you remember, Bob?'

I saw a fair young woman's face peer over the muslin of the little door at me.

'Thank you,' I replied, 'then I go straight on?'

'That's it, sir; past the pond, bear up the hill a bit to the left, and then there's the station lights before your eyes.'

We looked intelligently into each other's faces in the beam of the smoky lamp. But not one of the many questions in my mind could I put into words.

And again I paused irresolutely a few paces further on. It was not, I fancy, merely a foolish apprehension of what the raw-boned butcher might 'think' that prevented my going back to see if I could find Seaton's grave in the benighted churchyard. There was precious little use in pottering about in the muddy dark merely to discover where he was buried. And yet I felt a little uneasy. My rather horrible thought was that, so far as I was concerned—one of his extremely few friends—he had never been much better than 'buried' in my mind.

CREWE

*

When murky winter dusk begins to settle over the railway station at Crewe its first-class waiting-room grows steadily more stagnant. Particularly if one is alone in it. The long grimed windows do little more than sift the failing light that slopes in on them from the glass roof outside and is too feeble to penetrate into the recesses beyond. And the grained massive black-leathered furniture becomes less and less inviting. It appears to have been made for a scene of extreme and diabolical violence that one may hope will never occur. One can hardly at any rate imagine it to have been designed by a really *good* man!

Little things like this of course are apt to become exaggerated in memory, and I may be doing the Company an injustice. But whether this is so or not—and the afternoon I have in mind is now many years distant—I certainly became more acutely conscious of the defects of my surroundings when the few fellow-travellers who had been sharing this dreadful apartment with me had hurried out at the clang of a bell for the down train, leaving me to wait for the up. And nothing and nobody, as I supposed, but a great drowsy fire of cinders in the iron grate for company.

The almost animated talk that had sprung up before we parted, never in this world to meet again, had been occasioned

by an account in the morning's newspapers of the last voyage
of a ship called the *Hesper*. She had come in the evening before, and some days overdue, with a cargo of sugar from the
West Indies, and was now berthed safely in the Southampton
Docks. This seemed to have been something of a relief to
those concerned. For even her master had not refused to
admit that certain mysterious and tragic events had recently
occurred on board, though he preferred not to discuss them
with a reporter. He agreed, even with the reporter, however,
that there had been a full moon at the time, that, apart from a
heavy swell, the sea was 'as calm as a mill-pond', and that his
ship was at present in want of a second mate. But the voyage
of the *Hesper* is now, of course, an old tale many times told.
And I myself, having taken very little part in the discussion,
had by that time wearied of her mysteries and had decided to
seek the lights and joys and coloured bottles of the refreshment room when a voice from out of the murk behind me
suddenly broke the hush. It was an unusual voice, rapid,
incoherent and internal, like that of a man in a dream or under
the influence of a drug.

I shifted my high-backed ungainly chair and turned to look.
Evidently this, the only other occupant of the room, had until
that moment been as unaware of my presence in it as I of his.
Indeed he seemed to have been completely taken aback at
finding he was not alone. He had started up from out of his
obscure corner beyond the high window and was stating
across at me out of his flat greyish face in unconcealed stupefaction. He seemed for a moment or two to be in doubt even
of what I was. Then he sighed, a sigh that ended in a long
shuddering yawn. 'I am sorry,' I said, 'I supposed——'

But he interrupted me—and not as if my company, now
that he had recognized me as a fellow creature, was any the
less welcome for being unexpected.

'Merely what I was saying, sir,' he was mildly explaining,
'is that those gentlemen there who have just left us had no

more notion of what they were talking about than an infant in the cradle.'

This elegant paraphrase, I realized, bore only the feeblest resemblance to the violent soliloquy I had just overheard. I looked at him. 'How so?' I said. 'I am only a landsman myself, but. . . .'

It had seemed unnecessary to finish the sentence—I have never seen anyone less marine in effect than *he* was. He had shifted a little nearer and was now, his legs concealed, sitting on the extreme edge of his vast wooden sofa—a smallish man, but muffled up in a very respectable greatcoat at least two sizes too large for him, his hands thrust deep into its pockets.

He continued to stare at me. 'You don't have to go to sea for things like that,' he went on. 'And there's no need to argue about it if you do. Still it wasn't my place to interfere. They'll find out all right—all in good time. They go their ways. And talking of that, now, have you ever heard say that there is less risk sitting in a railway carriage at sixty miles an hour than in laying alone, safe, as you might suppose, in your own bed? That's true, too.' He glanced round him. 'You know where you are in a place like this, too. It's solid, though——' I couldn't catch the words that followed, but they seemed to be uncomplimentary to things in general.

'Yes,' I agreed, 'it certainly looks solid.'

'Ah, "looks",' he went on cantankerously. 'But what *is* your "solid", come to that? I thought so myself once,' He seemed to be pondering over the *once*. 'But now', he added, 'I know different.'

With that he rose and, dwarfed a little perhaps by the length of his coat, sallied out of his obscure corner beyond the high window and came to the fire. After warming his veined shrunken hands at the heap of smouldering cinders in the grate under the black marble mantelpiece—he seated himself opposite to me.

At risk of seeming fastidious, I must confess that now he was near I did not much care for the appearance of this stranger. He might be about to solicit a small loan. In spite of his admirable greatcoat he looked in need of a barber, as well as of medicine and sleep—a need that might presently exhibit itself in a hankering for alcohol. But I was mistaken. He asked for nothing, not even sympathy, not even advice. He merely, it seemed, wanted to talk about himself. And perhaps a complete stranger makes a better receptacle for a certain kind of confidences than one's intimates. He tells no tales.

Nevertheless I shall attempt to tell Mr. Blake's, and as far as possible in his own peculiar idiom. It impressed me at the time. And I have occasionally speculated since whether his statistics in relation to the risks of railway travel proved trustworthy. *Safety first* is a sound principle so far as it goes, but we are all of us out-manœuvred in the end. And I still wonder what end was his.

He began by asking me if I had ever lived in the country— 'In the depps of the country'. And then, quickly realizing that I was more inclined to listen than talk, he suddenly plunged into his past. It seemed to refresh him to do so.

'I was a gentleman's servant when I began,' he set off; 'first boot-boy under a valet, then footman and helping at table, then pantry work and so on. Never married or anything of that; petticoats are nothing but encumbrances in the house. But I must say if you keep yourself *to* yourself, it sees you through—in time. What you have to beware of is those of your own calling. Domestic. That's the same everywhere; nobody's reached much past the cat-and-dog stage in that. Not if you look close enough; high or low. I lost one or two nice easy places all on that account. Jealousy. And if you don't stay where you are put there's precious little chance of pickings when the funeral's at the door. But that's mostly changed, so I'm told; high wages and no work being the order of the day; and gratitude to follow suit. They are all rolling stones nowadays, and never mind the moss.'

As a philosopher this white-faced muffled-up old creature seemed to affect realism, though his reservations on the 'solid' had fallen a little short of it. Not that *my* reality appeared to matter much—beyond, I mean the mere proof of it. For though in the rather intimate memories he proceeded to share with me he frequently paused to ask a question, he seldom waited for an answer, and then ignored it. I see now this was not to be wondered at. We happened to be sharing at the moment this—for my part—chance resort and he wanted company—human company.

'The last situation I was in' (he was going on to tell me), 'was with the Reverend W. Somers, M.A.: William. In the depps of the country, as I say. Just myself, a young fellow of the name of George, and a woman who came in from the village to char and cook and so on, though I did the best part of that myself. The finishing touches, I mean. How long the Reverend hadn't cared for females in the house I never knew; but parsons have their share of them, I'm thinking. Not that he wasn't attached enough to his sister. They had grown up together, nursery to drawing-room, and that covers a multitude of sins.

'Like *him*, *she* was, but more of the parrot in appearance; a high face with a beaky nose. Quite a nice lady, too, except that she was mighty slow in being explained to. No interference, generally speaking; in spite of her nose. But don't mistake me; we had to look alive when she was in the house. Oh, yes. But that, thank God, was seldom. And in the end it made no difference.

'She never took to the Vicarage. Who would? I can hear her now—Blake this, and Blake that. Too dark, too vaulty, too shut in. And in winter freezing cold, laying low maybe. Trees in front, everlastings; though open behind with a stream and cornfields and hills in the distance; especially in summer, of course. They went up and down, and dim and dark, according to the weather. You could see for miles from those upper corridor windows—small panes that take a lot of cleaning. But George did the windows. George had come from the village, too, if you could call it a village. But he was a permanency. Nothing much but a few cottages, and an outlying farmhouse here and there. Why the old brick church lay about a mile away from it, I can't say. To give the Roaring Lion a trot, perhaps. The Reverend had private means—naturally. I knew that before it came out in the will. But it was a nice fat living notwithstanding—worked out at about fifty pounds to the pig-sty, I shouldn't wonder, with the vicarage thrown in. You get what you've got in this world, and some of us enjoy a larger slice than we deserve. But the Reverend, I must say, never took advantage of it. He was a gentleman. Give him his books, and to-morrow like yesterday, and he gave no trouble —none whatever.

'Mind you, he liked things as they should be, and he had some of the finest silver I ever lay finger on; and old furniture to match. I don't mean furniture picked up at sales and such like, but real old family stuff. That's where the parrot in the family nose came from. Everything punctual to the minute and the good things *good*. Soup or fish, a cutlet, a savoury, and a glass of sherry or madeira. No sweets—though he was a lean, spare gentleman, silvery beard and all. And I have never seen choicer fruit than came from his houses and orchard, though it was here the trouble began. Cherries, gages, peaches, nectarines—old red sun-baked walls nine or ten feet high and a sight like wonder in the spring. I used to go out specially to have a look at them. He had his fancies, too, had the Reverend. If any smoking was to be done it must be in the shrubbery with the blackbirds, not under the roof. And sitting there in his study, sir, he could detect the whiff of a cigarette even in the furthest of the attics!

'But tobacco's not *my* trouble, never was. Keep off what you don't need, and you won't want it when you can't get it. That's my feeling. It was, as I say, an easy place, if you forgot how quiet it was—not a sound, no company, and not a soul to be seen. Fair prospects, too, if you could wait. He had no fancy for change, had the Reverend; made no concealment of it. He told me himself that he had remembered me in his will —"if still in his service". You know how these lawyers put it. As a matter of fact he had given me to understand that if in the meantime for any reason any of us went elsewhere, the one left was to have the lot. But not death. *There*, as it turned out, I was in error.

'But I'm not complaining of that now. He was a gentleman; and I have enough to see me through however long I'm left. And that might be for a good many years yet.'

The intonation of this last remark suggested a question. But my confidant made no pause for an answer and added argumentatively, 'Who *wants* to go, I should like to ask? Early *or* late. And nothing known of what's on the other side?' He lifted his grey eyebrows a little as if to glance up at me as he sat stooped up by the fire, and yet refrained from doing so. And again I couldn't enlighten him.

'Well, there, as I say, I might have stayed to this day if the old gentleman's gardener had cared to stay too. *He* began it. Him gone, we all went. Like ninepins. You might hardly credit it, sir, but I am the only one left of that complete establishment. Gutted. And that's where these fine gentlemen here were talking round their hats. What I say is, keep on this side of the tomb as long as you can. Don't meddle with that hole. Why? Because while some fine day you will have to go down into it, you can never be quite sure while you are here what mayn't come back out of it.

'*There'll be no partings there*—I have heard them trolling that out in them chapels like missel-thrushes in the spring. They seem to forget there may be some mighty unpleasant *meetings*. And what about the further shore? It's my belief there's some kind of a ferry plying on that river. And coming back depends on what you want to come back *for*.

'Anyhow the Vicarage reeked of it. A low old house, with lots of little windows and far too many doors; and, as I say, the trees too close up on one side, almost brushing the glass. No wonder they said it was what they call haunted. You could feel that with your eyes shut, and like breeds like. The Vicar—two or three, I mean, before my own gentleman—had even gone to the trouble of having the place exercised. Candles and holy water, that kind of thing. Sheer flummummery, *I* call it. But if what I've heard there—and long before that gowk of a George came to work in the house—was anything more than mere age and owls and birds in the ivy, it must badly have needed it. And when you get accustomed to noises, you can tell which from which. By usual, I mean. Though more and more I'm getting to ask myself if any thing is anything much more than what you think it is—for the time being.

'Same with noises of course. What's this voice of conscience that they talk about but something you needn't hear if you don't want to? I am not complaining of that. If at the beginning there was anything in that house that was better out than in, it never troubled me; at least, not at first. And the Reverend, even though you could often count his congregation on your ten fingers, except at Harvest Festival, was so wove up in his books that I doubt if he'd have been roused up out of 'em even by the Last Trump. It's my belief that in those last few weeks—when I stepped in to see to the fire—as often as not he was sitting asleep over them.

'No, I'm not complaining. Live at peace with who you can, I say. But when it comes to as crusty a customer, and a Scotchman at that, as was my friend the gardener, then there's a limit. Mengus he called himself, though I can't see *how*, if you spell it with a z. When I first came into the place it was all gold that glitters. I'm not the man for contentiousness, if let alone. But afterwards, when the rift came, I don't suppose we ever hardly exchanged the time of day but what there came words of it. A long-legged man *he* was, this Mr. Menzies; too long I should have thought for strict comfort in grubbing and hoeing and weeding. He had ginger hair, scanty, and the same on his face, whiskers—and a stoop. He lived down at the lodge; and his widowed daughter kept house for him, with one little boy as fair as she was dark. Harmless enough as children go, the kind they call an angel, but noisy, and not for the house.

'Now why, I ask you, shouldn't I pick a little of this gentleman's precious fruit, or a cucumber for a salad, if need be, and him not there? What if I wanted a few grapes for dessert or a nice apricot tart for the Reverend's luncheon, and our Mr. Menzies gone home or busy with the frames? I don't hold with all these hard and fast restrictions, at least outside the house. Not he, though! We wrangled about it week in, week out. And him with a temper which once roused was past all reasoning.

'Not that I ever took much notice of him until it came to a point past any man's enduring. I let him rave. But duty is duty, there's no getting away from that. And when, apart from all this fuss about his fruit, a man takes advantage of what is meant in pure friendliness, well, one's bound to make a move. Job himself.

'What I mean to say is, I used occasionally—window wide open and all that, the pantry being on the other side of the house and away from the old gentleman's study—I say I used occasionally, and all in the way of friendliness, to offer our friend a drink. Like as with many of Old Adam's trade, drink was a little weakness of his, though I don't mean I hold with it because of that. But peace and quietness is the first thing, and to keep an easy face to all appearances, even if you do find it a little hard at times to forgive and forget.

'When he was civil, as I say, and as things should be, he could have a drink, and welcome. When not, not. But it came to become a kind of habit; and to be expected; which is always a bad condition of things. Oh, it was a thousand pities! There was the Reverend, growing feeble as you could see, and him believing all the while that everything around him was calm and sweet as the new Jerusalem, while there was nothing but strife and agrimony, as they call it, underneath. There's many a house looks as snug and cosy as a nut. But crack it and look inside! Mildew. Still, our Mr. Mengus had "prospects," up to then.

'Well, there came along at last a mighty hot summer—five years ago, you may remember. Five years ago, next August, an extraordinary hot summer. And an early harvest—necessarily. Day after day I could see the stones in the stubble fields shivering in the sun. And gardening is thirsty work; I will say that for it. Which being so, better surely virgin water from the tap or a drop of cider, same as the harvesters have, than ardent spirits, whether it is what you are bred up to or not! It stands to reason.

'Besides, we had had words again, and though I can stretch a point with a friend and no harm done, I'm not a man to come coneying and currying favour. Let him get his own drinks, was my feeling in the matter. And you can hardly call me to blame if he did. *There* was the pantry window hanging wide open in the shade of the trees—and day after day of scorching sun and not a breath to breathe. And there was the ruin of him within arm's reach from outside, and a water tap handy, too. Very inviting, I'll allow.

'I'm not attesting, mind you, that he was confirmed at it, no more than that I'm a man to be measuring what's given me to take charge of by tenths of inches. It's the principle of the thing. You might have thought, too, that a simple honest pride would have kept him back. Nothing of the sort; and no matter, wine or spirits. I'd watch him there, though he couldn't see me, being behind the door. And practices like that, sir, as you will agree with me, can't go on. They couldn't go on, vicarage or no vicarage. Besides, from being secret it began to be open. It had gone too far. Brazen it out: that was the lay. I came down one fine morning to find one of my best decanters smashed to smithereens on the stone floor, Irish glass and all. Cats and sherry, who ever heard of it? And out of revenge he filled the pantry with wasps by bringing in over-ripe plums. Petty waste of time like that. And some of the green-houses thick with blight!

'And so things went, from bad to worse, and at such a pace as I couldn't have credited. A widower, too, with a married daughter dependent on him; which is worse even than a wife, who expects to take the bad with the good. No, sir, I had to call a halt to it. A friendly word in his ear, or keeping everything out of his reach, you may be thinking, might have sufficed. Believe me, not for him. And how can you foster such a weakness by taking steps out of the usual to prevent it? It wouldn't be proper to your self-respect. Then I thought of George; not com*prom*ising myself in any way, of course, in so doing. George had a face as long as your arm, pale and solemn, enough to make a cat laugh. Dress him up in a surplice and hassock, he might have been the Reverend's curate. Strange that, for a youth born in the country. But curate or no curate, he had eyes in his head and must have seen what there was to be seen.

'I said to him one day, and I remember him standing there in the pantry in his black coat against the white of the cupboard paint, I said to him, "George, a word in time saves nine, but it would come better from you than from me. You take me? Hold your peace till our friend's sober again and can listen to reason. Then hand it over to him—a word of warning, I mean. Say we are muffling things up as well as we *can* from the old gentleman, but that if he should hear of it there'd be fat in the fire; and no mistake. He would take it easier from you, George, the responsibility being mine."

'Lord, how I remember George! He had a way of looking at you as if he couldn't say *Boh* to a goose—swollen hands and bolting blue eyes, as simple as an infant's. But he wasn't stupid, oh no. Nobody could say that. And now I reflect, I think he knew our little plan wouldn't carry very far. But there, whatever he might be thinking, he was so awkward with his tongue that he could never find anything to say until it was too late, so I left it at that. Besides, I had come to know he was, with all his faults, a young man you could trust for doing what he was told to do. So, as I say, I left it at that.

'What he actually did say I never knew. But as for its being of any use, it was more like pouring paraffin on a bonfire. The very next afternoon our friend came along to the pantry window and stood there looking in—swaying he was, on his feet; and I can see the midges behind him zigzagging in a patch of sunshine as though they were here before my very eyes. He was so bad that he had to lay hold of the sill to keep himself from falling. Not thirst this time, but just fury. And then, seeing that mere flaunting of fine feathers wasn't going to inveigle *me* into a cockfight, he began to talk. Not all bad language, mind you—*that's* easy to shut your ears to—but cold reasonable abuse, which isn't. At first I took no notice, went on about my business at my leisure, and no hurry. What's the use of arguing with a man, and him one of these Scotchmen to boot, that's beside himself with rage? What was wanted was *peace* in the house, if only for the old gentleman's sake, who I thought was definitely under the weather and had been coming on very poorly of late.

' "Where's that George of yours?" he said to me at last—with additions. "Where's that George? Fetch him out, and I'll teach him to come playing the holy Moses to my own daughter. Fetch him out, I say, and we'll finish it here and now." And all pitched high, and half his words no more English than the mewing of a cat.

'But I kept my temper and answered him quite moderate and as pleasantly as I knew how. "I don't want to meddle in *any*body's quarrels," I said. "So long as George so does his work in this house as will satisfy *my* eye, I am not responsible for his actions in his off-time and out of bounds."

'How was I to know, may I ask, if it was *not* our Mr.

Mengus who had smashed one of my best decanters? What proof was there? What *reason* had I for thinking else?

' "George is a quiet, unbeseeming young fellow," I said, "and if he thinks it's his duty to report any misgoings-on either to me or to the Reverend, it doesn't concern anybody else."

'That seemed to sober my fine gentleman. Mind you, I'm not saying that there was anything unremidibly wrong with him. He was a first-class gardener. I grant you that. But then he had an uncommonly good place to match—first-class wages; and no milk, wood, coals or house-rent to worry about. But breaking out like that, and the Reverend poorly and all; that's not what he thought of when he put us all down in his will. I'll be bound of that. Well, there he stood, looking in at the window and me behind the table in my apron as calm as if his wrangling meant no more to me than the wind in the chimmeny. It was the word "report", I fancy, that took the wind out of his sails. It had brought him up like a station buffer. And he was still looking at me, and brooding it over, as though he had the taste of poison on his tongue.

'Then he says very quiet, "So that's his little game, is it? You are just a pair, then?"

' "If by pair you're meaning me," I said, "well, I'm ready to take my share of the burden when it's ready to fit my back. But not before. George may have gone a bit beyond himself, but he meant well, and you know it."

' "What I am asking is this," says our friend, "have you ever seen me the worse for liquor? Answer me that!"

' "If I liked your tone better," I said, "I wouldn't say how I don't see why it would be necessarily the *worse*."

' "Ehh? You mean, Yes, then?" he said.

' "I mean no more than what I say," I answered him, looking at him over the cruet as straight as I'm looking at you now. "I don't ask to meddle with your private affairs, and I'll thank *you* not to come meddling with mine." He seemed taken aback at that, and I noticed he was looking a bit pinched, and hollow under the eyes. Sleepless nights, perhaps.

'But how was *I* to know this precious grandson of his was out of sorts with a bad throat and that—seeing that he hadn't mentioned it till a minute before? I ask you! "The best thing you and George there can do," I went on, "is to bury the hatchet; and out of hearing of the house, too."

'With that I turned away and went off into it myself, leaving him there to think things over at his leisure. I am putting it to you, sir, as a free witness, what else could I have done?'

There was little light of day left in our cavernous waiting-room by this time. Only the dulling glow of the fire and the phosphorescence caused by a tiny bead of gas in the 'mantles' of the great iron bracket over our heads. My realist seemed to be positively in want of an answer to this last question. But as I sat looking back into his intent small face nothing that could be described as of a helpful nature offered itself.

'If he was anxious about his grandson,' I ventured at last, 'it might explain his being a little short in temper. Besides. . . . But I should like to hear what came after.'

'What came after, now?' the little man repeated, drawing his right hand gingerly out of the depths of his pocket and smoothing down his face with it as if he had suddenly dis-covered he was tired. 'Well, a good deal came after, but not quite what you might have expected. And you'd hardly go so far as to say perhaps that anxiety over his grandson would excuse him for what was little short of manslaughter, and him a good six inches to the good at that? Keeping facts as facts, if you'll excuse me, our friend waylaid George by the stables that very evening, and a wonderful peaceful evening it was, shepherd's delight and all that. But to judge from the looks of the young fellow's face when he came into the house there hadn't been much of that in the quarter of an hour they had had together.

'I said, "Sponge it down, George, sponge it down. And by good providence maybe the old gentleman won't notice anything wrong." It wasn't to reason I could let him off his duties and enter into a lot of silly peravications which in the long run might only make things worse. It's that you have to think of when you are a man in my position. But as for the Reverend's not noticing it, there, as luck would have it, I was wrong myself.

'For when the two of us were leaving the dining-room that evening after the table had been cleared and the dessert put on, he looked up from round the candles and told George to stay behind. Some quarter of an hour after that George came along to me snuffling as if he'd been crying. But I asked no questions, not me; and, as I say, he was always pretty slow with his tongue. All that I could get out of him was that he had decocted some cock-and-bull story to account for his looks the like of which nobody in his senses could credit, let alone such a power of questioning as the old gentleman could bring to bear when roused, and apart from what comes, I suppose, from reading so many books. So the fat *was* in the fire and no mistake. And the next thing I heard, after coming back late the following evening, was that our Mr. Mengus had been called into the house and given the sack there and then, with a quarter's wages in lieu of notice. Which, after all, mind you, was as good as three-quarters a gift. What I'm saying is that handsome is as handsome does, and that was the Reverend all over; though I agree, mind you, even money isn't necessarily everything when there's what they call character to be taken into account. But if ever there was one of the quality fair and upright in all his dealings, as the saying goes, then that was the Reverend Somers. And I abide by that. He wouldn't have any truck with drink topped with insolence. That's all.

'Well, our friend came rapping at the back door that evening, shaken to the marrow if ever man was, and just livid. I told him, and I meant it too, that I was sorry for what had occurred: "It's a bad ending", I said, "to a tale that ought never to have been told." I told him too, speaking as quiet and pleasant as I am to you now, that the only hope left was to let bygones be bygones; that he had already had his fingers on George, and better go no further. Not he. He said, and he was sober enough then in all conscience, that, come what come may, here or hereafter, he'd be even with him. Ay, and he made mention of me also, but not so rabid. A respectable man, too; never a word against him till then; and not far short of sixty. And by rabid I don't mean violent. He spoke as low and quiet as if there was a judge on the bench there to hear him, sentence said and everything over. And then. . . .'

The old creature paused until yet another main-line train had gone roaring on its way. 'And then,' he continued, 'though he wasn't found till morning, he must have gone straight out—and good-bye said to nobody. He must, I say, have gone straight out to the old barn and hanged himself. The midmost rafter, sir, and a drop that would have sufficed for a Giant Goliath. All night. And it's my belief, good-bye or no good-bye, that it wasn't so much the *disgrace* of the affair but his daughter—Mrs. Shaw by name—and his grandson that were preying on his mind. And yet—why, he never so much as asked me to say a good word for him! Not one.

'Well, that was the end of that. So far. And it's a curious thing to me—though they say these Romans aren't above making use of it—how, going back over the past clears everything up like; at least for the time being. But it's what you were saying just now about what's *solid* that sets me thinking and keeps repeating itself in my mind. Solid was the word you used. And they look it, I agree.' He deliberately twisted his head and fastened a prolonged stare on the bench on which he had been seated. 'But it doesn't follow there's much comfort in them even if they are. Solid or not, they go at last when all's said to what's little else but gas and ashes once they're fallen to pieces and been put on the fire. Which holds good, and even more so, for them that sit on them. Peculiar habit that, too—sitting! Yes, I've been told, sir, that after what they call this cremation, and all the moisture in us gone up in steam, what's left would scarcely turn the scales by a single *hounce*!'

If sitting *is* a peculiar habit, it was even more peculiar how etherealizing the effect of my new acquaintance's misplaced aspirate had been—his one and only lapse in this respect throughout his interminable monologue.

'Yes, they say that so far as this *solid* goes, we amount to no more than what you could put into a walnut. And my point, sir,' he was emphasizing with a forefinger that only just showed itself beyond the long sleeve of his greatcoat, 'my point is *this*—that if *that's* all there is to you and me, we shouldn't need much of the substantial for what you might call the mere sole look of things, if you follow me, if *we* chose or chanced to come back. When gone, I mean. Just enough, I suppose, to be obnoxious, as the Reverend used to say, to the naked eye.

'But all that being as it may be, the whole thing had tided over, and George was pretty nearly himself again, and another gardener advertised for—and I must say the Reverend, though after this horrible affair he was never the same man again, treated the young woman I mentioned as if he himself had been a father—I say, the whole thing had tided over, and the house was as silent as a tomb again, ay, as the sepulchre itself, when I began to notice something peculiar.

'At first maybe, little more *than* mere silence. What, in the contrast, as a matter of fact, I took for *peace*. But afterwards not so. There was a strain, so to speak, as you went about your daily doings. A strain. And especially after dark. It may have been only in one's head. I can't say. But it was there: and I could see without watching that even George had noticed it, and *he'd* hardly notice a black-beetle on a pancake.

'And at last there came something you could put word to, catch in the act, so to speak. I had gone out towards the cool of the evening after a broiling hot day, to get a little air. There was a copse of beeches, which as perhaps you may know, is a very pleasant tree for shade, sir, at a spot a bit under the mile from the back of the Vicarage. And I sat there quiet for a minute or two, with the birds and all—they were beginning to sing again, I remember—and—you know how memory strays back, though sometimes it's more like a goat tethered to a peg on a common—I was thinking over what a curious thing it is how one man's poison is another man's meat. For the funeral over, and all that, the old gentleman had thanked me for all I had done. You see what had gone before had been a hard break in his trust of a man, and he looked up from his bed at me almost with tears in his eyes. He said he wouldn't forget it. He used the word substantial, sir; and I ought by rights to have mentioned that he was taken ill the night of the inquest; a sort of stroke, the doctor called it, though he came round, I must say, remarkably well considering his age.

'Well, I had been thinking over all this on the fringe of the woods there, and was on my way back again to the house by the field-path, when I looked up as if at call and saw what I take my oath I never remembered to have seen there before— a scarecrow. A scarecrow—and that right in the middle of the cornfield that lay beyond the stream with the bulrushes at the back of the house. Nothing funny in that, you may say. Quite so. But mark me, this was early September, and the stubble all bleaching in the sun, and it didn't look an *old* scarecrow, either. It stood up with its arms out and an old hat down over its eyes, bang in the middle of the field, its back to me, and its front to the house. I knew that field as well as I know my own face in the looking-glass. Then how could I have missed it? What wonder then I stood stock still and had a good long stare at it, first because, as I say, I had never seen it before, and next because—but I'll be coming to that later.

'That done, and *not* to my satisfaction, I turned back a little and came along on the other side of the hedge, and so, presently at last, indoors. Then I stepped up to the upper storey to have a look at it from the windows. For you never know with these country people what they are up to, though they may seem stupid enough. Looked at from there, it wasn't so much in the middle of the field as I had fancied, seeing it from the other side. But how, thought I to myself, could you have escaped me, my friend, if you had been there all through the summer? I don't see how it could; that's flat. But if not, then it must have been put up more recently.

'I had all but forgotten about it next morning, but as afternoon came on I went upstairs and had another look. There was less heat-haze or something, and I could see it clearer and nearer, so to speak, but not quite clear enough. So I whipped along to the Reverend's study, him being still, poor gentleman, confined to his bed, in fact he never got up from it; I whipped along, I say, to the study to fetch his glasses, his boniculars, and I fastened them on that scarecrow like a microscope on a fly. You will hardly credit me, sir, when I say that what seemed to me then most different about it—different from what you might expect—was that it didn't look in any ordinary manner of speaking, quite *real*.

'I could watch it with the glasses as plain as if it had been in touch of my hand, even to the buttons and the hat-band. It wasn't the first time I had set eyes on the *clothes*, either, though I couldn't have laid name to them. And there was something in the appearance of the thing, something in the way it bore itself up, so to speak, with its arms thrown up at the sky and its empty face, which wasn't what you'd expect of mere sticks and rags. Not, I mean, if they were nothing but just real—real like that there chair, I mean, you are sitting on now.

'I called George. I said, "George, lay your eye to these glasses"—and his face was still a bit discoloured, though his little affair in the stableyard was now a good three weeks old.

"Take a squint through these, George," I said, "and tell me what you make of *that* thing over there."

'George was a slow dawdling mug if ever there was one—clumsy-fingered. But he fixed the glasses at last, and he took a good long look. Then he gave them back into my hand.

' "Well?" I said, watching his face.

' "Why, Mr. Blake," he said, meaning me, "it's a scare-crow."

' "How would you like it a bit nearer?" I said. Just off-hand, like that.

'He looked at me. "It's near enough in *them*," he said.

' "Does the air round it strike you as funny at all?" I asked him. "Out-of-the-way funny—*quivering*, in a manner of speaking?"

' "That's the heat," he said, but his lip trembled.

' "Well, George," I said, "heat or no heat, you or me must go and have a look at that thing closer some time. But not this afternoon. It's too late."

'But we didn't, sir, neither me *nor* him, though I fancy he went on thinking about it on his own account in between. And lo and behold, when I got up next morning and had slid out of my bedroom early, and went along into the corridor to have another glance at it, and—believe me, sir, as you looked out into the morning the country lay as calm and open as a map—it wasn't there. The scarecrow, sir. It wasn't there. It was vanished. Nor could I get a glimpse of it from down-stairs through the bushes *this* side of the stream. And all so still and early that even there from the back door you could hear the water moving. Now who, thinks I to myself, is answerable for *this* jiggery-pokery?

'But it's no good in this world, sir, putting reasons more far-fetched to a thing than are necessary to account for it. That you *will* agree. Some farmer's lout, I thought to myself, must have come and moved the old mommet overnight. But, that being so, what was it ever put up for? Harvest done,

mind you, and the crows, one would think, as welcome to
what they could pick up in the stubble—if they hadn't picked
it all up already—as robins to house crumbs. Besides, what
about the peculiar looks of it?

'I didn't go out next day, not at all; and there being only
George and me in the Vicarage, and the Reverend shut off in
his room, I never remember such a holy quiet. The heavens
like a vault. Eighty-four in the shade by the thingamy in the
verandah and this the fourth of September. All day long, and
I'll vouch for it, the whole twenty acres of that field, but for
the peewits and the rooks running over it, lay empty. And
when, the sun going down, the harvest moon came up that
evening—and that summer she showed up punctual as a clock
the whole month round—you could see right across the flat
country to the hills. And the night-jars croaking too. You
could have cut the heat with a knife.

'What time the old gentleman's gruel was gone up and
George out of the way, I took yet another squint through the
glasses from the upper windows. And I am ready to own that
something inside of me gave a sort of a *hump*, sir, when, large
as life, I saw that the scarecrow was come back again, though
this is where you'll have, if you please, to go careful with me.
What I saw the instant before I began to look, and to that I'd
lay my affidavit, was something moving, and pretty rapid, too;
and it was only at the very moment I clapped the glasses on to
it that it suddenly fixed itself into what I already *supposed* I
should find it to be. I've noticed that—though in little things
not mattering much—before. It's your own mind that learns
you before what you look at turns out to be what you expect.
Else why should we be alarmed by this here *solid* sometimes?
It *looks* all so; but *is* it?

'You might be suggesting that both shape and scarecrow
too were all my eye and Betty Martin. But we'll see later on
about that. And what about George? You don't mean to infer
that he could borrow to order a mere fancy clean out of my

head and turn it into a scarecrow in the middle of a field and in broad daylight too? That would be the long bow, and no mistake. Ay, and take it in some shape for what we *did*! No. Yet, as I say, even when I first cast eyes on it, it looked too real to be real. So there's the two on the one side, and the two on the other, and they don't make four.

'Well, sir, I must say that from that moment on I didn't like the look of things, and never have I shared a meal so mum as when George and me sat to supper that evening. From being a hearty eater his appetite was fallen almost to a cipher. He munched and couldn't swallow. I doubt if his vittles had a taste of them left. And we both of us knew as though it had been printed on the tablecloth what the other was thinking about.

'It was while we sat there, George and me alone, him on the right and the window opposite, and me on the cupboard side in what was called the servants' hall, that we heard some words said. Not what you could understand, but still, words. I couldn't tell from where, except that it wasn't from the Reverend, and I couldn't tell what. But they dropped upon us and between us as if there was a parrot in the room, clapping its horny bill, so to say, motionless in the air. At this George stopped munching for good, his face little short of green. But except for a cockling up inside of me, I didn't make any sign I'd heard. After all, it was nothing that made any difference to *me*, though what was going on was, to say the least of it, not all as it should be. And if you knew the old Vicarage you'd agree.

'Lock-up time came at last. And George took his candle and went up to bed. Not quite as willing as usual, I fancied; though he had always been a glutton for his full meed of sleep. You could notice by the sound of his feet on the stairs that he was as you might say pushing of himself on. As for me, it had always been my way to sit up after him reading a bit with the Reverend's *Times*. But that night, I went off early. I gave a

last look in on the old gentleman, and I might as well mention
—though dilatory isn't the word for these doctors, even when
they *are* called in in reasonable time—I say a nurse had been
sent for, and his sister was now expected any day from Scot-
land. All well there, and him lying as peaceful on his bed as if
the end had come already. Well, sir, that done, coming back
along the corridor I blew out my candle and stood waiting.
The candle out, the moon came streaming in, and the outside
from the window lay spread out beneath me almost bright as
day. I looked this ways and I looked that ways, back and
front; but nothing to be seen, nor heard neither. Yet it seemed
not more than one deep breath after I had closed my eyes in
sleep that night that I was stark wideawake again, trying to
make sense of some sound I'd heard.

'Old houses—I'm used to them; the timbers crinkle like a
bee-hive. But this wasn't timbers, oh no! It might maybe have
been wind, you'll say. But what chance of wind with not a
hand's breadth of cloud moving in the sky, and such a blare
of moonlight as would keep even a field mouse from peeping
out of its hole? What's more, not to know whether what you
are listening to is in or outside of your head isn't much help
to a good night's rest. Still I fell off at last, unnoticing.

'Next morning, as George came back from taking up the
breakfast tray, I had a good look at him in the sunlight, but
you couldn't tell whether the marks round his eyes were
natural—from what had gone before with the other, I mean—
or from *insommia*. Best not to meddle, I thought; just wait. So
I gave him good morning and poured out the coffee and we
sat to it as usual, the wasps coming in over the marmalade as
if nothing had happened.

'All quiet that day, only rather more so, as it always is in a
sick-room house. Doctor come and gone, but no nurse yet;
and the old gentleman I thought looking very ailing. But he
spoke to me quite cheerful. Just like his old self, too, to be
sympathizing with me for the double-duty I'd been doing in

the house. He asked after the garden, too, though there was as fine a bunch of black grapes on his green plate as any out of Canaan. It was the drought was in his mind. And just as I was leaving the room, my hand on the door, he mentioned one or two compliments about my having stayed on with him so long. "You can't pay for that out of any Bank," he said to me, smiling at me almost merry-like, his beard over the sheet.

' "I hope and trust, sir," I said, "while I am with you, there will be no further fuss." But I had a surety even as I said the words that he hadn't far to go, so that fusses, if come they did, didn't really much matter to him. I don't see how you would be likely to notice them when things are drawing to a last conclusion; though I am thankful to say that what did occur, was kept from him to the end.

'That night there came something sounding about the house that wasn't natural, and no mistake. I had scarcely slept a wink, and as soon as I heard it, I was on with my tail-coat over my night-shirt in a jiffy, though there was no need for light. I had fetched along my winter overcoat, too, one the Reverend himself had passed on to me—this very coat on my back now —and with that over my arm, I pushed open the door and looked in on George. Maybe he had heard my coming, maybe he had heard the other, I couldn't tell which, but there he was, sitting up in bed—the moonlight flooding in on his long white face and tousled hair—and his trousers and braces thrown down anyhow on the chair beside it.

'I said to him, "What's wrong, George? Did you hear anything? A voice or anything?"

'He sat looking at me with his mouth open as if he couldn't shut it, and I could see he was shaken to the very roots. Now, mind you, here I was in the same quandary, as they call it, as before. What I'd heard might be real, some animal, fox, badger, or the like, prowling round outside, or it might not. If not, and the house being exercised, as I said, though a long way back, and the Reverend gentleman still in this world himself, I had a kind of trust that what was there, if it *was* anything, couldn't get in. But naturally I was in something of a fever to make sure.

' "George," I said, "you mustn't risk a chill or anything of that sort"—and it had grown a bit cold in the small hours—"but it's up to us—our duty, George—with the Reverend at death's door and all, to know what's what. So if you'll take a look round on the outside I'll have a search through on the in. What we must be cautious about is that the old gentleman isn't disturbed."

'George went on looking at me, though he had by this time shuffled out of bed and into the overcoat I had handed him. He stood there, with his boots in his hand, shivering, but more maybe because he felt cold after the warmth of his sheets than because he had quite taken in what I had said.

' "Do you think, Mr. Blake," he asked me, sitting down again on his bed, "—you don't think he is come back again?"

'*Come back*, he said, just like that. And you'd have supposed from the quivering of his mouth I might have stopped it!

' "Who's, George, come back?" I asked him.

' "Why, what we looked through the glasses at in the field," he said. "It had his look."

' "Well, George," I said, speaking as moderate and gentle as you might to a child, "we know as how dead men tell no tales. Let alone scarecrows, then. All we've got to do is just to make sure. You do as you're bid, then, my lad. You go your ways, and I'll go mine. There's never any harm can befall a man if his conscience is easy."

'But that didn't seem to satisfy him. He gave a gulp and stood up again, still looking at me. Stupid or not, he was always one for doing his duty, was George. And I must say that what I call courage is facing what you're afraid of in your very innards, and not mere crashing into danger, eyes shut.

' "I'd lief as not go down, Mr. Blake," he said. "Leastways, not alone. He never took much of a liking to me. He said he'd be evens. Not *alone*, Mr. Blake."

' "What have you to fear, George, my lad?" I said. "Man or spectre, the fault was none of yours."

'He buttoned the coat up, same as I am wearing it now, and he gave me just one look more. It's hard to say all that's in a fellow-creature's eyes, sir, when they are full of what no tongue in him could tell. But George had shut his mouth at last, and the moon on his face gave him a queer look, far away-like, as if all that there was of him, this world or the next, had come to keep him company. I will say that.

'And when the hush that had come down on the house was broken again, and this time it *was* the wind, though away high up over the roof, he didn't look at me any more. It was the last between us. He turned his back on me and went off out into the passage and down the stairs, and I listened until I could hear him in the distance scrabbling with the bar at the back. It was one of those old-fashioned doors, sir, you must understand, just loaded with locks and bolts, like in all old places.

'As for myself, I didn't move for a bit. There wasn't any hurry that I could see. Oh, no. I just sat down on the bed on the place where George had sat, and waited. And you may depend upon it, I stayed pretty quiet there—with all that responsibility, and not knowing what might happen next. And then presently what I heard was as though a voice had said something—very sharp and bitter; then said no more. There came a sort of moan, and then no more again. But by that time I was on my way on my rounds inside the house, as I'd promised; and so, out of hearing: and when I got back to my bedroom again everything was still and quiet. And I took it of course that George had got back safe to his. . . .'

Since the fire had faded and the light of day was gone, the fish-like phosphorescence of the gas-mantles had grown brighter, and this elderly man, whose name was Blake, I understood, was looking at me out of his white, almost leper-like face in this faint gloom as steadily almost as George must have been looking at him a few minutes before he had descended the back stairs of the Vicarage, never, I gathered, to set foot on them again.

'Did you manage to get any more sleep that night?' I said.

Mr. Blake seemed to be pleasingly surprised at so easy a question.

'That was the mistake of it,' he said. 'He wasn't found till morning. Cold for hours, and precious little to show why.'

'So you did manage to get a little sleep?'

But this time he made no answer.

'Your share, I suppose, was quite a substantial one?'

'Share?' he said.

'In the will. . . ?'

'Now, didn't I tell you myself,' he protested with some warmth, 'that that, as it turned out, wasn't so; though why, it would take half a dozen or more of these lawyers to explain. And even at that, I don't know as what I did get has brought me anything much to boast about. I'm a free man, that's true. But for how long? Nobody can stay in this world here for ever, can he?'

With a peculiar rocking movement of his small head he peered round and out of the door. 'And though in this world,' he went on, 'you may have not one *iota* of harm to blame yourself for *to* yourself, there may still be misunderstandings, and them that have been deceived by them may be waiting for you in the next. So when it comes to what the captain of the *Hesper*——'

But at this moment our prolonged *tête-à-tête* was interrupted by a thickset vigorous young porter carrying a bucket of coals in one hand, and a stumpy torch of smouldering brown paper in the other. He mounted one of our chairs and with a tug of finger and thumb instantly flooded our dingy quarters with an almost intolerable gassy glare. That done, he raked out the ash-grey fire with a lump of iron that may once have been a poker, and flung all but the complete contents of his bucket of coal on to it. Then he looked round and saw who was sitting there. Me he passed over. I was merely a bird of passage. But he greeted my fellow derelict as if he were an old acquaintance.

'Good evening, sir,' he said, and in that slightly indulgent and bantering voice which suggests past favours rather easily earned. 'Let in a little light on the scene. I didn't notice you when I came in and was beginning to wonder where you had got to.'

His patron smirked back at him as if any such trifling human attention was a peculiar solace. This time the porter deliberately caught my eye. And his own was full of meaning. It was as if there were some little privy and ironical understanding between us in which this third party was unlikely to share. I ignored it, rose to my feet and clutched my bag. A passenger train had come hooting into the station, its gliding lighted windows patterning the platform planks. Alas, yet again it wasn't mine. Still—such is humanity, I preferred my own company, just then.

When I reached the door, and a cold and dingy prospect showed beyond it, I glanced back at Mr. Blake, sitting there in his greatcoat beside the apparently extinguished fire. With a singularly mournful look, as of a lost dog, on his features, he was gazing after me. He seemed to be deploring the withdrawal even of my tepid companionship. But in that dreadful gaseous luminosity there was nothing, so far as I could see, that any mortal man could by any possibility be afraid of, alive or dead. So I left him to the porter. And—as yet—we have not met again.

MISSING

*

It was the last day of a torrid week in London—the flaming crest of what the newspapers call a *heat wave*. The exhausted inmates of the dazzling, airless streets—plate-glass, white stone, burnished asphalt, incessant roar, din, fume and odour —have the appearance at such times of insects trapped in an oven of a myriad labyrinthine windings and chambers; a glowing brazen maze to torture Christians in. To have a *mind* even remotely resembling it must be Satan's sole privilege!

I had been shopping; or rather, I had been loafing about from one department on to another in one of the huge 'stores' in search of bathing-drawers, a preventative of insect bites, and a good holiday 'shocker', and had retired at last incapable of buying anything—even in a world where pretty well everything except peace of mind can be bought, and sold. The experience had been oppressive and trying to the temper.

Too hot, too irritable even to lunch, I had drifted into a side street, and then into a second-hand bookshop that happened still to be open this idle Saturday afternoon; and having for ninepence acquired a copy of a book on psycho-analysis which I didn't want and should never read, I took refuge in a tea shop.

In spite of the hot-water fountain on the counter it was a

degree or two cooler in here, though even the marble-top tables were tepid to the touch. Quiet and drowsy, too. A block of ice surmounted the dinner-wagon by the counter. The white clock face said a quarter to three. Few chairs were now occupied; the midday mellay was over. A heavy slumbrousness muffled the place—the flies were as idle as the waitresses, and the waitresses were as idle as the flies.

I gave my order, and sat back exhausted in a listless vacancy of mind and body. And my dazed eyes, having like the flies little of particular interest to settle on, settled on the only fellow reveller that happened to be sitting within easy reach. At first glimpse there could hardly be a human being you would suppose less likely to attract attention. He was so scrupulously respectable, so entirely innocent of 'atmosphere'. Even a Chelsea psychic would have been compelled to acknowledge that this particular human being had either disposed of his aura or had left it at home. And yet my first glimpses of him had drawn me out of the vacuum into which I had sunk as easily as a cork is drawn out of an empty bottle.

He was sitting at a table to the left, and a little in front of me. The glare from the open door and the gentler light from the cream-blinded shop window picked out his every hair and button. It flooded in on him from the sparkling glittering street, focused him, 'placed' him, arranged him—as if for a portrait in the finest of oils for next year's Academy. Limelight on the actor-manager traversing the blasted heath is mere child's play by comparison.

Obviously he was not 'the complete Londoner'—though that can hardly be said to be a misfortune. On the other hand, there was nothing rural, and only a touch or so of the provincial in his appearance. He wore a neat—an excessively neat —pepper-and-salt tweed suit, the waistcoat cut high and exhibiting the points of a butterfly collar and a triangle of black silk cravat slipped through a gold mourning ring. His ears maybe were a little out of the mode. They had been attached rather high and flat on either side of his conical head with its dark, glossy, silver-speckled hair.

The nose was straight, the nostrils full. They suggested courage of a kind; possibly, even, on occasion, bravado. He looked the kind of man, I mean, it is well to keep out of a corner. But the eyes that were now peering vacantly down that longish nose over a trim but unendearing moustache at the crumbs on his empty plate were too close together. So, at least, it seemed to me. But then I am an admirer of the wide expressive brow—such as our politicians and financiers display. Those eyes at any rate gave this spruce and respectable person just a hint, a glint of the fox. I have never heard, though, that the fox is a dangerous animal even in a corner; only that he has his wits about him and preys on geese—whereas my stranger in the tea shop had been refreshing himself with Osborne biscuits.

It was hot. The air was parched and staled. And heat—unless in Oriental regions—is not conducive to exquisite manners. Far otherwise. I continued to watch this person, indolently speculating whether his little particularities of appearance did not match, or matched too precisely. Those ears and that cravat, for example; or those spruce-moustached nostrils and the glitter of the close-neighbouring eyes. And why had he brought to mind a tightly-packed box with no address on it? He began to be a burden, yet I could not keep my eyes away from him—nor from his hands. They were powerful and hairy, with large knuckles; and now that they were not in use he had placed them on his knees under the dark polished slab of his marble table. Beneath those knees rested his feet (the toes turned in a little) in highly polished boots, with thickish soles and white socks.

There is, I agree, something peculiarly vulgar in thus picking a fellow-creature to pieces. But even Keats so dissected Miss Brawne; and even when he was in love with her: and it was certainly not love at first sight between myself and this stranger.

Whether he knew it or not, he was attaching himself to me; he was making his influence felt. It was odd, then, that he could remain so long unconscious of so condensed a scrutiny. Maybe that particular nerve in him had become atrophied. He looked as if a few other rather important nerves might be atrophied. When he did glance up at me—the waitress having appeared with my tea at the same moment—there was a far-away startled look in his bleak blue-black eyes—as if he had been called back.

Nothing more; and even at that it was much such a look as had been for some little time fixed on the dry biscuit crumbs in his empty plate. He seemed indeed to be a man accustomed to being startled or surprised into vigilance without reason. But having seen me looking at him, he did not hesitate. He carefully took up his hat, his horn-handled and gold-mounted umbrella, and a large rusty scaling leather bag that lay on a chair beside him; rose; and stepping gently over with an almost catlike precision, seated himself in the chair opposite to mine. I continued to pour out my tea.

'You will excuse me troubling you,' he began in a voice that suggested he could sing tenor though he spoke bass, 'but would you kindly tell me the number of the omnibus that goes from here to King's Cross? I am a stranger to this part of London.'

I called after the waitress: 'What is the number of the bus,' I said, 'that goes from here to King's Cross?'

'The number of the bus, you si, that goes from here to King's Cross?'

'Yes,' I said, 'to King's Cross.'

'I'm sure *I* don't know,' she said. 'I'll ask the counter.' And she tripped off in her silk stockings and patent leather shoes.

'The counter will know,' I assured him. He looked at me,

moving his lips over his teeth as if either or both for some reason had cause to be uneasy.

'I am something of a stranger to London altogether,' he said, 'and I don't usually come these ways: it's a novelty to me. The omnibuses are very convenient.'

'Don't you? Is it?' I replied. 'Why not?' They were rather point-blank questions (and a gentleman, said Dr. Johnson, does not ask questions) but somehow they had slipped out as if at his pressing invitation.

He looked at me, his eyes seeming to draw together into an intenser focus. He was not exactly squinting, but I have noticed a similar effect in the eyes of a dog when its master is about to cry 'Fetch it!'

'You see,' he said, 'I live in the country, and only come to London when I seem to need company—badly, I mean. There's a great contrast between the country and this. All these houses. So many strange faces. It takes one out of oneself.'

I glanced round at the sparsely occupied tables. A cloud apparently had overlaid the sun, for a dull coppery glow was now reflected from the drowsy street. I could even hear the white-faced clock ticking. To congratulate him on his last re-mark would hardly have been courteous after so harmless an advance. I merely looked at him. What kind of self, I was vaguely speculating, would return into his hospitality when he regained his usual haunts.

'I have a nice little place down there,' he went on, 'but there's not much company. Lonely: especially now. Even a few hours makes all the difference. You would be surprised how friendly a place London can be; the people, I mean. Helpful.'

What can only be described as a faint whinny had sounded in his voice as he uttered that 'helpful'. Was he merely to prove yet another of those unfortunate travellers who have lost the return halves of their railway tickets? Had he marked me down for his prey!

'It is not so much what they say,' he continued, laying his hand on the marble table; 'but just their being about, you know.' I glanced at the heavy ring on its third finger and then at his watch-chain—woven apparently of silk or hair—with little gold rings at intervals along it to secure the plait. His own gaze continued to rest on me with so penetrating, so corkscrew-like an intensity, that I found myself glancing over my shoulder in search of the waitress. She however was now engaged in animated argument with the young lady at the pay-desk.

'Do you live *far* from London?' I ventured.

'About seventy miles,' he replied with an obvious gulp of relief at this impetus to further conversation. 'A nice old house too considering the rent, roomy enough but not too large. Its only drawback in some respects is there's nothing near it—not within call, I mean; and we—I—suffer from the want of a plentiful supply of water. Especially now.'

Why so tactless a remark on this broiling afternoon should have evoked so vivid a picture of a gaunt yellow-brick building perched amid sloping fields parched lint-white with a tropical drought, its garden little more than a display of vegetable anatomies, I cannot say. It was a house of a hideous aspect; but I confess it stirred my interest. Whereupon my stranger, apparently, thought he could safely glance aside; and I could examine him more at leisure. It was not, I have to confess, a taking face. There was a curious hollowness in its appearance. He looked like the shell of a man, or rather, like a hermit crab—that neat pepper-and-salt tweed suit and so on being a kind of second-hand accumulation on his back.

'And of course,' he began again, 'now that I am alone I become'—he turned sharply back on me—'I become more conscious of it.'

'Of the loneliness?' I suggested.

Vacancy appeared on his face, as if he had for the instant stopped thinking. 'Yes,' he replied, once more transfixing me with those bleak close eyes of his, 'the loneliness. It seems to worsen more and more as the other slips away into the past. But I suppose we most of us have much the same experience; just of that, I mean. And even in London. . . .'

I busied myself with my tea things, having no particular wish at the moment to continue the conversation. But he hadn't any intention of losing his victim as easily as all that.

'There's a case now here in the newspaper this morning,' he went on, his glance wandering off to a copy of the *Daily Mail* that lay on the chair next the one he had just vacated. 'A man not much older than I am—"found dead". Dead. The only occupant of quite a good-sized house, I should judge, at Stoke Newington—though I don't know the place personally. Lived there for years on end without even a charwoman to do for him—to—to work for him. Still even there there was some kind of company, I suppose. He could look out of the window; he could hear people moving about next door. Where I am, there isn't another house in sight, not even a barn, and so far as I can see, what they call Nature doesn't become any the more friendly however long you stay in a place—the birds and that kind of thing. It may get better in time; but it's only a few months ago since I was left quite like this. When my sister died.'

Obviously I was hooked beyond hope of winning free again until this corkscrew persistent creature had had his way with me. The only course seemed to be to get the experience over as quickly as possible. It is not easy, however, to feign an active sympathy; and mention of his dead sister had produced in my mind only a faint reflex image of a dowdy lady no longer young in dingy black. Still, it was an image that proved to be not very far from the actuality.

'Any close companionship like that', I murmured, 'when it is broken is a tragic thing.'

He appeared to have seen no significance in my remark.

'And you see, once there were three of us. Once. It never got into the papers—at least not into the London papers, except just by mention, I mean.' He moistened his lips. 'Did you ever happen to come across a report about a lady, a Miss Dutton, who was "missing"?'

It was a pretty stupid question, for after all, few human beings are so gifted as to be able to recall the names even of the protagonists in genuine *causes célèbres*. To bear in mind every sort of Miss Dutton whose disappearance would be referred to only in news-snippets borrowed by the Metropolitan press from the provincial, would be rather too much of a tax even for those interested in such matters. I sipped my tea and surveyed him as sagaciously as possible; 'Not that I can actually recall,' I said. 'Miss—Dutton? It isn't a very uncommon name. You knew her?'

'Knew her!' he repeated, placing his hands on his knees and sitting stiffly back in his chair, his eyes unflinchingly fixed on mine. 'She lived with us a matter of two years or more. It was us she left. It was my house she was missing from. It caused quite a stir in the neighbourhood. It was the talk of the countryside. There was an Inquiry; and all that.'

'How long ago?'

'Pretty near a year ago. Yes; a year yesterday.'

'Do you mean the inquiry, or when Miss Dutton disappeared?'

'The inquiry,' he replied in a muffled fashion, as if a little annoyed at my want of perspicacity. 'The other was—oh, a month or more before that.'

The catechism was becoming a rather laborious way of extracting a story, but somehow its rudiments had begun to interest me. I had nothing to do. To judge from the look of the street, the quicksilver in the thermometer was still edging exquisitely upwards. I detested the thought of emerging into that oven. So apparently did my companion, unless the mere sound of his voice seemed to him better entertainment than, say, the nearest 'picture palace'—where at least one would be out of sight and it would be dark.

'I should have thought,' I began again in a voice as unconcerned as I could manage, 'that living as you do, a stir in the neighbourhood would not much matter, though I agree that the mystery itself must have mattered a good deal more. That of course must have been a great shock to you both.'

'Ay,' he said, with a gleam in his eye, 'but that's just what you Londoners don't seem to understand. You have your newspapers and all that. But in most ways you don't get talked about much. It's not so in the country. I guarantee you might be living right in the middle of the Yorkshire Moors and yet, if it came to there being anything to keep their tongues wagging, you'd know that your neighbours were talking of you, and what about, for miles around. It gets across—like those black men's drums one hears about in West Africa. As if the mere shock of the thing wasn't enough! What I feel about it is that nowadays people don't seem to show any sympathy, any ordinary feeling with—with those in such circumstances; at least, not country people. Wouldn't you say yourself,' he added, with feline rapidity, 'that if *you* were reported as missing it would be rough luck if nobody cared?'

'I don't quite see what you mean,' I replied. 'I thought you said that the disappearance of your friend made a stir in the neighbourhood.'

'Yes; but they were not thinking so much of *her* as of the cause of it.'

We exchanged a long glance, but without much addition to my own small fund of information. 'But surely,' I ventured, 'that must depend upon where she was supposed to have disappeared *to*?'

'That,' he replied, 'they never knew. We couldn't find out not one iota about it. You've no idea'—he drew his hands down over his face as if to clear away a shadow from his eyes —'you've no idea. Since she has gone I feel almost sometimes as if she can never have been real. *There*, but not real; if you understand me. I see her; and then the real thing goes again. It never occurred to me, that.'

'The psychologists would tell us something about that.'

'The what?' he asked sharply.

'Oh, those who profess to explain the workings of the mind. After all, we can't definitely say whether that teapot there is real—what it is in itself, I mean. And merely to judge from its looks,' I added, 'one might hope it was a pure illusion.'

He looked hard at the teapot. 'Miss Dutton was a very well-preserved woman for her age,' he said. 'And when I say "not real", it's only in a manner of speaking, I mean. I've got her portrait in the newspaper in my pocket-book. That ought to prove her real enough. I never knew any one who was more "all there", as they say. She was a good friend to me—I have every reason to remember her. She came along of her own free will—just a chance meeting. In Scarborough, as a matter of fact. And she liked the comforts of a home after all those hotels and boarding houses.'

In the course of these ruminating and mournful remarks— and there was unmistakable 'feeling' in his tones—he was rather privily turning over the contents of an old leather pocket-book with an inelastic black band. He drew out a frayed newspaper cutting and put it down on the table beside the teapot.

'Looking at that, you wouldn't be in much doubt what Miss Dutton was in herself, now, would you? You'd recognize her,' he raised his eyes, 'if she were—if you met her, I mean, in these awful streets? I would myself.'

It was impossible to decide whether this last remark was ironical, triumphant, embittered, or matter-of-fact; so I looked at Miss Dutton. She was evidently a blonde and a well-preserved woman, as my friend had intimated; stoutish, with a plump face, a plump nose, infantile blue eyes, frizzy hair, and she wore (what a few years ago were old-fashioned and are now new-fashioned) long ear-rings.

It was curious what a stabilizing effect the ear-rings produced. They resembled the pole Blondin used to carry as he tripped across his rope over the Niagara Falls. Miss Dutton was looking out of her blurred image with a sort of insouciance, gaiety, 'charm', the charm that photographers aim at but rather seldom convey. Destiny, apparently, casts no retrospective shadow. I defy anybody to have found the faintest hint in that aware, vain, commonplace, good-natured face which would suggest Miss Dutton was ever going to be 'missed'—missed, I mean, in the sense of becoming indiscoverable. In the other sense her friends would no doubt miss her a good deal. But then boarding houses and hotels are the resorts rather of acquaintances than of friends.

The owner of the newspaper snippet was scrutinizing the gay, blurred photograph with as much interest as I was; though to him it was upside-down. There was a queer foolish look on his face, a little feline, perhaps, in its sentimentality.

I pushed back the cutting across the marble table and he carefully reinterred it in his pocket-book. 'I was wondering,' he rambled on as he did so, 'what you might have thought of it—without prejudice, so to speak, if you had come across it—casually-like; in the newspaper, I mean?'

The question was not quite so simple as it sounded. It appeared as if my new acquaintance were in wait for a comment which he himself was eager to supply. And I had nothing much to say.

'It's difficult, you know, to judge from prints in newspapers,' I commented at last. 'They are usually execrable even as caricatures. But she looks, if I may say so, an uncommonly genial woman: feminine—and a practical one, too. Not one, I mean, who would be likely to be missing, except on purpose—of her own choice, that is.' Our eyes met an instant. 'The whole business must have been very disturbing, a great

anxiety to you. And, of course, to Miss . . . to your sister,
I mean.'

'My name,' he retorted abruptly, shutting his eyes while a
bewildering series of expressions netted themselves on his
face, 'my name is Bleet.'

'Miss Bleet,' I added, glancing at the pocket into which the
book had by now disappeared, and speculating, too, why so
preposterous an *alias* should have occurred to apparently so
ready a tongue.

'You were saying "genial",' he added rapidly. 'And that is
what they all agreed. Even her only male relative—an uncle,
as he called himself, though I can swear she never mentioned
him in that or in any other capacity. She hadn't always been
what you might call a happy woman, mind you. But they
were bound to agree that those two years under my care—in
our house—were the happiest in Miss Dutton's life. We made
it a real home to her. She had her own rooms and her few bits
of furniture—photographs, what-nots and so on, quite private.
It's a pretty large house considering the rent—countrified, you
know; and there was a sort of a new wing added to it fifty
years or more ago. Old-fashioned, of course—open fireplace,
no bath, enormous kitchen range—swallows coal by the
bushel—and so on—very inconvenient but cheap. And though
my sister was not in a position to supervise the housekeeping,
there couldn't be a more harmless and affectionate creature.
To those, that is, who were kind to her. She'd run away from
those who weren't—just run away and hide. I must explain
that my poor sister was not quite—was a little weak in her
intellects—from her childhood. It was always a great responsibility. But as time went on,' he drew his hand wearily over
his face, 'Miss Dutton herself very kindly relieved me of a
good deal of that. You said she looked a practical woman; so
she was.'

His narrative was becoming steadily more personal, and
disconcerting. And yet—such is humanity—it was as steadily

intensifying in interest. A menacing rumble of thunder at that moment sounded over the street, and a horse clattered down with its van beyond the open door. My country friend did not appear to have noticed it.

'You never know quite where you are with the ladies,' he suddenly ejaculated, and glanced piercingly up—for at that moment our waitress had drawn near.

'It's a 'Ighteen,' she said, pencil on lip, and looking vacantly from one to the other of us.

' "Ighteen",' echoed her customer sharply; 'what's that? Oh the omnibus. You didn't say what you meant. Thank you.' She hovered on, check-book in hand. 'And please bring me another cup of coffee.' He looked at me as if with the intention of duplicating his order. I shook my head. 'One cup, then, miss; no hurry.'

The waitress withdrew.

'It looks as if rain was coming,' he went on, and as if he were thirsting for it as much as I was. 'As I was saying, you can never be quite sure where you are with women; and, mind you, Miss Dutton was a woman of the world. She had seen a good deal of life—been abroad—Gay Paree, Monte Carlo, and all that. Germany before the war, too. She could read French as free and easy as you could that mennoo there. Paper-bound books with pictures on them, and that kind of thing.' He was looking at me, I realized, as if there were no other way of intimating the particular kind of literature he had in mind.

'I used to wonder sometimes what she could find in us, such a lonely place; no company. Though, of course, she was free to ask any friends if she wanted to, and talked of them too when in the mood. Good class, to judge from what she said. What I mean is, she was quite her own mistress. And I must say there could not be more good humour and so on than what she showed my poor sister. At least, until later. She'd talk to her as if conversing; and my sister would sit there by the window, looking back at her and smiling and nodding just as if she were taking it all in. And who knows, perhaps she was. What I mean is, it's possible to have things in your head which you can't quite put into so many words. It's one of the things I look for when I come up to London: the faces that could tell a story though what's behind them can't.'

I nodded.

'I can assure you that before a few weeks were over she had got to be as much at home with us as if we had known her all our lives. Chatty and domesticated, and all that. And using the whole house just as if it belonged to her. All the other arrangements were easy, too. I can say now, and I said it then, that we never once up to then demeaned ourselves to a single word of disagreement about money matters or anything else. A woman like that, who has been all over the continent, isn't likely to go far wrong in that. I agree the terms were on the generous side; but then, you take me, so were the arrangements.

'She asked herself to raise them when she had been with us upwards of twelve months. But I said "No". I said, "A bargain's a bargain, Edna"—we were "Edna" and "William" to one another, by then, and my sister too. She was very kind to my poor sister; got a specialist up all the way from Bath—though for all his prying questions he did nothing, as I knew he wouldn't. You can't take those things so late. Mind you, as I say, the business arrangements were not all on one side. Miss Dutton liked things select and comfortable. She liked things to go smoothly; as we all do, I reckon. She had been accustomed to smart boarding-houses and hotels—that kind of thing. And I did my level best to keep things nice.'

My stranger's face dropped into a rather gloomy expression, as if poor humanity had sometimes to resign itself to things a little less agreeable than the merely smooth and nice. He laid down his spoon, which he had been using with some vigour, and sipped his coffee.

'What I was going to explain,' he went on, rubbing at his moustache, 'is that everything was going perfectly easy—just like clockwork, when the servant question came up. My house, you see, is on what you may call the large side. It's old in parts, too. Up to then we had had a very satisfactory woman —roughish but willing. She was the wife, or what you might just as well call the widow, of a sailor. I mean he was one of the kind that has a ditto in every port, you know. She was glad of the place, glad to be where her husband couldn't find her, even though the stipulation was that her wages should be permanent. That system of raising by driblets always leads to discontent. And I must say she was a fair tyrant for work.

'Besides her, there was a help from the village—precious little good *she* was. Slummocky—and *stupid*! Still, we had got on pretty well up to then, up to Miss Dutton's time, and for some months after. But cooking for three mouths is a different thing to two. Besides, Miss Dutton liked her meals dainty-like: a bit of fish, or soup occasionally, toast-rack, tantalus, serviettes on the table—that kind of thing. But all that came on gradual-like—the thin edge of the wedge; until at last, well, "exacting" wasn't in it.

'And I must say,' he turned his wandering eye once more on mine, 'I must say, she had a way of addressing menials which sometimes set even my teeth on edge. She was a lady, mind you—though what *that* is when the breath is out of your body it's not so easy to say. And she had the lady's way with them— those continental hotels, I suppose. All very well in a large establishment where one works up against another and you can call them names behind their backs. But our house wasn't an establishment. It wouldn't do there: not in the long run, even if you had an angel for a general, and a cook to match.

'Mind you, as I say, Miss Dutton was always niceness itself to my poor sister: never a hard word or a contemptuous look —not to her face nor behind her back, not up to then. I wouldn't have tolerated it either. And you know what talking to a party that can only just sit, hands in lap, and gape back at you means, or maybe a word now and then that doesn't seem to have anything to do with what you've been saying. It's a great affliction. But servants were another matter. Miss Dutton couldn't demean herself to them. She lived in another world. It was, "Do this"; and "Why isn't it done?"—all in a breath. I smoothed things over, though they got steadily worse and worse, for weeks, and weeks, ay, months. It wore me to a shadow.

'And one day the woman—Bridget was her name—Irish, you know—she flared up in earnest and gave her, as they say, as good as she got. I wasn't there at the time. But I heard afterwards all that passed, and three times over—on the one side at least. I had been into the town in the runabout. And when I came home, Mrs. Tantrums had packed up her box, got a gig from the farm, and was gone for good. It did me a world of harm, that did.

'Pretty well upset, I was too, as you can imagine. I said to Miss Dutton, "Edna," I said, "all I am saying is, was it necessary to go to such extremes? Not," I said, "mind you, Edna, that she was all sugar and honey even to me. I knew the wrong side of her mouth years before *you* appeared on the scene. What you've got to do with such people is—to manage—be firm, keep 'em low, but manage. It isn't commonsense to cut off your tongue to spite your teeth. She's a woman, and Irish at that," I said, "and you know what to expect of them."

'I was vexed, that's a fact, and perhaps I spoke rather more sharply than need have been. But we were good friends by that time: and if honest give-and-take isn't possible between friends, where are you? I ask you. There was by that time too, nothing left over-private between us, either. I advised her about her investments and so on, though I took precious good care not to be personally involved. Not a finger stirring unless she volunteered it first. That all came out too. But it was nothing to do with me, now, was it, as man to man, if the good lady took a fancy into her head to see that my poor sister was not left to what's called the tender mercies of this world after my death?

'And yet, believe me, they fixed on that, like leeches. My hell, they did! At the Inquiry, I mean. And I don't see how much further their decency could have gone if they had called it an Inquest; and. . . .'

Yet another low (almost gruff) volley of thunder interrupted his discourse. He left the sentence in the air; his mouth ajar. I have never met any one that made such active use of his chin in conversation, by the way, as Mr. Bleet did. It must have been exceedingly fatiguing. I fancy he mistook just then the expression on my face for one of inquiry. He leant forward, pushing down towards me that long hairy finger on the marble table-top.

'When I say "tender mercies",' he explained, 'I don't mean that my sister would have been left penniless, even if Miss Dutton or nobody like her had come into the house. There was money of my own too, though, owing to what I need not explain'—he half swallowed the words—'not much.' He broke off. 'It seems as if we are in for a bit of a thunderstorm. But I'd sooner it was here than down my way. When you're alone in the house you seem to notice the noise more.'

'I fancy it won't be much,' I assured him. 'It will clear the air.'

His eyes opened as if in astonishment that any mere act of nature could bring such consolation.

'You were saying,' I exclaimed, 'that you lost your maid?' He glanced up sharply. 'Though of course,' I added hastily, 'you mustn't let me intrude on your private affairs.'

'Not at all; oh, not at all,' he interrupted with relief. 'I thought you said, "lost my head". Not at all. It makes all the difference to me—I can assure you, to be able to go over it like this. Friendly like. To get a listener who has not been fed up on all that gossip and slander. It takes some living down, too. Nothing satisfies them: nothing. From one week's end to another you can't tell where they'll unearth themselves next.'

It was becoming difficult to prevent a steadily growing distaste for my companion from showing itself in my face. But then self-pity is seldom ingratiating. Fortunately the light where we sat was by now little better than dusk. Indeed, to judge from the growing gloom in our tea-shop, the heavens at this moment were far from gracious. I determined to wait till the rain was over. Besides, though my stranger himself was scarcely winning company, and his matter was not much above the sensational newspaper order, the mere zigzagging of his narrative was interesting. Its technique, I mean, reminded me of the definition of a crab: 'The crab is a little red animal that walks backwards.'

'The fact is,' he went on, 'on that occasion—I mean about the servant—Miss Dutton and I had words. I own it. Not that she resented my taking the thing up in a perfectly open and friendly way. She knew she had put me in a fair quandary. But my own private opinion is that when you are talking to a woman it's best not to bring in remarks about the sex in general. A woman is herself or nothing, if you follow me. What she thinks is no more than another skin. Keep her sex out of it, and she'll be reasonable. But no further. As a matter of fact, I never argue with ladies. But I soon smoothed that over. It was only a passing cloud. And I must say, considering what a lady she *was*, she took the discomforts of having nothing but a good-for-nothing slattern in the house very generously, all things considered.

'Mind you, I worked *myself*, fit for any couple of female servants: washed up dishes, laid the table, kept the little knick-knacks going. Ay, and I'd go into the town to fetch her out little delicacies,: tinned soups and peaches, and such like; anything she might have a taste to. And I taught her to use the runabout for herself, though to hear her changing gear was like staring ruin in the face. A gallon of petrol to a hank of crimson silk—that kind of thing. Believe me, she'd go all those miles for a shampoo-powder, or to have tea at a tea-shop—though you can't beat raw new-laid eggs and them on the premises. They got to know her there. She was a rare one for the fashions: scarves and motor-veils, and that kind of thing. But I never demurred. It wasn't for me to make objections, particularly as she'd do a little shopping on the house-keeping side as well, now and then. Though, mind you, she knew sixpence from a shilling, and particularly towards the last.

'What was the worst hindrance was that my poor sister seemed to have somehow come to know there were difficulties in the house. I mean that there had begun to be. You don't know how they do it; but they do. And it doesn't add to your patience, I grant, when what you have done at one moment is done wrong over again the next. But she meant well, poor creature: and scolding at her only made things worse. Still, we got along happily enough for a time, until'—he paused once more with mouth ajar—'until Miss Dutton took it into her head to let matters come to a crisis. Now judging from that newspaper cutting I showed you, what would you take the lady's age to be? Allowing, as you might say, for all that golden hair?'

It was an indelicate question. Though why the mere fact that Miss Dutton was now missing should intensify its in-delicacy, it is not easy to say.

'Happiness makes one look younger than one really is,' I suggested.

He gaped at me, as if in wonderment that in a world of woe he himself was not possessed of a white beard as long as your arm.

' "Happiness?" ' he echoed.

'Yes, happiness.'

'Well, what I mean is, you wouldn't say she was in the filly class; now, would you? High-spirited, easy-going, and all that; silly, too, at times: but no longer young. Not in her heyday, I mean.'

I pushed my empty cup aside and looked at him. But he looked back at me without flinching, as if indeed it was a pleasant experience to be sharing with a stranger sentiments so naïve regarding 'the fair sex'.

'Mind you, I don't profess to be a young man either. But I can assure you on my word of honour, that what she said to me that evening—I was doing chores in the kitchen at the time, and she was there too, arranging flowers in a vause for supper; she had a dainty taste in flowers—well, she asked me why I was so unkind to her, so unresponsive, and—it came on me like a thunderbolt.'

As if positively for exemplification, a violent clap of thunder at that moment resounded overhead. The glasses and crockery around us softly tinkled in sympathy. We listened in silence to its reverberations dying away across the chimney-tops; though my companion seemed to be taking them in through his mouth rather than through his ears. His cheek paled a little.

'That's what she asked me, I say. And I can tell you it took me on the raw. It was my turn to flare up. We had words again: nothing much, only a storm in a tea-cup.' Instead of smiling at this metaphor in the circumstances, he seemed astonished, almost shocked, at its aptitude. But he pushed on boldly.

'And then after I had smoothed things over again, she put her cards on the table. Leap Year, and all that tomfoolery, not a bit of it! She was in dead earnest. She told me what I had guessed already, that she had scarcely a friend in the world. Never a word, mind you, of the Colonel—interloping old Pepper-face! She assured me, as I say, she hadn't not only a single relative, but hardly a friend; that she was, as you might say, alone in life, and—well, that her sentiments had become engaged. In honour bound I wouldn't have breathed this to a living soul who knew the parties; but to a stranger, if I may say so, it isn't quite the same thing. What she said was—in the kitchen there, and me in an apron, mind you, tied round me—doing chores—she said—well, in short, that she wanted to make a match of it. She had taken a fancy to me, and was I agreeable.' There was no vanity in his face; only a stark un-philosophical astonishment. He seemed to think that to ex-plain all is to forgive all; and was awaiting my concurrence.

'You mean she proposed marriage,' I interrupted him with needless pedantry, and at once, but too late, wished the word back. For vestiges of our conversation had evidently reached the counter. Our waitress, still nibbling her pencil, was gazing steadily in our direction. And for some obscure reason this heat that we were sharing with the world at large, combined with this preposterous farrago, was now irritating me almost beyond endurance. The fellow's complacency was incredible.

I beckoned to the young woman. 'You said this gentleman's bus to King's Cross was an Eighteen, didn't you?'

'Yes, 'Ighteen,' she repeated.

'Then would you please bring him an ice.'

Mr. Bleet gazed at me in stupefaction; a thick colour had mounted into his face. 'You don't mean to say,' he spluttered, 'that *I* made any such mention of such a thing. I'm sure I never noticed it.'

My impulse had been nothing more than a protest against my own boredom and fatigue; but the way he had taken it filled me with shame. What could the creature's state of mind be like if his memory was as untrustworthy as that? The waitress retired.

'It's so devilishly hot in here,' I explained. 'And even talk-ing is fatiguing in this weather.'

'Ay,' he said in a low voice. 'It is. But you aren't having one yourself?'

'No, thank you,' I said, 'I daren't. I can't take ices. Indigestion—it's a miserable handicap. . . . You were saying that at the time of Miss Dutton's proposal, you were in the kitchen.'

There was a pause. He sat looking foolishly at the little glass dishful of ice-cream: as surprising a phenomenon apparently as to an explorer from the torrid zone earth's northern snows must first appear. There was a look upon his face as if he had been 'hurt', as if, like a child, at another harsh word he might burst out crying.

'I hardly know that it's worth repeating,' he said at last lamely. His fine resonant voice had lost its tone. 'I suppose she intended it kindly enough. And I wouldn't say I hadn't suspected which way the wind was blowing: Willie this, and Willie that. I've always been William to them that know me, except Bill at school. But it was always Willie with her; and a languishing look to match. Still, I never expected what came after that. It took me aback.

'There she was, hanging on my every word, looking volumes, and me not knowing what to say. In a way too, I was attached to her. There were two sides to her, I allow that.' He turned away but not, it seemed, in order to see the less conspicuous side more clearly. 'I asked her to let me think things over, and I said it as any gentleman would. "Let me think it over, Edna," I said. "You do me honour," I said. Her hand was on my arm. She was looking at me. God being my witness, I tried to spare her feelings. I eased it over, meaning it all for the best. You see that little prospect had no more than occurred to me. Married life wasn't what I was after. I shouldn't be as old as I am now—and unmarried, I mean—if that had been so. It was uncomfortable to see her carrying on like that: too early. But things having come to such a pass, well, as you might say, we glided into an understanding at last. And with what result? Why . . . she made it an occasion for putting her foot down all the way round. And hadn't I known it of old?'

He looked at me searchingly, with those dog-bright eyes,

those high-set ears, as if to discover where precisely I now was in relation to his confidences.

'She took the reins, as they say. All in good temper for the most part; but there was no mistaking it. Mistress first and Mrs. after, in a manner of speaking. But when it came to speaking sharply to my poor sister on a matter which you wouldn't expect even a full-witted person to be necessarily very quick about at the uptake—I began to suspect I had made a mistake. I knew it then: but forewarned isn't always fore-armed. And mistakes are easier to make than to put right. It had gone too far. . . .'

'If you really don't want that ice, I can easily ask the waitress to take it away,' I assured him, if only to bring back that wandering empty eye from the reverie into which he seemed to have fallen. Or was it that he was merely absorbed in the picture of the rain-drenched street that was reflected in the looking-glass behind my chair?

'Thank you,' he said, taking up the spoon.

'And Miss Dutton left you at last. Did she tell you she had any intention of going?'

'Never,' he asseverated. 'Not a word. No, not a single word. And if you *can't* explain it, well then, why go on trying? I say. Not at this late day. But you might as well argue with a stone wall. The heat had come by then. Last summer, you know: the drought. Not the great drought, I mean—but round our parts in particular. The whole place was dried up to a tinder; cracks in the clay; weeds dying; birds gone. Even the trees flagging: and the oaks half eaten up by caterpillars already. Meantime, I don't know how it was—unless, perhaps, the heat—but there had been another quarrel. They never got *that* out of me at the Inquiry, though; I can tell you. And that was patched up, too. I apologized because she insisted. But she had hurt me; she had hurt my feelings. And I couldn't see that marriage was going to be a very practical experiment on those lines. But she came round; and considering what an easy woman of the world she looks like in that photograph, you wouldn't have guessed, would you, that crying, weeping, I mean, was much in her way? I found that out, too. Fatiguing.

'And it didn't suit her, either. But she was what they call a woman made for affection. And I mean by *that*,' he broke in emphatically, 'she liked to monopolize. She wasn't a sharer. We were badly in want of a servant ourselves by that time, as you may imagine. Going from bad to worse, and me with a poisoned thumb, opening tins. But *she* was in want of a servant still more. She wanted me. Husbands often are nothing much better. What's more, I don't wish to say anything against the—against her now; but for the life of me I can't see any reason why she should have gone so far as to insult me. And not a week since we were like birds on one roost. To insult me, mind you, with my poor sister there, listening by!

'But I had learned a bit by then. I held my tongue, though there was a plenty of things to say in reply if I could have demeaned myself to utter them. Plenty. I just went on looking out of the window, easing myself with my foot—we were in the drawing-room at the time—and the very sight of the dried-up grass and the dead vegetables, and the sun pouring down out of the sky like lava from a volcano would have been enough in themselves to finish off most people's self-restraint. But as I say, I just stood there thinking of what I might have said, but saying nothing—just let her rant on.

'Why, for instance, do you suppose she had made out weeks before that her investments were bringing in twice as much as they really did? Why all that stuff about Monte Carlo and the lady from America when it was only Boulogne and what they call a *pension*, which in plain English is nothing more than lodgings? Mind you,' he said, as if to intercept the remark I had no intention of making, 'mind you, I agree there *was* a competence, and I agree that, apart from a silly legacy to the Home for Cats and Dogs and that Belgian knacker trade, she had left all there was to leave to my sister—and long before what I told you about just now. I saw that in black and white. It was my duty. That was all settled. On the other hand, how was I to know that she wouldn't change her mind; that she hadn't been paving the way, as you may call it? And why had she deliberately deceived me? I thought it then, and I think it now, more than ever—considering what I have been through. It wasn't treating me fairly, and particularly before she was in a position when things couldn't be altered, so to speak, as between husband and wife. Stretch it too far, and . . .'

Owing to the noise of the rain—and possibly in part to his grammar—it was only with difficulty that I could now follow what the creature was mumbling. I found my attention wandering. A miniature Niagara at least eighteen inches wide was at this moment foaming along the granite gutter while the rain in the middle of the street as it rebounded above the smoking asphalt was lifting into the air an exquisite mist of spray. I watched it enthralled; it was sweet as the sight of palm-trees to my tired hot eyes, and its roar and motion lulled me for a moment or two into a kind of hypnotic trance. When I came back to myself and my trivial surroundings, I found my companion eyeing me as if he had eagerly taken advantage of these moments of oblivion.

'That's the real thing,' he said, as if to humour me, beckoning with his thumb over his shoulder. 'That rain. But it's waste on only stones.' He eyed it pensively, turning his head completely round on his narrow shoulders to do so. But only for a moment. He returned to the business in hand as promptly as if we gossipers had been called to order by the Chairman of a Committee.

'Now it says in that report there, which you have just been reading, that Miss Dutton had not been seen after she left Crowstairs that afternoon of the 3rd of July. That's what it says—in so much print. And I say that's a lie. As it came out later on. And it doesn't make it any truer being in print. It's inaccurate—proved so. But perhaps I ought to tell you first exactly how the whole thing came about. Things get so confused in memory.' Once more he wearily drew his hand over his face as if to obliterate even the memory itself. 'But—quite apart from the others—it's a relief to get things clearer even in one's own mind. The fact is, the whole thing was over between us a day or two before. As I say, after the last little upset which I told you about, things were smoothed out again as usual. At least on her side, though there was precious little in which I was really myself at fault. But my own belief is that she was an hysterical woman. What I mean is, she didn't need anything to make a fuss about; to fire up over. No foundation except just her own mood and feelings. I never was what they call a demonstrative person; it isn't in our family. My father himself was a schoolmasterish kind of man. "It hurts me more than it hurts you"; that kind of man. And up to the age of ten I can honestly say that I never once heard my mother answer him back. She felt it, mind you. He thrashed me little short of savage at times. She'd look on, crying; but she kept herself in. She knew it only made matters worse; and she died when I was twelve.

'Well, what I think is this—that Miss Dutton made a mistake about me. She liked comfort. Breakfast in bed; slippers at night; hot water to wash in; that kind of thing. I'll go further: she was meant for luxury. You could see it in her habits. If she had been twice as well off, she'd have wanted three times as many luxuries: lady's maid, evening dress, tea-gowns, music in the drawing-room—that sort of thing. And maybe it only irritated her when she found that I could keep myself in and just look calm, whatever she did or said. Hesitate to say whatever came into her mind?—not she!—true or untrue. Nor actual physical violence, either. Why months before, she threw a vause full of flowers at me: snowdrops.'

The expression on his face suddenly became fixed, as if at an unexpected recollection.

'I am not suggesting,' he testified earnestly, 'considering—

considering what came after, that I bear her any grudge or malice on account of all that. All I mean is that I was pressed and pushed on to a point that some would say was beyond human endurance. Maybe it was. But what I say is, let', his voice trembled, 'bygones be bygones. I will say no more of that. My point is that Miss Dutton, after all, was to be, as they say, a bird of passage. There had been a final flare up and all was over between us. Insult on insult she heaped on me. And my poor sister there, in her shabby old black dress, peering out at us, from between her fingers, trembling in the corner like a dumb animal. She had called her in.

'And me at my wits' end, what with the servant trouble and the most cantankerous and unreasonable lot of tradespeople you could lay hands on, north or south. I can tell you, I was pretty hard pressed. They dragged all that up at the Inquiry. Oh, yes, bless you. Trust 'em for that. Once it's men against man, then look to it. Not a *public* Inquiry, mind you. No call for that. And I *will* say the police, though pressing, and leaving no stone unturned in a manner of speaking, were gentlemen by comparison. But such things leak out. You can't keep a penny-a-liner from gabbing, and even if there had been nothing worse to it they'd have made my life a hell upon earth.

'Nothing worse to it? How do you mean?'

His glance for the instant was entirely vacant of thought. 'I mean,' he said stubbornly, after a moment's hesitation, 'the hurt to my private feelings. That's what I mean. I can hear her now. And the first thing I felt after it was all over, was nothing but relief. We couldn't have hit it off together, not for long: not after the first few weeks, anyhow. Better, I say, wash your hands of the whole thing. I grant you her decision had left me in a nasty pickle. As a matter of fact, she was to go in a week, and me to clear up the mess. Bills all over the place— fresh butter, mind you, olives, wine, tinned mock turtle—that kind of thing; and all down to my account. What I feel is, she oughtn't to have kept on at me like that right up to the last.

Wouldn't you have thought, considering all things, any woman with an ounce of common sense—not to speak of common caution—would have let sleeping dogs lie?'

He was waiting for an answer.

'What did her uncle, the Colonel, say to that?'

'Oh, him,' he intimated with an incredible sneer. 'In the Volunteers! I was speaking as man to man.'

'And she didn't even wait the two or three days, then?'

'It was the 3rd of July,' he repeated. 'After tidying things up for the day—and by that time, mind you, every drop of water had to be brought in buckets across the burnt-up fields from a drying-up pond half a mile away. But it was done. I did it. After finishing, I say, all the rest of the morning chores, I was sitting there thinking of getting a snack of lunch and then what to do next, when I heard a cough—her door had opened; and then her footstep on the stairs—slippers.' He held up that forefinger as if at an auction, and he was speaking with extreme deliberation as if, with eyes and senses fixed on the scene, he were intent to give me the exactest of records in the clearest of terms. 'And I said to myself, "She's coming! and it's all to begin again!" I said it; I knew it. "And face it out? . . . then—me?"' He shook his head a little like a cat tasting water, but the eyes he showed me were like the glazed windows of an empty shop. 'No, I made myself scarce. I said to myself: "Better keep your distance. Make yourself scarce; keep out of it." And heaven help me I had been doing my best to forget what had passed the night before and to face what was to come. And so—I went out.

'It was early afternoon: sultry, like now. And I wandered about the fields. I must have gone miles and never met a soul. But if you ask me to say where, then all I can say is: Isn't one field the living image of another? And what do you see when your mind isn't there? All round Winstock way—lanes, hedges, cornfields, turnips—tramp and tramp and tramp. And it was not until about seven o'clock that evening that I got back again. Time for supper. I got out the crockery and—and raked out the fire. No sign of nobody, nor of my sister either —though there was nothing in that: she had a habit of sitting up at her bedroom window, and looking out, just with her hands in her lap. And the house as still as a—as still as a church.

'I loafed about a bit in the kitchen. Call *her*? Well, hardly! There was plenty to do. As usual. The supper, and all that. The village woman had left about eleven that morning—toothache. She owned to it. Not that that put me about. I can cook a boiled egg and a potato well enough for most Christians. But hot meals—meals for—well, anyhow, there was nothing hot that evening. It was about seven-thirty by then, I suppose; and I was beginning to wonder. Then I thought I'd go out in the yard and have a look at the runabout—an old Ford, you know—I hadn't had time then for weeks to keep it decent. When I got to the shed, there was a strange cat eating up some fish-bones; and when I looked in, it was gone.'

'You mean the Ford?'

'Yes, the Ford. There wasn't a sign of it. That froze me up, I can tell you, for there had been gipsies about a day or two before. I rushed into the house and called out up the stairs, "Edna! Edna! Are you there? The Ford's gone." No answer. I can tell you I was just like a frenzied man. I looked in the drawing-room—teapot and cup on a tray but empty: just sunshine streaming in as if nothing had happened. Then I looked into her little parlour: boudoir, she called it. Nothing doing. Then I went upstairs and tapped on her bedroom door. "Miss Dutton," I said, "have you seen anything of the Ford? It's gone." And then I looked in. That was the queer thing about it. They all said that. That it never occurred to me, I mean, that she was not in the car herself. But what I say is—how can you think of everything before you say it, and wasn't it I myself that *said* I had said it?

'Anyhow, I looked in: I suppose a man can do *that* in his

own house and his car gone from under his very nose! And believe me, the sight inside was shocking. I'm a great stickler myself for law and order, for neatness, I mean. I had noticed it before: it irritated me. In spite of all her finery, she was never what you would call a tidy woman. But that room beat everything. Drawers flung open, dresses hugger-mugger, slippers, bags, bead-work, boxes, gimcracks all over the place. But not a sign of her. I looked—everywhere. She wasn't there, right enough. Not—not a sign of her. She was gone. And— and I have never seen her since.'

The rain was over, and the long sigh he uttered seemed to fill the whole tea-shop as if it were a faint echo of the storm which had ceased as suddenly as it had begun. The sun was wanly shining again, gilding the street.

'You at once guessed, I suppose, the house had been broken into, while you were out?'

He kept his eyes firmly on mine. 'Yes,' he said. 'That's what I thought—at first.'

'But then, I think you said a minute or two ago that Miss Dutton *was* actually seen again?'

He nodded. 'That's just it,' he said, as if with incredulous lucidity. 'So you see, the other couldn't have been. The facts were against it. She was seen that very evening,' he said, 'and driving my Ford. By more than one, too. Our butcher happened to be outside his shop door; no friend of mine either. It was a Saturday, cutting up pieces for the 4d. and 6d. trays, and he saw her going by: saw the number too. It was all but broad daylight, though it's a narrow street. It was about seven then, he said, because he had only just wound his clock. There she was; and a good pace too. And who could be surprised if she looked a bit unusual in appearance? It's exactly what you'd expect. You don't bolt out of a house you have lived in comfortable for two or three years as neat as a new pin.'

'What was wrong with her?'

'Oh, the man was nothing better than a fool, though

promptitude itself when it came to asking a good customer to settle up. He said he'd have hardly recognized her. There, in my car, mind you, and all but broad daylight.'

'But surely,' I said as naturally as possible, 'even if it is difficult sometimes to trace a human being, it is not so easy to dispose of a car. Wasn't that ever found?'

He smiled at me, and in a more friendly way than I should have deemed possible in a face so naturally inexpressive.

'You've hit the very nail on the head,' he assented. 'They did find the car—on the Monday morning. In fact it was found on the Sunday by a young fellow out with his sweetheart, but they thought it was just waiting—picking flowers, or something. It had been left inside a fir-copse about a couple of hundred yards from a railway station, a mile or so out of the town.'

'Just a countryfied little railway station, I suppose? Had the porter or anybody noticed a lady?'

'Countryfied—ay, maybe: but the platform crowded with people going to and fro for their week's marketing, besides a garden party from the Rectory.'

'The platform going into the town?'

'Yes, that's it,' said my friend. 'Covering her tracks.'

At that moment I noticed one of our waitress's bright-red 'Eighteens' whirling past the tea-shop door. It vanished.

'She had had a letter that morning—postmark Chicago,' the now far-too-familiar voice edged on industriously. 'The postman noticed it, being foreign. It's my belief *that* caused it. But mind you, apart from that, though I'm not, and never was, complaining, she'd treated me, well——' But he left the sentence unfinished while he clumsily pushed about with his spoon in the attempt to rescue a fly that had strayed in too far in pursuit of his sweet cold coffee. He was breathing gently on the hapless insect.

'And I suppose, by that time, you had given the alarm?'

'Given the alarm?' he repeated. 'Why?'

The sudden frigidity of his tone confused me a little. 'Why,' I said, 'not finding Miss Dutton in the house, didn't you let anybody know?'

'Now my dear sir,' he said, 'I ask you. How was *I* to know what Miss Dutton was after? I wasn't Miss Dutton's keeper; she was perfectly at liberty to do what she pleased, to come and go. How was I to know what she had taken into her head? Why, I thought for a bit it was a friendly action considering all things, that she should have borrowed the car. Mind you, I don't say I wasn't disturbed as well, her not leaving a word of explanation, as she had done once before—pinned a bit of paper to the kitchen table—"Yours with love, Edna"—that sort of thing. Though that was when everything was going smooth and pleasant. What I did first was to go off to a cottage down the lane and inquire there. All out, except the daughter in the wash-house. Not a sight or sound of car or Miss Dutton, though she did recollect the honk of a horn sounding. "Was it my horn?" I asked. But they're not very observant, that kind of young woman. Silly-like. Besides, she wasn't much more than a child.'

'And your sister: where actually was she, after all?'

He looked at me as if once more in compliment of my sagacity.

'That, I take it—to find and question *her*, I mean, was a matter of course. I went up to her room, opened the door, and I can hear myself actually saying it now: "Have you seen anything of Edna, Maria?"

'It was very quiet in her room—stuffy, too, and for the moment I thought she wasn't there; and then I saw her—I detected her there—crouching in the farthest corner out of the light. I saw her white face turn round, it must have been covered up. "Where's Edna, Maria?" I repeated. She shook her head at me, sitting there beyond the window. I could scarcely see her. And you don't seem to have realized that any kind of direct or sudden question always confused her. It didn't seem she understood what I was saying. In my belief it was nothing short of brutal the way they put her through it. I mean that Colonel, as he calls himself. Over and over and over again.

'Well, we weren't in any mood for food, as you may guess, when eight, nine, went by—and no sign of her. At last it was no use waiting any longer; but just to make sure, I went over to the farm two miles or so away—a little off the road, too, she must have taken to the town. We were still pretty friendly there. It was about half-past nine, I suppose, and they had all gone to bed. The dog yelled at me as if it was full moon and he had never seen me before. I threw a handful of gravel up at the old man's window, and I must say, considering all things, he kept his temper pretty well. Specially as he had seen nothing. Nothing whatever, he said.

' "Well," I said, speaking up at him, and they were my very words, "I should like to know what's become of her." He didn't seem to be as anxious as I was—thought she'd turn up next morning. "That kind of woman knows best what she's about," he said. So I went home and went to bed, feeling very uneasy. I didn't like the feel of it, you understand. And I suppose it must have been about three or four in the morning when I heard a noise in the house.'

'You thought she had come back?'

'What?' he said.

'I say, you thought she had come back?'

'Yes, of course. Oh yes. And I looked out of my bedroom door over the banisters. By that time there was a bit of moonlight showing, striking down on the plaster and oilcloth. It was my sister, with an old skirt thrown over her nightgown. She was as white as a sheet, and shivering.

' "Where have you been, Maria?" I asked her in as gentle a voice as I could make it. The curious thing is, she understood me perfectly well. I mean she answered at once, because often I think really and truly she did understand, only that she couldn't as quickly as most people collect her wits as they say.

'She said, mumbling her words, she had been looking for her.

' "Looking for who?" I said, just to see if she had taken me right.

' "For her," she said.

' "For Edna?" I asked. "And why should you be looking for Edna this time of night?" I spoke a little more sternly.

'She looked at me, and the tears began to roll down her face.

' "For God's sake, Maria, why are you crying?" I said.

' "Oh," she said, "she's gone. And she won't come back now."

'I put my arm round her and drew her down on to the stairs. "Compose yourself," I said to her, "don't shiver and shake like that." I forgot she had been standing barefoot on the cold oilcloth. "What do you mean, Gone? Don't take on so. Who's to know she won't come back safe and sound?" I am giving you the words just as they came out of our mouths.

' "Oh," she said, "William, you know better than me—I won't say anything more. Gone. And never knowing that I hadn't forgotten how kind she was to me!"

' "Kind, my girl!" I said. "Kind! In good part, maybe," I said, "but not surely after what she said to you that day?"

'But I could get nothing more out of her. She shrank up moaning and sobbing. She had lost herself again, her hair all draggled over her eyes, and she kept her face averted from me, and her shoulders were all humped, shaking under my hands—you know what women are. So I led her off to her room and made her as comfortable as I could. But all through the night I could hear her afterwards when I went to listen, and talking too.

'You can tell I was by now in a pretty state myself. That was a long night for me. And what do you think: when I repeated that conversation to the Colonel, and the Inspector himself standing by, he as good as told me he didn't believe me. "Friendly questions"! I could have wrung his nose. But then by that time my poor sister couldn't put two words together, he bawled at her so; until even the Inspector said it was not fair on her, and that she wouldn't be any use, anyhow, whatever happened.'

Once again there fell a pause in my stranger's disjointed story. He took two or three spoonfuls in rapid succession of his half-melted ice-cream. Even though the rain and the storm had come and gone, the air was not appreciably cooler, or rather it was no less heavy and stagnant. Our waitress had apparently given us up as lost souls, and I glanced a little deprecatingly at the notice, 'No gratuities', on the wall.

'How long did the drought last after that?' I inquired at last.

'The drought?' said my friend. 'The questions you ask! Why, it broke that very night. Over an inch of rain we had in less than eight hours.'

'Well, that, at any rate, I suppose, was something of a comfort.'

'I don't see quite why,' he retorted.

'And then you informed the police?'

'On the Sunday.' He took out a coloured silk handkerchief from the pocket of his neat pepper-and-salt jacket, and blew his nose. It is strange how one can actually anticipate merely from the general look of a man such minute particulars as the trumpeting of a nose. Strange, I mean, that all the parts and properties of human beings seem to hang so closely together, as if in positive collusion. Anyhow, the noise resounded through the glass-walled marbled room as sharp as a cockcrow.

'Well,' he said, 'that's where I stand. Looking at me, you wouldn't suppose perhaps that everything that a man wants most in this world has been destroyed and poisoned away. I had no call perhaps to be confiding in a mere stranger. But you couldn't credit the relief. I have nothing left now. I came up here to lose myself in the noise—so shocking quiet it is, there, now. But I have to go back—can't sleep much, though: wake up shouting. But what's worst is the emptiness: it's all perished. I don't want anything now. I'd as lief die and have done with it, if I could do it undriven. I've never seen a desert, but I reckon I know what the inside of one's like now. I stop thinking sometimes, and get dressed without knowing it. You wouldn't guess that from my appearance, I dare say. But once begin living as you feel underneath living *is*, where would most of us be? They have hounded me on and they've hounded me down, and presently they'll be sealing me up, and me never knowing from one day to another what news may come of—of our friend. And my sister gone and all.'

'She isn't "missing" too, I hope?' As I reflect on it, it was a vile question to have put to the man. I don't see how anything could have justified it. His face was like a burnt-out boat. The effect on him was atrocious to witness. His swarthy cheek went grey as ashes. The hand on the marble table began to tremble violently.

'Missing?' he cried. 'She's *dead*. Isn't *that* good enough for you?'

At this, no doubt because I was hopelessly in the wrong, I all but lost control of myself.

'What do you mean?' I exclaimed in a low voice. 'What do you mean by speaking to me like that? Haven't I wasted the better part of a Saturday afternoon listening to a story which, if I cared, I could read in your own county newspaper? What's it all to me, may I ask? I want to have nothing more to do with it—or you either.'

'You didn't say that at the beginning,' he replied furiously, struggling to his feet. 'You led me on.'

'Let you on, by God! What do you mean by such a piece of impudence? I say I want nothing more to do with you. And if that's how you accept a kindness, take my advice and keep your troubles to yourself in future. Let your bygones *be* bygones. And may the Lord have mercy on your soul.'

It was a foul outburst, due in part, I hope, to the heat; in part to the suffocating dehumanizing fœtor which spreads over London when the sun has been pouring down on its bricks and mortar as fiercely as on the bones and sands of some Eastern mud village.

My stranger had sat down again abruptly, had pushed his ice away from him and covered his face with his hands. His shoulders were jumping as if with hiccups. It was fortunate perhaps that at the moment there was no other eater in the café. But the waitresses were clustered together at the counter. They must have been watching us for some little time. And the manageress was there, too, looking at us like a scandalized hen over her collar through her pince-nez. We were evidently causing a disturbance—on the brink of a 'scene'. A visionary placard flaunted across my inward eye: *Fracas in a Restaurant*.

I too sat down, and beckoned peremptorily to the young lady who had been so attentive about the bus.

'My bill, please,' I said—'this gentleman's and mine.' And then, foolishly, I added, 'It's hot, isn't it?'

She made no reply until, after damping her lead pencil, she had added up her figures and had handed me between her finger-tips the mean scrap of paper. Then she informed me crisply, in fastidious Cockney, that some people seemed to find it hotter than most, and that it was past closing time, and would I please pay at the desk.

My accomplice had regained a little of his self-restraint by now. He put out a wavering hand and took up his hard felt hat. It was almost incredible that so marked a change should have come over so insensitive a face in that brief space of time. Its touch of bravado, its cold clear stare as of a watchful dog, even the neatness of it, had disappeared. He looked ten years older—lost and abandoned. He put out his other hand for the check. It was a curious action for a man with an intense closeness—if not meanness—clearly visible on his features. 'I should prefer, if you don't mind, to pay my bill myself,' he said.

'Not at all,' I replied brusquely. 'It was my ice-cream. I must apologize for having been so abrupt.'

He tried to smile; and it was like the gleam of a sickly evening sunshine after heavy winter rain.

'It's broken me: that's all I can say,' he said. 'What I say is, you read such things in the newspapers, but you don't know what they mean to them as are most concerned. I don't see how you can. But anyhow, I *can* pay my way.'

I hesitated. A furious contest—dim spread-eagled figures silhouetted, as it were, against a background of utter black—seemed to be proceeding in some dream in my mind, a little beyond actual consciousness. 'Well,' I blurted, 'I hope time will make things better. I can guess what I should feel like myself in similar circumstances. If I were you, I should. . . .' But at sight of him, the words, I am thankful to say, faded out before I could utter them. 'If I were you'—how easy! But how is that metamorphosis conceivable?

He looked at his hat; he looked at his ice-cream, now an insipid mush; he looked anxiously and searchingly at the table—marked over with the hieroglyphics of dark ugly marble. And at last he raised his eyes—those inexpressive balls of glass—and looked at me. He changed his hat from his right to his left hand, and still looking at me, hesitated, holding the empty hand out a little above the table. Then turning away, he drew it back.

I pretended not to have noticed the action. 'There should be another Eighteen in a few minutes,' I volunteered. 'And I think I noticed a stopping-place a few yards down.'

Nevertheless I couldn't for the moment leave him there—to the tender mercies of those censorious young waitresses in their exquisitely starched caps. 'I am going that way,' I said. 'Shall I see you into it?'

'It's the heat,' he said. 'No, thank you. You have been a. . . .'

With a gasp I repelled as well as I could the distaste for him that was once more curdling as if with a few drops of vinegar my very blood. What monsters of hatred and uncharitableness we humans can be! And what will *my* little record look like, I wonder, when the secrets of all hearts are opened.

It seemed for the time being as though the whole of my right arm had become partially paralysed. But with an effort I put out my hand at last; and then he, too, his—a large green solitaire cuff-link showing itself against his wristband as he did so. We shook hands—though I doubt if a mere fleshly contact can express much while the self behind it is dumb with instinctive distaste.

Besides, the effect on him even of a friendly action as frigid as this was horribly disconcerting. It reminded me of ice pitted and crumbling in a sudden thaw. He seemed to have been reduced to a state of physical and spiritual helplessness as if by an extremity of emotion, or by a drug. It was nauseating. It confused me and made me ashamed and miserable. I turned away abruptly; paid our bill at the desk, and went out. And London enveloped me.

MISS MILLER

*

Because she had very little breath left, and because it must be far from easy to sob and run at the same time, the little girl with the square-bobbed flaxen hair dropped into a walk as she came in under the shade of the wide-spreading chestnut tree. And there, at sight of the figure that sat bolt upright in the middle of the seat, she at once stopped dead. So complete was her surprise that she had even forgotten to sob any more. She simply opened her tear-washed eyes and stared. And Miss Miller, in her tight soldierlike jacket and peculiar hat, seemed to be taking no more notice of her than a lighted lamp-post takes of a moth.

But Miss Miller had seen her right enough. Miss Miller had kept a weather-eye open, had watched her come tumbling across the gentle green grass slopes and under the trees and into the sunshine and into the shade again. It was only her funny little way to pretend not to have seen, though she could no more have explained *why* than she could explain why these long balmy summer mornings she always sat bolt upright on a seat that had clearly been constructed with such beautiful scroll-like curves at the back of it on purpose to make those who had time thus to idle the day away uncomfortable.

Not that this little creature had ever seen Miss Miller before, had even so much as suspected she was there. That was certain. Though, since they frequently shared the amenities of the park, she very well might have done so. The park-keepers knew Miss Miller all right, and there wasn't one that wouldn't nod her a jocular if slightly ironical good morning. So would the elephantine policeman at the gates—and then perhaps solemnly wink at the man who was piling up the dead leaves in his three-wheeled handcart. Hardly a day went by but Miss Miller was to be seen wandering about in these particular parts, observing the observable with a quick bird-like turn of the head, or sitting just as she was now, with her sharp black eyes and her long sharp nose, one cotton-gloved hand resting on the long-beaked stork's head of her umbrella, her gaze fixed on the sun-sheened waters of the ornamental pond, almost as though she were eternally on the point of being lost in some fantastically quizzical daydream.

Only 'almost', though; for Miss Miller had very little ultimate respect for daydreams. She preferred, or rather she restricted herself to, the actual—but with no excessive respect for that either. And however motionless her pose might be, however absent-looking the expression on her long, odd, sallow face, and in her coal-black cavernous eyes, she noticed positively everything that was going on around her—striding gluttonous starlings, clumsy, strutting, burnished wood-pigeons, fashionable nursemaids, smartly-stepping soldier-boys with their paper-squill puttees and funny little metal-headed swagger canes, ladies and gentlemen politely convers-ing on the gravel paths, or less politely colloguing under the trees, the swans for ever amorous of their own snowy images on the lustrous pale-blue water, and the wing-sailed toy-boats braving the breezes, their small round-behinded owners stoop-ing like Chinese dummies at the edge of the pond as they launched them out upon the deep. She even heard and heeded the changeable talk of the sparrows in the branches overhead, while their cousins of every degree dumpily hopped about her long feet with no more fear of casualties than if she were a dust-bin. And all the while some other Miss Miller sat trist-fully hearkening to the distant murmur of a fall of water feeding the shallow pond.

In the soft sweet air of that hot St. Martin's Summer morning her small tear-stained visitor must by now have stood staring at her under the tent of the chestnut tree for at least two whole minutes. And then softly and suddenly Miss Miller turned her sharp, black, coal-box eyes, and the long drooping nose that hung between them, straight at the child.

'Well, Rosie,' she said, 'and what's for you?'

But the question was neither sharp, tart, tradesman-like nor grown-up-ish. It merely asked for valuable information.

'Nothing at all, thank you,' said her visitor, 'I was only looking.'

'And so was I,' said Miss Miller. 'What's the harm in that?'

The bobbed head under the blue bonnet stooped a little forward. 'My name', she all but whispered, as though she didn't want to hurt anybody's feelings, 'is not Rosie; it's Nella.'

'And that's an odd thing too,' cried Miss Miller from in under her high hat, 'for mine is Miller—*Miss* Miller. At least that's what they call me:

> *Though only one had an umberella,*
> *There sat Miss Miller and there stood Nella.*'

'Can you make up *much*?' asked the little girl.

'It depends on who *for*, on the vocabulary, and the *rhymes*,' said Miss Miller. 'Some come, some won't. But the next and the next and the next thing to inquire is *why*, Rosie, you have run away? And who from? Or should we say, whom-m-m?

> *In life, so I'm told, there is no need to stammer,*
> *So long as we keep a sharp eye on our grammar.*

And be sure not to answer if you've *no* wish to say.'

The little girl looked stealthily over her shoulder, gazed

178

carefully once more at Miss Miller, turned, and breathed out her secret.

'It's my new nurse,' she said. 'She's *not* my real Nannie; *my* Nannie's ill. She's a beast, and I hate her.'

'Ah, now,' cried Miss Miller, clutching more firmly than ever her beaked umbrella; ' "a beast"! With four legs no doubt, but not, oh no, a tell-tale at the end of it! What did I *say*! Isn't that *just*, Rosie, what we have to expect? And I'll be bound she can't help it. That's *my* opinion. It's what's called ingrained. So you ran away. And what more likely? Though *not*, we must admit, allowed?

> *And there, maybe to mock the eye,*
> *Goes fluttering by a butterfly.*
> *But mark, dear Pilgrim, mark with me,*
> *How rational is the honey bee!*

Hey now, what about *that*? Nurses! It's years and years and years . . . but then you see after all it's only Time, Rosie, that divides us. By us meaning just you and me. And what is *Time*? Nothing I promise you but merely "wear and tear". Merely.'

Yet another prolonged shuddering sob shook the little girl from head to foot, but it was meaning little more now than that solemn foamless swell upon the Pacific which succeeds a storm.

'She won't let me do a single thing I want, and some day I'll run right away. Then even my daddy won't be able to find me.'

'I expect *not*,' said Miss Miller, 'and especially even if he shouldn't happen to look. You see, my poppet, even if we have the legs and the brrroth to run with, it's very very seldom really "right away". It can't be done. And *there's* the rub. I have frequently noticed it.'

She was still steadily surveying her visitor, her perched-up hat trembling a little in the process. The fair face looked far too young to have had so many troubles begin to show their markings in it. At which sad notion Miss Miller openly smiled at the little girl, though her smile rather more closely resembled a grimace.

'Now when *I* was about your size and for a good long time after ' she said, 'I didn't myself usually run away. I was run away *from*.'

'Didn't you have a nurse?'

'Three,' said Miss Miller. 'Black, yellow and brown. Turn and turn about. So it wasn't much good.'

'I don't think I quite understand that,' said her visitor.

'No? In such cases I am told it is better to explain. You will understand then, Pollie, that when I was young—which is exactly a hundred and forty-eight years ago now, not counting Sundays—I lived in a big, a *great* big house—a whacking great e*nor*mous house.'

'Why?'

'Because', said Miss Miller, 'it was there it had pleased God to call me. A house, Pollie, not parked as they say in a huge prairie like this one,' and she swept her umbrella across the ample view, '*not* with a bit of a pond in it like that one,' and she jabbed its point at the lake, 'but a river, my love, a wide r-r-rolling r-r-river, with cr-r-reeks in its cr-r-rumplings, and simply carpeted with water-lilies. Carpeted. A hop and a skip and a jump and there you were on the other side. And fish— *plop-plip-plopp*, and ducks—quack-quack—*quarkk*! And besides the woolly sheep, my love, *deer*! Herds of them, dappled and waggle-tailed and some of them horned, and ears like windmills. But believe me, Pollie, *one* flick of a finger and every single one of them clean out of sight! On the other hand, it was not the deer we were referring to, but the house. It had hundreds and hundreds and hundreds of windows. Specially up above, of course, where the corridors were—one after another and all the way round.' And Miss Miller spread out the black-gloved fingers of one lank left hand as if that would show exactly how. 'And to every window—or *two*—*or* three, as the case might be, a room or chamber: chiefly, as I say, bed. Not that I'd attempt to tell you exactly how many. Mistakes cannot always be put right. But imagine me there, if you please, looking *out* of the windows; and the OTHERS, you know, feasting in the HALL.'

'I have *my* dinner,' said her visitor, 'in the nursery; except on Sundays. Then it's with my daddy.'

'Halls and dining-rooms—much the same,' said Miss Miller. 'All depends on the *entourage*. Well', she planted her foot a little more firmly on the little patch of gravel that surrounded the seat, 'it was at one of those windows that I first saw it running away.'

'Saw what running away?'

'That, my love, is what I could never positively descry,' said Miss Miller, stooping her long nose and the brim of her hat in the direction of the little girl as if she were a cockatoo on a perch. 'There's some that run, and there's some who are run from, and it's distance lends enchantment to the view. What I can *say* is that it seemed to be something or somebody I didn't exactly want, you know, to go. *And* such a swimming moon! Every bit as the poem says,' and Miss Miller once more broke into rhyme:

> '*There were leaves on the branches like silver,*
> *And dew thick as frost on the grass,*
> *And nought but the moon in the shimmery-shammery,*
> *And me staring out through the glass.*

I say *staring*, Pollie, though we agree it's not polite. But *politesse* apart, as the barber said, it wasn't to be seen from *that* window. And why? Simply, my dear, because it had gone out of sight. So that's where we are.'

'Where?' said the little girl.

'Why, there,' said Miss Miller.

'What did you do?' asked the little girl.

'That's just it,' said Miss Miller. 'What would you have

done? And the answer to that is, I did just the same as that. I ran as fast as my trotters would carry me to the next—and then to the next, and then to *all* the nexteses. *Little* windows, every one of them, with round tops and small—er—panes. But no. *No*—and I repeat it on purpose—not a glimpse. I won't *say*, mind you,' she continued with due solemnity and with a longer face than ever, 'that all the little bedrooms had beds in them, or wash-hand-stands or even chests of drawer-seses. You'll pardon me, but I didn't really *look*. But I *will* say I went in and out, and out and in, and so of course out again of every single one there was, until after twice round the house and back, counting the corridors once and once only, I found myself in the very place I had started from. And by and large, my dear Miss Sheepshanks, that's what we all do. In time.'

Miss Miller thereupon burst out laughing, and even Miss Sheepshanks opened her mouth—not to laugh, but only because she was so intent on her new acquaintance that she couldn't help imitating her.

'What did you do then?' she said.

'Well, then,' said Miss Miller, drawing her cotton-gloved forefinger slowly down her nose as if in deep reflection, and the faded greying tip of it made a right-angle with the rest, 'then—I gave it up; and *it* gave *me* up. It was what's called mutual, my poppet. Then too about that time we were compelled to move—the Family, you know. Ups and downs, then downs again. So we dismissed the, the—well—the *entourage*. That *is* the best thing, don't you think?'

Nella nodded.

> 'Too-whit, *or* too-whoo,
> *Come now, or come soon,*
> *You won't miss the sun*
> *If you look at the moon.*

That', said Miss Miller, 'is how it goes in the *pome*. But oh,

Pollie, if *only* you could have seen the shadows on the cobble-stones and the silvering of the snails!'

'I don't *think*', said Nella, 'I quite like snails.'

Miss Miller merely beamed on her as though, if she had not entirely disagreed with her visitor, she could not have so easily comprehended a very natural aversion. 'There *are* such people; I admit it,' she cried cordially:

> *" "And whether one travels due East or due West,*
> *I'm inclined," said the Sailor, "to think truth is best."*

But as *I* was saying,' she went rapidly on, 'there might have been dew and there *were* snails, but there was positively nothing else. It had come, my dear; and it had gone, my dove. And if you should ask me what I mean by *it*, I should say it is called being *young*—like you and me, Miss Cosy. And as for that, and with all due respect for nursemaids and such, the first part of it is apt to be much nicer than the last.'

The little girl stared at this fantastic Miss Miller sitting so stiff and vertical on her scroll-shaped seat with its iron legs bent under her on the patch of gravel. It was deliciously cool under the fan-like fronds of the great spiky-fruited chestnut tree overhead. The leaves shed a dry fragrance, and the sun-burned grass, too; and there came floating on the air from afar the hypnotic whiff of an early autumn bonfire.

Miss Miller appeared for the moment to have forgotten she was not alone, while the round blue eyes of her visitor went on busily examining her from top to toe.

'Do you live in a great big enormous house now?' Nella presently inquired.

'By no means. Not at all,' Miss Miller replied, her black eyes fixed on the far-away. 'Still, for shelter from what are called the Ellimans, my child, only four walls are required, excluding floor and ceiling. What is *space*?'

'But you see,' said Nella, 'I didn't quite understand what

you meant it was when what you couldn't see ran away, out of all those little windows, I mean.'

Miss Miller penetrated the slight ambiguity of this sentence as if with a needle.

'And what more likely?' she agreed. 'No more did I. But you see, *me* never having noticed much that it was there, it wasn't scarcely right or proper to go laveering and lamenting up and down when it was gone. Which is what is called reasoning, Rosie. Besides, as I say, we moved. What is 17 from, say, 55?'

'I think', said Nella, after a long pause, 'it must be thirty something.'

'Well, then, it is about thirty something whatever-you-like-to-call-them ago since I climbed up the Tower for the last time.' Miss Miller suddenly stooped and pressed the fingers of her right hand on the toe of her left shoe. Her face had gone a little stiff and surprised-looking.

'Does that bump on your toe hurt you?' inquired her visitor courteously.

'Now and then,' replied Miss Miller in her richest tones. 'It does its best. It's what is called a bunion. Not John, of course, though it *may* come, they say, from walking about. And that, my dear, I am pretty well used to. Now the Tower, you must understand, please, was in our park. In what is called the centre, Rosie. Where we went to next, I mean. Two parks in all. But *not*, as I have said before, a public prairie like this!' And yet again Miss Miller swept the panorama with the point of her umbrella. 'This Tower I mention faced to the *east*, you will please imagine, and was of the fairest choicest marble. It might almost be ivory; something like a roly-poly jam-pudding, but pinker and more, as they say, diffused. And its top was like a pepper-pot, marble too, with heads and wings and faces, and cut out with holes like flowers for peeping places, and all, all of stone. Quite quite solid too. *And*'—Miss Miller paused and looked at her toe—'perhaps I ought to mention

that it was also in the middle of a box-wood. And, as dear
Alfred Lord Tennyson says:

> *"With here and there a cypress pricking*
> *Black against the blue,*
> *And here and there a dark but older*
> *Tree they call a yew."*

In the middle of a box-wood, Rosie; and you could see for
miles—if, that is, and you'll forgive the reminder, you troubled
to look. Well, I climbed that tower one morning, birds chim-
champing, grasshoppers whirring, larks in the sky, sun burning, and as I peered up the spiral staircase—you know what a
corkscrew is, my child—a twist, a wheeze and a pop?'

Nella, with a small dumpy forefinger pointing upward,
pushed that finger round and round and up and up under
the tree.

'Exactly. And just at the topmost bend of it, bless your
heart, what if I didn't go and see it yet again! Or something:
at any rate so much like it, you could scarcely tell them apart;
not at first.'

'What was it doing then?'

'*Just* the same as usual,' said Miss Miller airily. 'Running
away. And all as the old song goes.' She actually sang it too,
but not loud enough to get beyond the circuit of her chestnut
since she had her respectability to consider, and at times her
voice, even to her own ear, seemed almost too powerful:

> 'It's joys and cares and stri-i-ife
> I'm singing to you of,
> And some they call it li-i-ife,
> And some they call it lov.

So up I went, of course. Round and round and up
and up until at last I reached the top, and never a sign of it
*no*where.'

Miss Miller inhaled a deep breath of the thin autumnal air,

as if to restore her after that long climb in memory. But Nella still stood her ground.

'Not but what I might not say', said her new acquaintance a little craftily, 'there was no vestige of a sign of where it might have *been*. On the other hand it wasn't there then. And everything so calm and still and *trarn*quil you could have dined off thistledown. Why, it might have been carried off in its sleep the very moment I got to the top step and came out into the gallery. So, you see, once more, or, in other words, yet again'—and the lengthy angular face turned slowly about towards the little girl rather like the ominous top of an oast house—'I had been cheated of everything.

> '*No, no, papa, I cannot, since*
> *He whom I wed must be a* Prince.

Though how you can call it cheating when every single card from the Queen of Hearts to the Ace of Spades was on the table, I'll be dashed, Rosie, if I can see. And you will, I hope, excuse the vigour of the remark.

'Now when you say "It", my dear Miss Sheepshanks,' Miss Miller continued reflectively, 'I suppose we neither of us know exactly what we are talking about. What, I mean, we *mean*; even though it's something we might, given a good supper and a feather bed, dream of, say, every Monday, Wednesday and Friday for years and years. *And* on Tuesdays, Thursdays and Saturdays, including the Sabbath, be trusted to forget. But there is no need for high horses. None whatever.

> '*Come what come may; go what go will,*
> *There is such a thing as must.*
> *Then why be philo-so-sophical*
> *So long as one tries to be iust?*

You follow me?'

The round clear eyes under the compact little brow beneath

the fair straight fringe of hair and the rim of bonnet gazed steadily back. Then Nella nodded.

'Precisely,' said Miss Miller with a smile like that of the Conqueror at Hastings, as with a sharp little gesture she planted the point of her umbrella emphatically between the pebbles. 'Precisely. And so between you and me and the gatepost it has been ever since. This prairie, you understand, these here people, and all these trees; you sit, you scarcely need to look, but you know it just comes and goes. And the complete *entourage* dispersed! In fact, who would believe, Rosie, that looking out of one's *own* indefatigably poky little top-floor window, square this time, of course, or rather obbolongy, with a jar of geranium or mignonette on the sill—and I must say some of those young men who look after the gardens are very civil—*and* millions of chimney pots over the roofs of every shape and smell and size, and the wires simply humming in the breezes, not to speak of the noise and—er—odours from down below and only twopence-halfpenny to pay for it, *and* a land*lady* who *never* has *change*—who, I say, who would believe, my dear, there could be anything left at all?'

'In the chimney pots?'

'In the chimney pots.'

'Are there many smuts?'

'In winter, hosts,' said Miss Miller, 'and in summer, fewer.'

'Do you mean you can't see anything, of what you were saying, there, either? Not even now?' And Miss Miller's square-headed little visitor looked quite anxious about it.

'For certain; never: but of signs of it exactly a thousand and one. Now look at this,' Miss Miller with some little fumbling managed at last to unfasten an old leather vanity bag that hung on her arm, 'look at this.'

Nella with a deep sigh drew a step or two nearer, but not too close, while her odd friend held up between cotton-gloved finger and thumb an acorn with a long stalk. 'That,' said Miss Miller almost ingratiatingly as she rapidly twirled it, 'that is an acorn. No doubt of it. And did you ever in your life see any-thing that fitted better—John Bunyan apart, you know? As if the cup and the seed, or the "a" and the "corn" had been waiting for one another for ages on ages until at last there was no keeping them back. Now that, Rosie, dropped on to my hat as I was walking under its parent tree—this very hat, and not an hour ago. And what did I say to myself when I looked at it, come clean out of the blue sky, so to speak? I said: Observe, Miss Miller; it fits!

> '*It might be a lump of amber, ma'am,*
> *It might be a stick of coral;*
> *But what we have to remember, ma'am,*
> *Is to keep our eye on the moral.*

Ah, my dear Rosie, I have sat on that tower at noonday when the clocks were striking the hour, and in the height—though I prefer to say heighth—of the summer, and I have listened to the nightingales in the midst of the box-wood, though of course in the best families they come at night, and we mustn't get poetical. And bless my soul—now that your own smudged tears are dry upon your cheeks—I could weep about a bucket-ful at thought of it—and partly at what didn't fit, you know—if only it were not improper to do so in so public a resort as this.'

Nella watched Miss Miller closely, as if in hope of seeing at least one large tear course slowly down her cheek. It would probably keep very close to that long long nose. But far from weeping, Miss Miller was smiling with greater intensity than ever as she sat with that nose turned sidelong towards her little visitor in the shade of the chestnut tree.

'And now,' she said, 'instead, my dear Susie, of giving it to you, which might be troublesome, I will return my acorn to my bag. I shall plant it, as a matter of fact, in a pot, and after two or three leaves have appeared it will die. That, my child, is how things go. *And* come.' Up went her thin eyebrows,

'*And* go again. So why, why, make too much fuss about it?'

At the word 'come', Miss Miller's singularly attentive eye, which had ever and anon roved the green expanse beyond her canopying chestnut tree, had alighted on an enemy, and one rapidly approaching them.

'A fuss? Certainly not,' she added emphatically. 'We are simply *not* going to *lower* ourselves. And never, never, I say, because our horrid nurse, as I see, in her long grey odious coat and neat little bonnet is stamping after us at this moment like a buffalo over the savannas of the West. We are *not* going to make a fuss; oh, no! And it isn't even mere pride that stops us. What? Eh?'

Nella had turned her small head with extreme rapidity over her shoulder.

'I must say good-bye now,' she said, a little drily and sedately, turning once more to her friend. 'My nurse wants me. I suppose, you know, it must be nearly time for lunch. *Good* morning.'

'Lunch,' cried Miss Miller merrily. 'Why, certainly. *I* seldom think of it, you know, until I find that most of it isn't exactly *there*. And what's more, it's a long lane, Miss Sheepshanks, that has no turning, which is *not* to mention in any particular respect merely *red* lanes.'

When Nella had reached the big stone floriated vase that stood beside the bridge over the water—and she hadn't been listening very closely to the heated remarks which her nurse had been ejaculating from time to time during their walk— she turned her head and looked behind her; but the scroll-shaped seat under the chestnut tree was now vacant, and there was no sign at all of its late occupant.

But then, at this moment, any one of the 'prairie' trees might easily have hidden that long, spare, sharp-boned figure, including even its nose. And so intent was her small mind still upon her talk with this peculiar stranger, that when her nurse, snatching at her arm as if she were a tottering clockwork dummy which she intended to fling clean across the ornamental pond, said, 'Now, mind your *step*, you little imp! Just you wait till I get you home, my fine lady. Ooh, but *you*'ll be hearing of this! *You—mark—*ME!'—not the faintest change of expression showed on the child's face. It was almost as if one could learn to be a 'philo—so—sophoser' after one lesson, and that in the open, and without any fee.

THE ORGY: AN IDYLL

*

It was a Wednesday morning, and May-day, and London—
its West End too, crisp, brisk, scintillating. Even the horses
had come out in their Sunday best. With their nosegays and
ribbons and rosettes they might have been on their way to a
wedding—the nuptials of Labour and Capital, perhaps. As for
people, the wide pavements of the great street were packed
with them. Not so many busy idlers of the one sex as of the
other, of course, at this early hour—a top-hat here, a pearl-
grey Homburg there; but of the feminine a host as eager and
variegated as the butterflies in an Alpine valley in midsum-
mer; some stepping daintily down from their landaulettes like
'Painted Ladies' out of the chrysalis, and thousands of others,
blues and browns and speckleds and sables and tawnies and
high-fliers and maiden's blushes, from all parts of the world
and from most of the suburbs, edging and eddying along, this
way, that way, their eyes goggling, their tongues clacking, but
most of them, their backs to the highway, gazing, as though
mesmerized, in and through the beautiful plate-glass windows
at the motley merchandise on the other side. And much of that
on the limbs and trunks of beatific images almost as life-like
but a good deal less active than themselves.

The very heavens, so far as they could manage to peep
under the blinds, seemed to be smiling at this plenty. Nor had

they any need for care concerning the future, for nursemaids pushing their baby-carriages before them also paraded the pavements, their infant charges laid in dimpled sleep beneath silken awning and coverlet, while here and there a tiny tot chattered up into the air like a starling.

A clock, probably a church clock, and only just audible, struck ten. The sun from its heights far up above the roof-tops blazed down upon the polished asphalt and walls with such an explosion of splendour that it looked as if everything had been repainted overnight with a thin coat of crystalline varnish and then sprinkled with frozen sea-water. And every human creature within sight seemed to be as heart-free and gay as this beautiful weather promised to be brief. Every human creature—with one exception only—poor Philip Pim.

And why not? He was young—so young in looks, indeed, that if Adonis had been stepping along at his side they might have been taken for cousins. He was charmingly attired, too, from his little, round, hard felt hat—not unlike Mercury's usual wear, but without the wings—to his neat brogue shoes; and he was so blond, with his pink cheeks and flaxen hair, that at first you could scarcely distinguish his silken eyebrows and eyelashes, though they made up for it on a second glance. Care seemed never to have sat on those young temples. Philip looked as harmless as he was unharmed.

Alas! this without of his had no resemblance whatever to his within. He eyed vacantly a buzzing hive-like abandonment he could not share; first, because though he had the whole long day to himself he had no notion of what to do with it; and next, because only the previous afternoon the manager of the bank in which until then he had graced a stool specially reserved for him every morning, had shaken him by the hand and had wished him well—for ever. He had said how deeply he regretted Philip's services could not be indulged in by the bank any longer. He would miss him. Oh yes, very much indeed—but missed Philip must be.

The fact was that Philip had never been able to add up pounds, shillings, and pence so that he could be certain the total was correct. His 9's, too, often looked like 7's, his 5's like 3's. And as 'simple addition' was all but his sole duty in the bank, he would not have adorned its premises for a week if his uncle, Colonel Crompton Pim, had not been acquainted with one of its most stylish directors, and was not in the habit of keeping a large part of his ample fortune in its charge. He had asked Mr. Bumbleton to give Philip a chance. But chances—some as rapidly as Manx cats—come to an end. And Philip's had.

Now, if Colonel Pim had sent his nephew when he was a small boy to a nice public school, he might have been able by this time to do simple sums very well indeed. Philip might have become an accurate adder-up. It is well to look on the bright side of things. Unfortunately when Philip was an infant, his health had not been very satisfactory—at least to his widowed mother—and he had been sent instead to a private academy. There a Mr. Browne was the mathematical master— a Mr. Browne so much attached to algebra and to reading the *Times* in school hours that he hadn't much patience with the rudiments of arithmetic. 'Just add it up,' he would say, 'and look up the answer. And if it isn't right, do it again.'

It was imprudent of him, but in these early years poor Philip had never so much as dreamed that some day he was going to spend all day on a stool. If he had, he might not perhaps have been so eager to look up the answers. But then, his uncle was both fabulously rich and apparently unmarriageable, and Philip was his only nephew. Why, then, should he ever have paid any attention to banks, apart from the variety on which the wild thyme grows?

Term succeeded term, and still, though 'a promising boy', he remained backward—particularly in the last of the three R's. And his holidays, so called, would be peppered with such problems as (*a*) if a herring and a half cost three halfpence, how many would you eat for a shilling? (*b*) If a brick weighs just a pound and half a brick, what does it weigh? (*c*) If Moses was the son of Pharaoh's daughter, etc.; and (*d*) Uncles and brothers have I none, and so on. And since, after successive mornings with a sheet of foolscap and a stub of pencil, Philip's answers would almost invariably reappear as (*a*) 18; (*b*) 1½ lb.; (*c*) his sister, and (*d*) himself, Colonel Pim became more and more choleric and impolite, and Nature had long ago given him a good start.

He had a way, too, when carpeting at Philip, of flicking his shepherd-plaid trouser-leg with his handkerchief which was highly alarming to everyone concerned. At last, instead of transferring his nephew from Mr. Browne to Christ Church, Oxford, or to Trinity College, Cambridge, or to some less delectable resort at an outlying university, he first (before setting out in pursuit of big game all around the world), consigned him to a tutor, who thanked his lucky stars the expedition would take the Colonel a long time; and, on his return, he gave them both a prolonged vacation.

And *then* had fallen the bolt from the blue. On the morning of his twenty-first birthday, which had promised to be so cool, so calm, so bright, Philip received a letter from his uncle. He opened it with joy; he read it with consternation. It was in terms as curt as they looked illegible, and it was merely to tell him that what the Colonel called a post (but which was, in fact, a high stool) had been secured for his nephew, and that unless Philip managed to keep his seat on it for twelve consecutive months he would be cut off with a shilling.

Of these drear months about two and a half had somehow managed to melt away, and now not only was the stool rapidly following them into the limbo of the past, but at this very moment the Colonel was doubtless engaged, and with his usual zest, in keeping his promise. What wonder, then, Philip was not exactly a happy young man as he wandered this sunny populous May morning aimlessly on his way. There was nothing—apart from Everything around him—to make him so, except only one minute stroke of luck that had befallen him before breakfast.

When he had risen from his tumbled bed in his London lodgings, the sight of his striped bank trousers and his black bank coat and waistcoat had filled him with disgust. Opening the grained cupboard which did duty for a wardrobe—and in the indulgence of his tailor it was pretty full—he took down from a peg the festive suit he was now wearing, but which otherwise he had left unheeded since Easter. He found himself faintly whistling as he buttoned it on; but his delight can be imagined when, putting his finger and thumb into an upper waistcoat pocket, he discovered—a sovereign. And an excellent specimen of one, with St. George in his mantle and the dragon on the one side of it, and King Edward VII's head—cut off at the neck as if he had sat to its designer in his bath—on the other. This, with four others very much like it, had been bestowed on Philip many months ago by his Uncle Charles—a maternal uncle, who had since perished in Paris. As the rest of Philip's pockets contained only 7½d. in all, this coin—how forgotten, he simply could not conjecture—was treasure trove indeed.

Now, poor Philip had never really cared for money. Perhaps he had always associated it with herrings and half-bricks. Perhaps he had never needed it quite enough. Since, moreover, immediately opposite his perch at the Bank there hung a framed antique picture of this commodity in process of being shovelled out of receptacles closely resembling coal-scuttles into great vulgar heaps upon a polished counter, and there weighed in brass scales like so much lard or glucose, he had come to like it less and less. On the other hand, he dearly enjoyed spending it. As with Adam and the happy birds in the Garden of Eden—linnet and kestrel and wren—he enjoyed seeing it fly. In this he was the precise antithesis of his uncle.

Colonel Crompton Pim loved money. He exulted in it (not vocally, of course) *en masse*, as the Pharaohs exulted in pyramids. And he abhorred spending it. For this (and for many another) reason he had little affection for mere objects—apart, that is, from *such* objects as golf clubs, shooting boots, or hippopotamus-hoof inkstands, and he had not the smallest pleasure in buying anything for mere buying's sake.

His immense dormitory near Cheltenham, it is true, was full of furniture, but it was furniture, acquired in the 'sixties or thereabouts, for use and not for joy. Prodigious chairs with pigskin seats; tables of a solidity that defied time and of a wood that laughed at the worm; bedsteads of the Gog order; wardrobes resembling Assyrian sarcophagi; and ottomans which would seat with comfort and dignity a complete royal family. As for its 'ornaments', they came chiefly from Benares.

And simply because poor Philip delighted in spending money and hated such horrible impedimenta with the contempt a humming-bird must feel for a black-pudding, he had never been able to take to his uncle—not even for the sake of what he owned. And it was impossible—as he fondly supposed—for any human being to take to him for any other reason. No, there was nothing in common between them, except a few branches of the family tree. And these the Colonel might already have converted into firewood.

Now, as poor Philip meandered listlessly along the street, fingering his Uncle Charles's golden sovereign in his pocket, he came on one of those gigantic edifices wherein you can purchase anything in the world—from a white elephant to a performing flea, from a cargo of coconuts to a tin-tack. This was the 'store' at which his uncle 'dealt'. And by sheer force of habit, Philip mounted the welcoming flight of steps, crossed a large flat rubber mat, and went inside.

Having thus got safely in, he at once began to ponder how he was to get safely out—with any fraction, that is, of his golden sovereign still in his pocket. And he had realized in the recent small hours that with so little on earth now left to spend, except an indefinite amount of leisure, he must strive to spend that little with extreme deliberation.

So first, having breakfasted on a mere glance at the charred remnant of a kipper which his landlady had served up with his chicory, he entered a large gilded lift, or elevator, as the directors preferred to call it, *en route* to the restaurant. There he seated himself at a vacant table and asked the waitress to be so kind as to bring him a glass of milk and a bun. He nibbled, he sipped, and he watched the people—if people they really were, and not, as seemed more probable, automata intended to advertise the Ecclesiastical, the Sports, the Provincial, the Curio, the Export, and the Cast-Iron Departments.

With his first sip of milk he all but made up his mind to buy a little parting present for his uncle. It would be at least a gentle gesture. With his second he decided that the Colonel would be even less pleased to receive a letter *and*, say, a velvet smoking-cap, or a pair of mother-of-pearl cuff-links, than just a letter. By the time he had finished his bun he had decided to buy a little something for himself. But try as he might he could think of nothing (for less than a guinea) that would be worthy of the shade of his beloved Uncle Charles. So having pushed seven-fifteenths of all he else possessed under his plate for his freckled waitress, with the remaining fourpence he settled his bill and went steadily downstairs. Nineteen minutes past ten—he would have a good look about him before he came to a decision.

Hunger, it has been said, sharpens the senses, but it is apt also to have an edgy effect upon the nerves. If, then, Philip's breakfast had been less exacting, or his lunch had made up for it, he might have spent the next few hours of this pleasant May morning as a young man should—in the open air. Or he might have visited the British Museum, the National Gallery and Westminster Abbey. He might never, at any rate, in one brief morning of his mortal existence have all but died again and again of terror, abandon, shame, rapture and incredulity. He might never—but all in good time.

He was at a loose end, and it is then that habits are apt to prevail. And of all his habits, Philip's favourite was that of ordering 'goods' on behalf of his uncle. The Colonel in his fantastic handwriting would post him two weekly lists—one consisting of the 'wanted', the other of complaints about the previous week's 'supplied'. Armed with these, Philip would set out for the building he was now actually in. The first list, though not a thing of beauty, was a joy as long as it lasted. The second, for he had always flatly refused to repeat his uncle's sulphurous comments to any underling, he reserved for his old enemy, the secretary of the establishment, Sir Leopold Bull. And though in these weekly interviews Sir Leopold might boil with rage and chagrin, he never boiled over. For the name of Pim was a name of power in the secretary's office. The name of Pim was that of a heavy shareholder; and what the Colonel wanted he invariably in the long run got. A chest, say, of Ceylon tea, 'rich, fruity, bright infusion'; a shooting-stick (extra heavy Brugglesdon tube pattern); a double quart-size tantalus, with two double spring sterling silver Brahmin locks; a hundredweight of sago; a thousand black cheroots; a stymie, perhaps, or a click—something of that sort.

These 'order days' had been the balm of Philip's late existence. His eyes fixed on his ledger and his fancy on, say, 'Saddlery', or 'Sports', he looked forward to his Wednesdays —thirsted for them. Indeed, his chief regret at the bank, apart from little difficulties with his 9's and 3's, had been that his uncle's stores were closed on Saturday afternoons. And on Sundays. His hobby had, therefore, frequently given him indigestion, since he could indulge it only between 1 and 2 p.m. It was a pity, of course, that Colonel Pim was a man of wants so few, and these of so narrow a range. Possibly the suns of India had burned the rest out of him. But for Philip, any kind of vicarious purchase had been better than none.

And now these delights, too, were for ever over. His fountain had run dry. Sir Leopold had triumphed.

At this moment he found himself straying into an aisled medley of empties in hide. There is nothing like leather; here there was nothing *but* leather, and all of it made up into articles ranging in size from trunks that would contain the remains of a Daniel Lambert to card-cases that would hold practically nothing at all. And all of a sudden Philip fancied he would like to buy a cigarette-case. He would have preferred one of enamel or gold or ivory or tortoise-shell or lizard or shagreen; or even of silver or suede. But preferences are expensive. And as he sauntered on, his dreamy eye ranging the counters in search merely of a cigarette-case he could *buy*, his glance alighted on a 'gent's dressing-case'.

It was of pigskin, and, unlike the central figure in Rembrandt's 'Lesson in Anatomy', it so lay that the whole of its interior was in full view, thus revealing a modest row of silver-topped bottles, similar receptacles for soap, tooth-brushes, pomade, and hair-restorer; a shoe-horn, a boot-hook, an ivory paper-knife, and hair-brushes, 'all complete'. Philip mused on the object for a moment or two, perplexed by a peculiar effervescence that was going on in his vitals. He then approached the counter and asked its price.

'The price, sir?' echoed the assistant, squinnying at the tiny oblong of pasteboard attached by a thread to the ring of the handle; 'the price of that article is seventeen, seventeen, six.'

He was a tubby little man with boot-button eyes, and his snort, Philip thought, was a trifle unctuous.

'Ah,' he said, putting a bold face on the matter, 'it looks a sound vulgar workaday bag. A trifle blatant perhaps. Have you anything—less ordinary?'

'Something more expensive, sir? Why, yes, indeed. This is only a stock line—the "Archdeacon" or "Country Solicitor" model. We have prices to suit all purses. Now if you were thinking of something which you might call resshersy, sir'—

and Philip now was—'there's a dressing-case under the window over there was specially made to the order of Haitch
Haitch the Maharaja of Jolhopolloluli. Unfortunately, sir, the
gentleman deceased suddenly a week or two ago; climate, I
understand. His funeral obliquies were in the newspaper, you
may remember. The consequence being, his ladies not, as you
might say, concurring, the dressing-case in a manner of speaking is on our hands—and at a considerable reduction. Only
six hundred and seventy-five guineas, sir; or rupees to
match.'

'May I look at it?' said Philip. 'Colonel Crompton Pim.'

'By all means, sir,' cried the little man as if until that moment he had failed to notice that Philip was a long-lost son;
'Colonel Crompton Pim; of course. Here is the article, sir, a
very handsome case, and quite unique, one of the finest, in
fact, I have ever had the privilege of handling since I was
transferred to this Department—from the Sports, sir.'

He pressed a tiny knob, the hinges yawned, and Philip's
mouth began to water. It was in sober sooth a handsome
dressing-case, and the shaft of sunlight that slanted in on it
from the dusky window seemed pleased to be exploring it. It
was a dressing-case of tooled red Levant morocco, with gold
locks and clasps and a lining of vermilion watered silk, gilded
with a chaste design of lotus flowers, peacocks, and houris,
the 'fittings' being of gold and tortoise-shell, and studded
with so many minute brilliants and emeralds that its contents
even in that rather dingy sunbeam, appeared to be delicately
on fire.

Philip's light blue eyes under their silken lashes continued
to dwell on its charms in so spell-bound a silence that for a
moment the assistant thought the young man was about to
swoon.

'Thank you very much,' said Philip at last, turning away
with infinite reluctance and with a movement as graceful as
that of a faun, or of a *première danseuse* about to rest; 'I will

keep it in mind. You are sure the management can afford the reduction?'

Having made this rather airy comment, it seemed to Philip impolite, if not impossible, to ask the price of a 'job line' of mock goatskin cigarette-cases that were piled up in dreary disorder on a tray near at hand. So he passed out into the next Department, which happened to be that devoted to goods described as 'fancy', though, so far as he could see, not very aptly.

Still he glanced around him as he hurried on, his heart bleeding for the unfortunates, old and helpless, or young and defenceless, doomed some day to welcome these exacerbating barbarous jocosities as gifts. But at sight of an obscure, puffy, maroon object demonstratively labelled 'Pochette: Art Nouveau', his very skin contracted, and he was all but about to inquire of a large veiled old lady with an ebony walking-stick who was manfully pushing her way through this *mélange*, possibly in search of a *prie-dieu*, how such dreadful phenomena were 'begot, how nourished', and was himself preparing to join in the chorus, when a little beyond it his glance alighted on a minute writing-case, so frailly finished, so useless, so delicious to look at, handle, and smell, that even Titania herself might have paused to admire it. Philip eyed it with unconcealed gusto. His features had melted into the smile that so often used to visit them when as a little boy he had confided in his Uncle Charles that he preferred éclairs to doughnuts. Its price, he thought, was ridiculously moderate: only £67 10s.

'It's the décor, sir—Parisian, of course—that makes it a trifle costly,' the assistant was explaining. 'But it's practical as well as sheek and would add distinction to *any* young lady's boudoir, bedchamber, or lap. The ink, as you see, sir, cannot possibly leak from the bottle, if the case, that is, is held the right way up—so. The pencil, the "*Sans Merci*", as you observe, is of solid gold; and the pen, though we cannot guarantee the nib, is set with life-size turquoises. The flaps will hold

at least six sheets of small-size notepaper, and envelopes to—
or not to—match. And *here* is a little something, a sort of
calendar, sir, in fine enamel, sir, telling the day of the week of
any day of the month in any year in any century from one
A.D. to nine hundred and ninety-nine thousand, nine hundred
and ninety-nine. It could then be renewed.'

'M'm, very ingenious,' Philip murmured, 'and even Leap
Year, I see. Is it unique, and so on?'

'No doubt of it, sir. As a matter of fact, a lady from Philadelphia—the United States of America, sir—ordered fifty fac-
sillimies, platinum mounts, of this very article—only yesterday afternoon; they get married a good deal over there, sir;
wedding presents.'

'Quite, thank you, no,' said Philip, firmly but pleasantly.
'They say there is safety in numbers, but there seems to be
precious little else. Have you anything less reproducible?'

'Reproducible, sir? Why, naturally, sir. You see this is only
a counter article. While catering for the many, sir, we are
bound to keep an eye upon the few. For that very reason, the
management prefer to have the costlier specimens under
cover.'

'Again, thank you,' said Philip hurriedly. 'What evils are
done in thy name, O Philadelphia! I may return later.'

He emerged from the Fancy Goods Department, feeling at
the same moment crestfallen and curiously elated. His mind,
in fact, at this moment resembled a volcano the instant before
its gloom is fated to burst into a blazing eruption. Though
very hazily, he even recognized the danger he was in. So in
hope to compose himself he sat down for a minute or two on
a Madeira wicker chair intended perhaps by the management
for this very purpose, and found himself gazing at a large
black Chinese cat in the glossiest of glazed earthenware, and
as life-like as Oriental artifice could make it. It was seated in
a corner under a high potted palm, and it wore a grin upon
its features that may have come from Cheshire, but which

showed no symptom whatever of vanishing away. At sight of it—for Philip was not only partial to cats but knew the virtues of the black variety—a secret fibre seemed to have snapped in his head. 'Good luck!' the creature smirked at him. And Philip smirked back. A flame of anguished defiance and desire had leapt up in his body. He would show his uncle what was what. He would learn him to cut nephews off with shillings. He would dare and do and die!

He rose, refreshed and renewed. It was as if he had tossed off a bumper of 'Veuve Clicquot' of 1066. He must himself have come over with the Conqueror. A shopwalker lurking near was interrupted in the middle of an enormous gape by the spectacle of this Apollonian young figure now entering his department—Pianofortes and American Organs. There was something in the leopard-like look of him, something so princely and predatory in his tread, that this Mr. Jackson would have been almost ready to confess that he was moved. Frenchily dark and Frenchily sleek, he bowed himself almost double.

'Yes, sir?' he remarked out loud.

'I want, I think, a pianoforte,' said Philip. 'A Grand.'

'Thank you, sir; this way, please. Grand pianofortes, Mr. Smithers.'

'I want a Grand piano,' repeated Philip to Mr. Smithers, an assistant with a slight cast in his left eye and an ample gingerish moustache. But in spite of these little handicaps Philip liked him much better than Mr. Jackson. A far-away glimpse of Mrs. Smithers and of all the little Smitherses seated round their Sunday leg of mutton at Hackney or at Brondesbury had flashed into his mind.

'Grands, sir,' cried Mr. Smithers, moving his moustache up and down with a curious rotatory constriction of the lips; 'this way, please.'

The young man was conducted along serried ranks of Grands. They stood on their three legs, their jaws tight shut, as mute as troops on parade. Philip paced on and on, feeling very much like the late Duke of Cambridge reviewing a regiment of his Guards. He paused at length in front of a 'Style 8; 7 ft. 9 in., square-legged, black-wood, mahogany-trimmed Bismarck.'

'It *looks* spacious,' he smiled amiably. 'But the finish! And why overhung?'

'Overstrung, sir?' said Mr. Smithers. 'That's merely a manner of speaking, sir, relating solely to its inside. But this, of course, is not what we specificate as a *grand* Grand. For tone and timber and resonance and pedal work and solidity and *wear*—there isn't a better on the market. I mean on the rest of the market. And if you were having in mind an everlasting instrument for the nursery or for a practice room—and we supply the new padded partitioning—this would be precisely the instrument, sir, you were having in mind. The young are sometimes a little hard on pianofortes, sir. They mean well, but they are but children after all; and——'

'Now let—me—think,' Philip interposed. 'To be quite candid, I wasn't having anything of that sort in mind. My sentiments are England for the English; and Bismarck, you know, though in girth and so on a remarkable man, was in other respects, a little—well, miscellaneous. It is said that he mixed his champagne with stout—or was it cocoa? On the other hand, I have no wish to be insular, and I *may* order one of these constructions later—for a lady: the niece, as a matter of fact, of a governess of my uncle Colonel Crompton Pim's when he was young—as young at least, as it was possible for him to be—who is, I believe, thinking of taking—of taking in—pupils. But we will see to that later. Have you anything that I could really look at?'

Mr. Smithers's moustaches twirled like a weathercock. 'Why, yes, sir. Just now we are up to our eyes in pianos—flooded; and if I may venture to say so, sir, Bismarck was never no friend of *mine*. All this,' and he swept his thumb in the direction of the avenue of instruments that stretched behind them, 'they may be Grands, but they're most of them modern, and if you want a little something as nice to listen to as it is natty to look at, and *not* a mere menadjery fit only for an 'awl, there is a little what they call a harpsichord over yonder, sir. It's a bijou model, de Pompadour case, hand-painted throughout—cupids and scallops and what not, all English gut, wire, metal, and jacks, and I defy any dealer in London to approximate it, sir, in what you might call pure form. No noise and all music, sir, and that *mellow* you scarcely know where to look. A lady's instrument—a titled lady's. And only seven hundred and seventy-seven guineas, sir, all told.'

'Is it unique?' Philip inquired.

'Unique, sir? There's not another like it in Europe.'

Philip smiled at Mr. Smithers very kindly out of his blue eyes. 'But what about America?' he said.

The assistant curved what seemed an almost unnecessarily large hand round his lips. 'Between you and me, sir, if by America', he murmured, 'you're meaning the United States, why, Messrs. Montferas & de Beauguyou refuse to ship in that direction. It ruins their tone. In fact, sir, they are what's called *difficult*. They make for nobody and nowhere but as a favour; and that instrument over there was built for——!'

He whispered the sesame so low that water rustling on a pebbled beach would have conveyed to Philip tidings more intelligible. But by the look in Mr. Smithers's eye Philip guessed that the lady in question moved in a lofty, though possibly a narrow, circle.

'Ah!' he said; 'then that settles it. A home away from home. Charity begins there. I shall want it to-morrow. I shall want them both to-morrow. I mean the pianos. And perhaps a more democratic instrument for the servants' hall. But I will leave that to you.'

Mr. Smithers pretended not to goggle. 'Why, yes, sir, that can be easily arranged. In London, I ho—conjecture?'

'In London,' said Philip, 'Grosvenor Square.' For at that very instant, as if at the summons of a jinnee, there had wafted itself into his memory the image of a vacant and 'highly desirable residence' which his casual eye had glanced upon only the afternoon before, and which had proclaimed itself 'to be let'.

'Grosvenor Square, sir; oh yes, sir?' Mr. Smithers was ejaculating, order-book in hand. 'I will arrange for their removal at once. The three of them—quite a nice little set, sir.'

'Pim, Crompton, Colonel,' chanted Philip. 'R-O-M; deferred account; *thank* you. 4-4-4, yes, four hundred and forty-four, Grosvenor Square. I am—that is, *we* are furnishing there.'

But this gentle emphasis on the 'we' was so courtly in effect that it sounded more like an afterthought than a piece of information. Nevertheless it misled Mr. Smithers. Intense fellow-feeling beamed from under his slightly overhung forehead. 'And I am sure, sir, if I may make so bold, I wish you both every happiness, I am myself of a matrimonial turn. And regret it, sir? *never*! I always say if every——'

'That's very kind indeed of you,' said Philip, averting his young cheek, which having flushed had now turned a little pale. 'And, if *I* may be so bold, I am perfectly certain Mrs. Smithers is of the same way of thinking. Which is the best way to the Best Man's Department, if I take in Portmanteaux and the Fancies on my way?'

Mr. Smithers eyed him with the sublimest admiration. 'Straight through, sir, on the left beyond them Chappels. On the same floor, but right out on the farther side of the building. As far as you can go.'

'That is exactly what I was beginning to wonder—precisely how far I can go. This little venture of mine is a rather novel experience, and at the moment I am uncertain of its issue. But tell me, why is it our enterprising American friends have not yet invented a *lateral* lift?'

'Now that's passing strange, too, sir; for I've often fancied it myself,' said Mr. Smithers. 'But you see in a department like this there's not much time for quiet thought, sir, with so much what you might call hidden din about. As a matter of fact, when I was younger, sir—and that happens to us all—I did invent a harmonium key-stifler—rubber, and pith, and wool —*so*—and a small steel spring, quite neat and entirely unnoticeable. But the manufacturers wouldn't look at it; not they!'

'I don't believe', said Philip, folding up his bill, 'they ever look at anything. Not closely, you know. But if ever I do buy a harmonium,' he put his head a little on one side and again smiled at Mr. Smithers, 'I shall insist on the stifler. I suppose', he added reflectively, 'you haven't by any chance a nice pedigree Amati, or Stradivarius in stock? I have a little weakness for fiddles.'

Mr. Smithers, leaning heavily on the counter on both his thumbs, smiled, but at the same time almost imperceptibly shook his head.

'I fancied it was unlikely,' said Philip. 'What's that over there; in the glass case, I mean?'

'That, sir?' said Mr. Smithers, twinkling up, 'in that glass case there? That's a harp, sir. And a lovely little piece *that* is. Child's size, sir. What they call minnychoore, and well over a century old, but still as sweet as a canary. It was made, so they say, for Mozart, the composer, sir, as you might be aware, in 1760, and up in the top corner is scratched the letters A.W. No doubt of it, sir—A.W. I've seen a picture of the mite myself playing like an angel in his nightcap, and not a day over seven; you'd hardly believe it, and his parents coming in at the door. Surprising. Then Schumann, *he* had it, sir— I mean the harp; and Schumann, though I don't know how he could dissuade himself to part with it, *he* passed it on to Brahms, another composer—and very much thought of even though a bit nearer *our* day. But you'll find it all neatly set out on the brass label at the foot. It's all there, sir. There's many a custo——'

'Indeed!' said Philip, 'Brahms, Schumann, Mozart, what raptures we are recalling! And here it rests at last. The knacker's yard. How very, very sad. Why, of course, Mr. Smithers, we must have that sent on too—and packed very, very carefully. Is the glass case extra?'

Mr. Smithers gulped. 'I am exceedingly sorry, sir,' he said, 'exceedingly sorry, but it's not for sale; I mean—*except* the case.'

'Not for sale,' retorted Philip impulsively. 'But what is the use, Mr. Smithers, of a mercenary institution like this unless everything in it is for sale? You cannot mean for raw advertisement?'

Mr. Smithers was covered with confusion. 'I am sure, sir,' he said, 'that the directors would do their utmost to consider your wishes. They would be very happy to do so. But if you will excuse my mentioning it, I should myself very much miss that harp. I have been in this department thirteen years now. . . . My little boy. . . . It is the only thing. . . .'

It was Philip's turn to be all in confusion. 'Good gracious me, I quite understand,' he said; 'not another word, Mr. Smithers. I wouldn't *think* of pressing the point. None the less I can assure you that even if it *had* been for sale I should always have welcomed you whenever you cared to come to Grosvenor Square and take another look at it. And, of course, your little boy too—*all* your little boys.'

Mr. Smithers appeared to be lost in gratitude. 'If only', he began, a light that never was on sea or land in his eye—but words failed him.

At the other end of the 'Chappels' Philip again encountered the walker, Mr. Jackson, still looking as much like a self-possessed bridegroom as it is possible for a high collar and a barber to achieve.

'I see', said Philip, 'you exhibit specimens of the tuberphone (and, by the way, I would suggest *a* instead of "er")—the tuba-phone, the clog-box, and the Bombaboo, iniquities at the same time negroid and old-fashioned, but though in a recent visit to Budapest I found even the charming little linden-shaded shops—along the Uffelgang, you know, not, of course, a fashionable part of the city—crammed with models of the "Haba-Stein", a microtonic instrument with five keyboards and Hindu effects, intended, of course for the polytonal de-compositions of the "Nothing-but-Music" school—*most* inter-esting; I see *no* trace of it here. I am not a neotero-maniac, but still, we must keep abreast, we must keep abreast!'

He waved a not unfriendly glove over his head, smiled and went on.

Mr. Smithers had also watched the slim grey young figure until it had turned the corner and was out of sight. He then had a word with his 'floor chief'.

'Pim, eh, Crompton,' said Mr. Jackson, squinting morosely, at his underling's open order-book. ' "Setting up house"? Then I suppose the old gent must have sent in his checks. Not that I'm surprised this nephew of his hasn't bought his black yet. Close-fisted, purple-nosed, peppery old——! There won't be many to cry their eyes out over *his* arums and gardenias.'

Mr. Smithers, being a family man, felt obliged to seem to enjoy as much as possible his immediate chief's society.

'All I can say *is*,' he ventured, 'that young feller, and he's a gentleman if ever there was one, is making it fly.'

He *was*. At this moment Philip was assuring Assistant No. 6 in the Portmanteau Department that unless the Maharaja of Jolhopolloluli's dressing-case could be despatched next day to reach No. 444 Grosvenor Square by tea-time he need not trouble. 'A few other little things', he explained, 'are being sent at the same time.' No. 6 at once hastened to the house telephone and asked for the secretary's office. The line was engaged.

But he need not have hesitated, for when a young man with

a Pim for an uncle and of so much suavity and resource makes
his wishes known, this world is amiability itself. Philip was
warming up. However bland in outward appearance, he was
by this time at a very enlivening temperature. He had tasted
blood, as the saying goes; and he was beginning to see the
need of setting a good example. Customers, like the coneys,
are usually a feeble folk. His little sortie was turning into a
crusade.

By this time he had all but finished disporting himself in the
Furniture Department. 'Three large drawing-rooms, one of
them "extensive",' had run his rather naked catalogue, 'a ball-
room, a dining-room, a breakfast-room, and a little pretty
dumpy all-kinds-of-angles morning-room with a Cherubini
ceiling and a Venetian chimneypiece, eighteenth century, in
lapis lazuli and glass. Bedrooms, let me see, say, twenty-two
—just to go on with (but not in), eleven of them for personal
use, and the rest, staff. That, I think, will do for the present.
We face east or west as the case may be; and nothing, please,
of the "decorative", the quaint, or the latest thing out. Nothing shoddy, shapeless, or sham. I dislike the stuffy and the
fussy and mere trimmings; and let the beds be *beds*. Moreover,
I confess to being sadly disappointed in the old, the "antique",
furniture you have shown me. The choice is restricted, naïve
and incongruous, and I have looked in vain for anything that
could not be easily rivalled in the richer museums. However,
let there be as many so-called antique pieces as possible, and
those as antique as you can manage. Period, origin, design,
harmony—please bear these in mind.'

The assistants, clustering round him, bowed.

'If I have time I will look through the Department again
on my way down. Eight hundred guineas for the cheaper of
the Chippendale four-posters seems a little exorbitant; and
three hundred and fifty for the William and Mary wall-glass—
I fear it's been resilvered and patched. Still, I agree you can
but do your best—I say you can all of you but do your best—

and I must put up with that. What I *must* insist on, however, is
that everything I have mentioned—everything—must be in
its place to-morrow afternoon—carpets and so on will, of
course, precede them—by four o'clock. And let there be no
trace of that indescribable odour of straw and wrappings—
from Delhi, I should think—which accompanies removals.
444 Grosvenor Square. Pim—Crompton—Colonel: R-O-M.
Thank you. To the left? *Thank* you.'

This 'floor-chief' hastened on in front of his visitor as if he
were a Gehazi in attendance on a Naaman, and the young man
presently found himself in a scene overwhelmingly rich with
the colours, if not the perfumes, of the Orient. Here a complete quarter of an hour slid blissfully by. Mere wooden furniture, even when adorned with gilt, lacquer, ivory, or alabaster, can be disposed of with moderate ease; and especially
if the stock of the tolerable is quickly exhausted. But Persian,
Chinese, if not Turkey, carpets are another matter.

Philip sat erect on a gimcrack gilded chair, his cane and hat
in his left hand, his gloves in his right, while no less than three
sturdy attendants in baize aprons at one and the same moment
strewed their matchless offerings at his feet, and an infuriated
and rapidly multiplying group of would-be customers in
search of floorcloth, lino and coconut matting stood fuming
beyond. But first come first served is a good old maxim, and
even apart from it Philip was unaware of their company. He
lifted not so much as an eyebrow in their direction.

In the meantime, however, the cash balance in his uncle's
bank, and much else besides, had long since as rapidly vanished as the vapour from a locomotive on a hot summer's day.
From the Carpet Department, vexed that time allowed him
only one of London's chief treasuries to ransack—such are the
glories of Bokhara and Ispahan—he hastened down to the
wine counters. Here, childishly confident in the cellarage of
No. 444, Philip indulged a pretty palate *not* inherited from his
uncle: claret, Burgundy, hock, sherry, cherry brandy, green

Chartreuse, and similar delicate aids to good talk and reflection. He was ingenuous but enthusiastic. Port he ignored.

From 'Wines' he made his way through the galleries exhibiting curtains and 'hangings' (he shuddered), and china and glass—'most discouraging'. His spirits revived a little when yet another defunct and barbaric prince, this time from Abyssinia, supplied him in the Car Department with a vehicle whose only adequate use, to judge from the modesty of its dashboard, the simplicity of its engine and its price, would be a journey from this world into the next. Nevertheless His Highness had left it behind him.

Fleeting visits to counters bristling with ironmongery, turnery, kitchen utensils, and 'provisions'—and from motives of principle he omitted all mention of mulligatawny paste, chutney, West India pickles, and similar fierce and barbarous comestibles, vanished out of memory like the patterns of a kaleidoscope. The rather noisy annexe reserved for live stock Philip left unvisited. After deserts of dead stock it sounded inviting, but Philip's was a dainty nose and he was sorry for orang-outangs. Not so napery and damasks: he revelled.

So too with the books. He had clear convictions of what a gentleman's library should be without, but decided that it would take more leisure than he could spare this morning to expound them. Even the sight of a Work of Reference, however, is an excellent sedative; he ordered the choicest of obsolete dictionaries, old atlases, encyclopædias, bird, flower, and antique cookery books, ignored the Who's-whoo's—and retired.

As for pictures and statuary, one anguished glance into the dreadful chambers devoted to the fine arts had sent him scurrying on like a March hare. Nor, as he rather sadly realized, had he any need to linger at the portals of the Monumental Masonry Department, and he now suddenly found himself in the midst of a coruscating blaze of the precious metals and the still more precious stones. He had strayed into 'Jewellery'—a feast for Aladdin. Gold in particular—goblets and bowls and tankards, plates, platters, and dishes of it; clocks, chronometers, watches—from massive turnips, memorials of the Georges, to midgets like a three-penny-piece in crystal and enamel, many of them buzzing like bees, and all of them intent on the kind of time which is *not* wild or always nectarous, but of which Philip had always supposed there was an inexhaustible supply. But not, alas, for all purposes. Indeed, these officious reminders of the actual hour had for the first time a little scared him.

In the peculiar atmosphere that hangs over any abundant array of sago, cooked meats, candles, biscuits, coffee, tea, ginger, and similar wares, he had been merely a young bachelor on the brink of an establishment. But at sight of this otiose display of gewgaws in the lamplit mansion in which he now found himself, his fancy had suddenly provided him with a bride. She was of a fairness incomparably fair. The first faint hint of this eventuality had almost unnerved him. He lost his head and—his heart being unconcerned—his taste also. In tones as languid as the breezes of Arabia he had at once ordered her rings, bracelets, necklaces, pendants, brooches, ear-rings, not to speak of bediamonded plumes and tiaras, that would daunt the dreams even of the complete bevy of musical comedy young ladies on the British stage—not to mention that of Buenos Aires. And then, oddly enough, he had come to himself, and paused.

At the very moment of opening his mouth in repetition of a solo with which he was now entirely familiar—'R-O-M', and so on—he sat instead, gaping at the tall, calm, bald, venerable old gentleman on the other side of the counter. He had flushed.

'Have you', he inquired almost timidly at last, his eyes fixed on a chastely printed list of cutlery and silver ware that lay on the glass case at his elbow, 'have you just one really simple, lovely, rare, precious, and, well, unique little trinket suitable for a lady? Young, you know? An *un*-birthday present?'

The old gentleman looked up, looked at, looked *in*, smiled fondly, reminiscently, and, selecting a minute key on a ring which he had drawn out of his pocket, opened a safe not half a dozen yards away. 'We have this,' he said.

'This', at first, was a little fat morocco leather case. He pressed the spring. Its lid flew open. And for an instant Philip's eyesight failed him. But it was not so much the suppressed lustre of the jewels within that had dazed his imagination as the delicate marvel of their setting. They lay like lambent dewdrops on the petals of a flower. The old gentleman gazed too.

'The meaning of the word "simple",' he suggested ruminatively, 'is one of many degrees. This, sir, is a Benvenuto Cellini piece.' He had almost whispered the last few syllables as if what in workmanship were past all rivalry was also beyond any mortal pocket; as if, in fact, he were telling secrets of the unattainable. The tone piqued Philip a little.

'It is charming,' he said. 'But have you nothing then of Jacques de la Tocqueville's, or of Rudolph von Himmeldömmer's, nothing of—dear me, the name escapes me. The earlier Florentine, you will remember, no doubt referred to in *Sordello*, who designed the chryselephantine bowl for the Botticelli wedding-feast. But never mind. Nothing Greek? Nothing Etruscan—*poudre d'or*? Are you suggesting that the Winter Palace was thrice looted in vain?'

The old gentleman was accustomed to the airs and graces of fastidious clients and merely smiled. He had not been listening very intently. 'You will appreciate the difficulty, sir, of keeping anything but our more trifling pieces actually within reach of the nearest burglar with a stick of gun-cotton or an acetylene lamp. This'—he stirred the little leather case with his finger as lithely as a cat the relics of a mouse, and its contents seemed softly to sizzle in subdued flames of rose and amber and blue—'this', he said, 'happens not to be our property. It is merely in our keeping. And though to an article of such a nature it is absurd to put a price, we have been asked to dispose of it; and by—well, a client for whom we have the profoundest respect.'

'I see'; Philip pondered coldly on the bauble, though his heart was a whirlpool of desire and admiration. He swallowed. The remote tiny piping of a bird that was neither nightingale nor woodlark, and yet might be either or both, had called to him as if from the shores of some paradisal isle hidden in the mists of the future. He glanced up at the old gentleman, but his bald, long, grey countenance was as impassive as ever.

'I'll take it,' Philip said, and for a while could say no more. When speech was restored to him, he asked that it should be delivered not 'with the other things', and not to any butler or major-domo or other crustacean that might appear in answer to a knock at No. 444, but by special messenger into his own personal private hands.

'Precisely, at half-past four, if you please.' The old gentleman bowed. As there was not enough room in the money column of his order-book for the noughts, he had written in the price in longhand, and was engaged in printing the figures 444 in the place reserved for the customer's address, when a small but clearly actual little voice at Philip's elbow suddenly shrilled up into his ear——'Mr. Philip Pim, sir?' At echo of this summons Philip stood stock-still and stiff, his heart in his ears. 'The sekkertary, sir,' the piping voice piped on, 'asks me to say he'd be much obliged if you would be so kind as to step along into his office on your way *hout*, sir.'

The tone of this invitation, though a little Cockney in effect, was innocence and courtesy itself; yet at sound of it every drop of blood in Philip's body—though he was by no means a bloated creature—had instantly congealed. This was the end, then. His orgy was over. His morning of mornings was done. The afflatus that had wafted him on from floor to floor had wisped out of his mind like the smoke of a snuffed-out candle. Yet still the bright thought shook him: he had had a Run for his money. No—better than that: he had had a Run *gratis*.

He must collect his wits: they had gone wool-gathering. At last he managed to turn his head and look down at the small, apple-cheeked, maroon-tunicked page-boy at his side—apple-cheeked, alas, only because he had but that week entered the sekkertary's service and his parents were of country stock.

'Tell Sir Leopold Bull'—Philip smiled at the infant—'that I will endeavour to be with him in the course of the afternoon. Thank you. That, apart from the rest,' he added for the ear of his friend on the other side of the counter, 'that will be all.'

But Philip was reluctant to leave him. The last four words, as he had heard himself uttering them, sounded on in his ear with the finality of a knell. He was extremely dubious of what would happen if he let go of the counter. His knees shook under him. A dizzy vacancy enveloped him in. With a faint wan smile at the old gentleman, who was too busily engaged in returning his treasures to the safe to notice it, he managed to edge away at last.

Every mortal thing around him, gilded ceiling to grandfather clock, was at this moment swaying and rotating, as will the ocean in the eyes of a sea-sick traveller gloating down upon it from an upper deck. He felt ill with foreboding.

But breeding tells. And courage is a mistress that has never been known to jilt a faithful heart. Philip was reminded of this as he suddenly caught sight of a sort of enormous purple beefeater, resembling in stature a Prussian dragoon, and in appearance a Javanese Jimjam. This figure stood on duty in the doorway, and appeared to be examining him as closely as if he were the heir to the English throne (or the most nefarious crook from Chicago). As Philip drew near he looked this monster full in his fish-like eye, since he was unable to do anything else. But try as he might he couldn't pass him in silence.

'Ask Sir Leopold Bull, please,' he said, 'to send an official to show me the way to his office. He will find me somewhere in the building.'

'I can take you there meself,' replied the giant hoarsely. He could indeed—bodily.

'Thank you,' replied Philip. 'I have no doubt of it. But I should be much obliged if you would at once deliver my message.'

He then groped his way to yet another wicker chair not many yards along a corridor festooned with knick-knacks from Japan and the Near East, and clearly intended for speedy disposal. He eyed them with immense distaste and sat down.

'Nothing whatever, thank you,' he murmured to a waitress who had approached him with a card containing a list of soft drinks. Never in his life had he so signally realized the joys of self-restraint And though at the same moment he thrust finger and thumb into his waistcoat pocket in search of his Uncle Charles's last sovereign, it was with a view not to material but to moral support. Years before he had often tried the same device when as a small boy deadly afraid of the dark he had managed at last to thrust his fevered head up and out from under his bedclothes, and to emit a dreadful simulacrum of a croupy cough. He had never known it to fail of effect, and it was always nice to know his mother was *there*.

So, too, with his Uncle Charles's sovereign. It was nice to know it was there, though it was not the dark Philip was now afraid of but the light. Resting the ivory handle of his walking-stick on his lower lip, he began to think. What would his sentence be? A first offender, but not exactly a novice. Not, at any rate, he hoped, in taste and judgment. Months or years? Hard labour or penal servitude? So swift is the imagination that in a few seconds Philip found himself not only—his sentence served, the smiling governor bidden farewell—*out* and a free man again, but fuming with rage that he had not managed to retain a single specimen of his spoils. The Jobbli dressing-bag, for instance, or that tiny, that utterly and inimitably 'unique' little Sheraton Sheridan writing-desk.

He came back a little stronger from this expedition into the future. For reassurance, like hope, springs eternal in the human breast. His one regret was not so much that he had been found out (that might come later), but that he had been found out so soon. How much bolder, less humiliating, nobler, to have actually bearded that old curmudgeon of an uncle of his, swapp or bogey in hand, in his den!

That in any event he would have been 'found out' on the morrow, as soon, that is, as the first van arrived at No. 444, he had realized long ago. He certainly would not have been found 'in'! But even one brief night in May seems, in prospect, a long interval between being a Crœsus and a felon in Penton-ville.

He was recalled from these reflections by a young man whose sleek black hair was parted as neatly in front and in the middle as his morning coat was parted behind. A few paces distant, like a mass of gilded pudding-stone, stood the giant from the Jewellery Department. Were they in collusion? Philip could not decide.

'If you would step this way, sir, to the secretary's office,' said the young man, 'Sir Leopold Bull would be very much obliged.'

Philip mounted to his feet and, though he flatly refused to step *that* way, followed him—to his doom. That, however, was not to be instantaneous, for on his arrival Sir Leopold Bull, rising from his roll-top desk with a brief but thrilling smile, first proffered a plump white hand to his visitor and then a chair. It seemed to be a needlessly polite preamble to the interview that was to follow. Philip ignored the hand but took the chair.

'Thank you,' he said. 'I do hope you will some day take my advice, Sir Leopold, to *sim*plify the arrangement of this building. It is a perfect labyrinth, and I always miss my way.' With a sigh he sank down into the cushions. He was tired.

'My uncle, Colonel Crompton Pim,' he continued, 'is unable to spare a moment to see you this morning. I regret to say he strongly disapproved of the Bombay ducks, or was it the Clam Chowder, you sent him on Friday. They were beneath contempt.'

Sir Leopold smiled once more, but even more placatingly. 'I had the privilege of seeing Colonel Crompton Pim only yesterday afternoon,' he replied. 'He then expressed his satisfaction, for the time being, at the golf balls—the new *Excelsior* brand—with one of which we had the pleasure of supplying him *gratis* a week or two ago. The Bombay ducks shall be withdrawn immediately. I must apologize for not seeking you out in person, Mr. Pim, but what I have to say is somewhat of a private nature and——'

'Yes,' said Philip, realizing how thin was the end of the wedge which Sir Leopold was at this moment insinuating into the matter in hand. 'Yes, quite.' And he opened his innocent blue eyes as wide as he could, to prevent them from blinking. He kept them fixed, too, on the close-shaven face, its octopus like mouth and prominent eyes, with ill-suppressed repulsion. To be a fly that had fallen a victim to such a spider as this!

'It would please me better', he went on, 'if you would arrive as rapidly as possible at the matter you wish to discuss with me. I am free for five minutes, but I must beg you not to waste our time. And please tell your porter over there to go away. Such scenes are distasteful to me.'

The face of the porter who seemed to have been created solely for his bulk, turned as crimson as a specimen of *sang-du-boeuf*. He appeared to be hurt. But wages are of more importance than feelings, and he withdrew.

'You have had a busy morning, Mr. Pim,' said the secretary. 'No less than seven of my assistants who have had the privilege of waiting upon you have been monopolizing me for some time with telephone messages. I hope I am not being too intrusive if I venture to congratulate you, sir, on what I suppose to be Colonel Crompton Pim's approaching——'

'Candidly, Sir Leopold,' said Philip firmly, 'that *would* be venturing too far. Much too far. Let us say no more about it. What precise charge are you intending to bring against me?'

There was a pause while the world continued to rotate.

'For which article?' breathed Sir Leopold.

Philip gazed steadily at the full, bland, secretive countenance. It was as if once again he had heard that seraphic bird-like voice sounding in the remote blue sky above the storm-clouds that now hung so heavily over his beating heart.

'Oh, I mean for delivery,' he said. 'Mine was—was a large order.'

'But my dear sir, we shouldn't dream of making *any* such charge. *Any* service to Colonel Pim. . . . Even the Harp. . . .' The faint sob in the voice would have done credit to a Caruso.

Philip stooped to hide the cataract of relief that had swept over his face, then raised his head again. How could he be sure that this was anything more than play-acting—the torture of suspense? 'Ah, well,' he said, 'that is no matter now. I gather there was some other point you had in mind—in *view*, I should say.'

'Oh, only', said Sir Leopold, 'to ask if Colonel Pim would be so kind as to subscribe as usual to our Fund for the Amelioration of the Conditions of the Offspring of Super-annuated Shop Assistants. Mainly orphans, Mr. Pim. We must all die, Mr. Pim, and some of us have to die earlier in life than others. Still, our average here is little worse than that of any other large London establishment. In Petrograd—or was it Los Angeles?—I am given to understand, a shop assistant at two-and-thirty is a shop assistant with at least one foot in the grave. It is the little orphans, the fatherless ones, who from no apparent fault of their own, have to be left to the tender mercies of a busy world! It would grieve you, sir, which Heaven forbid, if I told you how many of these wee small things there are now on our hands. Chubby, joysome, rosebud little creatures, as happy as the day is long. Nevertheless it is a little thoughtless to marry, Mr. Pim, when it is only orphans one can leave behind one. On the other hand, there is a silver lining to *every* cloud. Without these infants we should be deprived of a good cause. An excellent cause. And it's causes that keep us going. Last year I think Colonel Pim very kindly contributed half a guinea.'

'In cash?' Philip inquired sharply.

'We debited his account,' said Sir Leopold.

'Well, then,' said Philip, 'please understand that my uncle *regrets* that little laxity. He has hardened. He now entirely disapproves of orphans and of orphanages. The shop assistant, he was saying to me only the other day, is a person who should be grateful to Providence that he has *no* justification for dabbling in matrimony. The more celibate they are, in his opinion, the better. But recollect, Sir Leopold, that until we arrive at the higher and fewer salaried officials in your establishment, I feel myself in no way bound to *share* my uncle's views. Your staff is as courteous and considerate as it appears to be unappreciated. A man's a man for a' that. And *a'* that. Let us talk of brighter things.'

Sir Leopold did his utmost to conceal the wound to his vanity. 'I am sorry to seem to be persistent,' he assured his client, 'but Colonel Pim only yesterday was so kind as to say he would *consider* my appeal. I take it, then, that he has changed his mind?

'My uncle', retorted Philip tartly, 'has a mind that is the better for being changed.' For an instant he saw the face before him as it would appear in due course in the witness-box; and his very soul revolted. That pitiless Machine called Society might have its merits, but not *this* cog in its wheel! 'I myself implored my uncle', he added bitterly, 'to give the orphans the cold shoulder. What in the chronic sirocco of his next world would be the use to him of a mere half-guinea's worth of cooling breezes? Scarcely a sop in the pan. Indeed, only a passion for the conventional prevented him from asking for his previous donations to be returned.'

Sir Leopold appeared to be engaged in rapidly bolting something—possibly his pride. It was at any rate no part of his secretarial duties to detect insanity in the family of any solvent shareholder.

'There is only one other little point,' he went on rather hollowly. 'Colonel Pim asked me to send him a detailed account of his purchases during the last month. We met by happy chance as he was yesterday alighting from a taxicab at the entrance to his bank. After to-day's purchases that will perhaps take an hour or two. But it shall reach him to-morrow morning—without fail.'

Philip had risen. It is better to stand when one is at bay. While with a gentle absent smile he stood drawing on his gloves he was faced with the wildest effort of his life—to make sure of what lay in hiding behind these last remarks. Anything *might*.

'Oh, he did—did he,' he remarked very softly. 'I fancy'— and at last he lifted his gentle eyes to meet his adversary's—'I *believe* there's an empty whisky jar that has not yet been credited to him. Perhaps that was on his mind.'

'Well, Mr. Pim,' said Sir Leopold, 'turning' at last, 'if *that's* his only jar it's soon adjusted.'

Philip took a deep breath. He playfully wagged a finger.

'Now *that*, Sir Leopold,' he said, 'was blank verse. I hope you don't intend to put my little purchases of this morning into *rhyme*! The effort, I assure you, would be wasted on my uncle.'

He wheeled lightly, and turned towards the door. Sir Leopold, his face now at liberty to resume its office of expressing his feelings, accompanied him. Indeed he continued to accompany him to the very entrance of his gigantic abode. And there Philip almost fainted. A deluge, compared with which that of Noah and his family was nothing but an April shower, was descending on the street.

'A taxi,' roared Sir Leopold at a group of his satellites in the porch, caparisoned in shiny waterproofs, and armed with gigantic *parapluies*.

But though at least nineteen of these vehicles were instantly battling their way towards this goal, Philip with incredible agility had eluded their attention. Before Sir Leopold had had time even to arrange his face to smile a farewell, our young friend had gone leaping up the staircase behind him, and had without a moment's pause vanished into the Tropical Department. One fugitive glance at its pith and pukka contents, and at the dusky assistants in attendance, had only accelerated his retreat. In less than half a minute he found himself confronting a young woman seated in the midst of a stockade of umbrellas.

The coincidence was too extreme to be ignored. He would at least carry off *some* little souvenir of his morning's outing. What better value could he get for hard cash than an implement that would be at the same time a refuge from the elements—for other he would soon presently have none—and a really formidable weapon at hand for his next interview with Sir Leopold?

He had but just enough breath left to express himself. He pointed.

'I *want* one, please,' he cried at the young woman. 'Cash.'

'One, two, three, four, *five* guineas?' she murmured, looking as if she were less in need of her stock than of her lunch. 'Partridge, malacca, horn, ivory, rhinoceros, natural, *gold*? Union, gloria, glacé, taffeta, cotton, mixture, *twill*?'

'Not a toy; an umbrella,' Philip expostulated. 'To keep off rain. A nephew returning to school—ten years' wear. Gingham, alpaca, calico, cast-iron—*anything*; so long as it is hefty, solid, endurable, awful, and *cheap*.'

'We have here what is *called* an umbrella,' replied the assistant a trifle coldly. 'The "Miss and Master Brand". Lignumvitæ stick, whalebone ribs, blunted ferrule, non-poisonous handle, guaranteed not to break, fray, fade, or scale. Nine and elevenpence complete.'

'Bill; in haste; cash; just as it is; thanks,' cried Philip and seized the dreadful object. With a groan he laid his Uncle Charles's sovereign in the narrow brass trough of the pay-desk. The obese young person in the wooden box seemed about to lift it to her lips, glanced at him again, put it aside, smiled, and gave him his change.

'The way to the back exit, I think, is over there?' Philip murmured, waving his gloves due west.

The young person smiled again, and he withdrew. He withdrew down the back steps and into the deluge: there to face a watery world, the possessor of ten shillings and a penny (in his pocket), a wardrobe of old suits, about a hundred and fifty books, three of them unmerited prizes for good conduct, a juvenile collection of postage stamps, a hypothetical legacy of a shilling, and an uncle who, if he faced his liabilities as an English gentleman must, had to all intents and purposes over-drawn his bank account that afternoon, by, say roughly, a couple of hundred thousand pounds.

THE NAP

*

The autumnal afternoon was creeping steadily on towards night; the sun after the morning's rain was now—from behind thinning clouds—glinting down on the chimney pots and slate roofs of Mr. Thripp's suburb. And the day being a Saturday, across Europe, across England, an immense multitudinous stirring of humanity was in progress. It had begun in remote Australia and would presently sweep across the Atlantic into vast America, resembling the rustling of an antheap in a pine wood in sunny June. The Christian world, that is, was preparing for its weekly half-holiday; and Mr. Thripp was taking his share.

As if time were of unusual importance to him, two clocks stood on his kitchen mantelpiece: one, gay as a peepshow in the middle, in a stained wood case with red and blue flowers on the glass front; the other an 'alarm'—which though it was made of tin had a voice and an appearance little short of the brazen. Above them, as if entirely oblivious to their ranting, a glazed King Edward VII stared stolidly out of a Christmas lithograph, with his Orders on his royal breast.

Mr. Thripp's kitchen table was at this moment disordered with the remains of a meal straggling over a tablecloth that had now gallantly completed its full week's service. Like all Saturday dinners in his household, this had been a hugger-

mugger dinner—one of vehement relays. Mr. Thripp himself
had returned home from his office at a quarter to two—five
minutes after his daughter Millie and Mrs. Thripp had already
begun. Charlie Thripp had made his appearance a little before
the hour; and James—who somehow had never become Jim
or Jimmie—arrived soon afterwards. To each his due, kept
warm.

But the hasty feeding was now over. Mr. Thripp in his
shirt-sleeves, and with his silver watch-chain disposed upon
his front, had returned once more from the scullery with his
empty tray. He was breathing heavily, for he inclined nowadays, as he would sometimes confess, to the *ongbongpong*. He
had remarkably muscular arms for a man of his sedentary
profession, that of ledger clerk in Messrs. Bailey, Bailey and
Company's counting house. His small eyes, usually half-
hidden by their plump lids, were of a bright, clear blue. His
round head was covered with close-cut hair; he had fullish
lips, and his ample jowl always appeared as if it had been
freshly shaved—even on Saturday afternoons.

Mr. Thripp delighted in Saturday afternoons. He delighted
in housework. Though he never confessed it to a living soul
(and even though it annoyed Tilda to hear him) he delighted
too in imitating the waitresses in the tea-shops, and rattled the
plates and dishes together as if they were made of a material
unshatterable and everlasting. When alone at the sink he
would hiss like a groom currying a full-grown mare. He
packed the tray full of dirty dishes once more, and returned
into the steam of the scullery.

'You get along now, Tilda,' he said to his wife who was
drying up. 'We shall have that Mrs. Brown knocking every
minute, and that only flusters you.'

Mrs. Thripp looked more ill-tempered than she really was
—with her angular face and chin, pitch-dark eyes, and black
straight hair. With long damp fingers she drew back a limp
strand of it that had straggled over her forehead.

'What beats me is, you never take a bit of enjoyment yourself,' she replied. 'It isn't fair to *us*. I slave away, morning, noon and night; but that's just as things are. But other husbands get out and about; why not you? *Let* her knock! She's got too much money to waste; that's what's the matter with *her*. I don't know what you wouldn't take her for in that new get-up she's got.'

Then what the devil do you go about with her for? were the words that entered Mr. Thripp's mind; and as for slaving, haven't I just *asked* you to give over? Have reason, woman! But he didn't utter them. 'That'll be all right,' he said instead, in his absurd genial way. 'You get on along off, Tilda; I'll see to all this. I enjoy myself my own way, don't you fear. Did you never hear of the selfish sex? Well, that's me!'

'Oh yes, I know all about that,' said his wife sententiously: 'a pinch of salt on a bird's tail! But there's no need for sarcasms. Now do be careful with that dish, there. It don't belong to us, but to next door. She gave me one of her pancakes on it—and nothing better than a shapeless bit of leather, eether. Just to show she was once in service as a cook-general, I suppose; though she never owns to it.'

A spiteful old mischief-maker, if you asked me, was Mr. Thripp's inward comment. But 'Oh well, Tilda, she means all right,' he said soothingly. 'Don't you worry. Now get along off with you; it's a hard day, Saturday, but you won't know yourself when you come down again.' As if forced into a line of conduct she deprecated and despised, Tilda flung her wet tea-cloth over a chair, and, with heart beating gaily beneath her shrunken breast, hastened away.

Mr. Thripp began to whistle under his breath as he turned on the hot water tap again. It was the one thing he insisted on —a lavish supply of hot water. He was no musician and only himself knew the tune he was in search of; but it kept him going as vigorously as a company of grenadiers on the march, and he invariably did his household jobs against time. It indulged a sort of gambling instinct in him; and the more he hated his job the louder he whistled. So as a small boy he had met the challenge of the terrors of the dark. 'Keep going,' he would say. 'Don't let things mess over. That's waste!'

At that moment, his elder son, James, appeared in the scullery doorway. James took after his mother's side of the family. In his navy-blue serge suit, light-brown shoes, mauve socks and spotted tie, he showed what careful dressing can do for a man. A cigarette sagged from his lower lip. His head was oblong, and flat-sided, and his eyes had a damp and vacant look. He thrust his face an inch or two into the succulent steam beyond the doorway.

'Well, dad, I'm off,' he said.

Oh, my God! thought his father; if only you'd drop those infernal fags. Smoke, smoke, smoke, morning to night; and you that pasty-looking I can't imagine what the girl sees in you, with your nice superior ways. 'Right you are, my son,' he said aloud, 'I won't ask you to take a hand! Enjoy yourself while you're young, I say. But slow and steady does it. Where might *you* be bound for this afternoon?'

'Oh, tea with Ivy's people,' said James magnanimously. 'Pretty dull going, I can tell you.'

'But it won't be tea all the evening, I suppose?' said his father, pushing a steaming plate into the plate-rack.

'Oh, I dare say we shall loaf off to a Revoo or something,' said James. He tossed his cigarette end into the sink, but missed the refuse strainer. Mr. Thripp picked it up with a fork and put it into the receptacle it was intended for, while James 'lit up' again.

'Well, so long,' said his father, 'don't spoil that Sunday-go-to-Meeting suit of yours with all this steam. And by the way, James, I owe you five shillings for that little carpentering job you did for me. It's on the sitting-room shelf.'

'Right ho. Thanks, dad,' said James. 'I thought it was six. But never mind.'

His father flashed a glance at his son—a glance like the smouldering of a coal. 'That so? Well, make it six, then,' he said. 'And I'm much obliged.'

'Oh, that's nothing,' replied James graciously. 'Cheerio; don't overdo it, dad.'

Mr. Thripp returned to his washing-up. He was thinking rapidly with an extraordinary medley of feeling—as if he were not one Mr. Thripp, but many. None the less, his whistling broke out anew as though, like a canary, in rivalry with the gushing of the tap. After loading up his tray with crockery for the last time, he put its contents away in the cupboard, and on the kitchen dresser; cleansed the drain, swabbed up the sink, swabbed up the cracked cement floor, hung up his dish-clout, rinsed his hands, and returned into the kitchen.

Millie in a neat, tailor-made costume which had that week marvellously survived dyeing, was now posed before the little cracked square of kitchen looking-glass. She was a pale, slim thing. Her smooth hair, of a lightish brown streaked with gold and parted in the middle, resembled a gilded frame surrounding her mild angelic face—a face such as the medieval sculptors in France delighted to carve on their altar-pieces. Whatever she wore became her—even her skimpy old pale-blue flannel dressing-gown.

She turned her narrow pretty face sidelong under her hat and looked at her father. She looked at every human being like that—even at her own reflection in a shop window, even at a flower in a glass. She spent her whole life subtly, instinctively, wordlessly courting. She had as many young men as the White Queen has pawns: though not all of them remained long in her service.

It's all very well to be preening yourself in that mirror, my girl, her father was thinking, but you'd be far better off in the long run if you did a bit more to help your mother, even though you do earn a fraction of your living. More thinking and less face, *I* say. And all that—— But 'Why, I never see such a girl as you, Millie,' he greeted her incredulously, 'for looking your best! And such a best, too, my dear. Which young spark is it to be *this* afternoon? Eh?'

'Sparks! dad; how you do talk. Why, I don't hardly know, dad. Sparks!' Millie's voice almost invariably ran down the scale like the notes of a dulcimer muted with velvet. 'I wasn't thinking of anybody in particular,' she went on, continuing to watch her moving mouth in the glass, 'but I promised Nellie Gibbs I. . . . One thing, I am not going to stay out long on a day like this!'

'What's the matter with the day?' Mr. Thripp inquired.

'The matter! Why, look at it! It's a fair filthy mug of a day.' The words slipped off her pretty curved lips like pearls over satin. A delicious anguish seemed to have arched the corners of her eyelids.

'Well, ain't there such a thing as a mackingtosh in the house, then?' inquired her father briskly.

'Mackingtosh! Over this? Oh, isn't that just like a man! I should look a perfect guy.' She stood gazing at him, like a gazelle startled by the flurry of a breeze across the placid surface of its drinking-pool.

Now see you here, my girl, that see-saw voice inside her father was expostulating once more, what's the good of them fine silly airs? I take you for an honest man's daughter with not a ha'penny to spare on fal-lals and monkey-traps. *That* won't get you a husband. But Mr. Thripp once more ignored its interruption. He smiled almost roguishly out of his bright blue eyes at his daughter. 'Ask *me* what I take you for, my dear? Why, I take you for a nice, well-meaning, though remarkably plain young woman. Eh? But there, there, don't worry. What I say is, make sure of the best (and the best that's *inside*) and let the other young fellows go.'

He swept the last clean fork on the table into the drawer and folded up the tablecloth.

'Oh, dad, how you do go on!' breathed Millie. 'It's always

fellows you're thinking of. As if fellows made any difference.' Her glance roamed a little startledly round the room. 'What *I* can't understand,' she added quickly, 'is why we never have a clean tablecloth. How can anybody ask a friend home to their own place if that's the kind of thing they are going to eat off of?' The faint nuance of discontent in her voice only made it the more enchanting and seductive. She might be Sleeping Beauty babbling out of her dreams.

A cataract of invective coursed through the channels of Mr. Thripp's mind. He paused an instant to give the soiled tablecloth another twist and the table another prolonged sweep of that formidable right arm which for twenty-three years had never once been lifted in chastisement of a single one of his three offspring. Then he turned and glanced at the fire.

'I wouldn't,' he said, seizing the shovel, 'I wouldn't let Mother hear that, my dear. We all have a good many things to put up with. And what I say is, all in good time. *You* bring that Mr. Right along! and I can promise him not only a clean tablecloth but something appetizing to eat off of it. A bit of a fire in the sitting-room too, for that matter.'

'You're a good sort, dad,' said Millie, putting up her face to be kissed—in complete confidence that the tiny powder-puff in her vanity bag would soon adjust any possible mishap to the tip of her small nose. 'But I don't believe you ever think *I* think of anything.'

'Good-bye, my dear,' said Mr. Thripp; 'don't kiss me. I am all of a smother with the washing-up.'

'Toodle-loo, ma,' Millie shrilled, as her father followed her out into the passage. He drew open the front door, secreting his shirt-sleeves well behind it in case of curious passers-by.

'Take care of yourself, my dear,' he called after her, 'and don't be too late.'

'Late!' tossed Millie, 'any one would think I had been coddled up in a hot-house.'

Out of a seething expense of spirit in Mr. Thripp's mind

only a few words made themselves distinct. 'Well, never mind, my precious dear. I'm *with* you for ever, whether you know it or not.'

He returned into the house, and at once confronted his younger son, Charlie, who was at that moment descending the stairs. As a matter of fact he was descending the stairs like fifteen Charlies, and nothing so much exasperated his father as to feel the whole house rock on its foundations at each fresh impact.

'Off to your Match, my boy?' he cried. 'Some day I expect you will be taking a hand in the game yourself. Better share than watch!'

Every single Saturday afternoon during the football season Mr. Thripp ventured to express some such optimistic sentiment as this. But Charlie had no objection; not at all.

'Not me, dad,' he assured him good-humouredly. 'I'd sooner pay a bob to see other fellows crocked up. You couldn't lend me one, I suppose?'

'Lend you what?'

'Two tanners; four frippenies; a twelfth of a gross of coppers.'

Good God! yelled Mr. Thripp's inward monitor, am I *never* to have a minute's rest or relief? But it yelled in vain.

'Right you are, my son,' he said instead, and thrusting his fleshy hand into his tight-fitting trouser-pocket he brought out a fistful of silver and pence. 'And there,' he added, 'there's an extra sixpence, free, *gratis*, and for nothing, for the *table d'hôte*. All I say is, Charlie, better say "give" when there isn't much chance of keeping to the "lend". I don't want to preach; but that's always been *my* rule; and kept it too, as well as I could.'

Charles counted the coins in his hand, and looked at his father. He grinned companionably. He invariably found his father a little funny to look at. He seemed somehow to be so remote from anything you could mean by things as they are, and things as they are now. He wasn't so much old-fashioned, as just a Gone-by. He was his father, of course, just as a jug is a jug, and now and then Charlie was uncommonly fond of him, longed for his company, and remembered being a little boy walking with him in the Recreation Ground. But he wished he wouldn't be always giving advice, and especially the kind of advice which he had himself assiduously practised.

'Ta, dad,' he said; 'that's doing me proud. I'll buy you a box of Havanas with what's over from the *table d'hôte*. And now we're square. Good-bye, dad.' He paused as he turned to go. 'Honour bright,' he added, 'I hope I shall be earning a bit more soon, and then I shan't have to ask you for anything.'

A curious shine came into Mr. Thripp's small lively eyes; it seemed almost to spill over on to his plump cheeks. It looked as if those cheeks had even paled a little.

'Why, that's all right, Charlie, me boy,' he mumbled, 'I'd give you the skin off me body if it would be of any use. That's all right. Don't stand about too long but just keep going. What I can't abide is these young fellows that swallow down their enjoyments like so much black draught. But we are not that kind of a family, I'm thankful to say.'

'Not me!' said Charles, with a grimace like a good-humoured marmoset, and off he went to his soccer match.

Hardly had the sound of his footsteps ceased—and Mr. Thripp stayed there in the passage, as if to listen till they were for ever out of hearing—when there came a muffled secretive tap on the panel of the door. At sound of it the genial podgy face blurred and blackened.

Oh, it's you, you cringing Jezebel is it?—the thought scurried through his mind like a mangy animal. Mr. Thripp indeed was no lover of the ultra-feminine. He either feared it, or hated it, or both feared *and* hated it. It disturbed his even tenor. It was a thorn in the side of the Mr. Thripp who not only believed second thoughts were best, but systematically refused to give utterance to first. Any sensible person, he would say, ought to know when he's a bit overtaxed, and act according.

The gloved fingers, Delilah-like, had tapped again. Mr. Thripp tiptoed back into the kitchen, put on his coat, and opened the door.

'Oh, it's you, Mrs. Brown,' he said. 'Tilda won't be a moment. She's upstairs titivating. Come in and take a seat.'

His eyes meanwhile were informing that inward censor of his precisely how many inches thick the mauvish face-powder lay on Mrs. Brown's cheek, the liver-coloured lipstick on her mouth, and the dye on her loaded eyelashes. Those naturally delicate lashes swept down in a gentle fringe upon her cheek as she smiled in reply. She was a graceful thing, too, but practised; and far more feline, far far more body-conscious than Millie. No longer in the blush of youth either; though still mistress of the gift that never leaves its predestined owner—the impulse and power to fascinate mere man. Still, there were limitations even to Mrs. Brown's orbit of attraction, and Mr. Thripp might have been the planet Neptune, he kept himself so far out in the cold.

He paused a moment at the entrance to the sitting-room, until his visitor had seated herself. He was eyeing her Frenchified silk scarf, her demure new hat, her smart high-heeled patent-leather shoes, but his eyes dropped like stones when he discovered her own dark languishing ones surveying him from under that hat's beguiling brim.

'Nice afternoon after the rain,' he remarked instantly. 'Going to the pictures, I suppose? As for meself, these days make me want to be out and in at the same time. It's the musty, fusty, smoky dark of them places *I* can't stand.'

Mrs. Brown rarely raised her voice much above a whisper. Indeed it appeared to be a physical effort to her to speak at all. She turned her face a little sidelong, her glance on the carpet. 'Why, it's the dark I enjoy, Mr. Thripp,' she said. 'It'—and she raised her own—'it rests the eyes so.'

For an instant Mr. Thripp's memory returned to Millie, but he made no comment.

'Here's Mrs. Brown, Tilda,' he called up the staircase. Good heavens, the woman might as well be the real thing, the voice within was declaring. But the words that immediately followed up this piece of news were merely, 'You'll be mighty surprised to hear, Tilda, Mrs. Brown's got a new hat.' A faint catcall of merriment descended the stairs.

'Oh, now, Mr. Thripp, listen to that!' whispered the peculiar voice from out of the little airless sitting-room. 'you always did make fun of me, Mr. Thripp. Do I deserve it, now?'

A gentle wave of heat coursed over Mr. Thripp as he covertly listened to these accents, but he was out of sight.

'Fun, Mrs. Brown? Never,' he retorted gallantly; 'it's only my little way:' and then to his immense relief, on lifting his eyes, discovered Tilda already descending the stairs.

He saw the pair of them off. Being restored to his coat, he could watch them clean down the drying street from his gate-post. Astonishing, he thought, the difference there can be between two women's backs! Tilda's, straight, angular, and respectable, as you might say; and that other—sinuous, seductive, as if it were as crafty a means of expression as the very smile and long-lashed languishments upon its owner's face. 'What can the old woman see in her!' he muttered to himself; 'damned if *I* know!' On this problem Mr. Thripp firmly shut his front door. Having shut it he stooped to pick up a tiny white feather on the linoleum; and stooping, sighed.

At last his longed-for hour had come—the hour for which his very soul pined throughout each workaday week. Not that it was always his happy fate to be left completely alone like this. At times, indeed, he had for company far too much housework to leave him any leisure. But to-day the dinner things were cleared away, the washing-up was over, the tables fair as a baker's board, the kitchen spick and span, the house

empty. He would just have a look round his own and Tilda's
bedroom (and, maybe, the boys' and Millie's). And then the
chair by the fire; the simmering kettle on the hearth; and the
soft tardy autumnal dusk fading quietly into night beyond the
window.

It was a curious thing that a man who loved his family so
much, who was as desperately loyal to every member of it as
a she-wolf is to her cubs, should yet find this few minutes'
weekly solitude a luxury such as only Paradise, one would
suppose, would ever be able to provide.

Mr. Thripp went upstairs and not only tidied up his own
and Tilda's bedroom, and went on to Millie's and the boys',
but even gave a sloosh to the bath, slid the soap out of the
basin where Charlie had abandoned it, and hung up the draggled towels again in the tiny bathroom. What a place looks
like when you come back to it from your little enjoyments—
it's *that* makes all the difference to your feelings about a home.
These small chores done, Mr. Thripp put on an old tweed coat
with frayed sleeves, and returned to the kitchen. In a quarter
of an hour that too more than ever resembled a new pin.

Then he glanced up at the clocks; between them the time
was a quarter to four. He was amazed. He laid the tea, took
out of his little old leather bag a pot of jam which he had
bought for a surprise on his way home, and arranged a bunch
of violets in a small jar beside Tilda's plate. But apart from
these family preparations, Mr. Thripp was now depositing a
demure little glossy-brown teapot all by itself on the kitchen
range. This was his Eureka. This was practically the only
sensual *secret* luxury Mr. Thripp had ever allowed himself
since he became a family man. Tilda's cooking was good
enough for him provided that the others had their little dainties now and then. He enjoyed his beer, and could do a bit of
supper occasionally with a friend. But the ritual of these
solitary Saturday afternoons reached its climax in this small
pot of tea. First the nap, sweet as nirvana in his easy-chair,

then the tea, and then the still, profound quarter of an hour's musing before the door-knocker began again.

Having pulled down the blind a little in order to prevent any chance of draught, Mr. Thripp eased his bootlaces, sat himself in his chair, his cheek turned a little away from the window, his feet on the box that usually lay under the table, and with fingers clasped over his stomach composed himself to sleep. The eyelids closed; the lips set; the thumbs twitched now and again. He breathed deep, and the kettle began a whispered anthem—as if a myriad voices were singing on and on without need of pause or rest, a thousand thousand leagues away.

But now there was none to listen; and beyond, quiet hung thick in the little house. Only the scarce-perceptible hum of the traffic at the end of the narrow side street was audible on the air. Within, the two clocks on the chimney-piece quarrelled furiously over the fleeting moments, attaining unanimity only in one of many ticks. Ever and again a tiny scutter of dying ashes rejoined those that had gone before in the pan beneath the fire. Soon even these faint stirrings became inaudible and in a few moments Mr. Thripp's spirit would have wafted itself completely free awhile from its earthly tenement, if, suddenly, the image of Millie—more vivid than even the actual sight of her a few minutes before—had not floated up into the narrow darkness of her father's tight-shut eyes.

But this was not the image of Millie as her father usually saw her. A pathetic earthly melancholy lay over the fair angelic features. The young cheek was sunken in; the eye was faded, dejected, downcast; and that cheek was stubbornly turned away from her father, as if she resented or was afraid of his scrutiny.

At this vision a headlong anxiety darted across Mr. Thripp's half-slumbering mind. His heart began heavily beating: and then a pulse in his forehead. Where was she now? What forecast, what warning was this? Millie was no fool. Millie knew her way about. And her mother if anything was perhaps a little too censorious of the ways of this wicked world. If you keep on talking at a girl, hinting of things that might otherwise not enter her head—that in itself is dangerous. Love itself even must edge in warily. The tight-shut lids blinked anxiously. But where was Millie now? Somewhere indoors, but where? Who with?

Mr. Thripp saw her first in a tea-shop, sitting opposite a horrid young man with his hair greased back over his low round head, and a sham pin in his tie. His elbows were on the marble-top table, and he was looking at Millie very much as a young but experienced pig looks at his wash-trough. Perhaps she was at the Pictures? Dulcet accents echoed into the half-dreaming mind—'But I enjoy the dark, Mr. Thripp. . . . It rests the eyes.' Why did the woman talk as if she had never more than half a breath to spare? Rest her eyes! She never at any rate wanted to rest the eyes of any fool in trousers who happened to be within glimpse of her own. It was almost unnaturally dark in the cinema of Mr. Thripp's fancy at this moment; yet he could now see his Millie with her pale, harmless, youthful face, as plainly as if she were the 'close-up' of some star from Los Angeles on the screen. And now the young man in her company was almost as fair as herself, with a long-chinned sheepish face and bolting eyes; and the two of them were amorously hand in hand.

For a moment Mr. Thripp sat immovable, as if a bugle had sounded in his ear. Then he deliberately opened his eyes and glanced about him. The November daylight was already beginning to fade. Yes, he would have a word with Millie— but not when she came home that evening. It is always wiser to let the actual coming-home be pleasant and welcoming. To-morrow morning, perhaps; that is, if her mother was not goading at her for being late down and lackadaisical when there was so much to be done. Nevertheless, all in good time he would have a little quiet word with her. He would say only what he would not afterwards regret having said. He had meant to do that ages ago; but you mustn't flood a house with water when it's not on fire. She was but a mere slip of a thing —like a flower; not a wild flower, but one of those sweet waxen flowers you see blooming in a florist's window— which you must be careful with and not just expose anywhere.

And yet how his own little place here could be compared with anything in the nature of a hot-house he could not for the life of him understand. Delicate-looking! Everybody said that. God bless me, perhaps her very lackadaisicalness was a symptom of some as yet hidden malady. Good God, supposing! . . . He would take her round to see the doctor as soon as he could. But the worst of it was you had to do these things on your own responsibility. And though Mr. Thripp was now a man close on fifty, sometimes he felt as if he could no longer bear the burden of all these responsibilities. Sometimes he felt as if he couldn't endure to brood over them as he was sometimes wont to do. If he did, he would snap. People *looked* old; but nobody was really old inside; not old at least in the sense that troubles were any the lighter, or forebodings any the more easily puffed away; or tongues easier to keep still; or tempers to control.

And talking of tempers reminded him of Charlie. What on earth was going to be done with Charlie? There was no difficulty in conjuring up, in seeing Charlie—that is if he really did go every Saturday to a football match. But Charlie was now of an age when he might think it a fine manly thing to be loafing about the counter of a pub talking to some flaxen barmaid with a tuppeny cigar between his teeth. Still, Mr. Thripp refused to entertain more than a glimpse of this possibility. He saw him at this moment as clearly as if in a peepshow, packed in with hundreds of other male creatures close as sardines in a tin, with their check caps and their 'fags', and their staring eyes revolving in consort as if they were all attached to one wire, while that idiotic ball in the middle of the arena coursed on its helpless way from muddy boot to muddy boot.

Heaven knows, Mr. Thripp himself was nothing much better than a football! You had precious small chance in this life of choosing which boot should give you the next kick. And what about that smug new creeping accountant at the office with his upstart airs and new-fangled book-keeping methods!

Mr. Thripp's mouth opened in a yawn, but managed only to achieve a fraction of it. He rubbed his face; his eyes now shut again. It was not as if any of your children were of much practical help. Why should they be when they could never understand that what you pined for, what you really needed was not only practical help but some inward grace and clearness of mind wherewith they could slip in under your own thoughts and so share your point of view without all that endless terrifying argumentation. He didn't *always* give advice to suit his own ends; and yet whenever he uttered a word to James, tactfully suggesting that in a world like this—however competent a man may be and however sure of himself—you *had* to push your way, you had to make your weight felt, James always looked at him as if he were a superannuated orang-outang in a cage—an orang-outang with queer and not particularly engaging habits.

He wouldn't mind even that so much if only James would take his cigarette out of his mouth when he talked. To see that bit of stained paper attached to his son's lower lip wagging up and down, up and down, beneath that complacent smile and those dark helpless-looking eyes, all but sent Mr. Thripp stark staring mad at times. Once, indeed, he had actually given vent to the appalling mass of emotion hoarded up like water in a reservoir in his mind. The remembrance of the scene that followed made him even at this moment tremble in his chair. Thank God, thank God, he hadn't often lost control like that.

Well, James would be married by this time next year, he supposed. And what a nice dainty pickle he was concocting for himself! Mr. Thripp knew that type of young woman, with the compressed lips, and the thin dry hair, and the narrow hips. She'd be 'a good manager', right enough, but there's a point in married life where good managing is little short of being in a lunatic asylum between two iron-faced nurses and yourself in a strait waistcoat. The truth of it was, with all his fine airs and neat finish, James hadn't much common sense. He had a fair share of brains; but brains are no good if you are merely self-opinionated and contemptuous on principle. James was not like anybody in Mr. Thripp's own family. He was a Simpkins.

And then suddenly it was as if some forgotten creature in Mr. Thripp's mind or heart had burst out crying; and the loving look he thereupon cast on his elder son's face in his mind was almost maudlin in its sentimentality. He would do anything for James within reason: anything. But then it would have to be within James's reason—not his own. He knew that. Why he would himself marry the young woman and exult in being a bigamist if only he could keep his son out of her way. And yet, and yet; maybe there were worse women in the world than your stubborn, petulant, niggardly, half-sexed nagger. Mr. Thripp knew a nagger of old. His brother's wife, Fanny, had been a nagger. She was dead now, and George was a free man—but drinking far too much.

Well, as soon as he could get a chance, Mr. Thripp, sitting there in his chair decided, he would have another good think; but that probably wouldn't be until next Saturday, if then. You can't think to much purpose—except in a worried disjointed fashion—when you are in the noise of an office or keeping yourself from saying things you have no wish to say. The worst of it was it was not much good discussing these matters with Tilda. Like most women, she always went off at a tangent. And when you came down to it, and wanted to be reasonable, there was so little left to discuss. Besides, Tilda had worries enough of her own.

At this moment Mr. Thripp once more opened his eyes wide. The small kitchen loomed beatifically rosy and still in the glow of the fire. Evening had so far edged on its way now that he could hardly see the hands of his two clocks. He could but just detect the brass pendulum—imperturbably chopping up eternity into fragments of time. He craned forward; in five minutes he ought to be brewing his little private pot of tea. Even if he nodded off now, he would be able to wake in time, but five minutes doesn't leave *much* margin for dropping off. He shifted a little on his chair, and once more shut his eyes. And in a moment or two his mind went completely blank.

He seemed to have been suddenly hauled up helpless with horror into an enormous vacancy—to be dangling unconfined and motionless in space. A scene of wild sandy hills and spiky trees—an illimitable desert, came riding towards him out of nothingness. He hung motionless, and was yet sweeping rapidly forward, but for what purpose and to what goal there was not the smallest inkling. The wilderness before him grew ever more desolate and menacing. He began to be deadly afraid; groaned; stirred—and found himself with fingers clenched on its arms sitting bolt upright in his chair. And the hands of the clock looked to be by a hair's breadth precisely in the same position as when he had started on that ghastly nightmare journey. His face blanched. He sat appalled, listening to an outrageous wauling of voices. It was as though a thousand demons lay in wait for him beneath his window and were summoning him to his doom.

And all this nightmare horror of mind was due solely to a conversazione of cats! Yet, as with flesh still creeping he listened on to this clamour, it was so human in effect that it might be multitudinous shades of the unborn that were thronging about the glass of his window. Mr. Thripp rose from his chair, his face transfigured with rage and desire for revenge. He went out into the scullery, opened the back door, and at sound of him the caterwauling instantly ceased.

And almost as instantly his fury died out in him. The cold evening air fanned his forehead. He smiled quixotically, and looked about him. There came a furtive rustle in the bushes. 'Ah, there you are!' he sang out gently into the dark. 'Have your play while you can, my fine gentlemen! Take it like your betters, for it's a sight too soon over.'

Above the one cramped leafless elder-tree in his yard a star was pricking the sky. A ground mist, too, was rising, already smelling a little stale. Great London and its suburbs appeared to be in for one of its autumnal fogs. A few of the upper windows opposite loomed dim with light. Mr. Thripp's neighbours, it seemed, were also preparing to be off to the pictures or the music-halls. It was very still, and the air was damp and clammy.

As he stood silent there in the obscurity a deepening melancholy crept over his mind, though he was unaware into what gloomy folds and sags his face had fallen. He suddenly remembered that his rates would have to be paid next week. He remembered that Christmas would soon be coming, and that he was getting too old to enter into the fun of the thing as he used to do. His eyes rolled a little in their sockets. What the . . . ! his old friend within began to suggest. But Mr. Thripp himself did not even enunciate the missing 'hell'. Instead, he vigorously rubbed his face with his stout capable hand. 'Well, fog anyhow don't bring rain,' he muttered to himself.

And as if at a signal his own cat and his next-door neighbour's cat and Mrs. Brown's cat and the cat of the painter and decorator whose back garden abutted his own, together with the ginger-and-white cat from a newsvendor's beyond, with one consent broke out once more into their Sabbath eve quintette. The many-stranded strains of it mounted up into the heavens like the yells of demented worshippers of Baal.

'And, as I say, I don't blame ye neether,' Mr. Thripp retorted, with a grim smile. 'If you knew, my friends, how narrowly you some of you escaped a bucket of cold water when you couldn't even see out of your young eyes you'd sing twice as loud.'

He shut the door and returned to his fireside. No more hope of sleep that afternoon. He laughed to himself for sheer amusement at his disappointment. What kids men were! He stirred the fire; it leapt brightly as if intent to please him. He pushed the kettle on; lit the lamp; warmed his little privy glossy-brown tea-pot, and fetched out a small private supply of the richest Ceylon from behind some pots in the saucepan cupboard.

Puffs of steam were now vapouring out of the spout of the kettle with majestic pomposity. Mr. Thripp lifted it off the coals and balanced it over his tea-pot. And at that very instant the electric bell—which a year or two ago in a moment of the strangest caprice Charles had fixed up in the corner—began jangling like a fire-alarm. Mr. Thripp hesitated. If this was one of the family, he was caught. Caught, that is, unless he was mighty quick in concealing these secret preparations. If it was Tilda—well, valour was the better part of discretion. He poured the water into the pot, replaced the lid, and put it on to the oven-top to stew. With a glance of satisfaction at the spinster-like tidiness of the room, he went out, and opened the door.

'Why, it's Millie!' he said, looking out at the slim-shouldered creature standing alone there under the porch; 'you don't mean to say it's you, my dear?'

Millie made no reply. Her father couldn't see her face, partly because the lamp-post stationed in front of the house three doors away gave at best a feeble light, and partly because her features were more or less concealed by her hat. She pushed furtively past him without a word, her head still stooping out of the light.

Oh, my God, what's wrong now? yelled her father's inward monstrous monitor, frenziedly clanging the fetters on wrist and ankle. 'Come right in, my pretty dear,' said Mr. Thripp seductively, 'this *is* a pleasant surprise. And what's more, between you and me and the gatepost, I have just been making myself a cup of tea. Not a word to mother; it's *our* little secret. We'll have it together before the others come in.'

He followed his daughter into the kitchen.

'Lor, what a glare you are in, pa!' she said in a small muffled voice. She turned the wick of the lamp down so low that in an instant or two the flame flickered and expired, and she seated herself in her father's chair by the fire. But the flamelight showed her face now. It was paler even than usual. A strand of her gilded pale-brown hair had streaked itself over her blue-veined temple. She looked as if she had been crying. Her father, his hands hanging down beside him as uselessly as the front paws of a performing bear, watched her in an appalling trepidation of spirit. This then was the secret of his nightmare; for this the Cats of Fate had chorused!

'What's wrong, Millie love? Are you overtired, my girl? There! Don't say nothing for a minute or two. See, here's my little pot just meant for you and me!'

Millie began to cry again, pushing her ridiculous little handkerchief close to her eyes. Mr. Thripp's hand hovered awkwardly above her dainty hat and then gently fumbled as if to stroke her hair beneath. He knelt down beside her chair.

For heaven's sake! for heaven's sake! for heaven's sake! a secret voice was gabbling frenziedly in his ear. 'Tell your old dad, lovey,' he murmured out loud, softly as the crooning of a wood-pigeon.

Millie tilted back her pretty hat and dropped her fair head on his shoulder. 'It's nothing, Dad,' she said. 'It's only that they are all the same.'

'What are all the same?'

'Oh, fellows, Dad.'

'Which one, precious?' Mr. Thripp lulled wooingly. God strike him dead! muttered his monster.

'Oh, only young Arthur. Like a fool I waited half an hour for him and then saw him with—with that Westcliff girl.'

A sigh as voluminous as the suspiration of Niagara swept over Mr. Thripp; but it made no sound. Half a dozen miraculous words of reassurance were storming his mind in a frenzy of relief. He paused an instant, and accepted the seventh.

'What's all that, my precious?' he was murmuring. 'Why, when I was courting your mother, I saw just the same thing happen. She was a mighty pretty young thing, too, as a girl, though not quite so trim and neat in the figure as you. I felt I could throttle him where he stood. But no, I just took no notice, trusting in my own charms!'

'That's all very well,' sobbed Millie, 'but you were a man, and *we* have to fight without seeming to. Not that I care a fig for him: he can go. But——'

'Lord, Millie!' Mr. Thripp interrupted, smoothing her cheek with his squat forefinger, 'you'd beat twenty of them Westcliffs, with a cast in both eyes and your hands behind your back. Don't you grieve no more, my dear; he'll come back safe and sound, or he's less of a—of a nice young feller than I take him for.'

For a moment Mr. Thripp caught a glimpse of the detestable creature with the goggling eyes and the suede shoes, but he dismissed him sternly from view.

'There now,' he said, 'give your poor old dad a kiss. What's disappointments, Millie; they soon pass away. And now, just take a sip or two of this extra-strong Bohay! I was hoping I shouldn't have to put up with a lonely cup and not a soul to keep me company. But mind, my precious, not a word to your ma.'

So there they sate, father and daughter, comforter and comforted, while Mr. Thripp worked miracles for two out of a tea-pot for one. And while Millie, with heart comforted, was musing of that other young fellow she had noticed boldly watching her while she was waiting for her Arthur, Mr.

Thripp was wondering when it would be safe and discreet to disturb her solacing daydream so that he might be busying himself over the supper.

It's one dam neck-and-neck worry and trouble after another, his voice was assuring him. But meanwhile, his plain square face was serene and gentle as a nestful of halcyons, as he sat sipping his hot water and patting his pensive Millie's hand.

PHYSIC

❋

Emilia and William had been keeping one another company in the kitchen. Mary, her trusty substantial cook-general was 'out', and would not be knocking at the door until half-past ten. After that there might be another hour to wait. But then Emilia would be alone. Meanwhile, just like man and wife, William and she would soon be having supper together at two corners of the kitchen table, and William would have an egg—with nine bread-and-butter fingers.

This, once fortnightly, now weekly, Wednesday-night feast had become a kind of ritual, a little secret institution. They called it their covey night. Not even Daddie ever shared it with them; and it was astonishing what mature grown-up company William became on these occasions. It was as if, entirely unknown to himself, he had swallowed one of Jack's bean-seeds and had turned inside into a sort of sagacious second-husband. All that Emilia had to do, then, was merely to become again the child she used to be. And that of course needs only a happy heart.

He was a little dark-skinned boy, William—small for his age. A fringe of gilt-edged fair hair thatched a narrow forehead over his small, restless eyes. His sister Sallie—poor gaunt Aunt Sarah, whom she had been called after, having departed this life when less than a month had passed since the gay

248

christening party—little Sallie, after a restless and peevish afternoon and a wailful bath, was asleep now, upstairs, in her crib. You could tell that almost without having to creep out every now and again to listen at the foot of the stairs.

William had been even more lively and hoppity than usual. He and Emilia had been playing Beggar-my-Neighbour, and he had become steadily more excited when with something very like sheer magic, every sly knave in the pack had rapidly abandoned poor Emilia and managed to slide into his hand. And when—after an excited argument as to where the Queen of Hearts had best be hidden—they changed the game, he laughed and laughed till the tears came into his eyes to see her utter confusion at finding herself for the third time an abject Old Maid! And when supper-time came—plates, spoons, forks—he had all but danced from dresser to table, from table to dresser again. They had borrowed Mary's best blue-check kitchen tablecloth; he had said it looked cooler. 'Don't you *think* so, Mummie?' And every now and again he had ejaculated crisp shrill remarks and directions at Emilia, who was looking after the cooking in the outer room, a room she had steadfastly refused to call the 'scullery'. Merely because she disliked the word! Though one day in a sudden moment of inspiration she had defended his priggishness by exclaiming, 'Well, spell it with a *k* and then see what you think of it!'

It was a little way Emilia had. As tenaciously as she could she always put off until to-morrow even what it was merely difficult to put up with to-day. Never trouble trouble till trouble troubles you, was her motto when driven into a corner. She hated problems, crises, the least shadow of any horror, though they would sometimes peer up at her out of her mind—and from elsewhere—when she wasn't looking, like animals at evening in the darkening hills. But when they actually neared, and had to be faced; well, that was quite another matter.

For some minutes now, busied over her sizzling pan at the

gas stove, she hadn't noticed that William's galvanic sprightly conversation piped up from the kitchen had been steadily dwindling, had almost ceased. He had decided to have his supper egg fried, though 'lightly boiled' was the institution. And Emilia had laughed when, after long debate, he had declared that he had chosen it fried because then it was more indigestible. She was dishing it up from the smoke and splutter—a setting sun on a field of snow, and with a most delicate edging of scorch.

When she came back into the kitchen William was standing by the table, gazing across it at the window. He couldn't be looking *out* of the window, for although there was a crevice a few inches wide between the flowered chintz curtains that had been drawn over it and where the blue linen blind had not been pulled down to the very bottom, it was already pitch dark outside. Yet even at this distance she saw that he couldn't also be staring solely at his own reflection.

He stood motionless, his eyes fixed on this dark glassy patch of window, his head well above the table now. He had not even turned at sound of her footsteps. So far as Emilia's birdlike heart was concerned it was as if a jay had screeched in a spinney. But best not to notice too much. Don't put things into people's heads. 'There!' she exclaimed, 'Well now, you *have* cut the bread and butter thick, Mr. Stoic! *I'm* going to have that scrap of cold fish. Eat this while it's hot, my precious!'

But William had continued to wait.

'I don't think, Mummie,' he said, slowly as if he were reciting something he had been learning by heart, 'I don't *think* I'll have my egg after all. I don't think I feel very hungry just now.'

All his eagerness and excitement seemed to have died down into this solemn and stagnant reverie; and for a child to have the air and appearance of a sorrowful old dwarf is unutterably far away from its deliciously pretending to be a sedate grown-up.

'Not to have it!' cried Emilia. 'Why, look, blessing, it's cooked! Look! Lovely. You wouldn't know it wasn't a tiny half of a peach in cream. Let's pretend.'

'I couldn't like even that, mummie,' he said, glancing at it, a slight shudder ending in a decisive shake of the head as he hastily looked away again. 'I don't think, you know, I want *any* supper.'

Emilia's eyes widened. She stood perfectly still a moment, the hot plate in her hand, staring at him. Then she hurriedly put it down on the table, knelt with incredible quickness beside him, and seized his hand.

'That's what it is,' she said. 'You don't feel very well, William. You don't feel very well? Your hands are hot. Not sick? Not sore throat? Tell mummie.'

'I'm *not* ill,' wailed William obstinately. 'Just because I don't want the egg! You *can't* like that horrid cold fish, and if I did feel sick, wouldn't I say so? That's only what *you* say.' He paused as if the utmost caution and precision were imperative, then added, nodding his head mournfully and sympathetically in time to the whispered words, 'I *have* got a teeny tiny headache, but I didn't notice it until just now.' His mouth opened in a prodigious yawn, leaving tears in his eyes. 'Isn't it funny, mummie—you can't really see anything out of the window when it's black like that, yet you needn't look at your*self* in the glass. It's just as if. . . .'

His eyes came round from examining the window, and fixed themselves on her face.

'That's what it is,' said Emilia, raising herself abruptly from the floor. 'That's what it is.' She kept squeezing the thin, unresponsive fingers of his hand between her own. 'You're feverish. And I knew it. *All* the time. Yes—*how* stupid of me.' And instantly her voice had changed, all vain self-recriminations gone. 'I'll tell you what we'll *do*, William. First, I'll fill a hot-water bottle. Then I'll run up and get the thermometer. And *you* shall be the doctor. That's much the best thing.' And she did not even pause for his consent.

'I expect you know, Dr. Wilson,' she had begun at once, 'it's something that's disagreed with my little boy. I expect so. Oh, yes, I expect so.'

William, pale and attentive, was faltering. 'Well, yes, Mrs. Hadleigh, p'raps,' he said at last, as if his mouth were cramfull of plums. 'You *may* be right. And that depends, you know, on what he has been *eating*.'

'Yes, yes, I quite understand, doctor. Then would you perhaps wait here just for one moment, while I see if my little boy is ready for you. I think, you know, he might like to wash his hands first and brush his hair. And *pray* keep on your overcoat in case you should feel cold.' She took a large dry Turkey towel that was airing on a horse near by, and draped it over William's shoulders. 'I won't be a moment,' she assured him. 'Not a moment.'

Yet she paused to glance again at his shawled-in pale face and fever-bright eyes, as if by mere looking she could bore clean through his body; and stooping once more, she pressed her cheek against his, and then his hand to her lips.

'You said,' half tearfully chanted the little boy, 'that I was the doctor; and now you are kissing me, mummie!'

'Well, I could often and often kiss lots of doctors,' said his mother, and in a flash she was gone, leaving him alone. She raced up the dark staircase as if she were pursued by twenty demons, not even waiting to switch on the light. And when she came to her bedroom it was as if everything in it were doing its utmost to reassure her. The shining of the street lamp was quietly dappling its walls with shadow. The whole room lay oceans deep in silence; the duskily mounded bed, the glass over the chimney-piece, the glass on the dressing-table. They may until that very moment have been conferring together, but now had, as usual, instantly fallen mute, their profound confabulations for the time being over. But she did not pause even so much as to sip of this refreshing stillness. Her finger touched the electric switch, and in an instant the harmless velvety shadows—frail quivering leaf-shadows—the peace, the serenity, had clean evaporated. It was as if the silence had been stricken with leprosy, so instantaneous was the unnatural glare—even in spite of the rose-pink lamp-shades. For now Emilia was staring indeed.

How, she was asking herself, how by any possibility could that striped school tie of her husband's have escaped from its upper drawer on to the bedspread? How by an utter miracle had she failed to see it when she had carried Sallie into the room only an hour or two ago? Ties don't wriggle out of top-drawers across carpets and climb up valances like serpents in the tropics. Husbands miles away cannot charm such things into antics like *these*!

Mary had been out all the afternoon. She herself had been out for most of it with the children, and she could have vowed, taken her oath, *knew*, that *that* couldn't have been there when she had come up to put on her hat. In the instant that followed, before even she could insist on raising her eyes from this queer scrap of 'evidence', her mind suddenly discovered that it was dazed and in the utmost confusion. It was as if, like visitors to a gaudy Soho restaurant, a jostling crowd of thoughts and images, recollections, doubts, memories, clues, forebodings, apprehensions and reiterated stubborn reassurances had thronged noisy and jostling into consciousness—and then were gone again. And at that, at once, as if by instinct and as unforeseeably as a night moth alights on one out of a multitude of flowers, her stricken glance had encountered her husband's note.

At sight of it her heart had leapt in her body, and then cowered down like a thing smitten with palsy. Novels told you of things like these, but surely not just ordinary life! The note had been scribbled on a half-sheet of her own notepaper, and hastily folded into a cocked hat—perhaps the only old-fashioned device she had ever known that husband to be capable of. It seemed that she had learned by heart the message it contained before even she had unfolded the paper and read it. Indeed, it did not matter what it had to say. It hardly even mattered *how* it had said it. So considerately, yet so clumsily, so blastingly. 'She'—that alone was enough. When shells explode why be concerned with fuse or packing? Edward was gone. That was all that mattered. She had been abandoned— she and the children.

So far, so inevitably. You can in vile moments of suspicion, incredulity and terror foresee things like that. Just that he was gone—and for good. But to have come stealing back in the afternoon into a vacant house, merely for a few clothes or a little money, and she out, and Mary out, and the children out —and everything else out; well, that seemed a funny, an unnecessary thing to do!

'I wouldn't have so much minded . . .' she began to mutter to herself, and then realized that her body was minding far too much. A thin acid water had welled into her mouth. Unlike William, she felt sick and dizzy. She had gone stiff and cold and goose-flesh all over. It was as if some fiendish hand were clutching her back hair and dragging the scalp from her forehead taut as the parchment of a drum over her eyes. It was as if she had swallowed unwittingly a dose of some filthy physic. Her knees trembled. Her hands hung down from her arms as though they were useless. And the only thing she could see at this instant was the other woman's face. But it wasn't looking at her; on purpose. It was turned all but three-quarters away —a becoming angle for the long, fair cheekbone, the drooping eyelashes, the lips, the rounded chin Clara. And then, suddenly, she saw them both together, stooping a little; at a railway station, it seemed; talking close. Or was it that they had just got out of a cab?

Emilia might as well have been dreaming all this, since although these picturings, this misery, this revulsion of jealousy, and the horror of what was to come persisted in a hideous activity somewhere in her mind, she herself had refused for the time being to have anything to do with it. There was something infinitely more important that must be done at once, without a moment's delay. Husbands may go, love *turn*, the future slip into ruin as silently and irretrievably as a house of cards. But children must not be kept waiting; not sick children. She was already clumsily tugging at the tiny middle drawer of the old mirror, one of their first bargains, on the dressing-table, and she caught at the same instant a glimpse of the face reflected in its glass; but so instantaneously that the eyes of the image appeared to be darkened and shut, and therefore blind.

What a boon a little methodicalness may be. What a mercy that in this world *things* stay where they are put; do not hide, deceive, play false, forsake and abandon us. Where she always kept it, *there* lay the slim, metal, sharp-edged case of the thermometer. It was as if it had been faithfully awaiting this very reunion—ever since she had seen it last. In the old days, before she was married and had children, even if she had possessed such a thing, she might have looked for it for hours before discovering it. She had despised thermometers. Now, such a search would have resembled insanity.

She hesitated for scarcely the breadth of a sigh at the door, and then with decision switched off the light. Stuffing her husband's scribbled note into her apron pocket, she flew into the next room, put a match to the fire laid in the grate, pushed the hot-water bottle between the sheets of the bed, and hastened downstairs. Her legs, her body, her hand flitting over the banisters, were as light and sure again as if she had never experienced so much as an hour even of mere disappointment in her life. Besides, for some little time now, that body had been habitually told what it had to do. And so long as her orders came promptly and concisely, it could be trusted to continue to act in the same fashion, to be instantly obedient. That was what being a mother taught you to become, and even taught to you try within limits to teach a young child to become—an animated automaton

'Dr. Wilson' stood where she had left him beside the table and in precisely the same attitude. He had not even troubled to sit down. He had, apparently, not even so much as moved his eyes.

'Now, doctor,' said Emilia.

At this, those eyes first settled on her fingers, then quietly shifted to her face.

'You were a long time gone, Mrs. Hadleigh,' he remonstrated in a drawling voice, as if his tongue were sticking to the roof of his mouth. 'A very long time.' He took the thermometer and pushed it gingerly between his lips, shutting them firmly over the thin glass stem. Then his blue and solemn eyes became fixed again, and, without the faintest stir, he continued to watch his mother, while she in turn watched him. When half a minute had gone by, he lifted his eyebrows. She shook her head. In another half-minute he himself took the thermometer out of his mouth, and, holding it between finger and thumb, gravely scrutinized it under the light. 'A hundred and forty-seven,' he announced solemnly. 'H'm.' Then he smiled, a half-secret, half-deprecatory smile. '*That*'s nothing to worry about, Mrs. Hadleigh. Nothing at all. It looks to me as if all you did was to worry. Put him to bed; I will send him round a bottle of very nice medicine—*very* nice medicine. And . . .' his voice fell a little fainter, 'I'll look in again in the morning.'

His eyes had become fixed once more, focused, it seemed, on the far-away. 'Mummie, I do wish when Mary pulls down the blinds she would do it to the very bottom. I *hate* seeing—seeing myself in the glass.'

But Emilia had not really attended to this fretful and unreasonable complaint. She herself was now examining the thermometer. She was frowning, adjusting it, frowning again. Then she had said something—half-muttered, half-whispered—which Dr. Wilson had failed to catch.

'I'd give him,' he again began wearily, 'some rice pudding and lemonade, and——' But before the rest of his counsel could be uttered she had wrapped him tighter in his bath towel, had stooped down to him back to front so that he could clasp his hands round her neck, pick-a-back; and next moment he was being whisked up the dark staircase to the blue and white nursery. There she slid him gently down beside the fender, took off his shoes, smoothed his fringe, and tenderly kissed him.

'You have very bright eyes, Dr. Wilson. You mustn't let them get too bright—just for my sake.'

'Not at all, Mrs. Hadleigh,' he parroted, and then suddenly his whole body began to shiver.

'There,' she said, 'now just begin to take off your clothes, my own precious, while I see to the fire—though *that*, Dr. Wilson, should have been done *first*. Look, the silly paper has just flared up and gone out. But it won't be a minute. The sticks are as dry as Guy Fawkes' Day. Soon cosy in bed now.'

William with unusually stupid fingers was endeavouring to undo his buttons. He was already tired of being the doctor. 'Why', he said, 'do your teeth chatter, mummy, when you are very hot? That seems funny. And why do faces come in the window, horrid faces? Is *that* blind right down to the very bottom? Because I would like it to be. Oh dear, my head does ache, mummie.'

It was extraordinary with what cleverness and dexterity Emilia's hands, unlike her son's, were now doing as they were bidden. The fire, coaxed by a little puffing in lieu of bellows, in a wondrous sheet of yellow, like crocuses, was now sweeping up the chimney as if to devour the universe. A loose under-blanket had been thrust into the bed, the hot bottle wrapped up in a fleecy old shawl, the coal scuttle had been filled, a second pair of small pyjamas had been hung over the fender to air, a saucepan of milk had been stood on the stove with its gas turned low—like a circlet of little blue wavering beads;

and William himself, half-naked for less than the fraction of a second, had been tucked up in his bed, one of her own tiny embroidered handkerchiefs sprinkled with lavender water for company. There, he had instantly fallen asleep, though spasmodic jerks of foot and hand, and flickering eyelids showed that his small troubles had not wholly been left behind him.

So swiftly and mechanically had her activities followed one upon the other that Emilia had only just realized that she was still unable to make up her mind whether to telephone at once to the doctor or to venture—to dare—to look in on Sallie.

Blind fool! *Blind* fool!—foreseeing plainly every open or half-hidden hint and threat of to-night's event, smelling it, tasting it, hearing it again and again knocking at the door of her mind, she had yet continually deferred the appalling moment when she must meet it face to face, challenge and be done with it, and accept its consequences. The mere image in her mind of her husband's school tie left abandoned on the bed had made the foreboding of looking at Sallie a last and all but insupportable straw. The futility, the cowardice! What needs most daring must be done instantly. There had not been the least need to debate such a question. You can't do twenty-*one* things at once!

Having stolen another prolonged scrutiny of William's pale dream-distorted face and dilating nostrils, she hastened into her own bedroom again, groped for the tiny switch-pull that dangled by the bed-rail, stooped over the cot beside it, and, screening its inmate's face as much as possible from the glare, looked down and in. The small blonde creature, lovelier and even more delicate to the eye than any flower, had kicked off all its bedclothes, the bright lips were ajar, the cheeks flushed —an exquisite coral red. And the body was breathing almost as fast and shallowly as a cat's. That children under three years old should talk in their sleep, yes; but with so minute a vocabulary! Still, all vocabularies are minute for what they are sometimes needed to express—or to keep silent about.

PHYSIC

No sickness, no sore throat; but headache, lassitude, pains all over the body, shivering attacks and fever—you just added up the Yes's and subtracted the Noes; and influenza, or worse, was the obvious answer. Should she or should she not wheel the cot into William's room? Sallie might wake, and wake William. Whereas if she remained here and she herself lay down in the night even for so much as an hour—and began to think, she wouldn't be alone, not hopelessly alone. It was the fear of waking either patient that decided the question. She very gently drew blanket and counterpane over Sallie's nakedness, draped a silk handkerchief over the rose-coloured shade, switched on the electric stove in the fireplace, and ran downstairs. There for a few moments, eyes restlessly glancing, she faced the stark dumbness and blindness of the mouthpiece of the telephone.

Dr. Wilson *was* in. Thank Heaven for that. Incredible, that was his voice! There might have been a maternity case—hours and hours. He might have had a horde of dispensary patients. But no, he would be round in a few minutes. Thank Heaven for that. She put back the receiver with a shuddering sigh of gratitude. All that was now needed—superhuman ordeal— was just to wait.

But this Emilia was to be spared. For midway up the stair-case, whose treads now seemed at least twice their usual height, she had suddenly paused. Fingers clutching the banister rail, she stood arrested, stock still, icy, constricted. The garden gate had faintly clicked. There could be only one explanation of that—at least on a Wednesday. Edward's few friends and cronies, every one of them, must have discovered long ago that Wednesdays were now *his* 'evenings out'. And she—she hadn't much fancied friends or company recently. It was he himself, then. He had come back. What to do now? A ghastly revulsion took possession of her, a gnawing ache in the pit of her stomach, another kind of nausea, another *kind*, even, of palpitation.

If only she could snatch a few minutes to regain her balance, to prepare herself, to be alone. Consciousness was like the scene of a fair—a dream-fair, all distortion, glare, noise, diablerie and confusion. And before she was even aware of her decision—to make use of a deceit, a blind, a mere best-thing-for-the-time-being—she had found herself in her bedroom again, had somehow with cold and fumbling fingers folded the note into its pretty cocked-hat shape again, and replaced it where she had first set eyes on it, beside the charming little travelling clock, the gift of Aunt Sarah, in the middle of the mantelpiece.

What light remained in the room behind the blinded and curtained windows could not possibly have been detectable outside. That was certain. In an instant she was in William's room once more—listening, her heart beating against her ribs like the menacing thumping of a drum. She had not long to wait. The latch of the front door had faintly squeaked, the lower edge of the door itself had scraped very gently across the coarse mat within, had as softly and furtively shut.

'Is that you, Edward?' she heard herself very gently and insidiously calling over the banisters from the landing. 'How lovely! You *are* home early. I didn't expect you for—for hours and hours!'

And now she had met and kissed him, full in the light of the hall-lamp. 'Why, what's the matter, darling . . . ? You are ill!' She was peering as if out of an enormous fog at the narrow, beloved, pallid countenance, the pale lips, the hunted, haunted, misery-stricken light-brown eyes in those pits of dark entreaty and despair.

'Is it *that*'s brought you home?'

He continued to stare at her as if, spectacles lost, he were endeavouring to read a little book in very small print and in an unfamiliar language. His mouth opened, as if to yawn; he began to tremble a little, and said, 'Oh, no; nothing much. A headache; I'm tired. Where *were* you?'

'Me?' But her lips remained faintly, mournfully, sympathetically smiling; her dark eyes were as clear and guileless and empty of reflections as pools of water under the windless blue of the sky. 'I was in William's room. It's hateful to say it now, Edward—now that you are so tired yourself—but—but I'm rather afraid, poor mite, he's in for another cold—a little chill—and I shouldn't be surprised if Sallie. . . . But don't worry about that—because, because there's nothing of course at all yet to worry about. It's you I'm thinking of. You look so dreadfully fagged and—what a welcome! . . . There's nothing . . . ?'

Her vocabulary had at last begun to get a little obstinate and inadequate, 'You don't mean, Edward, there's anything *seriously* wrong? I fancy, you know'—she deliberately laid her hand for an instant on his, 'I fancy *you* may be the least little bit feverish yourself—you too. Well. . . .' She turned away, flung up a hand as if to flag off a railway train, 'I'll get you something hot at once.

'And Edward'—she turned her head over her shoulder, to find him as motionless as she had left him, in almost as stolid and meaningless an attitude as 'Dr. Wilson's' had been in the kitchen, as he stood brooding on the nightmare faces in the darkness of the glass. 'There is just one thing, if you could manage it. Just in *case*, would you in a moment or two first wheel Sallie's cot into William's room. I've lit the fire—and I *had* to ask Dr. Wilson to come. I'm so dreadfully stupid and anxious, when—even when there's no reason to be.

The two faces had starkly confronted one another again, but neither could decipher with any absolute certainty the hitherto unrevealed characters now inscribed on them. Each of them was investigating the map of a familiar country, but the cartographer must now have sketched it from an unprecedentedly eccentric angle. The next moment she had turned away, had whisked upstairs and down again, leaving him free, at liberty, to dispose of himself—and of anything else he might be inclined to. In every family life there are surely potential keepsakes that would be far better destroyed; and perhaps a moment *some* time might come. But now. . . .

When she returned with her tray and its contents—a steaming tumbler of milk, a few biscuits and a decanter containing a little whisky—she found him standing beside William's bedroom fire. He watched her, as with the utmost care she put down her burden on the little wicker table.

'Millie,' he said, 'I'm not sure. . . . But, well—it was, I suppose, because of William's being ill that you haven't yet been into—into the other room, our bedroom. And so'—he had gulped, as if there was some little danger of producing his very heart for her inspection—'you have not seen *this*?' He was holding towards her the unfolded note, and with trembling fingers she found herself actually pretending to read its scribbled lines again.

Her face had whitened; she had begun to despair of herself, conscious beyond everything else—the tumult in her mind, the ravaging of her heart—that she could hardly endure the mingled miseries, remorse, humiliation in his eyes, in the very tones of his voice, yet listening at the same time to a message of ineffable reassurance. He has not then deceived me again! At last she had contrived to nod, her chin shaking so stupidly for a while that she could scarcely utter a word. 'Yes. I *have* read it. I put it back . . . couldn't face it when I heard you. The children—I had to have time. I'm *sorry*, Edward.'

' "*Sorry!*" ' he echoed.

'I mean—it *was* an awful, well, revelation; but I was stupid; I ought to have seen . . . I did see. But we won't—I *can't* go into that now. You are tired, ill; but you are back . . . for the present.'

Her eyes had managed at last to glance at him, and then to break away, and to keep from weeping. And, as if even in his sleep his usual tact and wisdom had not deserted him, William had suddenly flung back his scorching sheet and in a gasping voice was muttering to an unseen listener in some broken, unintelligible lingo that yet ended with a sound resembling the word faces. 'There, darling,' she answered him, smoothing back his fair fringe from his forehead, '*I* know. They are gone; all gone now; and the blind *is* down—to its very last inch.'

She stayed watching him, couldn't look back just yet.

'You see, Millie . . . She'—her husband was trying to explain—'that is, *we* had arranged to meet. It's hopeless to attempt to say anything more just now. . . . I waited. She sent. . . . She didn't come.'

'I see. And so?'

'Millie, Millie. It wasn't, it wasn't *you*. Oh, I can't bear it any longer. If I had dreamed—the children!' He had flung himself into a pretty round basket chair and sat shuddering, his face hidden in his lean, bloodless hands.

The few minute sounds in the room, the peevish creakings of the chair, William's rapid, snoring breathing, the fluttering of the fire, were interrupted by the noise of brakes and wheels rasping to a standstill in the street below. A brisk yet cautious knocking had followed, awakening an echo, it seemed, in the very hollow of her breast bone.

'Look,' she said, 'that's where *that* goes. There's no *time* now.' The scrap of paper, more swiftly than a vanishing card in a conjuring trick, had been instantly devoured by the voracious flames, had thinned to an exquisitely delicate fluttering ash, and then, as if with a sudden impulse, wafted itself out of sight like a tiny toy balloon into the sooty vacancy of the chimney.

'Listen. Must *you* see the doctor, to-night? Unless it's not—you know—well *bad* 'flu? Wouldn't it be better not? I'll tell him; I could find out; I could say you had gone to bed. Quick, I must go.' Every nerve in her body was clamouring for motion, action, something to face, something to do.

He nodded. 'And you'll come back?'

'Yes. . . . I'll try. Oh, Edward, I'm sorry, sorry. If only there were words to say it. It must have been awful—awful!' She hesitated, gazing at his bent head, the familiar hands. . . .

And now the doctor, having deftly packed up Sallie again, burning hot but seemingly resigned to whatever fate might bring, and having carefully wiped his thermometer on the clean huckaback towel Emilia had handed him, was stuffing his stethoscope back into his little brown case. An almost passionate admiration filled her breast at his assured, unhurried movements, and with it a sort of mute, all-reconciling amusement to see how closely, deep within, behind these gestures, and the careful choice of words, he resembled his small and solemn understudy, William.

She was returning earnestly glance for glance, intently observant of every least change of expression in his dark decisive face, of timbre in his voice. Practically every one of the hungered-for, familiar, foreseen, all-satisfying assurances— like a tiny flock of innocent sheep pattering through a gateway —had been uttered and sagaciously nodded to: 'It may be just a feverish attack; it might, it *might* be 'flu.' 'Don't forget, Mrs. Hadleigh, they are down one moment and up the next!' 'I'll send round a bottle of medicine to-night, almost at once, and some powders.' 'I'll look in again first thing in the morning.' Then he had paused, little leather case in hand, his eyes fixed on the fire.

Some day, she told herself, she *must* retaliate in kind: 'You must understand, Dr. Wilson, that at this hour of the night it would be utterly stupid of you to breathe the word *pneumonia*, which takes weeks and weeks and weeks; may easily be fatal; and one has just to wait for the crisis!' Or, 'Don't be mistaken, Dr. Wilson, even if you were at death's door yourself I shouldn't hesitate to ring you up if their temperatures go over 103'—that kind of thing.

'You know, Mrs. Hadleigh,' he was beginning again, 'it just beats me why you mothers—quite rational, sensible, almost cynically practical creatures some of you, simply wear yourselves out with worry and anxiety when there's scarcely a shred of justification for it. Quite uselessly. Getting thin and haggard, wasting away, losing all that precious youth and beauty. I say I often *think* these things—wish I could express them. You simply refuse to heed *the* lesson in life: that really great Englishman's, Mr. Asquith's—"Wait and See". *Condensing*, don't you see, and not squandering all energy, impulse and reserves. "Never trouble trouble until trouble troubles you." Isn't *that* good sense? It's what's called an old wives' saying, of course—not a mother's. But I could have saved dozens of precious lives and bodies and all but souls, if only ... well, literally saved them, I mean, a deuce of a lot of wear and tear.'

She was drinking in his words, this delicious lecture, these scoldings; devouring them, as if they were manna dipped in honey, the waters of life. They were a rest and peace beyond expression. A ready help in time of trouble. He shall lead his flock like a shepherd. Yea, though I walk. . . . Why all this Bible? Dr. Wilson was not a parson; he was just a doctor. And then another Dr. Wilson had piped up in memory again, ' "You *said* that I was the doctor; and now you are kissing me, Mummie!" . . . "I could often kiss lots of doctors!" '

'I know, I know,' she heard herself meekly assuring him. 'I'm utterly stupid about these things. And of course if we were all sensible savages or gipsies there wouldn't be. . . . Even—oh, but you can't think what a comfort it is to—to be reassured.'

He was eyeing her now more closely, totting up and subtracting yes's and noes, it seemed, on his own account, and on hers. It was with difficulty she met the straight clear scrutiny. 'Well, there we are,' he decided. 'Just look what lovely babies you have. Everything a woman could wish for! Gipsies be dashed. There are, I assure you, my dear Mrs. Hadleigh, spinsters galore in this parish who. . . . How's your husband?'

Her dark shining eyes had now at last quivered in their sockets, if only for the fraction of a second.

'It sounds very silly,' the words were squeezing out like cooing turtle doves through too narrow an exit, 'but *he's* not very well either! It's, it's almost funny, ridiculous—all three at once. Isn't it? He came home rather late from—from the office, and he's gone to bed.' It seemed a pity that one's cheeks should flatly refuse not to flame up, when one's eyes were hard as brass. 'The fact is, Dr. Wilson, he refused to see you. You know what men are. But could it be, do you think', a little nod towards William's bed had helped her out, 'that too?'

'I think,' Dr. Wilson had replied drily, a scarcely perceptible forking frown between his eyebrows, 'it might very well be that too. But listen, Mrs. Hadleigh. Husbands, of course, are not really of much importance in life—not really. Necessities perhaps; but here to-day and gone to-morrow. *Children* are what the kernel is to the nut; the innermost part of it. And so must be taken great care of. *Therefore*—and this is not advice; this is *orders*: I forbid you to worry; forbid it. I shall throw up the case! If you *must* stay up—you have a maid, a good solid, stolid one too. Wake up her and chance it; she'll love you all the better. And you can share the night between you. Otherwise—unless of course you need me again, and you won't, though I should be *easily* handy—you are not only not to worry (more than you can help) but you are on no account to get up more than twice until the morning to look at your patients—at *our* patients, mind you. It's bad for them, worse for you. When they've had their dose, they'll soon quieten down—unless I'm *wrong*. And—imagine it!—I sometimes am.' He was holding out his hand, a look of unadulterated, generous, wholly masculine admiration on his vigilant, assured features.

'By gad!' he said. 'All three! But then *you* know *I* know what you can manage when hard pressed. So that's all right.' He was plunging downstairs into the night, and Emilia was trying in vain to keep up with him.

'And after the first dose and the powders, Dr. Wilson, I shouldn't, I suppose, wake either of them up to give them any *more* medicine—not until the morning?'

'As a general rule, Mrs. Hadleigh,' replied the doctor, carefully putting on his hat and glancing as he did so into the strip of looking-glass on the wall, 'it's wiser never to wake *anybody* up, merely to give them physic—and certainly not mere doctor's physic.'

THE PICNIC

*

There was an empty, pensive look on Miss Curtis's face as she stood there, solitary, by the (as yet unblinded) shop-door, the finger and thumb of her small firm hand idly twisting the pencil stuck in between the two little black buttons of her black bodice. She was looking out through the glass of the door into the street, while Miss Mavor on the further side of the shop was drawing down the other blinds—a swoop and a swish to each, in turn. Miss Mavor did everything like that.

It was the first week of a hot September. The homeward stream of people in the street outside had long since begun to ebb. A late evening sky hung over London, painting with its faint colours the glassy windows of the houses opposite—right down, Miss Curtis noticed, to the top of the first floor. There the darker parts began. All quiet; all serene; and the close of another busy competent day.

With her set, square, capable face, its dark eyes in curious contrast to the pallor of the skin, she seemed to have fallen into a reverie. She herself with her neat handbag and her admirable umbrella would soon be returning to her lodgings. All lights out, she would open this door, shut it, lock the padlock, give it a tug and, after one look to left and right just in case of 'suspicious characters', she would go off home. And anybody who happened to meet and look at her would know that she was a woman well able to take care of herself—or of anybody or anything else, for that matter.

Miss Curtis wasn't proud of it, but she knew she could be relied on. And so she had got on in the world, and was still getting on. You can never tell, indeed, into what comfortable port a capable head will not finally conduct you if softly and steadily you follow its nose. Miss Curtis's nose stood out straight and able. She would have made a formidable figure-head if, head and bust, she had been modelled in wood and dyed with woad and crimson for the purpose. But though, since she was now manageress of the 'establishment' and to that extent her own mistress, she could in most things have her own way, yet she was always the first to come, and to-night as on all other nights she would be the last to go. She just lived for her business; that's what it came to.

Silly pretty little Phyllis had left the shop at least an hour before. Miss Curtis had been reminded of her by the sight of yet another belated tip-tap young woman tripping along in her champagne stockings to her own particular tryst. The child had asked her for time off—and much too soon after the last occasion. But it is difficult to say No, even to a butterfly —when it happens to be in love. Miss Curtis had always be-lieved in a firm hand, but not in *too* firm a hand. You must keep up appearances, and you must keep the rules—or discipline will suffer. But the rod of iron was not one of her fetishes, except in relation to herself.

Nobody was watching her now, the day was over, and for the moment she could let appearances take care of themselves. So every sign of competence and efficiency had gradually drained out of her features as she went on looking out into the street. Her face had become gentle, almost demure. It now resembled, quite unknown to herself, the plush-framed photo-graph on her mantelpiece which had been taken of her as a fat little girl in a round hat. She had sunk into the deeps as much as that, reducing her to the wish that this pensive coloured scene might go on for ever.

But it wouldn't. Life wasn't like that, though you *had* to stand aside sometimes and have a look at it, if only in order to keep on taking your part. Otherwise the less attention you gave it the better. It was hopeless to let it interfere with your —career. Still you had your melting moments—silly ones, too; even dangerous perhaps. Mere memories of them did no harm, though. They helped. They made even really silly people more intelligible—and there was scarcely a moment in Miss Curtis's day when there wasn't some silly person about. They also kept a firm hand flexible. Indeed there were little events even in Miss Curtis's past—just a few—that would occasionally intrude into her mind like shy exotic animals into a highly conventional park—as if positively on purpose to amuse her.

Perhaps the queerest of all, the most absurd and ridiculous, yet in some ways the easiest to recall without minding much —simply because it *was* so absurd, so meaningless—was that few days' holiday she had spent at the seaside, about five years ago. Some memories are like ghosts. So was this. Miss Curtis, at any rate, never knew when it was not going to reappear. And she was almost sure to find it lurking in wait for her at this particular hour of this particular sort of day.

And here, as if to prove it, was that blind man again, with his black goggles and his tin and his stick and his dog, tapping and groping along the darkening pavement outside. He never failed to call its cue. No marvel in that. Occasionally, if nobody was looking, Miss Curtis had slipped out to put a soundless penny into his tin, and he would lift his unshaven chin at her as if he still hoped he could take a look at so unexpected a patron through those awful lantern-like spectacles. Once, one summer evening, she had actually dropped a shilling into his tin. It wasn't sentiment; she knew he wasn't to be pitied so much as all that; but there are ways of letting *yourself* down, if you harden right off. But to-night—well, Miss Mavor was close upon her. 'There goes that old one-eyed humbug with the dog,' she was saying, and down came her last blind. 'I bet *he's* got some money in the bank.'

Miss Curtis watched him absently out of sight. She didn't reply; Miss Mavor said everything like that. As for the blind beggar's having money in the bank, so had Miss Curtis, and a good deal more than this time five years ago. That particular summer indeed she had not only been out of a job for a few weeks, but instead of at once looking for another she had taken a holiday and just blued some of her savings. In really nice apartments, too. But then of course Miss Curtis, at her age, was never in any doubt of a job when she wanted one. She wasn't exactly lucky; she was efficient. Yet heavens, what a fool she had been! What a simpleton!—and absolutely nothing to show for it, not even to herself when the lights were out, and she was alone.

Simply because she *was* so efficient, and looked so ungullible and was so completely trustworthy, it was almost a solace now to realize that she could ever have been quite so fantastically silly—idiotic. Still, with memories of that kind silence is best. There are limits. Miss Curtis would no more have dreamed of sharing this old ghost with, say, Miss Mavor, than a crocus would dream of blossoming at the foot of the North Pole. And the funny thing was, it was partly because it hadn't been bad *enough*—looked at in cold blood. You can stand up to the really tragic and—and brazen things out. At least Miss Curtis supposed you could.

It had been at Newhampton—a nice quiet select little place. And it hadn't been in the horrible height of August either—the Newhampton 'season'—but at the end of May, when only the idle rich can afford to enjoy such resorts. She remembered it as clearly as if she had been reading about it the night before in a novel. For the matter of that she remembered even *what* novel she had been reading about an hour or two before she had set out that afternoon on her last solitary picnic—the picnic that had never come off. Oh dear me, how amusing!—with her broken thermos flask, her raspberry-jam sandwiches and her currant bun. After that little *contretemps* she had sat alone under the sand-dunes, staring at the sea, or with her eyes tight shut—for three solid hours; and then at last by a long way round had come back, sandwiches and bun still uneaten, to her apartments.

Lying half inside her bedroom, in shadow, and half on its canopied balcony, in the sun, she had spent the first part of that afternoon in a deck-chair—dressed ready to go out—her rather dingy-looking novel in her hand. By stooping forward a little and peeping round the brick corner of the balcony to the left she could see the placid English channel, steadfastly intent on its imitation of the colour of a baby's eyes. A tang of salt and sea-weed and stale fish was in the air, and that queer fizz of expectation which frequents all seaside places was in her mind.

'Mind!' Why your very inside gives a little happy jump every time even an idle boatman suggests a sail. She could even recall the exact look of the table at her mid-day meal—some dry cold tongue and stewed gooseberries and cream—though she hadn't eaten very much of either. That done, and cleared away, there she had lolled—yes, lolled—two cushions behind her head, her legs drawn up sideways under her, but very very carefully so that neither blouse nor tailor-made skirt should suffer from creases, while she continued to devour that precious novel. Simply to make the time go by. Not think of two things at once! What utter nonsense. Yet how silly a story it had been. Even Phyllis would have turned up her nose at such a 'fullyton' as that.

It was so silly that she herself had never finished it, and now never would. She had even forgotten to return the book to the stuffy little circulating library that had seemed such a ravishing addition to Newhampton the day after she had arrived. That was the queerest thing of all, perhaps—why (when her own little affair—affair!—was over), a story so silly, so exaggerated, so unreal should have become positively nauseating in memory—almost as if it had been an extract from her own autobiography.

Hearts Aflame: that was the title. And its author had chosen for his hero a man positively made and designed for victories over the inflammable sex. Nothing very original in that, perhaps. He was always most beautifully dressed, either in plusfours or for the evening, and with one glance of his piercing blue eyes, with one befondlement, and with the iciest *sang-froid* he broke hearts wherever he went, never even turning aside to glance at the remains. And yet so far as Miss Curtis could see he never got the least bit of pleasure out of any heart in any condition—green, ripe, or rotten. It was merely a habit. He was just a Don Juan. On the other hand he was a Don Juan who had made a slip—before the story opened. For an Italian Countess had somehow succeeded in marrying him in spite of his efforts (even then apparent) to practise the part of Henry VIII without incurring its responsibilities. Poor hysterical racked drugged creature, by Chapter XXIII she had long ago of course lost every shred of belief or faith in him. And yet she had continued to hope (though nothing the author could say persuaded Miss Curtis that the Countess had *really* hoped), he would some day turn over a new leaf—one, that is, that would not be merely tantamount to turning over a new lady-love. As if such men had any leaves to turn!

The frail little night-orbed Countess had had her wits about her too. She had remained an angler long after she had caught her fish—or rather had been caught by her fish. But in Chapter XXIV she had begun doing what Miss Curtis had often noticed ladies, especially titled ladies, often do in novels—she had decided to win back her husband by means of her charms. That was odd, too. The author kept on talking about the Countess's charms, but even Miss Curtis had felt bound to agree with her promiscuous husband that some of them weren't very conspicuous. They were at any rate hopelessly unpractical, and unlikely even, according to Miss Curtis's secondhand experience of such matters, to last out a honeymoon. Perhaps this was because she was so foreign. Whether or not, Miss Curtis couldn't have supposed that any one— even an Italian Countess, could be of her own sex and yet be so, well, shameless. In such a stupid way, too. She had positively no reserve. She said things to her husband, even when she knew he didn't care, that you couldn't possibly say to *any* body if you remembered you were ever going to be alone again. She entreated him, she besought him—that was the word—to be 'kinder', to return to her, to remember all her sacrifices. 'Oh,' she would cry, grovelling at his feet, her sultry lambent eyes raining tears down her pale olive cheeks. 'Oh, how I love you! How I love you!' And then in the same breath those very same eyes would be snapping crackers at him, 'Oh, how I *hate* you! *How* I hate you!' Remarks like that, of course, are like holding the candle of your life in the middle and asking *any* Don Juan to burn it up at both ends.

And then had come Chapter XXV. In a desperate effort to retrieve her husband's affections the Countess had sent to Paris for the most seductive of new confections in ivory silk with jewels to match that Worth could supply—for she had still managed somehow to cling to the remnant of her prenuptial fortune. Miss Curtis had not cared much for the look of this 'model' as it appeared in print. Perhaps that was because the book had been written by a man. But how silly of him not to ask his wife or his sister or his mother or a female friend what she thought of it. Anyhow the Countess had sent for it, and it had come, and there it lay, in its original package where her maid had put it—on her own little bed in her own little bedroom. And the Night of Nights was still to come. Alas, when the night did come her husband, morally speaking, had put even himself beyond the pale—though what the Countess thought of it Miss Curtis was never to discover. Miss Curtis had got thus far and no further. The wretched man, that is, at his wits' end to convince his last lady of his good intentions —though lady was perhaps hardly the word to use for her— had given the milliner's box precisely as it stood and with all its contents—and without even seeing if they would fit, *to* that last lady and—well, that was the end of it.

For at this point Miss Curtis had let the book fall back into her lap, had folded her hands on its open pages and—realizing that she must set off now if she was to set off at all—with a long-drawn shuddering sigh of relief, expectation, dread and sheer physical fatigue, all in one, had stared vacantly out at the houses on the other side of the street. She would read what came after in bed that night.

But she didn't read anything in bed that night. She had lain (though not for nearly so many hours as she had imagined next morning), staring into the dark, and every now and then softly laughing; and in a way in which she had never laughed since, and would never, if she could help it, laugh again.

For Miss Curtis in less than a week at Newhampton had fallen in love. She had fallen in love with a stranger sitting at a window at the other end of the esplanade. Not that she had ever confessed this in so many raw unrecallable words, even to herself. Not even at the time, when she had been at least five years younger. Five!—more like fifty. But one can know and never say: and if she had not been in love, why had the mere shadow of that homeward-bound, cadaverous blind man in the street made her feel slightly sick? And why, whenever the opportunity came, did she find herself staring like this out of the glass door of the shop into the darkening street if it were not something of a pleasure to feel a little sick like that?

Well, it didn't much matter now. She had long ago recovered her balance and could recall without a single pang every little incident that had followed the final putting aside of that utterly fatuous novel. Stories like that were of course *known* as 'sensational'. But life! Why the mere packing up of her sandwiches and her bun, her little talk with her landlady as she filled her flask with tea, the last glance of herself in the painted looking-glass between the photographs and the texts over the chimney-piece in her landlady's sitting-room, the mere catching up of her gloves, as with a whisk of her tailor-made skirt she turned aside and with chin a little raised, bloused shoulders a little squared, she once more faced an experience which had become the very elixir of her existence —what did it all amount to but proof that writers of novels only dabble in tinctures while the essence for ever escapes them! You don't have to be a clay-coloured little Countess with Southern blood in your veins to find *that* out!

Miss Curtis had met her landlady again at the foot of the stairs, and had caught the far-away little cockcrow in her own heart at sight of the faded old eyes 'taking her in'. Probably they were no longer merely faded now—she had never seen the old woman since, had only written that once, and then no more. And yet the house must still be there, sunning itself in the marine breezes, and may be somebody else's card with APARTMENTS in silver letters in the sitting-room window. Things went on whatever your idea of them might be. She remembered even what her landlady had said—just a few words. She had told her to enjoy herself while she was young —as had Solomon the Wise in other terms, and had added: 'What's the seaside *for* but to lay, as you might say, in that direction?'

Mrs. Evan's seaside, as Miss Curtis had heard two or three times on the very morning of her arrival, had lain so little in that direction that only once during her long married and widowed life at Newhampton had she ventured out to the end of the pier. And then she hadn't been able to see 'much in it what they fancy'. But you mustn't of course judge of good counsel by the counsellor. Miss Curtis had smiled at the old woman, with her head on one side, as if with the thought that, if you want to look as nice as you possibly can, it is as well to practice doing so at every opportunity.

And mention had been made of an egg—a nice fresh egg for her supper; she remembered that too, though not the egg itself. 'There's always a nice fresh egg'—they were her landlady's very words, and Miss Curtis had replied with the utmost gaiety and aplomb that if there weren't, why, there wouldn't be any more chickens and therefore there wouldn't be any more eggs. And they had both of them laughed. At that gush of inward exultation it hadn't seemed to matter the least bit in the world whether or not she was ever going to eat anything again as long as she lived. But she had none the less assured the old woman she would adore an egg—'As *you* boil them, you know!'—and had then sallied out into the hot air down the sleepy street, and turned off towards the blue, bright, salty, sea-sweet esplanade.

There, she had paused. She had not only paused, but seated herself in one of the little glass and cast-iron shelters and gazed out at the far-away flurry of smoke of a small steamer, that was steadily pushing its way round the extreme edge of the world, bound, like Miss Curtis, for some unknown port. And she had tried, and tried in vain, to take stock of herself.

Wasn't it really and truly worse than ridiculous, almost as silly as that black-eyed, painted-up, feather-witted little Italian Countess herself, and much, after all, in the same way, to be sitting there actually out of breath, almost *unable* to breathe, simply in expectation of seeing a strange man? And him not in the open, mind, but seated at a balconied window similar to but rather more spacious than the one she had just left, and gazing as she was now, out to sea? The crisis had come so suddenly too. One glimpse at that lonely face and shoulders and she was never, never to forget him, though she *was* to get over him, so to speak.

Like most things in life that seem to mean anything, it had all happened so instantly, so absolutely unforeseeably. Miss

Curtis had been just walking as usual along by herself—off to the sand-dunes once more, and a little absent in mind—and without in the least knowing why, as she came to the flagstaff she had lifted her eyes and looked straight up across at him. And there he was—up there on the other side of the street as if he had been waiting for her for months. There was something extraordinarily gentlemanly in his appearance—gentlemanly in the real sense. This was one of the first things she had noticed afterwards when she was back in her rooms again. And though he had been smiling—smiling straight out across at her, it was impossible to have taken the least offence at such boldness. It wasn't boldness. It was as natural as a child who likes the look of a stranger—of any sex—and of course doesn't mind showing it. There wasn't in fact the least little symptom of the cheeky, of the fast, in that smile. It was quiet, and faraway; *lonely*—that was the word.

And taken at a disadvantage like this, Miss Curtis had only been able to gaze blankly back. She was perfectly certain of that. And then after what had seemed an interminable exchange of secrets, she had lowered her head, averted her face, and hastened on to the dunes.

There, oddly enough, she had eaten up the whole of her tea at least half an hour before its usual time. A most curious thing—that just that first look from a stranger should have given her an appetite like a schoolgirl's at a birthday party, and that the next should have taken it almost completely away. For there had been a next. More than one. She simply couldn't help herself. The following afternoon she had no more been able to resist marching steadily along past the striped bathing-machines and the boats, with the sea-wash in her ears, and the marvellous vivacity of it all tingling her senses, and she herself openly bound—she didn't deny it—for that shallow bow-window and its occupant, than she could stop herself yawning when she was tired.

And the one gnawing anxiety that followed was not that

she ever scanned that window in vain, but that nothing else ever happened at all. There the young man would be—not in the least *too* young, of course—with that marvellous quiet dark face of his which she knew now by heart if ever woman can, yet with precisely the same remote welcoming smile on its features. That; and nothing more.

As for herself—and Miss Curtis had never minded acknowledging this the least little bit—why should she?—the third time she had, quite definitely, smiled back. She had raised her square face—and she knew she wasn't so bad-looking—and welcoming, all-hospitable, had given him smile for smile, and so openly that if they had met in the street, it couldn't else but have resulted in his raising his hat! And he, not in the least shocked—she wasn't such an idiotic judge of character as all that—had simply smiled on: a smile not exactly wistful, not exactly melancholy or sad, but as if its owner were in search of something of which he was only vaguely aware.

But why vaguely? Why vaguely? If only Miss Curtis hadn't been a little short-sighted, or had had the courage to wear *pince-nez*—which she did not consider suited her—she might have been able to explore that question more closely. All that she knew for certain was this, that day after day and *after* she had first smiled back, that dark pale handsome romantic face was always turned in her direction when she came stepping along the sandy esplanade, and that it always wore the same look of genuine expectation, if not exactly of increasing interest. Of all this she was sure. And it had almost in her own phrase worn the inside out of her—the joy and expectation and waiting and doubting and longing of the whole thing.

And what if it had? Wasn't every seaside resort frequented by dark piratical creatures, or fresh curly-haired fair ones, on the look-out for conquests? And much older ones, too: and much worse. But far from bothering about them, Miss Curtis had never paid any more attention to the species than she had to the Dad-and-Mum-and-three-little-nippers kind of tripper at Easter or in August, or to the let-the-world-go-by young lovers on the beach. This young man at the window hadn't the faintest resemblance to such buccaneers. Obviously he wasn't even a visitor. He didn't even wear clothes different from the clothes you wear in London; just dark blue or dark grey, so far as she could see, and always, unless her short sight misled her, as nicely finished off as if he had just left the hands of a valet.

At first her heart had sunk at the thought that he was perhaps a 'resident'. Residents of course never take the smallest notice of mere visitors. Far from it. Except on Sundays at church-time or when they go shopping they don't even appear on the esplanade, and if they do, they take good care to show that they are used to it and not much enjoying it. Why merely living at the seaside should make you so haughty and exclusive Miss Curtis had never troubled to consider. Besides, this young man at the window—he must be a *little* under thirty, she supposed—wasn't haughty and he was obviously not absolutely exclusive. Perhaps then he couldn't be a resident. But if he were neither a resident nor a visitor, what on earth could he be? And if he was a resident would he ever come out?

While Miss Curtis was only at Chapter XXI of *Hearts Aflame* she had ventured on in speculation even as far as that. And it was not because of any—well, whatever you like to call it—but because she couldn't be quite certain what the smile meant, that she hadn't quite consciously ventured further yet. Worse, she had begun to realize that though still far-away, his was a smile neither serene nor happy but a little pathetic. It was the smile of someone who is in search of something. What? Understanding? Companionship? Sympathy? Miss Curtis simply didn't know. And if it was any of these things, what ought she to do? If only—not the sexes themselves—but the conduct of the sexes could be sometimes reversed! Without any fatal results. If only she could have marched up to the door, knocked, asked for him and said, 'Well, here I am, you see. You want me? I have come. What can I do? Positively anything you ask of me.' A smile can sink as deep into one's innermost consciousness as that!

Miss Curtis, who was at this moment quite alone—for Miss Mavor was now putting on her things—as she gazed on vacantly out into the London street, all its sunset colours now faded, didn't care a jot now *what* he had wanted. The only thing that mattered was that he hadn't wanted her. Not that she bore him any ill-will on that score. Not only would she never see him again; she would never see his like again. On his account she had given up all interest in men absolutely and for ever. Her every faculty was now centred on the practical— on her 'career'. The only male creature she still had any interest in was a nephew and she was going to leave him all her savings. Besides, look at that flossy little fly-away Phyllis and the dark secretive Miss Mavor and the rest. What a stupid waste, when every hour even of their working day was merely a wait between the acts of some silly love affair. The 'Pictures', a joy-ride, *some* young man always sapping their efficiency.

Miss Curtis's affair would never have been a mere love affair; it would have been a life affair. She knew that, at any rate. She knew perfectly well that if that smiling one at the window had suggested—quite simply even at their first meeting—that he wanted her to spend the rest of her life in his service, she wouldn't have hesitated. She knew that if for some reason best known to himself, he had merely nodded his head at her, to let her know that only her dead body washed up from out of the sea next morning would be of any use to him, in she'd have gone.

That would have been a funny eventuality if you like. But are eventualities that don't occur of the slightest importance? No smile now would ever bring Miss Curtis's sound healthy body to any such pass as that. Old age might, but so far as she knew she was not intolerably terrified at the thought that her sea might then be a trifle cold. Even the fact that five years ago, she was already tending towards the spinsterish hadn't seemed to matter in the least. It made the shock when it came the more amusing to recall. It was almost her last little lesson, so to speak, on the brink. That thermos flask of tea, for example —and what an indescribable flavour it always had, like tepid metal, and those damp raspberry-jam sandwiches! In a moment of weakness she had owned that raspberry jam was her favourite of all jams, and her landlady had remembered it.

Anyhow, no one really young and silly and gullible and romantic would have taken food on such an expedition. It was not as though the face at the window would share it. She knew perfectly well that it was for her own sustenance alone —though it had quickly ceased to be. In fact the flavour of raspberry jam even as a memory was slightly indigestible. Miss Curtis was sorry her inside could betray her like that. Sitting among the sand-dunes with the long grey-green nodding grasses, the faint winds stirring their surface under those sunny heavens, and the bright platter of the empty sea—that would only have been pleasanter and pleasanter to remember. But not so the raspberry jam!

And now, in memory, Miss Curtis had come out of the glass and cast-iron shelter to which her feverish excitement had consigned her. It had been for only a very few minutes— to quiet down. With a glance at its one other occupant, an old gentleman, of whose countenance—since he was muffled up to the eyes in shawls—nothing was visible except spectacles, she had set out once more. It had been her new rule to keep her eyes fixed firmly on the barometer under the flagstaff on the front until she was nearly opposite the balcony, and then to cast only one firm straight intent glance up at the window, before—and this was the most horrible abyss to remember— before sitting down on a neighbouring seat, a few yards further on. Yes, she could be frank with herself about even that now. She had accustomed herself to sit down there—in wait for him. She had definitely broken herself in to that, and solely with the intention of lying in wait for him. Of lying in wait for him—like other women. Her one scrap of redeeming decency being that once she was seated she never by a fraction of an inch turned her head. Indeed sitting there—horribly stiff and hot and self-conscious—she *might* be out of sight of him— unless of course, he changed his position at the window to look. And wasn't that perhaps the least one could expect— when at any rate one had oneself sunk so low? It was on this afternoon however she was to learn that it is actually possible in this world to sink as low as that, and nobody, no human being anyhow, be a penny the richer. While you yourself might remain—well, what? Indescribably poorer? Just because you have been humbled to the dust? Because you've been taught your lesson? Had there been need to learn *that*? And supposing it had not been a lesson—a holiday task?

A slow smile had stolen into Miss Curtis's face—not sour but extraordinarily resolute, even a little grim. But never mind all that. It was the *last* afternoon of her degradation she was now thinking of. Questions were useless now.

She had found him there at his window just as usual, just as immobile, and almost excruciatingly alone, as if simply stricken with solitude. Smiling, oh yes; but—she hadn't any doubt of it now—unhappy. It was absurd to deny it any longer. He was alone, he was desperate, he needed help. At this it seemed that an emotion of infinite understanding, of selfless abandonment, had swamped over her. She didn't even smile back *that* afternoon. She only looked. But with all her self—mind, heart, and soul and all these thirty years of long waiting—welling over in her eyes. It was no good mincing matters. She had felt like that: just swamped—like some clumsily-handled Sunday tripper's rowing-boat that has landed wrong side on on the beach with a smart sea running. Every drop of blood in her body seemed at that moment to have come to a standstill. Then the gulp, the clutch at her bag, and she had sat down.

She had sat down, her back to the high pleasant house behind her and a few paces to her left, with its late Georgian greenish balconies. And there she had simply waited on and on and on. She had to do so; there was no help for it; to-morrow—or the next day—she must be going back. She couldn't blue all her savings, not to the very last stiver. Why then he must realize it; his very intelligence would reveal it if only she gave him time. She would wait, and he would declare himself. To ignore her now! With a face like that, a smile so unmotived, so wistful! Perfidy like *that* was not possible even in this perfidious world. The bottom of things didn't come out quite like that.

So she had sat on and on, only once drifting on, for fifty yards or so, very very slowly, her eyes on the sea, and then returning—without so much as an eyelash lifted towards the window. And as she sat down there the second time—her heart grown a little cold, her mind miserable with wrangling voices, there had presented itself in the skies opposite to her the most astonishing sunset she had ever seen.

It appeared as if the clouds must have been waiting in the wings all day for this last huge transformation scene. They were journeying, rank on rank, each to its appointed place, not only drenching heaven and earth with an enormous pomp of colour, but widening, shallowing, patterning the whole western horizon and even the zenith arched over her simple head. It was an amazingly joyful spectacle. One could hardly believe that again and again and again throughout the centuries of the earth's solitary and peopled existence just such vast preparations as these must often have been made before —as if for the entry of some all-powerful and all-merciful potentate. Yet one who never actually appeared. And it didn't occur to Miss Curtis that, strictly speaking, the immense scene she was contemplating was hers alone; that every instant it was beginning a little further westward to some other spectator; indeed—sobering thought—that sunset was always going on for someone; and daybreak too, for that matter.

For herself that evening the two extremes seemed to have combined into one. And then, night. During those last brief minutes she had realized as she watched what it is to be in the presence of a life of infinite possibilities, crammed, brimmed with joys and anguish and responsibilities and delights that no foresight could apprehend. She was to realize too at the end of those few minutes what it is—so far as she was concerned—to see it instantaneously fade away and die, while still these lovely apparitions of the heavens burned on, in their turn too to fade away. For this life of which she had caught this marvellous glimpse had itself never even been a possibility—merely an illusion. Worse, a delusion.

Miss Curtis was not smiling now as she stood looking out into the street. Her face had never worn an expression so assured and resolute and indomitable. What a solace is a career, what a never-wearisome refuge plenty to do! How wise, how sagacious to retire and just look on. At least so it seemed now.

At Newhampton that evening an awful moment had intervened, a moment almost appallingly ridiculous to recall. For you can't actually remember racking pain of mind and spirit any more than you can remember bodily agony. Voices had sounded out behind her as she sat with her little bag clutched in her tailor-made lap, her whole person positively blazing with the preternatural dyes of the west. And one of those voices she was to remember—it had sounded familiar too, though she had never heard it before—to her dying day. It was the voice of the Destroyer.

The esplanade at this moment had been all but deserted—

empty. Two men—and as if a tocsin had proclaimed him she *knew* who one of them was—two men had come straight across from the house behind her, had passed the seat on her left about twenty yards away, had then turned right, and now were but a pace or two distant. She positively saw all this, as if she had eyes between her shoulder-blades. And she had sat on, motionless, half-suffocated with suspense, unable for an instant to stir hand or foot.

Then, with that vast western light for help, she had looked up—straight into the unknown one's face, straight into his eyes. And though they were fixed in her direction they had made no sign. None—just none. How could they? For though they were wide open they were veiled by a peculiar film, and even if the unknown one's hand had not been resting on his companion's arm, she would have realized at once that he was blind.

It was curious, perhaps, that being so, he could be capable —as that curiously vague gentle smile seemed to testify—of enjoying this spectacle of light and colour and refulgence, of sea, air, and sky. But Miss Curtis had never thought it curious. She had first heard only the voice, without catching the words, and then had gulped down the heart that had come into her mouth, and had so clumsily clutched at the wrong end of her bag, that her thermos flask had slipped out of it, had rolled with extraordinary animation out of her lap and fallen with an incredible crash on to the asphalt beneath.

'What's that, what's that?' the voice had cried out, and a panic-stricken expression had transfigured the mute pale face.

'It's all right,' the other replied. 'It's only a lady who has dropped something.' And then as if in confidence: 'As a matter of fact, a bottle of tea, poor thing.'

The last words had been scarcely more than muttered. But in moments of extreme torture the senses may be exceedingly acute and the whole soul observant. They had remained fixed in Miss Curtis's mind as finally as if they had been recorded in wax for the gramophone. 'A bottle of tea.' But since something that seemed very much like her whole being, her very heart itself had at this moment been shattered into bits, it wasn't till some little time after, when the deeper wounds were numbing, that she felt the full destructiveness of that 'poor thing'. To see ourselves as others see us and not through the distortion of self-deception, rapture, and romance—'Poor thing!'—in the very words with which she herself had sometimes compassionated in silence some blowsy bedraggled tripper—or worse! 'And so—*ad infinitum.' That*, anyhow, only amused her now.

And that had been the end of it. Miss Curtis had stooped—the blood rushing to her head and staining her vision as she did so—and had picked up her broken flask. It looked a little disgusting but she had stuffed it back into her bag with her raspberry-jam sandwiches and her bun. Then she had swept her hands down over her lap almost as if she had finished a most delicious meal and wanted to get rid of the crumbs. And then she had got up and gone off on her picnic to the sand-dunes. And then. . . .

But now Miss Mavor, having finished her last few little jobs—and all lip-sticked and freshly powdered for the evening—was ready to go. Miss Curtis herself pulled down the last dark-blue blind, the blind that covered the glass of the door. And she herself turned the handle and opened that door.

'Good night, Miss Curtis,' said Miss Mavor.

'Good night,' said Miss Curtis; then turned back into the vacant and half-lighted shop to get her own neat hand-bag and admirable umbrella, and to put on her hat and coat.

ALL HALLOWS

*

*'And because time in itselfe . . . can receive no alteration, the
hallowing . . . must consist in the shape or countenance which we put
upon the affaires that are incident in these days.'*

RICHARD HOOKER

It was about half-past three on an August afternoon when
I found myself for the first time looking down upon All
Hallows. And at glimpse of it, fatigue and vexation passed
away. I stood 'at gaze', as the old phrase goes—like the two
children of Israel sent in to spy out the Promised Land. How
often the imagined transcends the real. Not so All Hallows.
Having at last reached the end of my journey—flies, dust,
heat, wind—having at last come limping out upon the green
sea-bluff beneath which lay its walls—I confess the actuality
excelled my feeble dreams of it.

What most astonished me, perhaps, was the sense not so
much of its age, its austerity, or even its solitude, but its air
of abandonment. It lay couched there as if in hiding in its
narrow sea-bay. Not a sound was in the air; not a jackdaw
clapped its wings among its turrets. No other roof, not even
a chimney, was in sight; only the dark-blue arch of the sky;
the narrow snowline of the ebbing tide; and that gaunt coast
fading away into the haze of a west over which were already
gathering the veils of sunset.

We had met, then, at an appropriate hour and season. And yet—I wonder. For it was certainly not the 'beauty' of All Hallows, lulled as if into a dream in this serenity of air and heavens, which was to leave the sharpest impression upon me. And what kind of first showing would it have made, I speculated, if an autumnal gale had been shrilling and trumpeting across its narrow bay—clots of wind-borne spume floating among its dusky pinnacles—and the roar of the sea echoing against its walls! Imagine it frozen stark in winter, icy hoar-frost edging its every boss, moulding, finial, crocket, cusp!

Indeed, are there not works of man, legacies of a half-forgotten past, scattered across this human world of ours from China to Peru, which seem to daunt the imagination with their incomprehensibility? Incomprehensible, I mean, in the sense that the passion that inspired and conceived them is incomprehensible. Viewed in the light of the passing day, they might be the monuments of a race of demi-gods. And yet, if we could but free ourselves from our timidities, and follies, we might realize that even we ourselves have an obligation to leave behind us similar memorials—testaments to the creative and faithful genius not so much of the individual as of Humanity itself.

However that may be, it was my own personal fortune to see All Hallows for the first time in the heat of the Dog Days, after a journey which could hardly be justified except by its end. At this moment of the afternoon the great church almost cheated one into the belief that it was possessed of a life of its own. It lay, as I say, couched in its natural hollow, basking under the dark dome of the heavens like some half-fossilized monster that might at any moment stir and awaken out of the swoon to which the wand of the enchanter had committed it. And with every inch of the sun's descending journey it changed its appearance.

That is the charm of such things. Man himself, says the philosopher, is the sport of change. His life and the life around him are but the flotsam of a perpetual flux. Yet, haunted by ideals, egged on by impossibilities, he builds his vision of the changeless; and time diversifies it with its colours and its 'effects' at leisure. It was drawing near to harvest now; the summer was nearly over; the corn would soon be in stook; the season of silence had come, not even the robins had yet begun to practice their autumnal lament. I should have come earlier.

The distance was of little account. But nine flinty hills in seven miles is certainly hard commons. To plod (the occupant of a cloud of dust) up one steep incline and so see another; to plod up that and so see a third; to surmount that and, half-choked, half-roasted, to see (as if in unbelievable mirage) a fourth—and always stone walls, discoloured grass, no flower but ragged ragwort, whited fleabane, moody nettle, and the exquisite stubborn bindweed with its almond-burdened censers, and always the glitter and dazzle of the sun—well, the experience grows irksome. And then that endless flint erection with which some jealous Lord of the Manor had barricaded his verdurous estate! A fly-infested mile of the company of that wall was tantamount to making one's way into the infernal regions—with Tantalus for fellow-pilgrim. And when a solitary and empty dung-cart had lumbered by, lifting the dumb dust out of the road in swirling clouds into the heat-quivering air, I had all but wept aloud.

No, I shall not easily forget that walk—or the conclusion of it—when footsore, all but dead beat—dust all over me, cheeks, lips, eyelids, in my hair, dust in drifts even between my naked body and my clothes—I stretched my aching limbs on the turf under the straggle of trees which crowned the bluff of that last hill still blessedly green and verdant, and feasted my eyes on the cathedral beneath me. How odd Memory is—in her sorting arrangements. How perverse her pigeon-holes.

It had reminded me of a drizzling evening many years ago. I had stayed a moment to listen to an old Salvation Army officer preaching at a street corner. The sopped and squalid houses echoed with his harangue. His penitents' drum resembled the block of an executioner. His goatish beard wagged at every word he uttered. 'My brothers and sisters,' he was saying, 'the very instant our fleshly bodies are born they begin to perish; the moment the Lord has put them together, time begins to take them to pieces again. *Now* at this very instant if you listen close, you can hear the nibblings and frettings of the moth and rust within—the worm that never dies. It's the same with human causes and creeds and institutions—just the same. O, then, for that Strand of Beauty where all that is mortal shall be shed away and we shall appear in the likeness and verisimilitude of what in sober and awful truth we are!'

The light striking out of an oil-and-colourman's shop at the street corner lay across his cheek and beard and glassed his eye. The soaked circle of humanity in which he was gesticulating stood staring and motionless—the lassies, the probationers, the melancholy idlers. I had had enough. I went away. But it is odd that so utterly inappropriate a recollection should have edged back into my mind at this moment. There was, as I have said, not a living soul in sight. Only a few sea-birds—oyster-catchers maybe—were jangling on the distant beach.

It was now a quarter to four by my watch, and the usual pensive 'lin-lah-lone' from the belfry beneath me would soon no doubt be ringing to evensong. But if at that moment a triple bob-major had suddenly clanged its alarm over sea and shore I couldn't have stirred a finger's breadth. Scanty though the shade afforded by the wind-shorn tuft of trees under which I lay might be—I was ineffably at peace.

No bell, as a matter of fact, loosed its tongue that stagnant half-hour. Unless then the walls beneath me already concealed a few such chance visitors as myself, All Hallows would be empty. A cathedral not only without a close but without a congregation—yet another romantic charm. The Deanery and the residences of its clergy, my old guide-book had long since informed me, were a full mile or more away. I determined in due time, first to make sure of an entry, and then having quenched my thirst, to bathe.

How inhuman any extremity—hunger, fatigue, pain, desire —makes us poor humans. Thirst and drouth so haunted my mind that again and again as I glanced towards it I supped up in one long draught that complete blue sea. But meanwhile, too, my eyes had been steadily exploring and searching out this monument of the bygone centuries beneath me.

The headland faced approximately due west. The windows of the Lady Chapel therefore lay immediately beneath me, their fourteenth-century glass showing flatly dark amid their traceries. Above it, the shallow V-shaped, leaden ribbed roof of the chancel converged towards the unfinished tower, then broke away at right angles—for the cathedral was cruciform. Walls so ancient and so sparsely adorned and decorated could not but be inhospitable in effect. Their stone was of a bleached bone-grey; a grey that none the less seemed to be as immaterial as flame—or incandescent ash. They were substantial enough, however, to cast a marvellously lucent shadow, of a blue no less vivid but paler than that of the sea, on the shelving sward beneath them. And that shadow was steadily shifting as I watched. But even if the complete edifice had vanished into the void, the scene would still have been of an incredible loveliness. The colours in air and sky on this dangerous coast seemed to shed a peculiar unreality even on the rocks of its own outworks.

So, from my vantage place on the hill that dominates it, I continued for a while to watch All Hallows; to spy upon it; and no less intently than a sentry who, not quite trusting his own eyes, has seen a dubious shape approaching him in the dusk. It may sound absurd, but I felt that at any moment I too might surprise All Hallows in the act of revealing what in very truth it looked like—and *was*, when no human witness was there to share its solitude.

Those gigantic statues, for example, which flanked the base of the unfinished tower—an intense bluish-white in the sunlight and a bluish-purple in shadow—images of angels and of saints, as I had learned of old from my guide-book. Only six of them at most could be visible, of course, from where I sat. And yet I found myself counting them again and yet again, as if doubting my own arithmetic. For my first impression had been that seven were in view—though the figure furthest from me at the western angle showed little more than a jutting fragment of stone which might perhaps be only part and parcel of the fabric itself.

But then the lights even of day may be deceitful, and fantasy plays strange tricks with one's eyes. With exercise, none the less, the mind is enabled to detect minute details which the unaided eye is incapable of particularizing. Given the imagination, man himself indeed may some day be able to distinguish what shapes are walking during our own terrestrial midnight amid the black shadows of the craters in the noonday of the moon. At any rate, I could trace at last frets of carving, minute weather marks, crookednesses, incrustations, repairings, that had before passed unnoticed. These walls, indeed, like human faces, were maps and charts of their own long past.

In the midst of this prolonged scrutiny, the hypnotic air, the heat, must suddenly have overcome me. I fell asleep up there in my grove's scanty shade; and remained asleep, too, long enough (as time is measured by the clocks of sleep), to dream an immense panoramic dream. On waking, I could recall only the faintest vestiges of it, and found that the hand of my watch had crept on but a few minutes in the interval. It was eight minutes past four.

I scrambled up—numbed and inert—with that peculiar sense of panic which sometimes follows an uneasy sleep. What folly to have been frittering time away within sight of my goal at an hour when no doubt the cathedral would soon be closed to visitors, and abandoned for the night to its own secret ruminations. I hastened down the steep rounded incline of the hill, and having skirted under the sunlit expanse of the walls, came presently to the south door, only to discover that my forebodings had been justified, and that it was already barred and bolted. The discovery seemed to increase my fatigue four-fold. How foolish it is to obey mere caprices. What a straw is a man!

I glanced up into the beautiful shell of masonry above my head. Shapes and figures in stone it showed in plenty—symbols of an imagination that had flamed and faded, leaving this signature for sole witness—but not a living bird or butterfly. There was but one faint chance left of making an entry. Hunted now, rather than the hunter, I hastened out again into the full blazing flood of sunshine—and once more came within sight of the sea; a sea so near at last that I could hear its enormous sallies and murmurings. Indeed I had not realized until that moment how closely the great western doors of the cathedral abutted on the beach.

It was as if its hospitality had been deliberately designed, not for a people to whom the faith of which it was the shrine had become a weariness and a commonplace, but for the solace of pilgrims from over the ocean. I could see them tumbling into their cockle-boats out of their great hollow ships—sails idle, anchors down; see them leaping ashore and straggling up across the sands to these all-welcoming portals —'Parthians and Medes and Elamites; dwellers in Mesopotamia and in the parts of Egypt about Cyrene; strangers of Rome, Jews and Proselytes—we do hear them speak in our own tongue the wonderful works of God.'

And so at last I found my way into All Hallows—entering by a rounded dwarfish side-door with zigzag mouldings. There hung for corbel to its dripstone a curious leering face, with its forked tongue out, to give me welcome. And an appropriate one, too, for the figure I made!

But once beneath that prodigious roof-tree, I forgot myself and everything that was mine. The hush, the coolness, the unfathomable twilight drifted in on my small human consciousness. Not even the ocean itself is able so completely to receive one into its solacing bosom. Except for the windows over my head, filtering with their stained glass the last western radiance of the sun, there was but little visible colour in those great spaces, and a severe economy of decoration. The stone piers carried their round arches with an almost intimidating impassivity.

By deliberate design, too, or by some illusion of perspective, the whole floor of the building appeared steadily to ascend towards the east, where a dark wooden multitudinously figured rood-screen shut off the choir and the high altar from the nave. I seemed to have exchanged one universal actuality for another: the burning world of nature, for this oasis of quiet. Here, the wings of the imagination need never rest in their flight out of the wilderness into the unknown.

Thus resting, I must again have fallen asleep. And so swiftly can even the merest freshet of sleep affect the mind, that when my eyes opened, I was completely at a loss.

Where was I? What demon of what romantic chasm had swept my poor drowsy body into this immense haunt? The din and clamour of an horrific dream whose fainting rumour was still in my ear, became suddenly stilled. Then at one and the same moment, a sense of utter dismay at earthly surroundings no longer serene and peaceful, but grim and forbidding, flooded my mind, and I became aware that I was no longer alone. Twenty or thirty paces away, and a little this side of the rood-screen, an old man was standing.

To judge from the black and purple velvet and tassel-tagged gown he wore, he was a verger. He had not yet realized, it seemed, that a visitor shared his solitude. And yet he was listening. His head was craned forward and leaned sideways on his rusty shoulders. As I steadily watched him, he raised his eyes, and with a peculiar stealthy deliberation scanned the complete upper regions of the northern transept. Not the faintest rumour of any sound that may have attracted his attention reached me where I sat. Perhaps a wild bird had made its entry through a broken pane of glass and with its cry had at the same moment awakened me and caught his attention. Or maybe the old man was waiting for some fellow-occupant to join him from above.

I continued to watch him. Even at this distance, the silvery twilight cast by the clerestory windows was sufficient to show me, though vaguely, his face: the high sloping nose, the lean cheekbones and protruding chin. He continued so long in the same position that I at last determined to break in on his reverie.

At sound of my footsteps his head sunk cautiously back upon his shoulders; and he turned; and then motionlessly surveyed me as I drew near. He resembled one of those old men whom Rembrandt delighted in drawing: the knotted hands, the black drooping eyebrows, the wide thin-lipped ecclesiastical mouth, the intent cavernous dark eyes beneath the heavy folds of their lids. White as a miller with dust, hot and draggled, I was hardly the kind of visitor that any self-respecting custodian would warmly welcome, but he greeted me none the less with every mark of courtesy.

I apologized for the lateness of my arrival, and explained it as best I could. 'Until I caught sight of you,' I concluded lamely, 'I hadn't ventured very far in: otherwise I might have found myself a prisoner for the night. It must be dark in here when there is no moon.'

The old man smiled—but wryly. 'As a matter of fact, sir,' he replied, 'the cathedral is closed to visitors at four—at such times, that is, when there is no afternoon service. Services are not as frequent as they were. But visitors are rare too. In winter, in particular, you notice the gloom—as you say, sir. Not that I ever spend the night here: though I am usually last to leave. There's the risk of fire to be thought of and . . . I think I should have detected your presence here, sir. One becomes accustomed after many years.'

There was the usual trace of official pedantry in his voice, but it was more pleasing than otherwise. Nor did he show any wish to be rid of me. He continued his survey, although his eye was a little absent and his attention seemed to be divided.

'I thought perhaps I might be able to find a room for the night and really explore the cathedral to-morrow morning. It has been a tiring journey; I come from B——'

'Ah, from B——; it *is* a fatiguing journey, sir, taken on foot. I used to walk in there to see a sick daughter of mine. Carriage parties occasionally make their way here, but not so much as once. We are too far out of the hurly-burly to be much intruded on. Not that them who come to make their worship here are intruders. Far from it. But most that come are mere sightseers. And the fewer of them, I say, in the circumstances, the better.'

Something in what I had said or in my appearance seemed to have reassured him. 'Well, I cannot claim to be a regular churchgoer,' I said. 'I am myself a mere sightseer. And yet— even to sit here for a few minutes is to be reconciled.'

'Ah, reconciled, sir:' the old man repeated, turning away. 'I can well imagine it after that journey on such a day as this. But to live here is another matter.'

'I was thinking of that,' I replied in a foolish attempt to retrieve the position. 'It must, as you say, be desolate enough in the winter—for two-thirds of the year, indeed.'

'We have our storms, sir—the bad with the good,' he agreed, 'and our position is specially prolific of what they call sea-fog. It comes driving in from the sea for days and nights together—gale and mist, so that you can scarcely see your open hand in front of your eyes even in broad daylight. And the noise of it, sir, sweeping across overhead in that wooliness of mist, if you take me, is most peculiar. It's shocking to a stranger. No, sir, we are left pretty much to ourselves when the fine-weather birds are flown. . . . You'd be astonished at the power of the winds here. There was a mason—a local man too—not above two or three years ago was blown clean off the roof from under the tower—tossed up in the air like an empty sack. But'—and the old man at last allowed his eyes to stray upwards to the roof again—'but there's not much doing now.' He seemed to be pondering. 'Nothing open.'

'I mustn't detain you,' I said, 'but you were saying that services are infrequent now. Why is that? When one thinks of——' But tact restrained me.

'Pray don't think of keeping me, sir. It's a part of my duties. But from a remark you let fall I was supposing you may have seen something that appeared, I understand, not many months ago in the newspapers. We lost our dean—Dean Pomfrey—last November. To all intents and purposes, I mean; and his office has not yet been filled. Between you and me, sir, there's a hitch—though I should wish it to go no further. They are greedy monsters—those newspapers: no respect, no discretion, no decency, in my view. And they copy each other like cats in a chorus.

'We have never wanted to be a notoriety here, sir: and not of late of all times. We must face our own troubles. You'd be astonished how callous the mere sightseer can be. And not only them from over the water whom our particular troubles cannot concern—but far worse—parties as English as you or me. They ask you questions you wouldn't believe possible in a civilized country. Not that they care what becomes of us—not one iota, sir. We talk of them masked-up Inquisitors in olden times, but there's many a human being in our own would enjoy seeing a fellow-creature on the rack if he could get the opportunity. It's a heartless age, sir.'

This was queerish talk in the circumstances: and after all I myself was of the glorious company of the sightseers. I held my peace. And the old man, as if to make amends, asked me if I would care to see any particular part of the building. 'The light is smalling,' he explained, 'but still if we keep to the ground level there'll be a few minutes to spare; and we shall not be interrupted if we go quietly on our way.'

For the moment the reference eluded me: I could only thank him for the suggestion and once more beg him not to put himself to any inconvenience. I explained, too, that though I had no personal acquaintance with Dr. Pomfrey, I had read of his illness in the newspapers. 'Isn't he,' I added a little dubiously, 'the author of *The Church and the Folk*? If so, he must be an exceedingly learned and delightful man.'

'Ay, sir.' The old verger put up a hand towards me. 'You may well say it: a saint if ever there was one. But it's worse than "illness", sir—it's oblivion. And, thank God, the newspapers didn't get hold of more than a bare outline.'

He dropped his voice. 'This way, if you please'; and he led me off gently down the aisle, once more coming to a standstill beneath the roof of the tower. 'What I mean, sir, is that there's very few left in this world who have any place in their minds for a sacred confidence—no reverence, sir. They would as lief All Hallows and all it stands for were swept away to-morrow, demolished to the dust. And that gives me the greatest caution with whom I speak. But sharing one's troubles is sometimes a relief. If it weren't so, why do those Catholics have their wooden boxes all built for the purpose? What else, I ask you, is the meaning of their fasts and penances?

'You see, sir, I am myself, and have been for upwards of twelve years now, the dean's verger. In the sight of no re- specter of persons—of offices and dignities, that is, I take it— I might claim to be even an elder brother. And our dean, sir, was a man who was all things to all men. No pride of place, no vauntingness, none of your apron-and-gaiter high-and- mightiness whatsoever, sir. And then that! And to come on us without warning; or at least without warning as could be taken as *such*.' I followed his eyes into the darkening stony spaces above us; a light like tarnished silver lay over the soundless vaultings. But so, of course, dusk, either of evening or daybreak, would affect the ancient stones. Nothing moved there.

'You must understand, sir,' the old man was continuing, 'the procession for divine service proceeds from the vestry over yonder out through those wrought-iron gates and so under the rood-screen and into the chancel there. Visitors are admitted on showing a card or a word to the verger in charge; but not otherwise. If you stand a pace or two to the right, you will catch a glimpse of the altar-screen—fourteenth-century work, Bishop Robert de Beaufort—and a unique example of the age. But what I was saying is that when we proceed for the services *out* of here *into* there, it has always been our custom to keep pretty close together; more seemly and decent, sir, than straggling in like so many sheep.

'Besides, sir, aren't we at such times in the manner of an *array*; "marching as to war", if you take me: it's a lesson in objects. The third verger leading: then the choristers, boys and men, though sadly depleted; then the minor canons; then any other dignitaries who may happen to be present, with the canon in residence; then myself, sir, followed by the dean.

'There hadn't been much amiss up to then, and on that afternoon, I can vouch—and I've repeated it *ad naushum*— there was not a single stranger out in this beyond here, sir— nave or transepts. Not within view, that is: one can't be expected to see through four feet of Norman stone. Well, sir, we had gone on our way, and I had actually turned about as usual to bow Dr. Pomfrey into his stall, when I found to my consternation, to my consternation, I say, he wasn't there! It alarmed me, sir, and as you might well believe if you knew the full circumstances.

'Not that I lost my presence of mind. My first duty was to

see all things to be in order and nothing unseemly to occur. My feelings were another matter. The old gentleman had left the vestry with us: that I knew: I had myself robed 'im as usual, and he in his own manner, smiling with his "Well, Jones, another day gone; another day gone." He was always an anxious gentleman for *time*, sir. How we spend it and all.

'As I say, then, he was behind me when we swepp out of the gates. I saw him coming on out of the tail of my eye—we grow accustomed to it, to see with the whole of the eye, I mean. And then—not a vestige; and me—well, sir, nonplussed, as you may imagine. I gave a look and sign at Canon Ockham, and the service proceeded as usual, while I hurried back to the vestry thinking the poor gentleman must have been taken suddenly ill. And yet, sir, I was not surprised to find the vestry vacant, and him not there. I had been expecting matters to come to what you might call a head.

'As best I could I held my tongue, and a fortunate thing it was that Canon Ockham was then in residence and not Canon Leigh Shougar, though perhaps I am not the one to say it. No, sir, our beloved dean—as pious and unworldly a gentleman as ever graced the Church—was gone for ever. He was not to appear in our midst again. He had been'—and the old man with elevated eyebrows and long lean mouth nearly whispered the words into my ear—'he had been absconded—abducted, sir.'

'Abducted!' I murmured.

The old man closed his eyes, and with trembling lids added, 'He was found, sir, late that night up there in what they call the Trophy Room—sitting in a corner there, weeping. A child. Not a word of what had persuaded him to go or misled him there, not a word of sorrow or sadness, thank God. He didn't know us, sir—didn't know *me*. Just simple; harmless; memory all gone. Simple, sir.'

It was foolish to be whispering together like this beneath these enormous spaces with not so much as a clothes-moth for sign of life within view. But I even lowered my voice still further: 'Were there no premonitory symptoms? Had he been failing for long?'

The spectacle of grief in any human face is afflicting, but in a face as aged and resigned as this old man's—I turned away in remorse the moment the question was out of my lips; emotion is a human solvent and a sort of friendliness had sprung up between us.

'If you will just follow me,' he whispered, 'there's a little place where I make my ablutions that might be of service, sir. We would converse there in better comfort. I am sometimes reminded of those words in Ecclesiastes: "And a bird of the air shall tell of the matter." There is not much in our poor human affairs, sir, that was not known to the writer of that book.'

He turned and led the way with surprising celerity, gliding along in his thin-soled, square-toed, clerical springside boots; and came to a pause outside a nail-studded door. He opened it with a huge key, and admitted me into a recess under the central tower. We mounted a spiral stone staircase and passed along a corridor hardly more than two feet wide and so dark that now and again I thrust out my fingertips in search of his black velveted gown to make sure of my guide.

This corridor at length conducted us into a little room whose only illumination I gathered was that of the ebbing dusk from within the cathedral. The old man with trembling rheumatic fingers lit a candle, and thrusting its stick into the middle of an old oak table, pushed open yet another thick oaken door. 'You will find a basin and a towel in there, sir, if you will be so kind.'

I entered. A print of the Crucifixion was tin-tacked to the panelled wall, and beneath it stood a tin basin and jug on a stand. Never was water sweeter. I laved my face and hands and drank deep; my throat like a parched river-course after a drought. What appeared to be a tarnished censer lay in one corner of the room; a pair of seven-branched candlesticks shared a recess with a mouse-trap and a book. My eyes passed wearily yet gratefully from one to another of these mute discarded objects while I stood drying my hands.

When I returned, the old man was standing motionless before the spike-barred grill of the window, peering out and down.

'You asked me, sir,' he said, turning his lank waxen face into the feeble rays of the candle, 'you asked me, sir, a question which, if I understood you aright, was this: Was there anything that had occurred *previous* that would explain what I have been telling you? Well, sir, it's a long story, and one best restricted to them perhaps that have the goodwill of things at heart. All Hallows, I might say, sir, is my second home. I have been here, boy and man, for close on fifty-five years—have seen four bishops pass away and have served under no less than five several deans, Dr. Pomfrey, poor gentleman, being the last of the five.

'If such a word could be excused, sir, it's no exaggeration to say that Canon Leigh Shougar is a greenhorn by comparison; which may in part be why he has never quite hit it off, as they say, with Canon Ockham. Or even with Archdeacon Trafford, though he's another kind of gentleman altogether. And *he* is at present abroad. He had what they call a breakdown in health, sir.

'Now in my humble opinion, what was required was not only wisdom and knowledge but simple common sense. In the circumstances I am about to mention, it serves no purpose for any of us to be talking too much; to be for ever sitting at a table with shut doors and finger on lip, and discussing what to most intents and purposes would hardly be called evidence at all, sir. What is the use of argufying, splitting hairs, objurgating about trifles, when matters are sweeping rapidly on from bad to worse. I say it with all due respect and not, I hope, thrusting myself into what doesn't concern me: Dr. Pomfrey might be with us now in his own self and reason if only common caution had been observed.

'But now that the poor gentleman is gone beyond all that, there is no hope of action or agreement left, none whatsoever. They meet and they meet, and they have now one expert now another down from London, and even from the continent. And I don't say they are not knowledgable gentlemen either, nor a pride to their profession. But why not tell *all*? Why keep back the very secret of what we know? That's what I am asking. And, what's the answer? Why simply that what they don't want to believe, what runs counter to their hopes and wishes and credibilities—and comfort—in this world, that's what they keep out of sight as long as decency permits.

'Canon Leigh Shougar *knows*, sir, what *I* know. And how, I ask, is he going to get to grips with it at this late day if he refuses to acknowledge that such things are what every fragment of evidence goes to prove that they are. It's *we*, sir, and not the rest of the heedless world outside, who in the long and the short of it are responsible. And what I say is: no power or principality here or hereunder can take possession of a place while those inside have faith enough to keep them out. But once let that falter—the seas are in. And when I say no power, sir, I mean—with all deference—even Satan himself.' The lean lank face had set at the word like a wax mask. The black eyes beneath the heavy lids were fixed on mine with an acute intensity and—though more inscrutable things haunted them —with an unfaltering courage. So dense a hush hung about us that the very stones of the walls seemed to be of silence solidified. It is curious what a refreshment of spirit a mere tin basinful of water may be. I stood leaning against the edge of the table so that the candlelight still rested on my companion.

'What is *wrong* here?' I asked him baldly.

He seemed not to have expected so direct an inquiry. 'Wrong, sir? Why, if I might make so bold,' he replied with a wan, far-away smile and gently drawing his hand down one of the velvet lapels of his gown, 'if I might make so bold, sir, I take it that you have come as a direct answer to prayer.'

His voice faltered. 'I am an old man now, and nearly at the end of my tether. You must realize, if you please, that I can't get any help that I can understand. I am not doubting that the gentlemen I have mentioned have only the salvation of the cathedral at heart—the cause, sir; and a graver responsibility yet. But they refuse to see how close to the edge of things we are: and how we are drifting.

'Take mere situation. So far as my knowledge tells me, there is no sacred edifice in the whole kingdom—of a piece, that is, with All Hallows not only in mere size and age but in what I might call sanctity and tradition—that is so open— open, I mean, sir, to attack of this peculiar and terrifying nature.'

'Terrifying?'

'*Terrifying*, sir; though I hold fast to what wits my Maker has bestowed on me. Where else, may I ask, would you expect the powers of darkness to congregate in open besiegement than in this narrow valley? First, the sea out there. Are you aware, sir, that ever since living remembrance flood-tide has been gnawing and mumbling its way into this bay to the extent of three or four feet *per annum*? Forty inches, and forty inches, and forty inches corroding on and on: Watch it, sir, man and boy as I have these sixty years past and then make a century of it. Not to mention positive leaps and bounds.

'And now, think a moment of the floods and gales that fall upon us autumn and winter through and even in spring, when this valley is liker paradise to young eyes than any place on earth. They make the roads from the nearest towns well-nigh impassable; which means that for some months of the year we are to all intents and purposes clean cut off from the rest of the world—as the Schindels out there are from the mainland. Are you aware, sir, I continue, that as we stand now we are above a mile from traces of the nearest human habitation, and them merely the relics of a burnt-out old farmstead? I warrant that if (and which God forbid) you had been shut up here during the coming night, and it was a near thing but what you weren't—I warrant you might have shouted yourself dumb out of the nearest window if window you could reach—and not a human soul to heed or help you.'

I shifted my hands on the table. It was tedious to be asking questions that received only such vague and evasive replies: and it is always a little disconcerting in the presence of a stranger to be spoken to so close, and with such positiveness.

'Well', I smiled, 'I hope I should not have disgraced my nerves to such an extreme as that. As a small boy, one of my particular fancies was to spend a night in a pulpit. There's a cushion, you know!'

The old man's solemn glance never swerved from my eyes. 'But I take it, sir,' he said, 'if you had ventured to give out a text up there in the dark hours, your jocular young mind would not have been prepared for any kind of a congregation?'

'You mean,' I said a little sharply, 'that the place is haunted?' The absurd notion flitted across my mind of some wandering tribe of gipsies chancing on a refuge so ample and isolated as this, and taking up its quarters in its secret parts. The old church must be honeycombed with corridors and passages and chambers pretty much like the one in which we were now concealed: and what does 'cartholic' imply but an infinite hospitality within prescribed limits? But the old man had taken me at my word.

'I mean, sir,' he said firmly, shutting his eyes, 'that there are devilish agencies at work here.' He raised his hand. 'Don't, I entreat you, dismiss what I am saying as the wanderings of a foolish old man.' He drew a little nearer. 'I have heard them with these ears; I have seen them with these eyes; though whether they have any positive substance, sir, is beyond my small knowledge to declare. But what indeed might we expect their substance to *be*? First: "I take it," says the Book, "to be such as no man can by learning define, nor by wisdom search out." Is that so? Then I go by the Book. And next: what does the same Word or very near it (I speak of the Apocrypha) say of their *purpose*? It says—and correct me if I go astray—"Devils are creatures made by God, and *that for vengeance*."

'So far, so good, sir. We stop when we can go no further. Vengeance. But of their power, of what they can *do*, I can give you definite evidences. It would be a byword if once the rumour was spread abroad. And if it is *not* so, why, I ask, does every expert that comes here leave us in haste and in dismay? They go off with their tails between their legs. They see, they grope in, but they don't believe. They *invent* reasons. And they *hasten* to leave us!' His face shook with the emphasis he laid upon the word. 'Why? Why, because the experience is beyond their knowledge, sir.' He drew back breathless and, as I could see, profoundly moved.

'But surely,' I said, 'every old building is bound in time to show symptoms of decay. Half the cathedrals in England, half its churches, even, of any age, have been "restored"— and in many cases with ghastly results. This new grouting and so on. Why, only the other day. . . . All I mean is, why should you suppose mere wear and tear should be caused by any other agency than——'

The old man turned away. 'I must apologize,' he interrupted me with his inimitable admixture of modesty and dignity. 'I am a poor mouth at explanations, sir. Decay— stress—strain—settling—dissolution: I have heard those words bandied from lip to lip like a game at cup and ball. They fill me with nausea. Why, I am speaking not of dissolution, sir, but of *repairs, restorations*. Not decay, *strengthening*. Not a corroding loss, an awful *progress*. I could show you places—and chiefly obscured from direct view and difficult of a close examination, sir, where stones lately as rotten as pumice and as fretted as a sponge have been replaced by others fresh-quarried—and nothing of their kind within twenty miles.

'There are spots where massive blocks a yard or more square have been *pushed* into place by sheer force. All Hallows is safer at this moment than it has been for three hundred years. They meant well—them who came to see, full of talk and fine language, and went dumb away. I grant you they meant well. I allow that. They hummed and they hawed. They smirked this and they shrugged that. But at heart, sir, they were cowed—horrified: all at a loss. Their very faces showed it. But if you ask me for what purpose such doings are afoot—I have no answer; none.

'But now, supposing you yourself, sir, were one of them, with *your* repute at stake, and you were called in to look at a house which the owners of it and them who had it in trust were disturbed by its being re-edificated and restored by some agency unknown to them. Supposing that! *Why*,' and he rapped with his knuckles on the table, 'being human *and not one of us* mightn't you be going away too with mouth shut, because you didn't want to get talked about to your disadvantage? And wouldn't you at last dismiss the whole thing as a foolish delusion, in the belief that living in out-of-the-way parts like these cuts a man off from the world, breeds maggots in the mind?

'I assure you, sir, they don't—not even Canon Ockham himself to the full—they don't believe even me. And yet, when they have their meetings of the Chapter they talk and wrangle round and round about nothing else. I can bear the other without a murmur. What God sends, I say, we humans deserve. We have laid ourselves open to it. But when you buttress up blindness and wickedness with downright folly, why then, sir, I sometimes fear for my own reason.'

He set his shoulders as square as his aged frame would permit, and with fingers clutching the lapels beneath his chin, he stood gazing out into the darkness through that narrow inward window.

'Ah, sir,' he began again, 'I have not spent sixty years in this solitary place without paying heed to my own small wandering thoughts and instincts. Look at your newspapers, sir. What they call the Great War is over—and he'd be a brave man who would take an oath before heaven that *that* was only of human designing—and yet what do we see around us? Nothing but strife and juggleries and hatred and contempt and discord wherever you look. I am no scholar, sir, but so far as my knowledge and experience carry me, we human beings are living to-day merely from hand to mouth. We learn to-day what ought to have been done yesterday, and yet are at a loss to know what's to be done to-morrow.

'And the Church, sir. God forbid I should push my way into what does not concern me; and if you had told me half an hour gone by that you were a regular churchman, I shouldn't be pouring out all this to you now. It wouldn't be seemly. But being not so gives me confidence. By merely listening you can help me, sir; though you can't help *us*. Centuries ago—and in my humble judgement, rightly—we broke away from the parent stem and rooted ourselves in our own soil. But, right or wrong, doesn't that of itself, I ask you, make us all the more open to attack from him who never wearies in going to and fro in the world seeking whom he may devour?

'I am not wishing you to take sides. But a gentleman doesn't scoff; you don't find him jeering at what he doesn't rightly understand. He keeps his own counsel, sir. And that's where, as I say, Canon Leigh Shougar sets me doubting. He refuses to make allowances; though up there in London things may look different. He gets his company there; and then for him the whole kallyidoscope changes, if you take me.'

The old man scanned me an instant as if inquiring within himself whether, after all, I too might not be one of the outcasts. 'You see, sir,' he went on dejectedly, 'I can bear what may be to come. I can, if need be, live on through what few years may yet remain to me and keep going, as they say. But only if I can be assured that my own inmost senses are not cheating and misleading me. Tell me the worst, and you will have done an old man a service he can never repay. Tell me, on the other hand, that I am merely groping along in a network of devilish *delusion*, sir—well, in that case I hope to be with my master, with Dr. Pomfrey, as soon as possible. We were all children once; and now there's nothing worse in this world for him to come into, in a manner of speaking.

'Oh, sir, I sometimes wonder if what we call childhood and growing up isn't a copy of the fate of our ancient forefathers. In the beginning of time there were Fallen Angels, we are told; but even if it weren't there in Holy Writ, we might have learnt it of our own fears and misgivings. I sometimes find myself looking at a young child with little short of awe, sir, knowing that within its mind is a scene of peace and paradise of which we older folk have no notion, and which will fade away out of it, as life wears on, like the mere tabernacling of a dream.'

There was no trace of unction in his speech, though the phraseology might suggest it, and he smiled at me as if in reassurance. 'You see, sir—if I have any true notion of the matter—then I say, heaven is dealing very gently with Dr. Pomfrey. He has gone back, and, I take it, his soul is elsewhere and at rest.'

He had come a pace or two nearer, and the candlelight now cast grotesque shadows in the hollows of his brows and cheekbones, silvering his long scanty hair. The eyes, dimming with age, were fixed on mine as if in incommunicable entreaty. I was at a loss to answer him.

He dropped his hands to his sides. 'The fact is,' he looked cautiously about him, 'what I am now being so bold as to suggest, though it's a familiar enough experience to me, may put you in actual physical danger. But then, duty's duty, and a deed of kindness from stranger to stranger quite another matter. You seem to have come, if I may say so, in the nick of time; that was all. On the other hand, we can leave the building at once if you are so minded. In any case we must be gone well before dark sets in; even mere human beings are best not disturbed at any night-work they may be after. The dark brings recklessness: conscience cannot see as clear in the dark. Besides, I once delayed too long myself. There is not much of day left even now, though I see by the almanac there should be a slip of moon to-night—unless the sky is over-clouded. All that I'm meaning is that our all-in-all, so to speak, is the calm untrammelled evidence of the outer senses, sir. And there comes a time when—well, when one hesitates to trust one's own.'

I have read somewhere that it is only its setting—the shape, the line, the fold, the angle of the lid and so on—that gives its finer shades of meaning and significance to the human eye. Looking into his, even in that narrow and melancholy illumination, was like pondering over a grey, salt, desolate pool—such as sometimes neighbours the sea on a flat and dangerous coast.

Perhaps if I had been a little less credulous, or less exhausted, I should by now have begun to doubt this old creature's sanity. And yet, surely, at even the faintest contact with the insane, a sentinel in the mind sends up flares and warnings; the very landscape changes; there is a sense of insecurity. If, too, the characters inscribed by age and experience on a man's face can be evidence of goodness and simplicity, then my companion was safe enough. To trust in his sagacity was another matter.

But then, there was All Hallows itself to take into account. That first glimpse from my green headland of its louring yet lovely walls had been strangely moving. There are buildings (almost as though they were once copies of originals now half-forgotten in the human mind) that have a singular influence on the imagination. Even now in this remote candlelit room, immured between its massive stones, the vast edifice seemed to be gently and furtively fretting its impression on my mind.

I glanced again at the old man: he had turned aside as if to leave me, unbiased, to my own decision. How would a lifetime spent between these sombre walls have affected *me*, I wondered? Surely it would be an act of mere decency to indulge their worn-out hermit! He had appealed to me. If I were ten times more reluctant to follow him, I could hardly refuse. Not at any rate without risking a retreat as humiliating as that of the architectural experts he had referred to—with my tail between my legs.

'I only wish I could hope to be of any real help.'

He turned about; his expression changed, as if at the coming of a light. 'Why, then, sir, let us be gone at once. You are with me, sir: that was all I hoped and asked. And now there's no time to waste.'

He tilted his head to listen a moment—with that large, flat, shell-like ear of his which age alone seems to produce. 'Matches and candle, sir,' he had lowered his voice to a whisper, 'but—though we mustn't lose each other; you and me, I mean—*not*, I think, a naked light. What I would suggest, if you have no objection, is your kindly grasping my gown. There is a kind of streamer here, you see—as if made for the purpose. There will be a good deal of up-and-downing, but I know the building blindfold and as you might say inch by inch. And now that the bell-ringers have given up ringing it is more in my charge than ever.'

He stood back and looked at me with folded hands, a whimsical childlike smile on his aged face. 'I sometimes think to myself I'm like the sentry, sir, in that play by William Shakespeare. I saw it, sir, years ago, on my only visit to London—when I was a boy. If ever there were a villain for all his fine talk and all, commend me to that ghost. I see him yet.'

Whisper though it was, a sort of chirrup had come into his voice, like that of a cricket in a baker's shop. I took tight hold of the velveted tag of his gown. He opened the door, pressed the box of safety matches into my hand, himself grasped the candlestick and then blew out the light. We were instantly marooned in an impenetrable darkness. 'Now, sir, if you would kindly remove your walking shoes,' he muttered close in my ear, 'we should proceed with less noise. I shan't hurry you. And please to tug at the streamer if you need attention. In a few minutes the blackness will be less intense.'

As I stooped down to loose my shoe-laces I heard my heart thumping merrily away. It had been listening to our conversation apparently! I slung my shoes round my neck—as I had often done as a boy when going paddling—and we set out on our expedition.

I have endured too often the nightmare of being lost and abandoned in the stony bowels of some strange and prodigious building to take such an adventure lightly. I clung, I confess, desperately tight to my lifeline and we groped steadily onward —my guide ever and again turning back to mutter warning or encouragement in my ear.

Now I found myself steadily ascending; and then in a while, feeling my way down flights of hollowly worn stone steps, and anon brushing along a gallery or corkscrewing up a newel staircase so narrow that my shoulders all but touched the walls on either side. In spite of the sepulchral chill in these bowels of the cathedral, I was soon suffocatingly hot, and the effort to see became intolerably fatiguing. Once, to recover our breath we paused opposite a slit in the thickness of the masonry, at which to breathe the tepid sweetness of the outer air. It was faint with the scent of wild flowers and cool of the sea. And presently after, at a barred window, high overhead, I caught a glimpse of the night's first stars.

We then turned inward once more, ascending yet another spiral staircase. And now the intense darkness had thinned a little, the groined roof above us becoming faintly discernible. A fresher air softly fanned my cheek; and then trembling fingers groped over my breast, and, cold and bony, clutched my own.

'Dead still here, sir, if you please.' So close sounded the whispered syllables the voice might have been a messenger's within my own consciousness. 'Dead still, here. There's a drop of some sixty or seventy feet a few paces on.'

I peered out across the abyss, conscious, as it seemed, of the huge superincumbent weight of the noble fretted roof only a small space now immediately above our heads. As we approached the edge of this stony precipice, the gloom paled a little, and I guessed that we must be standing in some coign of the southern transept, for what light the evening skies now afforded was clearer towards the right. On the other hand, it seemed the northern windows opposite us were most of them boarded up, or obscured in some fashion. Gazing out, I could detect scaffolding poles—like knitting needles—thrust out from the walls and a balloon-like spread of canvas above them. For the moment my ear was haunted by what appeared to be the droning of an immense insect. But this presently ceased. I fancy it was internal only.

'You will understand, sir,' breathed the old man close beside me—and we still stood, grotesquely enough, hand in hand— 'the scaffolding over there has been in position a good many months now. It was put up when the last gentleman came down from London to inspect the fabric. And there it's been left ever since. Now, sir!—though I implore you to be cautious.'

I hardly needed the warning. With one hand clutching my box of matches, the fingers of the other interlaced with my companion's, I strained every sense. And yet I could detect not the faintest stir or murmur under that wide-spreading roof. Only a hush as profound as that which must reign in the Royal Chamber of the pyramid of Cheops faintly swirled in the labyrinths of my ear.

How long we stayed in this position I cannot say; but minutes sometimes seem like hours. And then, without the slightest warning, I became aware of a peculiar and incessant vibration. It is impossible to give a name to it. It suggested the remote whirring of an enormous mill-stone, or that—though without definite pulsation—of revolving wings, or even the spinning of an immense top.

In spite of his age, my companion apparently had ears as acute as mine. He had clutched me tighter a full ten seconds before I myself became aware of this disturbance of the air. He pressed closer. 'Do you see that, sir?'

I gazed and gazed, and saw nothing. Indeed even in what I had seemed to *hear* I might have been deceived. Nothing is more treacherous in certain circumstances—except possibly the eye—than the ear. It magnifies, distorts, and may even invent. As instantaneously as I had become aware of it, the murmur had ceased. And then—though I cannot be certain—it seemed the dingy and voluminous spread of canvas over there had perceptibly trembled, as if a huge cautious hand had been thrust out to draw it aside. No time was given me to make sure. The old man had hastily withdrawn me into the opening of the wall through which we had issued; and we made no pause in our retreat until we had come again to the narrow slit of window which I have spoken of and could refresh ourselves with a less stagnant air. We stood here resting awhile.

'Well, sir?' he inquired at last, in the same flat muffled tones.

'Do you ever pass along here alone?' I whispered.

'Oh, yes, sir. I make it a habit to be the last to leave—and often the first to come; but I am usually gone by this hour.'

I looked close at the dim face in profile against that narrow oblong of night. 'It is so difficult to be sure of oneself,' I said. 'Have you ever actually *encountered* anything—near at hand, I mean?'

'I keep a sharp look-out, sir. Maybe they don't think me of enough importance to molest—the last rat, as they say.'

'But *have* you?'—I might myself have been communicating with the phantasmal *genius loci* of All Hallows—our muffled voices; this intense caution and secret listening; the slight breathlessness, as if at any instant one's heart were ready for flight: 'But *have* you?'

'Well yes, sir,' he said. 'And in this very gallery. They nearly had me, sir. But by good fortune there's a recess a little further on—stored up with some old fragments of carving, from the original building, sixth-century, so it's said: stone-capitals, heads and hands, and such like. I had had my warning, and managed to lep in there and conceal myself. But only just in time. Indeed, sir, I confess I was in such a condition of terror and horror I turned my back.'

'You mean you heard, but didn't look? And—something came?'

'Yes, sir, I seemed to be reduced to no bigger than a child, huddled up there in that corner. There was a sound like clanging metal—but I don't think it was metal. It drew near at a furious speed, then passed me, making a filthy gust of wind. For some instants I couldn't breathe; the air was gone.'

'And no other sound?'

'No other, sir, except out of the distance a noise like the sounding of a stupendous kind of gibberish. A calling; or so it seemed—no human sound. The air shook with it. You see, sir, I myself wasn't of any consequence, I take it—unless a mere obstruction in the way. But—I have heard it said somewhere that the rarity of these happenings is only because it's a pain and torment and not any sort of pleasure for such beings, such apparitions, sir, good or bad, to visit our outward world. That's what I have heard said; though I can go no further.

'The time I'm telling you of was in the early winter—November. There was a dense sea-fog over the valley, I remember. It eddied through that opening there into the candlelight like flowing milk. I never light up now: and, if I

316

may be forgiven the boast, sir, I seem to have almost forgotten how to be afraid. After all, in any walk of life a man can only do his best, and if there weren't such opposition and hindrances in high places I should have nothing to complain of. What is anybody's life, sir (come past the gaiety of youth), but marking time. . . . Did you hear anything *then*, sir?'

His gentle monotonous mumbling ceased and we listened together. But every ancient edifice has voices and soundings of its own: there was nothing audible that I could put a name to, only what seemed to be a faint perpetual stir or whirr of grinding such as (to one's over-stimulated senses) the stablest stones set one on top of the other with an ever slightly varying weight and stress might be likely to make perceptible in a world of matter. A world which, after all, they say, is itself in unimaginably rapid rotation, and under the tyranny of time.

'No, I hear nothing,' I answered: 'but please don't think I am doubting what you say. Far from it. You must remember I am a stranger, and that therefore the influence of the place cannot but be less apparent to me. And you have no help in this now?'

'No, sir. Not now. But even at the best of times we had small company hereabouts, and no money. Not for any substantial outlay, I mean. And not even the boldest suggests making what's called a public appeal. It's a strange thing to me, sir, but whenever the newspapers get hold of anything, they turn it into a byword and a sham. Yet how can they help themselves?—with no beliefs to guide them and nothing to stay their mouths except about what for sheer human decency's sake they daren't talk about. But then, who am I to complain? And now, sir,' he continued with a sigh of utter weariness, 'if you are sufficiently rested, would you perhaps follow me on to the roof? It is the last visit I make—though by rights perhaps I should take in what there is of the tower. But I'm too old now for that—clambering and climbing over naked beams; and the ladders are not so safe as they were.'

We had not far to go. The old man drew open a squat heavily-ironed door at the head of a flight of wooden steps. It was latched but not bolted, and admitted us at once to the leaden roof of the building and to the immense amphitheatre of evening. The last faint hues of sunset were fading in the west; and silver-bright Spica shared with the tilted crescent of the moon the serene lagoon-like expanse of sky above the sea. Even at this height, the air was audibly stirred with the low lullaby of the tide.

The staircase by which we had come out was surmounted by a flat penthouse roof about seven feet high. We edged softly along, then paused once more; to find ourselves now all but *tête-à-tête* with the gigantic figures that stood sentinel at the base of the buttresses to the unfinished tower.

The tower was so far unfinished, indeed, as to wear the appearance of the ruinous; besides which, what appeared to be scars and stains as if of fire were detectable on some of its stones, reminding me of the legend which years before I had chanced upon, that this stretch of coast had more than once been visited centuries ago by pillaging Norsemen.

The night was unfathomably clear and still. On our left rose the conical bluff of the headland crowned with the solitary grove of trees beneath which I had taken refuge from the blinding sunshine that very afternoon. Its grasses were now hoary with faintest moonlight. Far to the right stretched the flat cold plain of the Atlantic—that enormous darkened looking-glass of space; only a distant lightship ever and again stealthily signalling to us with a lean phosphoric finger from its outermost reaches.

The mere sense of that abysm of space—its waste powdered with the stars of the Milky Way; the mere presence of the stony leviathan on whose back we two humans now stood, dwarfed into insignificance beside these gesturing images of stone, were enough of themselves to excite the imagination. And—whether matter-of-fact or pure delusion—this old verger's insinuations that the cathedral was now menaced by some inconceivable danger and assault had set my nerves on edge. My feet were numb as the lead they stood upon; while the tips of my fingers tingled as if a powerful electric discharge were coursing through my body.

We moved gently on—the spare shape of the old man a few steps ahead, peering cautiously to right and left of him as we advanced. Once with a hasty gesture he drew me back and fixed his eyes for a full minute on a figure—at two removes—which was silhouetted at that moment against the starry emptiness: a forbidding thing enough, viewed in this vague luminosity, which seemed in spite of the unmoving stare that I fixed on it to be perceptibly stirring on its windworn pedestal.

But no; 'All's well!' the old man had mutely signalled to me, and we pushed on. Slowly and cautiously; indeed I had time to notice in passing that this particular figure held stretched in its right hand a bent bow, and was crowned with a high weather-worn stone coronet. One and all were frigid company. At last we completed our circuit of the tower, had come back to the place we had set out from, and stood eyeing one another like two conspirators in the clear dusk. Maybe there was a tinge of incredulity on my face.

'No, sir,' murmured the old man, 'I expected no other. The night is uncommonly quiet. I've noticed that before. They seem to leave us at peace on nights of quiet. We must turn in again and be getting home.'

Until that moment I had thought no more of where I was to sleep or to get food, nor had even realized how famished with hunger I was. Nevertheless, the notion of fumbling down again out of the open air into the narrow inward blackness of the walls from which we had just issued was singularly un-inviting. Across these wide flat stretches of roof there was at least space for flight, and there were recesses for concealment. To gain a moment's respite, I inquired if I should have much difficulty in getting a bed in the village. And as I had hoped, the old man himself offered me hospitality.

I thanked him; but still hesitated to follow, for at that moment I was trying to discover what peculiar effect of dusk and darkness a moment before had deceived me into the belief that some small animal—a dog, a spaniel I should have guessed —had suddenly and surreptitiously taken cover behind the stone buttress nearby. But that apparently had been a mere illusion. The creature, whatever it might be, was no barker at any rate. Nothing stirred now; and my companion seemed to have noticed nothing amiss.

'You were saying', I pressed him, 'that when repairs— restorations—of the building were in contemplation, even the experts were perplexed by what they discovered? What did they actually say?'

'Say, sir!' Our voices sounded as small and meaningless up here as those of grasshoppers in a noonday meadow. 'Examine that balustrade which you are leaning against at this minute. Look at that gnawing and fretting—that furrowing above the lead. All that is honest wear and tear—constant weathering of the mere elements, sir—rain and wind and snow and frost. That's honest *nature*-work, sir. But now compare it, if you please, with this St. Mark here; and remember, sir, these images were intended to be part and parcel of the fabric as you might say, sentries on a castle—symbols, you understand.'

I stooped close under the huge grey creature of stone until my eyes were scarcely more than six inches from its pedestal. And, unless the moon deceived me, I confess I could find not the slightest trace of fret or friction. Far from it. The stone had been grotesquely decorated in low relief with a gaping crocodile—a two-headed crocodile; and the angles, knubs and undulations of the creature were cut as sharp as with a knife in cheese. I drew back.

'Now cast your glance upwards, sir. Is that what you would call a saintly shape and gesture?'

What appeared to represent an eagle was perched on the image's lifted wrist—an eagle resembling a vulture. The head beneath it was poised at an angle of defiance—its ears abnormally erected on the skull; the lean right forearm extended with pointing forefinger as if in derision. Its stony gaze was fixed upon the stars; its whole aspect was hostile, sinister and intimidating. I drew aside. The faintest puff of milk-warm air from over the sea stirred on my cheek.

'Ay, sir, and so with one or two of the rest of them,' the old man commented, as he watched me, 'there are other wills than the Almighty's.'

At this, the pent-up excitement within me broke bounds. This nebulous insinuatory talk!—I all but lost my temper. 'I can't, for the life of me, understand what you are saying,' I exclaimed in a voice that astonished me with its shrill volume of sound in that intense lofty quiet. 'One doesn't *repair* in order to destroy.'

The old man met me without flinching. 'No, sir? Say you so? And why not? Are there not two kinds of change in this world?—a building-up and a breaking-down? To give strength and endurance for evil or misguided purposes, would that be power wasted, if such was your aim? Why, sir, isn't that true even of the human mind and heart? We here are on the outskirts, I grant, but where would you expect the enemy to show himself unless in the outer defences? An institution may be beyond saving, sir: it may be being restored for a worse destruction. And a hundred trumpeting voices would make no difference when the faith and life within is tottering to its fall.'

Somehow, this muddle of metaphors reassured me. Obviously the old man's wits had worn a little thin: he was the victim of an intelligible but monstrous hallucination.

'And yet you are taking it for granted,' I expostulated, 'that, if what you say is true, a stranger could be of the slightest help. A visitor—mind you—who hasn't been inside the doors of a church, except in search of what is old and obsolete, for years.'

The old man laid a trembling hand upon my sleeve. The folly of it—with my shoes hanging like ludicrous millstones round my neck!

'If you please, sir,' he pleaded, 'have a little patience with me. I'm preaching at nobody. I'm not even hinting that them outside the fold circumstantially speaking aren't of the flock. All in good time, sir; the Almighty's time. Maybe—with all due respect—it's from them within we have most to fear. And indeed, sir, believe an old man: I could never express the gratitude I feel. You have given me the occasion to unbosom myself, to make a clean breast, as they say. All Hallows is my earthly home, and—well, there, let us say no more. You couldn't *help me*—except only by your presence here. God alone knows who can!'

At that instant, a dull enormous rumble reverberated from within the building—as if a huge boulder or block of stone had been shifted or dislodged in the fabric; a peculiar grinding nerve-wracking sound. And for the fraction of a second the flags on which we stood seemed to tremble beneath our feet.

The fingers tightened on my arm. 'Come, sir; keep close; we must be gone at once' the quavering old voice whispered; 'we have stayed too long.'

But we emerged into the night at last without mishap. The little western door, above which the grinning head had welcomed me on my arrival, admitted us to *terra firma* again, and we made our way up a deep sandy track, bordered by clumps of hemp agrimony and fennel and hemlock, with viper's bugloss and sea-poppy blooming in the gentle dusk of night at our feet. We turned when we reached the summit of this sandy incline and looked back. All Hallows, vague and enormous, lay beneath us in its hollow, resembling some natural prehistoric outcrop of that sea-worn rock-bound coast; but strangely human and saturnine.

The air was mild as milk—a pool of faintest sweetnesses—gorse, bracken, heather; and not a rumour disturbed its calm, except only the furtive and stertorous sighings of the tide. But far out to sea and beneath the horizon summer lightnings were now in idle play—flickering into the sky like the unfolding of a signal, planet to planet—then gone. That alone, and perhaps too this feeble moonlight glinting on the ancient glass, may have accounted for the faint vitreous glare that seemed ever and again to glitter across the windows of the northern transept far beneath us. And yet how easily deceived is the imagination. This old man's talk still echoing in my ear, I could have vowed this was no reflection but the glow of some light shining fitfully from within outwards.

We paused together beside a flowering bush of fuchsia at the wicket-gate leading into his small square of country garden. 'You'll forgive me, sir, for mentioning it; but I make it a rule as far as possible to leave all my troubles and misgivings outside when I come home. My daughter is a widow, and not long in that sad condition, so I keep as happy a face as I can on things. And yet: well, sir, I wonder at times if—if a personal sacrifice isn't incumbent on them that have their object most at heart. I'd go out myself very willingly, sir, I can assure you, if there was any certainty in my mind that it would serve the cause. It would be little to me if——' He made no attempt to complete the sentence.

On my way to bed, that night, the old man led me in on tiptoe to show me his grandson. His daughter watched me intently as I stooped over the child's cot—with that bird-like solicitude which all mothers show in the presence of a stranger.

Her small son was of that fairness which almost suggests the unreal. He had flung back his bedclothes—as if innocence in this world needed no covering or defence—and lay at ease, the dews of sleep on lip, cheek, and forehead. He was breathing so quietly that not the least movement of shoulder or narrow breast was perceptible.

'The lovely thing!' I muttered, staring at him. 'Where is he now, I wonder?' His mother lifted her face and smiled at me with a drowsy ecstatic happiness, then sighed.

And from out of the distance, there came the first prolonged whisper of a wind from over the sea. It was eleven by my watch, the storm after the long heat of the day seemed to be drifting inland; but All Hallows, apparently, had forgotten to wind its clock.

THE TRUMPET

*

'For Brutus, as you know, was Caesar's angel . . .'
'And he said . . . Am I my brother's keeper?'

The minute church, obscurely lit by a full moon that had not yet found window-glass through which her direct beams could pierce into its gloaming, was deserted and silent. Not a sound, within or without, disturbed its stony quiet—except only the insect-like rapid ticking of a clock in the vestry, and the low pulsating thump of a revolving cogwheel in the tower above the roof. Here and there a polished stone gleamed coldly in the vague luminous haze—a marble head, a wing-tip, a pointing finger, the claws and beak of the eagle on the brazen lectern, the two silvergilt candlesticks flanking the colourless waxen flowers upon the altar. So secret and secluded seemed the church within its nocturnal walls that living creature might never have been here at all—or creatures only so insignificant and transitory as to have left no perceptible trace behind them.

Like a cataleptic's countenance it hinted moreover at no inward activity of its own. And yet, if—fantastic notion— some unseen watcher through the bygone centuries had kept it perpetually within gaze, he might at last have concluded that it possessed a *sort* of stagnant life or animation, at least in its passive obedience to the influences of time, change, decay, and the laws of gravitation. Now it revealed not the faintest symptom of it. If, on the other hand, any immaterial sentinel were still, as ever, on guard within it, he made no sign of his presence here.

Unhasteningly, like water dripping from a fateful urn, the thump-recorded moments ebbed away; and it was approaching midnight and first cockcrow when from beyond the thick stone chancel walls there came the sound of a stealthy footfall, crunching the rain-soaked gravel. An owl squawked, the footsteps ceased; and after a brief pause, began again. The groping rattle of a key in the wards of a lock followed, and presently— with a motion so slow that it was barely perceptible—the heavy curtain that hung over the entrance to the vestry began as if with an extreme caution to be drawn aside; and the slender cone-shaped rays from the thick glass of a small bull's-eye lantern—its radiance thinning into the dusk of the moonlight as it expanded in area—to funnel inquisitively to and fro.

The lantern-bearer himself now appeared—a small boy. His thick fair hair was tousled over a pale forehead, his mouth was ajar and his lips were drawn back a little above his teeth, his eyes gleamed as they moved. The collar of his dark greatcoat had been turned up about his ears, but nevertheless disclosed in the crevice between its lapels the stripes of his pyjama's jacket which had been tucked into a pair of old flannel breeches. Stockinged ankles and damp mud-stained rubber shoes showed beneath the greatcoat. His cheeks at this moment were so pale as scarcely to be tinged with red, and since the pupils of his blue eyes were dilated to their full extent they appeared to be all but jet-black. He was shivering, in part by reason of the cold, in part because of certain inward qualms and forebodings. Only by an effort was he preventing his teeth from beginning to chatter. Still acutely cautious and intent, his head thrust forward, his eyes searching the darker recesses of the building around him as they followed the direction of his tiny searchlight, he stole a pace or two forward, the border of the heavy curtain furtively swinging-to behind him. In spite of the door-key safe in his pocket, he appeared to be divided in mind between hope and dread that he might prove to be not the sole occupant of the church.

Where there is space enough for the human cranium to pass, the shoulders, it is said, can follow; and particularly if they all three belong to a child. One small diamond-paned window in the vestry he had already observed was open. Images, too, less substantial in appearance than those of human beings were occupying his mind's eye. When then a little owl in the dark of the yew tree over the south gate in the moonlit churchyard again suddenly screeched, he started as if at an electric shock. And twice his mouth opened before he managed to call low and hoarsely, 'Are you there, Dick? . . . Dick, are you there?'

Not a stony eyelid in the heads around him had so much as flickered at this timid challenge. The stooping eagle—a large shut Bible on its outstretched wings—had stirred not a feather; the pulpit remained cavernously empty. But a few high-panelled pews, relics of the past, were within view, and even moonlight and lantern-light combined were powerless to reveal anything or anybody that might be hiding behind them. The trespasser appeared to be on the point of retiring as secretly as he had come, when a jangling gurgle, as of some monster muttering in its sleep, began to sound above his head, and the clock chimes rang out the second quarter of the hour. The vibrant metal ceased to hum; and, as if reassured by this interruption, he drew out of his pocket a large stone— a flint such as his remote ancestors would have coveted— roughly dumb-bell in shape, and now waisted with a thick and knotted length of old blindcord. This primitive weapon, long treasured for any emergency, he gently deposited on the shelf behind him, and then followed it into the pew.

Lantern still in hand, he seated himself on the flat faded red cushion that lay along the seat. It was that of one of the mighty, the rector's warden. Even in this half-light, as easily as a cat in the dark, he could spy out all about him now, organ-recess to gallery; but he opened his brand-new lantern none the less and trimmed as best he could with his finger nail its charred and oily wick. The fume and stench of the hot metal made him sneeze, whereupon he clicked-to the glass, covered it with his hand, and began listening again. 'Sneak,' he muttered, then suddenly plumped down on the hassock at his feet, rapidly repeated a prayer, with a glance over his shoulder half-covertly crossed himself, then as promptly sat up again; glancing as he did so at the pulpit over his head which he was accustomed to find comfortably brimmed with his father's portly presence.

Fortified by his prayer and by his wrath with the friend who it seemed at the last moment had abandoned their enterprise, he was now comparatively at ease. Tortoise-fashion he snuggled down in his great-coat in the corner of the pew, having discovered that by craning his neck a little he could fix his vacant eyes on the brilliant disc of the still-ascending moon.

She was the Hunter's moon, and her beams had now begun to silver a clear-glassed square-headed window high up in the south wall of the chancel. He watched her intently, lost in astonishment that at this very moment she should be keeping tryst with him here. But before she had edged far enough above the sill to greet the gilded figure of an angel that surmounted an ornate tomb opposite her peephole, a faint thief-like shuffle from the direction of the vestry door caught his ear. He instantly dropped out of sight into the shelter of his pew. The shuffling ceased, the door creaked. He crouched low; a smile at once apprehensive and malicious creasing his still-childish face. He would give his friend Dick a taste of his own physic.

In the hush, an anguished *Oh, oh, oh, oh!*—like the wailing of a lost soul, fountained up from his lips into the dusk of the roof. *Oh, oh, oh!* Then silence—and silence. And still there came no response. The smile faded out of his face; he had begun to shiver again. He was positively certain that this must be the friend whom he was expecting. And yet—suppose it was not! He leapt up, flashing at the same instant his toy lantern full into the glittering eyes of a dwarfish and motionless shape which were fixed on him through the sockets of a pitch-black battered mask—a relic of the last Fifth of November.

He had realized what trick was being played on him almost before he had time to be afraid. Nevertheless, for a few moments, his mouth wide-open, he had failed to breathe; and stood shuddering with rage as well as terror. His friend Dick, however, having emerged from his lair in the folds of the curtain, was now plunging about half doubled-up and almost helpless with laughter.

'You silly fool!' he fumed at him in a whisper, 'what did you want to do that for? Shut up! Shut *up*, I tell you! You think it's funny, I suppose. Well, I don't. You're hours late already, and I'm going home. Stop it, do you hear? Can't you remember you're in a *church*?'

From beneath its mask a small sharp-nosed and utterly sober face now showed itself—all laughter gone. 'Who began it, then?' Dick expostulated, dejectedly squeezing his pasteboard mask into his pocket. 'You tried it first on me, with your Oh-oh-oh-ing. And now just because . . . You didn't think of "church" then.'

'Well, I do now. Besides, it's near the time, and I might have broken my neck for all you cared, getting out of the window. What made you so late?'

Dick had been eyeing his friend as might a sorrowful mouse a slice of plum cake a few inches out of its reach. 'I'm sorry, Philip,' he said. 'I didn't mean any harm; honest, I didn't. It was only a lark.' He turned penitently away, and the next instant, as if all troubles were over and all discord pacified, began peeping about him with the movements and anglings of some little night-creature on unexpectedly finding itself in an utterly strange place.

'I say, Philip,' he whispered, 'doesn't it look creepy, just—the moon shining in? I had a dream, and then I woke. But I couldn't have come before. My father was downstairs with a lamp, reading. Besides I was waiting for you *out*side, under the trees. Why did you come *in*? It's by the gate you see them. That's what my mother heard *your* mother say. Oh, I'm glad I came; aren't you?'

The sentences were sprayed out in minute beads of words like the hasty cadenzas of a bird. The neat black head, the small bright eyes, the shallow wall of close-cropped hair, the sloping shoulders—every line, movement and quick darting variation of posture gave him a resemblance to a bird—including the alert, quick, shy yet fearless spirit within that neat skull's brittle walls.

Philip, who had been intently watching him meanwhile, had now recovered his equanimity, his pulse had sobered down, but he was still only partially placated, and querulous.

'Of course I came in. What was the good of loafing out there where *any*body might see us? It's cold and mouldy enough in here. You don't seem to remember I mustn't go out at night, because of my chest. I've been waiting until my feet are like stones. Did you hear that owl just now—or something?'

Dick having at last ventured in from the other end of the pew, had now seated himself beside his friend on the flat crimson cushion.

'Golly!' he exclaimed, his sharp eyes now fixed on the flint, 'what's that for? I shouldn't care to have a crump over the head with that!' He peered up winningly into his companion's fair face. 'I didn't really expect you would come, Philip. But', he sighed, 'I'm glad.'

'Didn't I *say* I would come?' retorted Philip in a small condescending voice. 'That's nothing.' He nodded at his stone. 'I always carry that at night. How was I to know. . .? *Didn't* I?'

The neat small head nodded violently. 'M'm.'

'Then why didn't you expect me to?'

'Oh, well, I didn't.' A thin ingratiating little smile passed over Dick's face and as quickly vanished. 'It wasn't so easy for you as it was for me. That's why.'

'That stone', said Philip incisively, 'keeps any harm from happening to me. It's got magic in it.'

'Has it, Philip? . . . What did *that*?' He was eyeing the patch of dried blood on the hand that clutched the bent wire handle of the lantern.

'Oh, that?' was the lofty reply. 'That's nothing; that was only the rope. It burned like billy-ho, and I fell half-way from my bedroom window-sill on to the lawn. An awful crack. But nobody heard me, even though the other windows were wide open round the corner. You could see them against the sky. My mother always sleeps with her windows open—all the year round. A doctor in London told her it would be good for her. I don't believe that about your father reading, though. When everybody is in bed and asleep! I didn't even know your father *could* read.'

'Well, he was, or I wouldn't have said so. He was reading the Bible. How could I tell that if he wasn't reading at all?'

'Anyhow, I bet it wasn't the Bible. Even my father wouldn't do that—not after evening prayers. Would he whack you much if he caught you?'

Dick shook his head. 'No fear. My mother won't have *him* punishing me, whatever happens. He preaches at me no end; and says I'll never be good for anything. Once,' he added pensively, as if scarcely able to believe his own ears, 'once he said I was a little imp of hell. Then my mother flared up. But he wouldn't beat me; oh no, he wouldn't beat me. Yesterday my mother came back with a big bundle of old clothes. There was a black silk jacket, and some stockings and hats and feathers and things, an *enormous* bundle. And this—look!'

He undid a button of his jacket and pulled out from underneath it a pinch of an old green silk dressing-gown.

'Why, that's mine!' said Philip. 'I've had it for ages.' He

stared at it censoriously, as if dubious whether or not to ask for it back. 'But I don't think I want it now, because it's miles too small for me. My grandmother gave it me for a Christmas present donkey's years ago. She's so rich she doesn't mind *what* things cost—when she gives me anything. That's real Spitalfields silk, that is; you can't get it anywhere now. You'll crumple it up and spoil it if you wear it stuffed in like that.' He peered closer. 'What have you got on underneath it? You're all puffed out like a turkey-cock.'

Dick promptly edged back from the investigating finger, a sly look of confusion passing swiftly over his face. 'That's my other clothes,' he explained.

'What *I* say,' said Philip, still eyeing his companion as if only a constant vigilance could hope to detect what he might not be up to next, 'what *I* say is, your mother's jolly lucky to get expensive things given to her—good things, even if they *are* left-offs. Most of our old stuff goes to the Jumble Sales. I bet,' he suddenly broke off, 'I bet if your *real* father found you skulking here, he'd whack you hot and strong.'

The alert and supple body beside his own had suddenly stiffened, and the dangling spindle legs beneath the pew ceased to swing.

'No, he wouldn't,' Dick hardly more than whispered.

'Why not?'

'For one thing he just wouldn't. He knows he's nothing to do with me; not now; and leaves me alone. For all that, I went out rabbiting with him one night last summer. And nobody knew. It was warm and still and pitch-dark—not like this; and when the moon began to come up over the woods, he sent me home. I know *he* wouldn't either. Besides,' he drew in his chin a little as if the words were refusing to come out of his throat, 'he's dead.'

'Dead! Oh, I say! I like that! Oh no, he isn't; *that's* not true. *H*e isn't dead. Why, I heard them reading out about him in the newspaper only a few weeks ago. That's what you *say*.

I know what has become of him; and I bet your tongue is burning. What's more, if your other father hadn't been Chapel you would never have had *any* father—not to show, I mean. Your mother would have been just like any other woman, though I don't suppose she could have gone on living in the village. But as he *is* Chapel, and, according to what you say, sits up as late as this reading in the Bible, I can't understand why he lets you sing in our choir. I call *that* a hypocrite. I'd like to see my father letting *me* go to Chapel. He must be just a hypocrite, Bible or not.'

Dick made no attempt whatever to examine this delicate moral question. 'Oh no, he isn't,' he retorted hotly. 'He's as good as yours any day. He goes by what my mother says: if you are Chapel, keep Chapel. *She's* not a hypocrite. And you'd better not say so, either.'

'I didn't say it. I didn't say that your mother was a hypocrite; not a *hypocrite*. I like your mother. And nobody's going to prevent me from going with you either, if I want to. Not if I want to. Your mother's been jolly decent to me—often. Mrs. Fuller sneaks: *she* doesn't.'

'So is your mother to me—when you aren't there. At least she talks to me sometimes then. And I'm glad you're my friend, Philip. The other day she gave me a hunch of cake, and she made me share a sip of wine from my mother's glass. Because it was her birthday. Some day I'm going to be a sailor, and going to sea. She had been crying, because her eyes were red; and *your* mother said that crying was no use at all—because I'm growing up more and more like her every day, and shall be a comfort to her when I'm a man. And so I will; you *see*!'

' "Wine"! Did she just? But that was only because she's always kind to people—to everybody. She doesn't mind *who* it is. That's why she likes being liked by everybody. But after what my father read out in the newspaper, he said he entreated her to be more careful. She must think of *him*, my father said.

He didn't want to have the village people talking. He tapped his eyeglasses on the paper and said it was a standing scandal. That's what he said. He was purple in the face.' His voice rather suddenly fell silent, as if, like a dog, he had scented indiscretions. 'But I say: *if* your real father is just dead, he would be the very person according to you to be coming here to-night. *Then* you'd look mighty funny, I should think.'

Dick's legs, like opposed pendulums, had begun very slug-gishly to swing again. 'Oh no, I wouldn't, because that's just what doesn't happen; and I told you so. It's the people who are going to die soon—next year—who come: *their* ghosts. Wouldn't they look white and awful, Philip, coming in under the yew tree. . . . I expect its roots go down all among the coffins. Shall we go out now and watch? It's as bright as day; you could see a bird hopping about.'

' "Ghosts"!' was the derisive reply. 'I like that! *You* can. I'm not. How can they be ghosts, silly, if they're still alive? Besides, even if there are such things, and even if what your mother told you is really true, you said yourself that they would come *into* the church. So if any *should* come and we keep here and hide and peep over the edge, they can't possibly see us—if ghosts do see. And then we shall be near the door in there. They would be surprised to find that one open, I should think. But even if they were, and ghosts don't mind doors, they wouldn't come in at a potty little door like that.'

He paused as if to listen, and continued more boldly. 'Not, mind you, that I believe a single word of anything you've said —all that stuff. Not really. I came . . .' he faltered, turning his head away, 'only just for a game, and because you dared me to. Why you asked me to come *really* is because you were frightened of being here alone. You wait and see, I'll dare *you* in a minute. Besides, how do you know anybody *is* going to die in the village next year—except old Mrs. Harrison? And she's been dying ever since I can remember. She takes snuff, but she can't stir a foot out of her bed. I bet she hasn't any ghost left. *She* wouldn't come.' The sentence suddenly concluded in a prodigious shuddering yawn. It reminded him that he was cold and that the fatal moment was rapidly nearing. 'Did they say, before, or after, the clock strikes?'

Dick paused a moment before replying, and then piped up confidently: 'It's the very second while the last clump of the bell is sounding. That's when they get to the church. Because it's midnight. And all the ghosts begin to walk then. Some come up out of their graves. But'—he sighed, as if saddened at the poverty of his expectations—'only very seldom. The people who go to heaven wouldn't want to, and the Devil wouldn't let the others out. At least that's what I think.'

'What *you* think! And yet,' retorted Philip indignantly, 'you talk all that stuff about ghosts; and believe it too. I'd just like to see your ghost. That'd be a skinny one if you like—like a starved bird. Would *you* come back?'

Dick leant his body forward; he was sitting on his hands; and at this his black, close-cropped head nodded far more vigorously than a china Mandarin's. 'I don't *know*,' he said; 'but I like being out at night. I like—oh, everything. . . . If ghosts can smell,' he began again in small matter-of-fact tones, 'they'd soon snuff *us* out. Look at it smoking.'

The two boys sat mute for a while, watching the tiny slender thread of sooty smoke from the lantern wreathing up in the luminous air; and in the silence—which, after their tongues had ceased chattering, immediately flooded the church fathoms deep—they stayed, listening; their senses avid for the faintest whisper. But the night was windless, and the earth coldly still in the deathly radiance of the moon. And if the Saints in their splendour were themselves assembled in the heavens to celebrate their earthly festival, no sound of their rejoicings reached these small pricked-up human ears.

'If,' at last Dick exploded, gazing up into the vaporous glooms of the roof above his head, 'if any more light comes

in, the walls will burst. I love the moon; I love the light. . . .
I'm going to have a peep.'

With a galvanic wriggle he had snatched his arm free from
Philip's grasp, had nimbly whipped out of the pew, and
vanished behind the curtain that concealed the vestry door.

Philip shuffled uneasily in his seat, hesitating whether or not
to follow him. But from a native indolence and for other
motives, and in spite of his incredulity, he decided to stay
where he was. It seemed safer than the churchyard. From a
few loose jujubes in his great-coat pocket he chose the cleanest,
and sat quietly sucking, his eyes fixed on the monument that
not only dominated but dwarfed the small but lovely chancel.
The figure of its angel was now bathed with the silver of the
moon. With long-toed feet at once clasping and spurning the
orb beneath them, it stood erect, on high. Chin out-thrust,
its steadfast sightless eyes were fixed upon the faded blue and
geranium red of the panelled roof. Its braided locks drawn
back from a serene and impassive visage, its left hand lay
flat upon its breast, and with the right it clasped a tapering,
uplifted, bell-mouthed, gilded trumpet, held firmly not against
but at a little distance from its lips.

Unlike Dick, Philip was not a chorister. He was none the
less his father's son, and as soon as he had learned to behave
himself, to put his penny in the plate and to refrain from
babbling aloud, he had been taken to church every Sunday
morning. This had been as natural an accompaniment of the
Sabbath as clean underclothes, Etons, and hot sausages for
breakfast. Thus he had heard hundreds of his father's sermons
—sermons usually as simple as they were short. If only he had
listened to them he might by now have become well-founded
in dogma, a plain but four-square theologian. Instead of
listening, however, he would usually sit 'thinking'. Side by
side with his mother, his cheek all but brushing her silks, with
their delicate odours, his fingers—rather clammy fingers when

the weather was hot—lightly clasping hers while he counted over and over the sharp-stoned rings on her dainty fingers, he had been wont to follow his fancies.

Morning service had been the general rule. During the last few years however his mother had become the victim of periodical sick headaches, of lassitude and palpitations, and had been given strict injunctions not to overdo things, to rest. Occasionally too she had worldly-minded visitors, including a highly unorthodox sister, whom it would be tactless even to attempt to persuade to spend her Sundays as, usually, she felt dutifully impelled to spend her own. All this she would confide to Philip. She must on no account, she repeatedly admonished him, be alarmed or worried, distressed or disturbed. As for his stout and rubicund father, who was at least ten years her senior, he adored every bone in her body. But though by nature placable and easy-going, he was also subject to outbursts of temper and fits of moroseness as periodical as her attacks of migraine. It was therefore prudent, if only for her sake, to avoid anything in the nature of a scene. 'So Philip,' she would cajole him, 'you will *promise* me to be a good boy, and you'll go to church this evening, won't you—instead of now? And you won't make any fuss about it? You know your father wishes it.'

Philip might demur, and, if it was practicable, bargain with her; but at heart he much preferred this arrangement. It meant that on these particular Sundays he was safe from interference, and could spend the whole morning as he pleased. It was too the darkening evenings about the time of the equinox, when it was not yet necessary to light the brass oil-lamps that hung in the nave, and two solitary candlesticks alone gleamed spangling in the pulpit—it was these he loved best. Only the village and farm people came to evening service, and not many even of them. Philip would sit in his pew, and, absorbed in his secret cogitations, enjoy the whole hour. The church changed then its very being. It welled over with mystery.

Even in the joy of a Harvest Festival, when he could admire the flowers and vegetables and the gigantic loaf of bread under the lectern, the bloom of grapes and apples, the minute sheaves of wheat and barley gently nodding their heads to the more impulsive strains of the organ, there was still a faint tinge of sadness. And the unheeded sermon drowsed his senses like an incantation. His father's honeyed pulpit voice rose and fell like that of some dulcet Old Man of the Sea; and he himself, though not, like Dick, sporting and whispering noiselessly with his surpliced choir-mates out of sight of the preacher, was at any rate beyond any direct scrutiny. Meanwhile the bulky family cook, his mother's usual proxy on these occasions, would settle down beside him into a state of apathy so complete, her cotton-gloved hands convulsively clasped over her diaphragm, that it was only by an occasional sniff he could tell that she was perhaps leading as active an internal life as he was, and was neither asleep nor dead.

Now and then he had himself been wafted away in sleep into regions of the most exorbitant scenery, events and vagaries; to be aroused suddenly by, 'And now to God, the Father . . .', blear-eyed, lost, and with so violent a start that it had all but dislocated his neck. The most beguiling and habitual of these reveries had been concerned with the angel. How and when his speculations on it had originated, what random bird had dropped this extravagant seed of a hundred daydreams into his mind, was beyond discovery now. But it was to the cook that he had confided his first direct questions concerning it.

One low thundery evening, during their brief solitary journey through the churchyard into the hedged-in narrow lane by the coach-house and stables, and so through the garden and back to the rectory, he had managed to blurt out, 'Mrs. Sullivan, why did they make the angel so as she can't *blow* the trumpet?' And this although his mind had been busied over the wholly different and more advanced problem

—What exactly would happen if for any reason she ever did?

Until this moment Mrs. Sullivan had been unaware of the angel's perpetual predicament, and her attitude was cautious and tentative.

'I *expect*', she said, 'it was because they couldn't help themselves. Besides, Master Philip, what you are talking about isn't a real angel, no more than what her trumpet is a real trumpet. And who's to say if even a real angel could blow a trumpet that isn't real. I wouldn't care to go so far as that myself. Besides who's to know as she is a she?'

Here, in this darker quiet, under the thick-leaved ilexes, Philip always drew a little nearer to his stout and panting companion; and sometimes for reassurance slipped a hand under her elbow. Free again, and the stars visible in the autumn sky, he had ventured to protest.

'But *why* couldn't they? And of course it's a she. Besides it was *I* who said she can't. *I* told *you*. It's three inches at least from her mouth. Like this. I've measured it heaps and heaps of times.'

'"*Measured* it"' Master Philip! Well, that's a nice thing to be getting up to! All I can say is if that's the kind of mischief you are after I don't know what your father wouldn't say.'

'I didn't mean *really*,' was the impatient reply. 'How could I? I meant by looking, of course. How *could* I mean "really"?' There was scorn in his voice, even though his question had fallen like a hint from heaven into the quiet of his mind.

'If it's just guessing,' Mrs. Sullivan had complacently decided, 'I wouldn't suppose it could be *three*. And, though *your* young eyes may be better than mine, it might be no more than just a shadow. . . . It looks as if it had been raining, according to all these puddles.'

Philip had paid no attention to the puddles, except that he had continued to enjoy quietly walking through them. 'But you said just now,' he persisted, 'that you'd never even seen the angel. So how can you possibly tell? Anyhow, it *is* three, it's more than three, it's more likely four or five. You don't seem to remember how far she is up under the roof. Why, the end of her trumpet nearly touches the ceiling. *I* think that was silly. *Why* didn't they?'

They were drifting back to his original riddle again. But Mrs. Sullivan, reminded of another kind of trumpet, was meditating vaguely at this moment on a deaf bedridden sister who lived in the Midlands. 'I never knew a boy with so many questions,' she answered him ruminatively, almost as if she were explaining the situation to a third party. 'I suppose it's because the Last Day hasn't risen on us as yet. That at least is what it was meant to mean for the gentleman that's laid in the tomb beneath it—and for all of us for that matter. God send it never may!'

'You mean *you* think *she* is waiting for the Last Day? I don't know what you mean by "never". There must be *a* Last Day, and that would be *the* Last Day. And if she's waiting for that, what will happen then—*after* the last?'

'Well, Master Philip, if you are the son of your own father, which I take you to be, you should best be able to answer that question for yourself. I don't hold with such pryings. It's far from ready *I'm* likely to be.'

'Why not?'

'Because', said Mrs. Sullivan, 'I'm getting old, and time is not what it was. When I was a young girl I nearly brooded all the blood out of my body thinking of things like that; though you might not suppose so now. Not that the young should or need be doing so, though I'm not saying there's no need even for *them* not to mind their p's and q's. There is.'

'What are p's and q's?'

But this tepid and lifeless inquiry might have been borne on the winds of Arabia, it seemed so far away.

'Goodness gracious, you've got a tongue like an empty

money-box. I see your mamma has gone to bed. Let's hope her sick headache is no worse. And here comes the Rector.'

Philip had accepted Mrs. Sullivan's complex solution of his difficulty with reservations, and had pondered continually on parts of it. After that, apart perhaps from a stray dog or bird, or a strange human face, nothing in church, or in the scriptures, not even Jezebel or the Scarlet Woman, or Gideon, or Og, or Samson's foxes in the wheat, or golden Absalom hanging in the oak tree, or hairy Esau with his mess of pottage, or Elisha and the widow's cruse—nothing had so instantly galvanized him into a rapt attention as the least word he heard uttered about an angel or a trumpet. He had even taken to searching the Bible on his own account to satisfy his craving.

To-night, none the less, was the first time he had ever been alone with his angel—wholly alone. And he had risked a good deal for her sake—a caning from his father; a break-neck fall from his bedroom window if the clothes-line had proved as rotten as it looked; a scurry, heart in mouth, through the fusty dark of the shrubbery; and the possibility, far more affrighting than he had confessed, of strange meetings at the lych gate. Besides there was the humiliation of having been beguiled into this crazy expedition by a friend who was frowned at if not forbidden, and who was not only one of the 'village boys', but clouded and compromised at that.

It was a companionship that fretted Philip at times almost beyond bearing, but from which he could not contrive to break free. Scrubbed and polished Dick might be, but he never *looked* clean. He could be stupider than an owl, and yet was as sharp and quick as a pygmy sparrow-hawk, and feared nothing and nobody. Sometimes even the mere sight of his intent, small-nosed face, and its dark eyes, now darting with life and eagerness, now laden with an inscrutable melancholy; of his very hands, even—small and quick, and his tiny pointed

ears filled Philip with an acute distaste. Yet there was a curious
and continual fascination in his company.

He was like a mysterious and unintelligible little animal,
past caging or taming, and possessed of a spirit of whose
secret presence he himself was completely unaware. Contrari-
wise, he could be as demure, submissive and affectionate as a
little girl, and it was past all hope to discover where his small
mind was ranging. Philip admired, despised, was jealous of,
and sometimes bitterly hated him.

Why, he wondered, did his father always become so flustered and unreasonable at the mere mention of his name; or
why his mother either, for that matter? If an unexpected
tradesman's bill from London or the county town accompanied his *Morning Post*, why was the heated discussion of this
particular topic almost bound sooner or later to follow? First
'words'—and these of a steadily densening drift; a desultory
wrangle; but at last his mother, flaming with anger, in tears,
would flare up like a loose heap of gunpowder, and his father
would subside into a sulky and cowed acquiescence.

Even if Dick was *not* the son of the sober and crusted old
wheelwright at the other end of the village, what did that
matter? And if Dick's mother *was* so close a confidante of his
own mother, what did that? Wasn't there every reason why
she should be? Only a few years before this, she had been
parlourmaid at the Rectory, a quiet, fair, meditative creature.
And then all of a sudden she had left and got married. But she
was still the best 'help' in the house imaginable. No one could
wait at table so deftly and sedately as she could; and not even
Philip's indolent and elegant mother was such a marvel with
her needle. And yet she was so quiet and so far-away that when
suddenly spoken to she would start and flush as if she had but
just come out of some secret hiding-place.

It was only the spiteful new cook, Mrs. Sullivan's successor,
who had steadily refused to be won over; and Philip hated *her*
anyhow. His father, on the other hand, took no more notice

of Dick when he passed him by in the Rectory garden than if he had been a toadstool.

It was a mystery. If ever on any rare feast or festival, there was a solo to be sung in the minute village choir, it was Dick who sang it—'As pants the hart', 'With verdure clad'—and as roundly and sweetly and passionlessly as the strains of some small woodland flute. His voice at any rate would need no angelic tuition—even in a better world. Nevertheless, although the Rector had been known to boast of the prowess of his choir, Philip could not recall a single word of commendation from his father after the service was over, not even so much as a pompous little pat on the head. So far as *he* was concerned, Dick might have been a deaf-mute.

Yet if nuts, or peppermints, or marbles, or a grasshopper, or a glow-worm in a matchbox were brought into church for furtive display, and Dick was discovered to be the culprit, very little happened. Other boys when they were caught were given a good lecture in the Rector's study, and one runagate far less enterprising than Dick had been expelled from the choir.

However closely he listened, Philip could never unravel the secret of this mystery. Even when he most enjoyed Dick's company, he could never for a moment conceal his own sense of superiority. At one moment he might be green with envy of Dick's silly, dare-devil, scatter-brained ways; at the next utterly despise him. There was a perpetual conflict in his mind between affection, jealousy and contempt. And Dick would detect these secret feelings, as they were expressed solely in his face and actions, as neatly and quickly as a robin pecks up crumbs. Yet he never referred to them, or for more than a minute or two together seemed to resent a single one.

Just now, however, his protective stone and the increasing stench of his lantern unheeded, Philip had all but forgotten what had brought him into his present extraordinary situation. Like the restless imp he always was, Dick had taken himself off. Let him stay away, then! Meanwhile he had himself sat stolidly on, lost in contemplation, the prey of the most fantastic and ridiculous hopes and forebodings.

The church was brimmed so full of limpid moonlight that at any moment, it seemed, the stone walls, the pulpit, the roof itself might vanish away like the fabric of a dream. Its contents appeared to have no more reality than the reflections in a glass. Every crevice in the mouldings of the arches, every sunken flower and leaf in the mullions of the windows, even the knot in the wood of the pew beneath his nose stood out as if it had been blacked in with Indian ink. Every jut and angle, corbel and finial, marble nose and toe and finger seemed to have been dipped in quicksilver. And Philip, his eyes fixed on the faintly-golden, winged, ecstatic figure—mutely 'shaking her gilded tresses in the air'—whose gaze he pined and yet feared even in imagination to meet, was lost for the time being to the world of the actual. He failed even to notice urgent reminders that one of his legs from knee to foot had gone numb, and that he was stone-cold.

The premonitory whirring rumble of the clock over his head and the chimes of midnight roused him at last from this lethargy. He 'came to', and listened starkly to the muffled, sullen booming of the bell, as if he had suddenly escaped from the mazes of a dream. '. . . Eleven . . . Twelve'. The sonorous vibrations ebbed into inaudibility, and a dead and empty silence again prevailed. He had steadily assured himself, from the moment the project had been decided on, that nothing would happen. Nothing *had* happened. He felt spiritless and vacant, and now realized miserably that in spite of this radiance and beauty, he was further away from his angel than he had ever been before. It was she who had withdrawn herself from him, and with that withdrawal a faltering speechless faith and belief in her had almost faded out of his heart.

And as he crouched there, chilled and sick, there rose suddenly into the night beyond the chancel windows a restrained yet fiendish screech, compared with which his own *Oh, oh, oh,* had been sweet as the lamentations of a mermaid. Even though he had instantly guessed its origin, he sat appalled. His eyes fixed on the heavy folds of the curtain that had softly swayed forward as if in a waft of the wind through the open door, he had in his horror almost ceased to breathe. What if he were mistaken? What ghoulish wraith might *not* be skulking there! All but indetectably the curtain was edging apart to disclose at length a lean faceless shape draped as if with a shroud from its flat-topped shapeless and featureless head downwards. Even in his consternation he marvelled at the delicate play of the moonlight in the folds of the cambric. With pointing sooty finger, this ridiculous scarecrow had now begun noiselessly edging towards his pew. The effort to prevent a yell of terror from escaping his throat had brought the taste of blood to Philip's lip; and he at once fell into a violent passion.

'You're nothing but a damn silly little fathead,' he bawled, as it were, under his breath, 'and it would serve you jolly well right if I gave you a good licking. Stop that rot! Stop it! Come *out*! I say!'

The spectre, notwithstanding had fallen into a solemn yet nimble negro shuffle and a voice out of its middle began to intone:

> *Dearly beloved brethren, is it not a sin*
> *To eat raw potatoes and throw away the skin?*
> *The skin feeds the pigs and the pigs feed you;*
> *Dearly beloved brethen, is—it—not—*TRUE?

Pat with the last word, and having flung off the Rector's surplice and discarded the semi-hairless broom of the old church charwoman, Dick edged out of his disguise, looking smaller and skinnier than ever. Then it was as if his high spirits, having learned that the same jest is seldom successful twice, had been crushed out of him for good by this last rebuke. He stood dumbly staring at Philip, like a stricken and downcast little monkey that has been chastised by its master.

'Keep your silly wig on,' he expostulated at last. 'That's what you always do. You can't take any joke unless you've made it yourself. I'm tired of being here. There's nothing coming—and there never was. Perhaps if you had been alone . . .' Unstable as water, his mood began to revive again. '*I* know! Let's go down to the mill-pond, Philip, and look at the fish. The moon's like glass. You could catch 'em with your hands with that lantern. Let's try. Come on.'

'Oh no, you don't,' retorted Philip morosely. 'You needn't suppose you're going to wriggle out like that. You dared me to come, and I dare *you* to stay. Anyhow, you shan't put your nose ever into our house again or into the garden, either, I can promise you, if you're nothing but a sneak—and afraid. I know something that will soon put a stop to that.'

Dick stood irresolute, eyeing him sharply, his high cheek-bones a bright red, his eyes shining, his mouth ajar.

'I'm not a sneak. And who'—a doleful quaver jarred his thin clear treble voice—'who *wants* to come into your silly old garden. If my mother . . . Besides, you know I'm not afraid!'

'Oh, do I!' A crafty stealthy designing look had crept into Philip's fair face, and a slight haze into his blue eyes. A faint ambiguous smile faded out of his angel features. He glanced covertly about him. 'What's more likely is you only want to show off,' he sneered. 'Wheedle.' He half yawned. 'You know perfectly well that I shouldn't be here now except for some silly story you told me and couldn't have understood. Dare for yourself! Why, you haven't even the pluck to climb up into the belfry and give the least tiny ding on one of the bells. Not all alone.'

'Oh, wouldn't I! Yes, I would. Where's the key? There's an old owl's nest in the belfry. . . . "*One!*"—why, even if anybody in the village woke and heard it, they'd think it was nothing but the wind.'

'Well, *three* dings, then. Anybody can make excuses. And

you knew I haven't the key! What's more, you wouldn't take a single flower, not even a scrap of a green leaf, from one of those vases up there.'

Dick's gaze angled swiftly over the silver candlesticks upon the altar, the snow-white linen, the rich silk embroidered frontal, with its design in gold thread—I.H.S., the flat hueless shields of hothouse flowers. 'Yes, I would, if I can reach them.'

'Oh, would you! And there you are again—"*if!*" But you shan't—not while *I'm* here. That would be worse than stealing even, because this is a church, and that's the altar. And that's holy. This is not one of your mouldy old chapels.' Once again he glanced about him. 'I bet this, then. You wouldn't go up into the gallery and scratch out the eye in *that*—not even if I lent you my knife to do it with. Why, you'd be scared even of falling off the chair!'

The 'that' he was referring to was an ancient painted lozenge-shaped hatchment, fastened by tenpenny nails in its clumsy black frame to the lime-washed western wall. It was blazoned with a coat of arms, and above the coat was a crest— the turbaned head of a Saracen in profile; and beneath the coat, in bold Gothic lettering, the one word, *Resurgam*.

Dick gazed motionlessly at its darkened green and vermilion and at the tilted head. 'Yes, I would,' he muttered. 'What does *Resurgam* mean?'

'It's Latin,' replied Philip, as if he were a little mollified by the modesty of the inquiry. 'And it means, *I shall rise up again*. But it *might* be the subjunctive. It's what's called a motto, and the head's the crest, and the body's down in the vault. I expect he was a crusader. Anyhow, *any*body could do that; because you know very well it mightn't be noticed for ages. Never, p'raps. Besides, what's the use? . . . I'll give you a last chance. I'll tell you what you *wouldn't* do, not if you stayed here for a month of Sundays, and not a single soul came into the church to see you!'

His cheek had crimsoned. He nodded his head violently. 'You wouldn't climb up that, and—and blow that trumpet.'

Dick wheeled about, lifting his dark squirrel-bright eyes as he did so towards the Angel, and looked. He continued to look: the angel at this moment of its nightly vigil, though already the hand that clasped the trumpet had lost its silver, seemed with an ineffable yearning as if about to leap into a cataract of moonlight, like a siren erecting her green-haired head and shoulders out of a rippleless sea to scan the shore.

'You *said*, what would be the use?' he protested at last in a small, scarcely audible voice, and without turning his head. 'Even if I did, no one would hear. . . . Why do you *want* me to?'

'*Who* "wants" you to!' came the mocking challenge. 'You asked me to give you a dare. And now—what did I say! Shouldn't *I* hear? I don't believe you've ever even looked at it, not even *seen* it before!'

'Oh, haven't I!' Dick faltered. 'You say that only because on Sundays I don't sit on your side. And what's the use? Staring up gives you a crick in the neck. But it's not because I am afraid. . . . Besides, she's only made of stone.' In spite of this disparagement he continued to gaze at the angel.

'*Is* she then! Stone! That's all you know about it. She's made of wood, silly. How could she be that colour if it were marble or even *any* stone? Anybody could see that! And even if she *is* only wood, there are people all over the world who worship idols and—and images. I don't mean just savages either. If she'—for an instant his eyes shut and revolved beneath their pale rounded lids—'if she or anybody else was to blow through that trumpet, it would be the Last Day. I say it, and I *know*. Even if your father has ever heard of angels, I bet he doesn't believe in them. I'm *sure* he doesn't. My father does believe in them, though. And if you had ever really listened to what he reads out about them in the Lessons you'd know too. *I—have*.'

He sat for a moment, torpid as a spider engaged in digesting
or contemplating a visitor to its nets. Dick's small, alert, yet
guileless face was still turned away from him, upwards and
sidelong. As one may put one's ear to a minute device in
clockwork and listen to the wheels within going round, the
very thoughts in his cropped, compact head seemed audible.
And then, as if after a sudden decision to dismiss the subject
from his mind, Philip casually picked up his bull's-eye lantern,
idly twisted its penthouse top, and directed first a greenish,
then a thin red beam of light towards the lustrous monument.
But the moon made mock of this trivial rivalry.

'What,' was Dick's husky inquiry at last, 'what *does* the
Bible say about angels? It must be a lovely place where they
are, Philip.'

Philip ignored the sentimental comment. 'Oh, heaps of
things. I couldn't tell you; not half of them, not a quarter.'
A mild, absent-minded, almost hypnotic expression now
veiled his pale cold features. He began again as though he were
repeating a lesson, in tones low yet so confident that the whole
church could easily play eavesdropper to his every word.
Nevertheless the sentences followed one another tardily and
piecemeal, as if, like a writer of books, he could not wholly
trust his faculties, as though words and ideas were stubborn
things to set in order and be made even so much as to hint at
what was pent up in his mind.

'Well, first there was St. Paul; he went to a man's house
who had *seen* an angel. Then there was the angel who came
to tell his mother about Samuel, when she was sitting alone
sewing in her bedroom.... And there was the angel that spoke
to a man called Lot before he came out of a place called Sodom
that was burned in the desert and his wife was turned into a
pillar of salt. Because she turned back. Oh, heaps! *You* seem to
suppose that because people can't see them now, there never
were angels. What about the sea-serpent, then; and what about

witches? And what about the stars millions and billions of miles out in space, and mites and germs and all that, so teeny-tiny *no*body ever saw them until microscopes and telescopes were invented? I've looked through a microscope, so I know.'

Dick nodded vacantly. 'If people can *see* them,' he admitted, 'there must be sea-serpents. And I *have* seen a witch. There's one lives in Colney Bottom, and everybody says she's a witch. She's humpty-backed, with straggly grey hair all over her shoulders. I crept in through the trees once and she was in her garden digging potatoes. At least I *think* it was potatoes. She was talking; but there was nobody there and it wasn't to *me*. But you were telling me about the angels, Philip. Won't you go on?'

' "Go on"!' echoed Philip in derision, and began again fumbling with his lantern. 'Good heavens, you don't expect me to tell you half the Bible, do you? Why don't you listen? I don't believe you've any more brains than a parrot. "Go on"! Why, *everybody* has heard of the angel that when Moses was with his sheep called to him out of the middle of the burning bramble bush on the mountains. Its leaves and branches were all crackling with flames. That's another. And when Elijah was once lying asleep in the desert under a juniper tree an angel came in the morning and touched him to wake him because he had brought him some cake, and some fresh water to drink. That,' he pondered a moment or two, 'that was before the ravens. And I suppose you've never even heard of Joshua either? He was a captain of Israel. And when he was standing dressed in his armour on the sand, with his naked sword in his hand, and looking at the enormous walls of Jericho, he saw an angel there beside him, in armour too, just as you might see a man in a wood at night. They stood there together looking at the *enormous* walls of Jericho. But you couldn't see them very plainly because it was getting dark, and there weren't any lamps or lights in the houses. So nobody inside knew that they were there, not even the woman who had talked to the two spies who had stolen the bunches of grapes.'

Philip, unperceived, had quickly and suddenly glanced at his friend, who, his face wholly at peace, had meanwhile been emptily watching the coloured lights succeeding one another in the round, glass, owl-like eye of the toy lantern.

'I should like to see an angel,' he said.

'Oh, would you? Then that's all you know about it. There are thousands upon thousands of them, most of them miles taller than any giant there ever was and others no bigger than —than ordinary. Not all of them have only two wings either; some of them have six—here, and here, and here; with two they fly and with two they cover their faces when they are asleep. And they have names too; else God wouldn't be able to call them. But don't you go and think they are like *us*; because they aren't. They are more like demons or ghosts— real ghosts, I mean, not the kind *you* were talking about. And I don't believe either that just because anything is made of wood or stone, it hasn't any life at all—not at *all*. Even savages couldn't be as stupid as all that. You only *think* you could touch angels. But you couldn't. And some angels, though I don't know even myself if they are most like women or men' —his voice ebbed away almost into a whisper, like that of a child murmuring in its sleep, as if he were not only nearing the end of his resources, but was losing himself in the rapture of some ineffable vision in his mind—'some angels are far far more beautiful to look at than any woman, even the most beautiful woman there ever was. And even than—*that*!'

Yet again Dick lifted his intense small eyes towards the image. It had, it seemed, as if in an instant, returned to an appearance of mute immobility; but only in the nick of time, to elude his silent questioning.

'I shouldn't mind any angel', he said, 'if it were only like that. Not *mind*, I mean. If she *looked* at me, perhaps I might. She's like Rebecca, the girl that lives up at the farm. My mother taught me a hymn once to say when I am in bed. I can't remember the beginning now, but some of it I can:

> *Four corners to my bed;*
> *Four angels round my head:*
> *One to bless, and one to pray,*
> *And one to bear my soul away....*

If you are not afraid, she says, not anywhere, ever, *nothing* can do anything against you.'

'Oh, they can't, can't they! That just shows all *you* know about it. Besides, what you've been saying is only a rhyme for children. It's only a rhyme. My nurse told me that ages ago. Those angels are only one kind. Why, there are angels so enormously strong that if one of them no more than touched even the roof of this church with the tip of his finger it would crumble away into dust. Like that'—he firmly placed his own small forefinger on the dried-up corpse of a tiny money-spider that had long since expired in the corner of the pew—'absolutely into dust. And their voices are as loud as thunder, so that when one speaks to another, the sound of their shouting sweeps clean across the sky. And some fly up out of the sea, out of the East, when the sun rises; and some come up out of a huge frightful pit. And some come up out of the water, deep dangerous lakes and great rivers, and they stand on the water, and can *fly*—straight across, as if it was lightning, from one edge of the world to the other—like tremendous birds. I should jolly well like to see what a pilot of an aeroplane would do at the edge of the night if he met one. They can'—he bent forward a little, his pale face now faintly greened with his own lantern—'they can see without looking; and they stay still, like great carved stones, in a light—why, this moon wouldn't be even a candle to it!

'And some day they will pour awful things out of vials down on the earth and reap with gigantic sickles not just ordinary corn, but men and women. Men and women. And besides the sea,' his rather colourless eyes had brightened, his cheeks had taken on a gentle flush, his nervous fingers were clasping and unclasping themselves over the warm metal of his lantern, 'and besides the sea, they can stand and live exulting in the sun. But on the earth here they are invisible, at least *now*, except when they come in dreams. Besides, everybody has two angels; though they never get married, and so there are never any children angels. They are called cherubs. And I know this too—you can tell they are there even when you cannot see them. You can hear them listening. If *they* have charge of you, nothing can hurt you, not the rocks—nor the ice—not even of the highest mountains. And that was why the angel spoke to Balaam's donkey when they were on the mountain pass, because he wished not to frighten him; and the donkey answered. But if you were cursed by one for wickedness, then you would wither up and die like a gnat, or have awful pains, and everything inside of you would melt away like water. And don't forget either that the devil has crowds of angels under his command who were thrown out of heaven millions of years ago, long before Adam and Eve. They are as proud as he is, and they live in hell. . . . They are awful.'

It was doubtful if Dick had been really attending to this prolonged, halting, almost monotoned harangue; his face at any rate suggested that his thoughts had journeyed off on a remote and marvelling errand of their own.

'Well,' he ventured at last, with a profound half-stifled sigh, 'I *would* climb it anyway. And not because you dared me to, either. Even *you* couldn't say what I might not see up there.'

He tiptoed a pace or two nearer the shallow altar steps and again fixed his eyes on his quarry. 'What about the trumpet?' he suddenly inquired, with a ring of triumph in his voice, as if he had at last managed to corner his learned friend. 'The trumpet? You didn't say a single word about the trumpet.'

'Well, what if I didn't?' was the flat acrimonious answer. 'I can't say two things at once, can I? You don't know *any*thing. And that is simply because you never pay any attention. You're just like a fly buzzing about among the plates seeing what you can pick up. I don't suppose, if I asked you even now, you could tell me a single word of *all* that I've been saying!'

Dick turned, glancing a little sadly and wistfully at his friend. 'I could, Philip. At least, I think I could. Besides flies do settle sometimes; I suppose then they are asleep.'

'Oh, well, anyhow,' replied Philip coldly, 'I don't think I want to. But I could if I had the time.' He sighed. 'You don't even seem to understand there are so many *kinds* of trumpets. You don't seem ever to have heard even of Gideon's trumpets. Some are made of brass and some are silver and some are great shells and some are made out of sheep's horns, rams'. And in the old days, ages ago, war-horses loved the sound of trumpets—I don't mean just men going hunting. It made them laugh and prance, with all their teeth showing. "*Ha-ha!*" —like that. Simply maddened to go into battle. And besides, clergymen, priests they were called in those days, used to have trumpets, but that was ages before Henry VIII. And they used to blow them, like that one, up there, when there was a new moon; and when,' he glanced sidelong, his eyelids drooping a little furtively over his full eyes, and his voice fell to a mumble, 'and when there was a *full* moon too. And at the end there will be incense, and dreadful hail, and fire, and scorpions with claws like huge poisonous spiders. And there's a Star called Wormwood; and there will be thousands and thousands of men riding on horses with heads like lions. . . .' He fell silent and sat fumbling for a few moments. 'But I wasn't really going to talk about all that. It's only because *I* have listened. And it's just what I've said already, and I know the very words too.' He nodded slowly as if he were bent on imparting a deathless and invaluable secret: ' "The trumpet shall sound and the dead shall be raised." Those are the very words. And *I* see what they mean.'

Dick had meanwhile become perfectly still, as if some inward self were lost in a strange land. He appeared to be profoundly pondering these matters. 'And supposing,' he muttered at length, as though like the prophet he had swallowed Philip's little book and it were sweet as honey, 'supposing *nothing* happens, Philip? If I do? Perhaps *that* trumpet is only solid wood all through. Then it wouldn't make *any* sound. Then you would only burst your cheeks, trying. Wouldn't it be funny—if I burst my cheeks, trying!'

'That,' replied Philip, disdaining the suggestion, 'that would only mean that it isn't really a trumpet. But you wouldn't even be *thinking* of that if you weren't too frightened to try. You're only talking.'

'*You* wouldn't.'

'I like that!' cried Philip, as if in a brief ecstasy. 'Oh, I like that! Who *thought* of the angel, may I ask? Who *asked* to be dared? Besides, as I have said again and again, this is my father's church; and chapel people don't believe in angels. They don't believe in anything that really matters.'

'You can say what you like about chapel people,' said Dick stubbornly, his eyes shining like some dangerous little animal's that has been caught in a snare. 'But I'm *not* afeard even if you won't go yourself.'

'Oh, well'—a cold and unforeseen fit of anxiety had stolen into Philip's mind as he sat staring at his friend. 'I don't care. Come on, let's clear out of this, I say. You can *try* if you want to, but I'm not going to *watch*. So don't get blaming anything on to me. It's nothing to do with me. That's just what you always do. You're a silly little weathercock. First, yes; then, no.'

Cramped and spiritless, he had got down from his pew and, as if absent-mindedly, had pushed his magic dumb-bell flint into his great-coat pocket and shut off the light of his lantern.

The moonlight, which a few moments before, from pavement to arching roof, had suffused the small church through and through, had begun to thin away into a delicate dusk again; and at the withdrawal even of the tiny coloured lights of the lantern, its pallor on the zigzag-fretted walls and squat thick stone shafts of the piers had become colder. Moreover the quietude around them had at once immeasurably deepened again now that the two boys' idle chirruping voices were stilled.

Philip took up the lantern, and looked at his friend. A curious, crooked, scornful alarm showed on his own delicate features. But it was the scorn in it that his ardent, undersized and peeping devotee had detected most clearly. His intensely dark eyes were searching Philip's face with an astonishing rapidity.

'You said, "blaming",' he half entreated. 'And did I ever? I—I . . . Haven't I always shown that we—I . . . ! It's only because I didn't think anything might happen. But I'm not afeard, whatever you may think. Besides, you asked me, Philip. And anything—*any*thing you asked me. . . . So it couldn't be *only* a dare.'

Like a cork on a shallow stream that has come momentarily to rest in the midst of rippling and conflicting currents, Philip stood motionless, his pondering eyes intent on the young adventurer whom he had at last decoyed into action. A faintly apprehensive, faintly melancholy expression had now crept into his features. The cold detaining fingers he had thrust out of his coat-sleeve fell slackly to his side again. For Dick had already straddled over the thick red plaited cord that dangled between nave and chancel, disclosing as he did so a frayed gaping hole in the canvas of one of his shoes. Their rubber soles made not the faintest sound as he trod lightly over the thick Persian rug and the stone slabs towards the great monument in the further corner, only a few paces from the altar.

It was a monument constructed of many ornate marbles, and these supplied cold couch and canopy for the effigy in alabaster of a worthy knight who, as its inscription declared, had long ago surrendered the joys and sorrows of this world. He reposed, rather uneasily, on his left elbow; his attire, ruff and hose, not less decorative and rococo than the wreathings and carvings, the cherubs and pilasters of his tomb. But like an Oriental bed in a small English bedroom, the tomb was a size or two too large for the church.

Until this moment Philip had not fully realized its loftiness, and how angularly its pinnacles soared up under the roof. Dark and dwarfed against the whiteness of its marble, Dick had now begun to climb. But he had mounted only a few feet from the ground when Philip noticed that the moon had now abandoned the carved ringlets, the rounded cheeks, the up-turned sightless face of his angel. Though her pinions and feet were still chequered with its silvering beams, her trump now lifted its mouth into a cold and sullen gloom. An unendurable misgiving had begun to stir in him.

'The moon's gone, Dick,' he whispered across. 'What's the good? Come down!'

'I say,' came the muffled but elated answer, 'the ledges are simply thick with dust, and don't they just cut into the soles of your feet. I can't hear what you're saying.'

'I said,' repeated Philip, still patiently, 'come down!' But he might as well have been pleading with the angel itself. There came no response. 'Dick, Dick,' he reiterated, 'I said, Come down! Oh, I'm going.' In a sudden fever he pushed his way under the curtain into the vestry and vanished. But it was only a ruse. He came flying back in a few moments as if in utter consternation.

'Quick, Dick; quick, I say!' he all but shouted. 'Come down! There's someone, something *coming*. It isn't a man and it isn't a woman. Quick! It won't be a minute before it's in the church. Oh you silly, silly fool! I tell you there's someone coming!'

His voice broke away into a sob of bewilderment, rage, apprehension and despair. 'My God,' he called, 'I'll tell my father
of this! You see if I don't.'

But the snail-slow groping figure, still radiantly lit with the
moon's downcast beams as it continued to scale the monument, was far too much engrossed in its mission to pay any
attention to him now, and hardly paused until with a small,
black, broken-nailed hand it had securely clasped the angel's
foot. 'I'm nearly up, Philip,' he called down at last. 'Look!
Look where I am! I'm even with the gallery now, and can
hardly see because of the dazzle. It's cold and still and awful,
but oh, *peace*ful; and I can see into the moon. The angel's
lovely too, close to, but much, much bigger. Supposing I blow
with all my might and the trumpet doesn't sound? It won't be
my fault, will it? And we will still keep friends, always, won't
we, Philip?'

'Oh, you fool, you idiot crock fool,' called Philip hoarsely.
'Didn't I *tell* you, didn't I tell you, what might come to *every*-
body? . . . And you believed it! Oh, it was all a story, a lie,
a story. Dick, I will give you anything in the world if you will
only come down.'

'I don't want anything in the world,' was the dull, stubborn
retort. Even as he spoke, the lower dust-dried hand had crept
cautiously up to join its fellow, and in a few moments, himself
half in and half out of the moonlight, his fingers were clutching the acorn tassels of the cord that bound its convoluted
hood to the angel's head. Philip was now all but past motion
or speech. He was shivering from head to foot, and praying
inarticulately in his terror, 'Oh God, make him come down!
Oh God, make him come down!'

'I believe', a calm but rapturous voice was declaring, 'it *is*
hollow, and I *think* she knows I'm here. You won't say I was
afraid now! Philip, I'd do anything in the world for you.'

But at this moment, it seemed, the ancient guardians of the
sanctity of the edifice had deemed it discreet to intervene. A

cock crowed from its perch in the hen-roost at the farm where
Rebecca now lay fast asleep. A vast solemn gust of wind
evoked from nowhere out of space had swept across the
churchyard and in at the open vestry door, powerful enough
in its gust to belly out the dark green felt curtain and to add
its edge of terror to Philip's appalled state of mind. 'Look!
Quick! It's coming. Didn't I *say* it was all . . .'

And this time the small human creature clinging to its goal,
a lean skinny arm outstretched above his head, had heard the
warning cry. 'Who? What's coming?' he called, faint and far.
'Oh, it's lovely up here. I'm alone. I can't stop now. I'm
nearly there.'

'I say, you are *not* to, you are *not* to.' Philip was all but
dancing in helpless fear and fury. 'It's wicked! It's *my* angel,
it's *my* trumpet! I hate you! Listen!—I tell you! I *command* you
to come down!'

But his adjurations had become as meaningless as is now
the song the Sirens sang.

A rending snap, abrupt as that of a pistol shot, had echoed
through the church. The tapering wooden trumpet, never
since its first fashioning visited by any other living creature
than capricious fly and prowling spider, had splintered off
clean from the angel's grasp. And without a cry, a syllable,
either of triumph or despair, Dick had fallen vertically on to
the flag-stones beneath, the thud of his small body, and the
minute crack as of some exquisitely delicate and brittle vessel
exposed to too extreme a tension being followed by a silence
soft, and thick, and deep as deep and heavy snow.

The stolid pendulum had resumed its imperturbable thumping again, the fussy vestry clock its protest against such indifference. By any miracle of mercy, *could* this be only yet another
of this intrepid restless little Yorick's infinite jests? The sharp-
nosed crusader continued alabaster-wise to stare into his
future. The disgraced angel, breast to lock-crowned head,

stood now in shadow as if to hide her shame. Her mute wooden trumpet remained clutched in a lifeless hand. . . No.

'Dick! Dick!' an anguished stuttering voice at last contrived to whisper. 'I didn't mean it. On my oath I didn't mean it. Don't let me down . . . Dick, are you dead?'

But since no answer was volunteered, and all courage and enterprise had ebbed into nausea and vertigo, the speaker found himself incapable of venturing nearer, and presently, as thievishly as he had entered it, crept away out into the openness of the churchyard, and so home.

THE HOUSE

*

Having ascended the three semi-circular damp-darkened steps into his porch, Mr. Asprey slipped his latch-key into its lock with a peculiar disrelish. He was utterly tired, exhausted —finished. Yet nothing, it seemed, could persuade his fevered mind to desist from its futile activities, although its one need was to be at rest. . . .

In a few brief hours he would be compelled to surrender this very key, since he would be leaving the house he knew so well: finally, if not 'for good'. Everything had been made ready for his departure. His two maid-servants, the ample Emily and the angular Ada, having muffled the furniture with their sepulchral dust-sheets, and left their charge neat and seemly had departed but a few hours before, bound for their new situations. How odd a destiny!

Mr. Asprey, being much older than either of them, had, he assumed, deeper roots. At daybreak it would be *his* turn, and as yet he was by no means certain of any particular 'place'. Indeed of recent years he had given little thought to this eventuality. He had merely stayed on.

And now his eviction was no longer a question of to-morrow and to-morrow and to-morrow. Why indeed should he 'wait' until then? And yet, taken for all in all, this house of his had proved a pleasant one; peculiar here and there in

361

'style' perhaps, yet not wildly eccentric; commodious yet compact, a heritage adjusted to his private purposes, fairly central and yet secluded. He had of course seen and envied residences with amenities more charming—a poor excuse for having neglected his own! But renovation had proved impracticable, and repairs far from satisfactory. In what sense and in what degree it actually *belonged* to him remained one of its many mysteries. Taxes fell due and he had been compelled to meet them. But of rent—hardly a peppercorn; of definite agreement, contract, in early life so frequently referred to by his spiritual pastors and masters—not a trace. If positive landlord there were (himself perhaps the architect) Mr. Asprey of late years had seldom 'called on' him, even in a merely metaphorical sense. And now—well, the one thing certain was that he had been given notice to quit.

Midnight had struck; the stars of the morning, though faintly hazed with a drift of dove-like cloud, were already traversing the heavens. In a little while it would be winter dawn. He had always hated change, and resented decay. Nevertheless destiny was spudding at his tap root.

The door ajar, and finger still on key, he turned reluctantly to look back. He had been wandering for hours alone in the darkness, and now he gazed forsakenly and forlornly at the gentle familiar prospect—the wooded downward slope, the faint line of low hills towards the south in the thin illumination of the night, and away, beyond the far horizon line, a soundless sea. The whole world was all but deathly still; and what weak fickle wind there was had lately changed its direction. The dark was turning colder.

And still—almost as if he were dubious whether he were being deceived by dream or wide awake—Mr. Asprey continued to ponder. However sharply he mistrusted the term, he realized that he had been a little *psychic* of late: that, prey of foreboding, he had been living much too closely secluded (even for him) in his own mind. His staid old family doctor, notoriously incompetent at any such extremity as this, had but yesterday morning given him up. A prying probing alienist, more skilful in analysing human puddingstone than quartz, might even have declared him a trifle 'mental'. The notion amused Mr. Asprey. Convinced of his own security, and aware that in these hazy matters silence is best, he had always enjoyed being a trifle mental. Partly perhaps for this reason he had no acute hankering to re-enter his house. He hated all good-byes. They entailed not only leaving but being left. Still, only the rankest discourtesy would admit of his posting off from so habitual and, despite its numerous defects and restrictions, so genial a residence with none; not even a grieved *adieu*, an ironic *au revoir*. And there was so much to say good-bye *to*! Houses, as the years collect, become densely populated. This is especially apparent, Mr. Asprey meditated, when they are about to be left vacant; and memories vividly revived may prove stubborn to exorcise.

They resemble a garden once beloved if seldom weeded, its wilder parts, its transitory solitudes, nearest to the heart and to the imagination. Tears cannot now refresh it, or sighs stir its seeded grasses, and the pitcher is broken at the well. This was the sad and enfeebling fact—Mr. Asprey was being victimized by his past. What folly! Since the future would see to his own interment, why not let that remain buried? 'Is thy servant a dog?' Of recent months, moreover—though often in a perfunctory fashion—it had been Mr. Asprey's odd custom to 'go over' his house before retiring for the night. He had become almost timidly apprehensive of fire, indeed of any 'act of God'; and he had acquired a belated passion for being tidy. Few hours for this were now left to him. He must make the most of them.

First, then, he would descend into the kitchen if merely to make sure that his breakfast would be ready for him at about half-past seven. Then he would go on his rounds, even more attentively and systematically than he usually did: Who goes there? *Qui vive?* How fortunate that this was so clearly not an occasion for electric light; since it is not only the most execrable of illuminants to be 'mental' by and in, but, owing to pure prejudice, Mr. Asprey had refrained from having it installed in his ancestral home. He might be in the nature of an introvert, but he was not a spy on himself. He had always enjoyed using his eyes, but seldom with the intention of showing anything or anybody up. He abhorred 'high lights'.

He withdrew the key, groped his way into the house, lit the candle which he had left ready in its old dish-shaped brass holder on a table, and shut the door. For a few moments he stood listening to the tardy and stentorian *Now-then: Now-then* of his grandfather's clock, then made his way to the back parts of the house and down the worn stone steps into the kitchen quarters. What mice were abroad at once scampered away with alacrity to warn their housemates that he was approaching: a few sluggish cockroaches were departing at leisure with the same tidings. Mr. Asprey scanned them an instant to make sure that they were real—aware at the same moment of the surmise that his next abode might be frequented by another species of vermin—then glanced about him. Everything was prepared. Everything was in order. That, of course, was Emily's doing.

Half the long speckless deal table was covered with a charming chequered tablecloth; the mound under the tea-cloth was without doubt a loaf of bread; the milk was creaming; and there the toast-rack, and the butter in its almost lordly dish. A conical coffee-pot dominated the neighbouring stove, for in spite of silly antiquated aversions, Mr. Asprey had been unable to evade gas. And two plump new-laid eggs stood side by side in their cups upon a plate. From their calm featureless faces they openly surveyed Mr. Asprey, and he them. Human existence, they seemed to be preaching, resembles an egg. In spite of a myriad apparent replicas it is unique, self-contained. Break the shell, you cannot repair it again. Some eggs are

good, others are horrid. The stale are an affliction to God and
man. And not every specimen need necessarily harbour a
chick. And as he stood thus quietly looking, he was also
listening. It was as though the vacant house over his head
were an echoing shell, and he its hermit crab.

Otherwise there was no reason to linger here; none whatever. Well, he would ascend to the attics and, room by room,
proceed slowly down again. The actual order mattered little,
except that it is perhaps the doors of a house that should be
examined last. They are the usual way out, and in.

Stair by stair went up poor weary Mr. Asprey; but, come to
the attics, made no attempt to enumerate, or to individualize
the many Emilys and Adas who had occupied them each in
turn. He had always prided himself on being by intention at
least a righteous master. He had never deliberately thought of
Emilys or Adas as being of else than flesh and blood. He knew
we are all human.

None the less he could clearly recall one or two of whose
felicity when they were under his roof he now felt a little
uncertain. And in retrospect even a discourtesy may seem a
crime. Nor, he noticed, had he hitherto been aware either that
his last Emily had had no mat on her old oilcloth, or that her
ewer was chipped; that a castor was wanting to Ada's bed and
that there was no fire-grate in her room. Pampering, oh no!
But he *might* have inquired, Are you quite happy here? And
if he *could* stay on a little, he would see that their successors.
. . . Alone on this uppermost landing close under the roof—
a trickle of water ding-donging there like funeral bells in the
old lead cistern bespeaking a leaky tap below—he could see
into either attic just as he pleased. Each in turn, he solemnly
bowed to them—it was the most he could manage—and went
on.

As fleeting a look into the lumber room also sufficed. It
would never do to botanize long there! But at the closed door
of the room at the foot of the top staircase he paused indeed.

It had been of old his nursery; and he was aware how easy it is to be otiose concerning one's early years. One is so seldom in retrospect a Child of the World. He opened the door and looked in—high fender, coloured pictures in their maple frames, rocking-horse, box of bricks. What dreadful emblems objects may become! And although, with that inward eye of his, which had recently been so active, he saw for a vivid instant his old nurse sitting beside the empty grate—slippered feet, stooping head, and clicking needles all complete—she immediately vanished. And instead, he was looking at a small boy, who was now exactly as far away in time as she was; though much further away in most things else.

He was sitting in a bare empty-looking room at a desk, stained with ink, and scarred with letters cut in the wood; and out of his blue eyes and plain face, pen between fingers, he was gazing through the window and over the low brick wall beyond it. It was a spring day out there in the meadows, and the towering clouds with their scarves of rain had but just drifted from over the face of the sun. So that at this moment the whole scene was lit—bright grass, green-beaded trees, tumbling stream—with a miraculously radiant panorama of delicate light. Mr. Asprey didn't look at things like that now, or rather no April morning ever enravished him like that now. His psychic skull must have contracted. It was as if all things were lovely if only you *could* see them—and in the proper light.

Yet in the very midst of this ecstatic reverie of looking, this inky boy—he realized—knew how intensely unhappy he was. He was homesick; he was a muff; he was being kept in; and he deserved to be. None the less, at sight of the child, Mr. Asprey had become aware of a peculiar compassion. Unhappy the creature might be, but there was no sign that he knew that he himself—whether unhappy or not—would soon be gone for ever. Also, Mr. Asprey was even more perfectly confident that in that young distant mind there was not a vestige of regret that when its owner grew up to be a man he would remain childless. How odd then that at the precise moment when he was abandoning his house for good, he should suddenly be convicting himself of the charge of deliberate heirlessness! To be leaving positively no one behind him who might some day be doing as he was doing now—well, he did not at all enjoy the look of the black cap that topped the bewigged, long, grey, thin-nosed judicial countenance already engaged in trying his case. Black cap apart, even the severest judge upon the bench, glancing up at his prisoner, may nod with a cold, 'Be calm, take your time; I am listening. One word even yet might put you right.'

This in mind, Mr. Asprey promptly took his little notebook out of his pocket—battered and dingy after more than eleven months' wear—and jotted down: 'Secure as soon as may be a natural, pleasant young woman, quiet, non-temperamental, easy, happy-looking, and in need of a good home—to ensure a son and heir. Leave her practically everything. This appears to be rather urgent.' It appeared to be so urgent that Mr. Asprey added his initials: *A.A.A.* Even in the act of writing he noticed, too, but did not stay to consider it, that a quite definite young woman for this purpose had emerged out of the groves of memory, was now in his mind's eye. But since he could not have been more than eight years old when she stole his heart away, not even a line in the Agony Column of the *Times*, that had so little to do with time absolute, would now be likely to have any effect. It was a pity. He was afraid it was now too late to be doing even 'his best'.

He closed the door, listened again a moment—what *habits* habits become!—meditating as he did so on the deep lovely blue of his candle flame, and passed on down the shabbily carpeted corridor to the next nearest bedroom. This was his father's and his mother's room or rather it had been theirs many years ago. Their son in the meantime, either in act or thought, had little visited it. It remained as they themselves had left it—the four-poster bed, the ponderous wardrobe, the grey marble-slabbed mahogany washstand, the Landseer engravings. Nor can you be said to *remember*—certainly not to remember a mother—if the happy event is dependent on some casual reminder.

The twin pair of old Venetian blinds now hung lowered to their very last slack slats. The old red damask curtains were undrawn. And there stood Mr. Asprey once more, peering in over his candle flame. And such was the unusual state of his mind that when he came to again he could not have said how long he had remained in this abstracted posture. His absent-mindedness however was chiefly due to the fact that his inward gaze meanwhile had been intent on a large visionary granite sarcophagus topped with an eighteenth-century urn and canopied over by the vast, fringed, heavily laden boughs of a prodigious cedar tree, its edges scintillating like a Maharaja with bead-like rows of full-sized raindrops.

It was engrossing to observe how apart from this transient jewellery the beam of his candle enlivened the delicate greys and browns and blacks of the corrosive lichens and the bright green of the moss on this vast emblem. The moss indeed was almost as vividly verdant as the meadows had been. But *did* moss grow on granite? Still stranger was it, in Mr. Asprey's experience, that he should be able to spell out the words that were graven on the stone. He would have supposed them to be long since indecipherable. Amazed at the incredibly gross egotism of the inscription, he read: HERE LIES MY F. . . . In plain honest lettering, too; nothing Gothic. For though he was unable to peer round to make sure, there was not a doubt in the world that ATHER followed immediately after the F. Actuality may be grossly abrupt and inartistic enough, but no *human* stonecutter, surely, had ever so clumsily divided the word *father* as that! It was merely yet another jape of the strange jinnee of the dream world—never busier, Mr. Asprey had frequently observed, than when one is wide awake.

However that might be, it was abysmally damp here and

atrociously dark. As for the brooding cedar that roofed the tomb, to judge by these gigantic water-crystalled twigs, it could hardly be less than a mile high. It all comes of neglect, thought Mr. Asprey. But whose? How much was all this his father's cumulative dark, how much his own? And why this dateless urn, when filial forgetfulness had been concerned solely with a Victorian angel in Portland stone? Mr. Asprey gave it up. Nor could he be certain whether a father who leaves his son so early an orphan, or that son grown old is the more to blame for any sad and protracted oblivion and neglect. Both surely had been indolent—his departed father in his son's dreams; and he himself in the waking day. Not that this was an hour for recriminations; he must merely strive to be fair. He had too the comfort of realizing that if his mother was lying side by side with that father within these dense cold lost stone walls, she seemed to be perfectly calm and happy. *She* hadn't even so much as turned to smile at him. And though this might be a consolation as dubious as it was sentimental, it was at least of her own sharing. Besides, like Mr. Asprey himself, she had always loved moss—'Look, Tony, the very instant rain comes! . . . It's just like a parrot!'

This time a little hesitantly then, out came his battered pocket-book again: 'Have f's grave attended to,' he scrawled in it. '? remove angel; ? replace it with some other kind? ? ?'

He paused in a fleeting attempt to petrify even in symbolic image one of Donne's angels, then added as an afterthought: 'If possible, go myself'. He trusted none the less that the expedition would not entail any attempt to fell that antediluvian cedar. He saw himself looking up at it, axe in hand, and the vast and vacant heavens beyond it.

Mr. Asprey closed his parents' bedroom door after him as reverently as he hoped that the less fickle-minded son and heir whom he had vowed some day to be responsible for would finally close his bedroom door after *him*. At grave risk of extinguishing his candle, he snuffed its wick between finger and thumb, and continued on his way down the corridor, thus creating the most fantastic shadows in leering and quixotic motion, but at the same time dispersing its narrow darkness as he went. His next two memoranda, or agenda, both of them concerned with a play-room that for many years— seemingly now how unjustly few!—had been used for his mature private work, were of so personal and secret a kind that he laboriously scribbled them into his book in an amateurish shorthand which he had invented in his youth. One of these, briefly translated, ran: 'Tell Self it didn't so *much* matter.' The other was decisively to the opposite effect.

His third and fourth memoranda, in longhand, related to a seldom-used guest-room. Even in the light of one brief candle, this was a room of a most charming pink and white; and particularly since its old-fashioned chintz curtains were at this moment concealing the view from the shuttered windows beyond them—of a dark, leafless, and fruitless orchard behind the house, and an empty dog-kennel. Once within this small sanctuary, and deeply relieved at having passed in furtive celerity his own shut bedroom door without personal and perilous interruption, Mr. Asprey might as well have ventured 'just as he was' into some evening Reception, so multitudinous was the silent company that had at once phantomwise thronged about him. With sharp febrile nose and dark begloomed eyes, his long lank fingers shielding his candle flame, Mr. Asprey paused until they had, so to speak, become accustomed to his intrusion among them, had thereupon mournfully thinned away, and had left him to himself. After all one *can't* possibly make things right with more than a mere fraction of one's past! No sinner, surely; hardly even a saint?

At length alone again, Mr. Asprey allowed his gaze to rest a little wistfully on a portrait in water-colour on the wall. The young woman depicted in it must have sat looking sideways at the artist. Thus the longer Mr. Asprey gazed at her, the clearer it became that in a peculiarly open and yet stealthy fashion she was sharing his scrutiny. Twenty years at least now severed him and her; and not a single faded petal or pinch of incense had Mr. Asprey recently offered at her shrine. It may, or may not, be discreet when you have fallen in love to 'tell'. That may depend on the degree of the infatuation, the attitude of the object, the propriety of the passion, and even the state of your health. The only alternative is to allow the toxin, the crisis, to become bygones as quietly and rapidly as de-'crystallization' permits. Mr. Asprey could not now choose between them. He had been more or less in love more than once, and having 'told' once or twice, had told no more. And *do* hearts warmed up become as indigestible as he had always feared?

This silent, reticent, searching creature here, with the side-long eyes and early Edwardian sleeves, was herself one of the told-no-mores. But as he continued to meet her motionless eyes, and himself at last ventured to smile faintly, surely she had smiled faintly back? He tried again; there was no doubt of it. How inadequate a word may 'reassurance' be! There could of course be only one solution to so arresting an enigma; and this, yet again, a tragically sentimental one. She must whatever *then* her state of being, have loved him 'all the time'; that is, always; and for ever. In other words, long before they had ever met; to meet no more. That is, until this very moment!

Mr. Asprey had turned slightly giddy. He was being 'mental' with a vengeance. Still, since he would have no further opportunities for self-adjustment in his earthly home, he was now striving to be strictly honourable. So he forthwith jotted into his diary: 'Explain somehow to Frances M. why I *had* to arrange about the pleasant-looking young woman—good-tempered, but not temperamental—because of an heir.' This entry much amused its writer. He looked up, and without question

Frances M.'s painted smile revealed an amusement at least equal to his own.

Thus complacent, he was about to continue on his valedictory pilgrimage when his glance, having vaguely wandered over the room, rested on a dark old wooden box in a shadow-infested corner on the other side of the flounced dressing-table. He could hardly believe anything so wooden could be so eloquent. It was as if Conscience had been actually searching for evidence against him—and evidence how stale! Yet there was no need—and in any case he had no wish to pass within range of the looking-glass on the table—there was no need to *open* the box. At sight of it Mr. Asprey had recalled instantly what it secreted; namely, the manuscript of a novel written by a friend. He had left it, long, long ago in Mr. Asprey's keeping in the hope of friendly criticism and appreciation; and three weeks afterwards he had been drowned at sea. Mr. Asprey's heart fell cold within him at remembering that he had let a full fortnight pass without even a glance at its first page; that he had, in fact, waited for his friend to be drowned before unsealing his MS. He had then, with increasing distaste and reluctance, read on to a breakfast 'scene' between three of the characters in the story one dismal morning in a dastardly December.

It described to perfection a virulent quarrel in which the unhappy human beings concerned had said everything they thought, or thought they thought, of human life and of one another. And in the course of this dispute a pot of liquid marmalade had been upset over an iniquitous love letter and the French tablecloth. Poe's raven's *Nevermore* was a cry of lyrical rapture by comparison with that marmalade. The whole chapter was one of the most vivid and caustic fragments of realism, or actualism, in fiction that Mr. Asprey had ever had the misfortune to share. And having heard of its author's tragic end, he had put the MS. away in this box, had entombed it there, with a relief beyond words. He had always fondly suspected that even naturalistic books may deeply affect their readers, and that, 'in parts', life is so real that it is wiser not to be too earnest about it. An overdose of honey, yes: but liquid marmalade?

Indeed, he himself, having finished this eighth chapter, had decided to read no more. And that no doubt had been grossly unfair. He acknowledged it; while his drowned fair-haired friend amid gently wavering sea-flowers out of his submarine ooze now quietly continued to watch him from beneath half-shut lids—an indefensible device, since his body had been recovered and interred inland! However that might be, his somnolent eyes *were* fixed on Mr. Asprey's, and Mr. Asprey continued serenely to meet them; with more serenity, indeed, than he had confronted Frances M. in the water-colour—all reservations over. He agreed, oh, yes! that there was money in the MS.; and, possibly, even a few years' fame. He agreed that his friend's widow would have enjoyed the money—though not perhaps the fame, since she had never inquired after her husband's masterpiece. None the less Conscience was astray this time, and he mustn't give in. With a little nervous nod at the mute drowned face, he put his candle down on the bed and opened his notebook again: 'At very first opportunity burn O.P.'s novel. And better not tell Mrs. P. (or the younger P.'s—not, at least, without a look at them first), when it is done; i.e. in this case *help* "the dead past".'

Thus poor Mr. Asprey proceeded on his way, tidying things up, placating as far as he was capable, his jinnee, his familiar—to the tune of at least ten small pages of illegible notes; until at length, the winter night very much older, he returned into the kitchen again. Poor gentleman, there was no need to remind himself that the small hours are an inept opportunity for the making of inventories, and that a house which one is about to leave for ever is not their happiest place. It entails far too hasty an elaboration; and sentimentalists and romanticists may be fully as conscientious as cynics. Was it not true that, whichever Dean Swift may have been, he bequeathed to a friend in his will his third best hat?

Mr. Asprey glanced at his watch. Gracious heaven, it was a quarter-past seven. Adieux may exhaust a large quantity of time. There was to be no more sleep for him now. In less than an hour the conveyance—to use as conciliatory a word for it as possible—would be calling for him, to take him away. Winter daybreak, indeed, was already thievishly groping on the glass behind the dark blue canvas blind and the rusted bars of the kitchen window. He shivered. But since he had attempted to lay so many ghosts on his rounds it was no wonder that this semi-subterranean chamber struck now so cold and so still. Foolishly, perhaps, he began listening again. This would never do. Besides, Mr. Asprey was tired of listening. He left his guttering stub of candle on the table, put his notebook down on the stove, and lit the gas under his antiquated tin coffee-pot. None of your new-fangled glass contrivances for Emily!

He turned about and glanced at his breakfast things. The shrouded loaf was on the table as he had left it: but the eggs were now mere eggs. They had lost all their looks. And where was his table-napkin? He recollected that even overnight he had noticed that something was missing, and nothing, of course, could be allowed to be missing on such an occasion as this; certainly not a napkin. As do the dinner-jacketed in the remotest oases of the Empire, Mr. Asprey felt he must keep up appearances. But where *was* the missing napkin? Upstairs in the sideboard, probably. Shunning what might be a fruitless journey, he hauled open one of the drawers in the kitchen dresser, just in case. And he did this so violently that it fell on to the floor at his feet, to be immediately followed by a small dark object that had apparently been wedged in and had long lain concealed behind it. And lo and behold, as he stooped to examine this nondescript object, with a most peculiar suggestion of the sea having yet again given up its dead, he recognized it.

It was a pocket-wallet, his: a wallet that had mysteriously vanished at least nine years ago. On the other hand it was a pocket-wallet that had vanished not quite so mysteriously as not to result in the dismissal with the usual month's notice of the reigning Emily-and-Ada dynasty at that time. It is impossible to discriminate in these matters. Under a common cloud they were, under a common cloud they went. And here, except that in this fuscous candle-gleam he couldn't tell at a glance whether the wallet now contained the treasure it had once contained—here was ample proof that he had been at least, say, *half* justified. Whether half or even wholly, however, should he have left the question where left it had been? He had never inquired into the fate of the two females concerned; he had merely left them to their future. To do so now would be a signally belated procedure, even if a practicable one. Well, then, that being so, should he or should he not examine the wallet? To be hesitating again—pestilent habit—at such a moment as this!

Elderly Mr. Asprey stood up, a little giddy after that few moments' concentration at such an angle; and there, standing immediately opposite to him, rounded, squat, in a large apron, with wisps of faded straw-coloured hair and a tallowish face, was none other than the very Emily in question. By no means a shy or demurring or furtive or embarrassed Emily either; she stood there looking at him, quietly, almost pensively, more than resignedly—as if perhaps she were waiting for morning orders. And what set her apart from all the other old friends he had been negotiating with up above was the fact—and it sharply interested him—that her apparition obstructed the view of what was immediately behind it. To this degree—and to this degree alone, no doubt—she was substantial; whereas what the mere jinnee of fevered memory produces for one's comfort or otherwise can very seldom be said to be that. And though Mr. Asprey had never succumbed to Materialism, this was a soothing discovery. He might need Emily later. Besides if she was not wholly ideal, pure fantasy, mere mind-stuff of the past, was there not less likelihood of sentimentality in this encounter? However that might be, here was this dumpy, anxious, tallow-faced Mrs. Grosvenor, quite as large as life, though obviously many years dead, looking up and back at him as if she had come to bid him a discreet god-speed, and was meanwhile asking for . . . what?

Mr. Asprey hesitated no longer. He stooped again, picked up the wallet, and there and then, without the least investigatory squeeze between finger and thumb, handed it over to the poor old soul. But why 'poor'? It is little short of idiotic to call the perfectly competent, whatever their 'state in life' may be, *poor*. 'And would you tell Ada?' Mr. Asprey smilingly added.

The one queer thing in this little interchange, was that as the wallet passed from Mr. Asprey's outstretched hand into Mrs. Grosvenor's—and she herself had hardly stretched out hers at all, not so much even as if she were suggesting a small gratuity or remembrance—it had ceased to be real. Unlike the marmalade in the MS., it had ceased even to be realistic. Or rather it had become Mrs. Grosvenor's real. And she had accepted it with so natural and benign a grace that it suggested nothing short of, 'Well, sir, I must say one good turn deserves another.' With which, almost as if she were on her way at once to keep the implied promise, her background reappeared. Mrs. Grosvenor was gone.

She had vanished so abruptly and irretrievably that a disastrous sense of dejection and loss and discomfort—cold, kitchen solitude, hushed mice, day-secreted cockroaches— had descended again like a veil of the dingiest crape upon Mr. Asprey's mind. Almost any interruption would be better than that.

And at once, and as if to order, an interruption came; and with it an overpowering, almost stifling, aroma of coffee. He turned about, but turned too late. Fountaining over in a miracle of iridescent bubbles stood his beautiful burnished coffee-pot, foaming like Etna with her billowing lava, its lid dancing—more fatefully than any receptacle James Watt had ever idly spied upon—above its froth. This, of course, in itself was a minor tragedy that could easily be remedied. The homely aroma was deliciously refreshing. But no expert of any museum of any country in the wide world would be able to decipher for him the sodden script which Mr. Asprey now gingerly attempted to rescue from this overwhelming cascade. It was a disaster. He had taken the utmost pains he could with his corrigenda, at what had seemed so brief a notice. There was no time now to begin again; and even if there were, any revised list, even if it were twice as long as the original, would prove, he knew, to be completely different. Indeed while, sad-eyed and breathless, having turned off the gas tap, Mr. Asprey continued to survey these sordid relics, he fancied he heard the sound of wheels. Wheels! Now! Surely, surely not!

Tragi-comedy by all means; but was there the least need to be ironical? His will hovered in an agony of hesitation; his eye discovered no help anywhere. There is no peace for the wicked. He hastened out of the kitchen as fast as—being so old and weary—he *could* hasten, without positively breaking into an undignified canter in his own house. And—oh, for a respite! Oh that his ears had misled him and there were even but one mere moment left! The instant he reached his front door he flung it open; and there and then, in astonishment, but not in dismay, Mr. Asprey all but fell down dead.

Another order of jinnee than his had also been busy in the small hours. The December sun was rising in the east. Out of the east came he. And above that sun, a strange celestiality had usurped the wide horizon: low luminous clouds, in tiers of dappling colour against the crystalline nought of space. Line upon line they lay, in horizontal glory, waiting. Where had Mr. Asprey seen before this description of beauty, marvellous and cold? So much for the far. And the near? From the tiniest of the leaves of the bushes at his elbow, from every two-edged blade of grass on the powdery path, to the remotest wood between his house and the calm sea, this private world of his was edged, skinned, furred with hoar-frost—hoar-frost of such a splendour that it seemed to be all the colours in earth and heaven, and eye and mind, blazing in a rapture of delight. Alas, Mr. Asprey!—how vulgar now and mean seemed all his efforts. He had ceased to breathe. It was as though his mortal being had become a mere organ of vision: '*Orgy in Silver* by Jinnium Naturæ'—a masterpiece! His very soul had begun pondering on the catalogue his nimble mind had presented him with. It *must* be merely Nature's; the blind enchantress's —it always had been. How else?

But before he could determine the question, though not the faintest motion of the air in this infinite waste of wasteless light was manifest, the door that he had left ajar behind him had, unperceived by Mr. Asprey, already begun to stir upon its hinges. There sounded a tiny click in the supreme silence. He turned his head. Too late, again!—the door was shut. And since between heaven and earth there followed not the remotest hint of an approaching *kloop-kloop* of hoof or muffled clatter of wheel, it looked as if he must be intended to walk. So he set out.

'WHAT DREAMS MAY COME'

*

Emmeline did not know what had happened to her, but at once supposed she had been asleep. Her body gently swaying and rocking in passive obedience to the almost soundless motion of the coach, she gazed out blankly into the window glass, cold and lustrous as a frozen pool in some outlandish and benighted valley. Vaguely reflected there, she scanned her pale and solemn face—'a nice tidy face', as a friend had once summarized it—wide brows, high-boned oval cheeks, a firm, quiet mouth, and these now darkly questing, searching, startled eyes. No answer to any question there. She turned towards the hunched-up shape of the driver seated in his glass cab; and continued awhile to survey the great hump of his shoulders and sprawling arms as if through a faint inward mist. He sat crouched together, his hands seemingly clasped on the steering wheel, his high-angled coat-collar helmeting a motionless head.

No wonder he was cold! A jagged hole gaped in his glass screen like a huge black star. This was no surprise, yet it filled her with perplexity. What was wrong? Surely the blazing light had dismally dimmed in the bulbs over her head? And how came it that she was *alone* now in the strange vacancy of the coach—a vacancy faint with fumes to which she herself could give no name? Fumes familiar enough, but not of petrol

379

—sweeter, more nebulous, dangerous, affrighting. Alone! Why, but an instant before, that faint image of herself had been smiling at another reflection beside it in this very glass! Her glance came to rest at last on the angle of the seat on which she was sitting, and there it stayed. What inconceivable, sudden and violent wrench could have twisted sidelong like that its heavy metal framework?

It must have been raining, too, while she slept—and slept through this! Raining heavily, if so; the dark stain on the thick grey fabric of the seat had soaked it through. She put out a tentative finger but refrained from touching it; then craned round her head in search of the conductor. The wreathing mist which dimmed her eyes obscured him too a little; but there he was, huddled and stooping forward on the backmost seat of all, elbows on knees, his face cupped in his hands, his eyes, it appeared, fixed on the floor. He might so have sat for ages, like a wax image immured in a museum, like Rodin's *Le Penseur*. Nevertheless of the immediate past the sight of him had recalled not a vestige.

Where had she come from? Where was she going to? Her mind was in a terrifying confusion. Apart from this deadly lethargy as of a profound and leaden slumber, she felt no pain, no discomfort even. The grey suede handbag beneath her clasped, gloved hands still lay in her lap. This she had instantly recognized. It was brand-new; it had been a gift. But when? From whom? Tears, it seemed, had begun forlornly rolling down her cheeks from out of her eyes. She opened the bag, fumbling hastily through its familiar contents, and found among them a scrap of paper—the remains of a broken envelope, scribbled over with what appeared to be a singularly eccentric handwriting.

This object, surely, she had *never* seen before, and yet in its dinginess, in its extreme familiarity, it seemed now far more actual than the rest. She stooped, gazing at it, then lifting it into the dingy light endeavoured in vain to read what it said.

The divisions between the words, the words themselves, arranged like those of an address, even the ridiculously prolonged loops of the letters—all this was clear enough, and yet she could decipher not a single syllable. A misery of misgiving swept over her; what dreadful fate had overtaken her? What next?

The cumbrous vehicle swayed stolidly on, its hidden engine throbbing hardly more audibly than if it were within her own breast. It was country here—bare, high, tangled trees to the left, skirting the road which glimmered on in front of her into the faint vague starlight; fields fading out obscurely on the right. She was lost—all memory gone. What next? And yet again those dark reflected panic-stricken eyes in the glass encountered her own; vividly, senselessly pleading for an answer.

Clutching in panic at the bar in front of her, she raised herself to her feet, turned, and stumbling unsteadily along from seat to seat, leaned close over the man, the conductor, where he sat by the yawning door. 'Where am I?' she called at him. 'Where are we going to? What is wrong?'

He did not stir. Only his eyes cold and blue as turquoises in his face, quietly lifted themselves and confronted her own, as if in some long-postponed and secret assignation. She thrust out her scrap of paper. He stared at it, but still said nothing. And she in turn continued to watch him, appalled yet not astonished.

'I want to stop,' she called at last. 'I want to get out. There was someone. . . .' It was as if the driver had himself been expecting the summons. The pace of the coach had instantly slackened, the wheels drew to a standstill.

'All I want to know is where we are—what has happened?' she called. 'But there,' her voice had softened as if she were addressing a child, 'I am sorry—sorry. I see you are ill. You, too, have suffered!' But *had* she spoken, or merely supposed that she had spoken? As if in unspeakable relief, his eyelids gently obscured again the bright blue eyes. He had resumed, it seemed, an inexhaustible reverie.

Her handbag clutched under her elbow, she descended from the coach. But before she could advance even a pace or two towards the driver, she heard the grinding of the gears; and the low, stertorous throbbing of the engine—so near and inward that it seemed a pulsation in her own body rather than a movement from the outer world—had become audible once more. He mustn't let *that* stop for long, she muttered cajolingly to herself; and smiled as if amused at the notion. And already, in utter silence now, the coach had vanished round the turn of the road.

It was odd that she should be less horrified, and even less confused now that she was alone, as completely alone, indeed, as a derelict ship at sea—a ship abandoned by her crew. She hesitated an instant, her eyes fixed on the constellation of the Great Bear. 'North'—an inward voice reminded her. At which, as if bidden, she at once began to walk in its direction, while she tried her utmost to restrain that voice from making any further comment, from asking any further questions.

Instead, she kept her inward eyes fixed on the reflected image of the face, of her own face, as she had seen it in the coach window glass. After all, she argued, so long as she kept *that* steadily in view she was sure of all that mattered most. She couldn't be utterly helpless, utterly astray, with her own inward eyes for guidance. You will always have *someone* with you, surely, so long as you have yourself, a self, she meant, still in some degree triumphant however dreadfully cowed at —well, at *this* kind of experience!

The death-still, leafless woods to her left hand had begun to thin a little, and presently high iron gates, shielded, it appeared, with coats of arms, revealed themselves, glistening faintly in the gloom. But not with dew. She had realized this instantly. They were coated with the winter night's first faint hoar-frost. She could detect the tiny, delicate crunch of the crystals even beneath her gloved fingers as she stood pondering, her hand clasping the iron bar. And at its cold, she had become suddenly as completely detached from her surroundings as a character who has escaped from a story.

A dense avenue of evergreen trees—ilex? holly? yew?—lay beyond the iron bars, a cave of impenetrable darkness. Still, this, too, was quite simple. She would go in. It seemed indeed that her dream in the coach from which she had been so rudely awakened had prepared her for this—and even for what might lie in wait.

The hinges made no sound at all as she pushed the gate open. It was as if they had been carefully oiled for her coming. There must be a well-kept and an old house beyond this, she thought to herself. Her foot fell silently on the gravel, owing, she supposed, to the moss beneath her shoe; since there were no weeds, and the turf fell gently away to its neatly trimmed edges under the dark prodigious branches. It occurred to her that ages, ages ago, she had once looked down into a place as full as this of stones. She could have counted them, although the place itself was past recollection; and very cold.

She fancied, too, she could discern wheel-marks; and even these dim rounded pebbles glimmered with the stars. So she went on, one urgent question on her lips. Apart from the diffused and dusky starshine, there was no light at all under the porch. To take breath she had paused again, her eyes on the iron bell-pull.

' "Emmeline",' she whispered to herself. ' "Emmeline", I must remember that!'

And then the door had swung gently open, as if into a softly glowing cavern of light, dazzling at first after the dark, like Ali Baba's. At which she secretly smiled to herself, for she had been on the very point of saying to the man who had so immediately answered her summons, *Sesame!* when but an instant before she had been steadily reminding herself to say, Emmeline.

Although not a single feature of it was perceptible, somewhere, *some*where, she had seen this dark lean meditative face before—these clothes even, the dove-grey waistcoat, the funereal morning coat. And, while she strove in vain to place this memory, she heard herself explaining, while he quietly listened—a face, however vigilant, that one could never suspect of eavesdropping!—that there had been an accident, a dreadful accident, and that the coach had gone on. 'You see, I'm really not sure, not at all sure, where I am; and—and what I am. Would, do you think, *this* be of any help?'

It was absurdly unconventional, she knew that well enough, talking to this butler-man as though he were her father confessor; but then what does one expect in such crises as these? She might have read of it all in a book.

The man had solemnly nodded over the scrap of paper—much too solemnly to be really convincing. He might have come out of one of the *Alices*! 'Yes, madam,' he said. And now she had been *definitely* reminded of something real—of an hotel, of a busy entrance hall, and of someone actually with her there whom she knew very well indeed, but who was out of sight, behind her.

'Yes, madam; this is right. This is the house. Have you any luggage?'

It seemed so preposterously meaningless a question that she had been quite unable to inquire *what* 'house'—how could it possibly be *the* house—before she had found herself following her guide's sinister coat-tails as he moved on swiftly and silently in front of her, as if on wheels, over the paving stones. Paving stones! Emmeline watched them closely, as she followed him, trying, like a child, with the utmost care to avoid stepping on the cracks between them. A strange house indeed, and yet again one not wholly unfamiliar. The hall, the succession of rooms, the corridors through which she followed on, were all of stone, nothing but frigid lifeless echoing stone. It was as if a pyramid had engulfed her. Her guide then must be Cheops. She knew *that* name well enough—Cheops. And yet the air, while thin and stifling, was laden with the delicious odour of flowers—of spring flowers, too, beneath which, none the less, hung and haunted the nameless fumes of the motor-coach.

'He seems to know *his* way,' she thought to herself, 'and soon. . . .' But the man had stopped, had opened a door, allowing her to pass on in front of him. 'This is the room,' he said. 'My master will be here directly.'

His 'master'! 'But I wanted . . .' she began; 'I shouldn't have come if. . . .' Her heart was throbbing now so thickly yet flutteringly—and faster far than any engine—that she could hardly utter the words. And then it was too late. The man had gone, had shut-to the door behind him. 'My paper! My paper!' she cried after him, in consternation.

But though she listened intently, not an echo of a footfall on the flagstones outside had answered her. She was alone again—abandoned. And this room also was of stone—floors, walls, and ceiling! and lit solely by two candles, flanking a wide chimneypiece—a chimneypiece far more closely resembling an altar stone than any she had ever seen before. And beyond it, that doorless vacancy—could that be another way out?

Out, and without an instant's delay, and before that other, the master, came, Emmeline *knew* she must get. But when, after listening again, she attempted to move, it was as if she were pushing her way through a deepening sea of heavy water, which threatened every instant to rise and engulf her. The faint light of the two candles scarcely blurred the gloom of the room beyond. But she could see there what appeared to be a bed, a bed which had no footboard and was draped with the dimly luminous whiteness of a vast sheet that hung in heavy vertical folds on either side of it down to the floor. And beneath it she knew there lay concealed what she dared not look at, and yet what also she knew with her whole soul now depended upon her. For what?

A dreadful terror seized her. She was shuddering from head

to foot, as if in an unearthly cold, as though every slender bone in her body were brittle as ice. Well, she must wait a moment. That might be all that was needed. Then she would perhaps have life and strength to face this fresh ordeal. Yet all that her *own* heart now thirsted for was an infinite peace and silence—a nothingness—wherein to be at rest.

Besides, the Master of the House, as the man had said, might be stealing in upon her at any moment; and what kind of personage would this be, if his own servant had a face so featureless, so cold, and so indifferent?

She turned instinctively towards the light of the candles. They stood as if in mute collusion on either side of a picture, of what appeared to be a portrait—obscure and sombre. Of a more intense blackness indeed even than the star in the broken window of the coach. Whose portrait? She drew near, and, as it seemed to her, these walls, of an unendurable frigidity, heightened, as if in a dream, as she did so; so that in order to see the picture fully she had to mount the stone that stood in front of this altar-like chimneypiece, with its fireless and yawning cavity.

With extreme stealth she gently pushed one of the candlesticks a little nearer and gazed up at the picture. And, as with a sheep that has scented the slaughter-house, a sudden paroxysm of misgiving swept over her mind; and then as swiftly, in an instant, was utterly gone. This, she realized, and as plainly as if the man himself had told her so—this must be the portrait of the Master of the House. And she mustn't stay too long to examine it because there was this other thing to do that she so much dreaded. Besides he himself would soon be here.

Nevertheless—and although the face in the portrait was as familiar to her as her own, and had been so even from her early childhood, it seemed that a complete lifetime's scrutiny could not exhaust its mysteries, its promises. She was terrified no longer, but consoled. Indeed it was against this very consolation that, utterly weak and weary, she knew she must strive. Yet still she gazed and hungered on, her glance roving insatiably over the arch of the bare bone above the brows, the fretted exquisite zigzag sutures, like brooks in a wilderness, traversing it north and south, and east and west. Once, however familiar, she could not have endured for long the fleshlessness of this countenance, the dark double vacancy where its nostrils should have been. But to say it 'grinned'—those even teeth set in that narrow arc in their regular sockets— why, even its owner, Emmeline almost smiled at the conviction, would have scoffed at such an insult!

And the vacant orbits gazed back at her, tonguelessly declaring their inexhaustible resources. If you peer down into a grave, it is nothing but a black shallow four-cornered cavity dug out of the passive surface of the earth. But these inscrutable hollows, surely, conveyed an assurance of the immortal mind that had had its dwelling behind them, even though all memory there (at which irony she again smiled softly to herself) appeared to have vanished.

'This, Emmeline,' she was repeating to herself, '*this*, Emmeline, is the Master of the House. This, Emmeline, is the Master of the House.' The childish syllables sounded on in consciousness like a tiny runlet of water threading a dried-up bed of pebbles.

So engrossed had she become that, although her inward attention had for many moments been aware of the inscription beneath the portrait, she had not yet attempted to read it. And now when she endeavoured to do so, the task proved all but as difficult as had been the deciphering of the scrap of paper which she had found in her bag. And yet again like a child she was compelled to spell out the letters. The candles bathed her eyelids with their beams as she stood there, almost *become* a child again. '*All hope abandon ye who enter here!*'

What? *What?* There must be some mistake! This couldn't be so—not after the serene silence of the blue-eyed conductor, his chin cupped in his hands. She leaned the candle closer till it guttered. No, no, not *'all'*. It was she herself who had made the mistake. It was not *'all* hope'; it was *'no* hope'. Why, then, if so, she promised the all-promising but unpromising sockets whence radiant eyes must once have shone, she need do nothing more than merely wait.

And at this, yet again the frenzied fear seized her that she must—that there was still that other ordeal to be faced, that on this depended her everlasting peace, and that in but another moment she would be too late. She seized one of the candlesticks and hastened into the further room, the stones beneath her feet seeming to withdraw themselves as she did so, so that this brief journey left her almost completely exhausted.

Come to the bed, she paused and listened, steadily surveying the shape that was now outlined there beneath her eyes. Sleeping Prince Charming, and she the Beauty! Again she smiled, but in a languid, self-pitying, wistful fashion, as if under the influence of a dense narcotic. 'What dreams may come . . .' she was whispering to herself. That was because of Yorick, of course. How cold these lips must be—*would* be! And did she really *want* to waken the sleeper? Even for his own sake?—when the Master of the House might. . . .

Hsst! What was that? *Had* a door opened? A chill breath as of jonquils and of that detestable, that odious other sweetness had rilled into the room. A sickening moment of agony followed. Why *try*? And then suddenly she had stooped and had lifted the uppermost corner of the sheet. . . .

And now it was not Emmeline who was the child, but this Naughty One whom she had found hiding under the sheet in the Master's house, pretending, shamming. Cold lips, indeed! Emmeline in all her dreams had never seen a face so youthful or more lovely. It was drawing nearer to her, too, the lips a little parted as if in astonished welcome of her kiss. . . .

And now she had really opened her eyes, to find herself gazing intently into the similitude of this very face, not a dream-face, but a real face, that of a fair young woman, her young head surmounted by a nurse's cap, her downcast gaze fixed on the hands of a watch which she held in her right hand, the fingers of the other hand gently but firmly encircling Emmeline's wrist. For a while Emmeline never so much as stirred. Hardly even her eyes moved except first to survey the strange spotless whiteness of the ceiling above her head, and then to slide tardily downwards and sideways until they rested on a glass-full of jonquils, that stood in the scintillating rays of a little electric lamp beside her bed. Theirs, then, was this delicious fragrance in the air. Motionless, their green stalks piercing the bright and vivid water. They refreshed her thirsty eyes—a miracle of beauty. For centuries, as it seemed—though it can but have been seconds, since the nurse herself was counting them—Emmeline then struggled to make her lips say but one word. They faltered, just like an infant's when it is about to cry, but at last the three syllables managed to escape from them.

'*Sesame!*' she whispered, solemnly. No less solemnly the young nurse had lifted her eyelids—eyes blue as the flower of the chicory.

'That's better!' she said. 'There's nothing to be afraid of. That's *all* you need say.'

'But I must,' began Emmeline, groping with hovering fingers over the bandage on her head, 'I must tell you just one thing. . . . I have been dreaming of you and—and. . . . Who was that?' she broke off to exclaim, as if in a momentary panic.

' 'Ssh now! You must keep very, very quiet,' said the nurse. 'That was only the doctor.'

'Ah, yes.' Emmeline tremblingly drew her hand down from her head, and in so doing caught the glimmer of the sapphires on her ring finger. The faintest frown of perplexity masking the clear pallor of her brow, she continued for a while steadily scrutinizing them. And then—as if a curtain had soundlessly lifted in the little theatre of her mind—recognition came.

'Look,' she said, holding the finger up to the nurse's inspection. 'Is—is he . . . *safe?*'

The blue eyes hadn't faltered. 'Waiting,' she replied.

'Well—in that case,' murmured an ever drowsier voice, 'I am . . .'—there was a long pause—'glad.'

And with that Emmeline had already escaped from actuality again, had fallen asleep; and not even the most vigilant and skilful of nurses can keep a chart of her patient's dreams.

THE VATS

*

Many years ago now—in that once upon a time which is the memory of the imagination rather than of the workaday mind, I went walking with a friend. Of what passed before we set out I have nothing but the vaguest recollection. All I remember is that it was early morning, that we were happy to be in one another's company, that there were bright green boughs overhead amongst which the birds floated and sang, and that the early dews still burned in their crystal in the sun.

We were taking our way almost at haphazard across country: there was now grass, now the faintly sparkling flinty dust of an English road, underfoot. With remarkably few humans to be seen, we trudged on, turning our eyes ever and again to glance laughingly, questioningly, or perplexedly at one another's, then slanting them once more on the blue-canopied countryside. It was spring, in the month of May, I think, and we were talking of Time.

We speculated on what it was, and where it went to, touched in furtive tones on the Fourth Dimension and exchanged 'the Magic Formula'. We wondered if pigs could see time as they see the wind, and wished we could recline awhile upon those bewitching banks where it grows wild. We confessed to each other how of late we had been pining in our secret hearts for just a brief spell of an *eternity* of it. Time wherein we could be and think and dream all that each busy, hugger-mugger, feverish, precipitate twenty-four hours would not allow us to be or to think or dream. Impracticable, infatuate desire! We desired to muse, to brood, to meditate, to embark (with a buoyant cargo) upon that quiet stream men call reverie. We had all but forgotten how even to sleep. We lay like Argus of nights with all our hundred eyes ajar.

There were books we should never now be able to read; speculations we should never be able to explore; riddles we should never so much as hear put, much less expounded. There were, above all, waking visions now past hoping for; long since shut away from us by the stream of the hasty moments—as they tick and silt and slide irrecoverably away. In the gay folly of that bright morning we could almost have vowed there were even other 'selves' awaiting us with whom no kind of precarious tryst we had ever made we had ever been faithful to. Perhaps they and we would be ready if only the world's mechanical clocks would cease their trivial moralisings.

And memories—surely they would come arrowing home in the first of the evening to haunts serene and unmolested, if only the weather and mood and season and housing we could offer were decently propitious. We had frittered away, squandered so many days, weeks, years—and had saved so little. Spendthrifts of the unborrowable, we had been living on our capital—a capital bringing in how meagre an 'interest'—and we were continually growing poorer. Once, when we were children, and in our own world, an hour had been as capacious as the blue bowl of the sky, and of as refreshing a milk. Now its successors haggardly snatched their way past our sluggard senses like thieves pursued.

Like an hour-glass that cannot tell the difference between its head and its heels; like a dial on a sunless day; like a timepiece wound-up—wound-up and bereft of its pendulum; so were we. Age, we had hideously learned, devours life as a river consumes flakes of the falling snow. Soon we should be beggars, with scarcely a month to our name; and none to give us alms.

I confess that at this crisis in our talk I caught an uncomfortable glimpse of the visionary stallions of my hearse—ink-black streaming manes and tails—positively galloping me off —wreaths, glass, corpse and all, to keep their dismal appointment with the grave: and even at that, abominably late.

Indeed, our minds had at length become so profoundly engaged in these pictures and forebodings as we paced on, that a complete aeon might have meanwhile swept over our heads. We had talked ourselves into a kind of oblivion. Nor had either of us given the least thought to our direction or destination. We had been following not even so much as our noses. And then suddenly, we 'came to'. Maybe it was the unwonted silence—a silence unbroken even by the harplike drone of noonday—that recalled us to ourselves. Maybe the air in these unfamiliar parts was of a crisper quality, or the mere effect of the strangeness around us had muttered in secret to our inward spirits. Whether or not, we both of us discovered at the same instant and as if at a signal, that without being aware of it, and while still our tongues were wagging on together on our old-fashioned theme, we had come into sight of the 'Vats'. We looked up, and lo!—they lay there in the middle distance, in cluster enormous under the cloudless sky: and here were we!

Imagine two age-scarred wolf-skinned humans of prehistoric days paddling along at shut of evening on some barbarous errand, and suddenly from a sweeping crest on Salisbury Plain descrying on the nearer horizon the awful monoliths of Stonehenge. An experience resembling that was ours this summer day.

We came at once to a standstill amid the far-flung stretches of the unknown plateau on which we had re-found ourselves, and with eyes fixed upon these astonishing objects, stood and stared. I have called them Vats. Vats they were not; but rather sunken Reservoirs; vast semi-spherical primeval Cisterns, of an area many times that of the bloated and swollen gasometers which float like huge flattened bubbles between earth and heaven under the sunlit clouds of the Thames. But no sun-beams dispread themselves here. They lay slumbering in a grave, crystal light, which lapped, deep as the Tuscarora Trough, above and around their prodigious stone plates, or slats, or slabs, or laminæ; their steep slopes washed by the rarefied atmosphere of their site, and in hue of a hoary green.

As we gazed at them like this from afar they seemed to be in number, as I remember, about nine, but they were by no means all of a size. For one or two of the rotundas were smaller in compass than the others, just as there may be big snails or mushrooms in a family, and little ones.

But any object on earth of a majesty or magnitude that recalls the pyramids is a formidable spectacle. And not a word passed between us, scarcely a glance, as with extreme caution and circumspection we approached—creeping human pace by pace—to view them nearer.

A fit of shivering came over me, I recollect, as thus advan-taged I scanned their enormous sides, shaggy with tufts of a monstrous moss and scarred with yard-wide circumambula-tions of lichen. Gigantic grasses stooped their fatted seedpods from the least rough ledge. They might be walls of ice, so cold their aspect; or of a matter discoverable only in an alien planet.

Not—though they were horrific to the *eye*—not that they were in themselves appalling to the soul. Far rather they seemed to be emblems of an ineffable peace; harmless as, centuries before Noah, were the playing leviathans in a then privy Pacific. And when one looked close on them it was to see myriads of animated infinitesimals in crevice and cranny, of a beauty, hue and symmetry past eye to seize. Indeed, there was a hint remotely human in the looks of these Vats. The likeness between them resembled that between generations of mankind, countless generations old. Contemplating them with the unparalleled equanimity their presence at last bestowed, one might almost have ventured to guess their names. And never have I seen sward or turf so smooth and virginally emerald as that which heaved itself against their brobding-nagian flanks.

My friend and I, naturally enough, were acutely conscious of our minuteness of stature as we stood side by side in this unrecorded solitude, and, out of our little round heads, peered up at them with our eyes. Obviously their muscous incrusta-tions and the families of weeds flourishing in their interstices were of an age to daunt the imagination. Their ancestry must have rooted itself here when the dinosaur and the tribes of the megatherium roamed earth's crust and the pterodactyl clashed through its twilight—thousands of centuries before the green acorn sprouted that was to afford little Cain in a fallen world his first leafy petticoats. I realized as if at a sigh why smiles the Sphinx; why the primary stars have blazed on in undiminish-ing midnight lustre during Man's brief history and his childish constellations have scarcely by a single inch of heaven changed in their apparent stations.

They wore that air of lively timelessness which decks the thorn, and haunts the half-woken senses with the odour of sweet-brier; yet they were grey with the everlasting, as are the beards of the patriarchs and the cindery craters of the Moon. Theirs was the semblance of having been lost, forgotten, aban-doned, like some foundered Nereid-haunted derelict of the first sailors, rotting in dream upon an undiscovered shore. They hunched their vast shapes out of the green beneath the sunless blue of space, and for untrodden leagues around them stretched like a paradisal savanna what we poor thronging clock-vexed men call Silence. Solitude.

In telling of these Vats it is difficult to convey in mere words even a fraction of their effect upon our minds. And not merely our minds. They called to some hidden being within us that, if not their coeval, was at least aware of their exquisite antiquity. Whether of archangelic or daemonic construction, clearly they had remained unvisited by mortal man for as many centuries at least as there are cherries in Damascus or beads in Tierra del Fuego. Sharers of this thought, we two dwarf visitors had whispered an instant or so together, face to face; and then were again mute.

Yes, we were of one mind about that. In the utmost depths of our imaginations it was clear to us that these supremely solitary objects, if not positively cast out of thought, had been abandoned.

But by whom? My friend and I had sometimes talked of the divine Abandoner; and also (if one can, and may, distinguish between mood and person, between the dream and the dreamer) of It. Here was the vacancy of His presence; just as one may be aware of a filament of His miracle in the smiling beauty that hovers above the swaying grasses of an indecipherable grave-stone.

Looking back on the heatless and rayless noonday of those Vats, I see, as I have said, the mere bodies of my friend and me, the upright bones of us, indescribably dwarfed by their antediluvian monstrosity. Yet within the lightless bellies of these sarcophagi were heaped up, we were utterly assured (though *how*, I know not) floods, beyond measure, of the waters for which our souls had pined. Waters, imaginably so clear as to be dense, as if of melted metal more translucent even than crystal; of such a tenuous purity that not even the moonlit branches of a dream would spell their reflex in them; so costly, so far beyond price, that this whole stony world's rubies and sapphires and amethysts of Mandalay and Guadalajara and Solikamsk, all the treasure-houses of Cambalech and the booty of King Tamburlane would suffice to purchase not one drop.

It is indeed the unseen, the imagined, the untold-of, the

fabulous, the forgotten that alone lies safe from mortal moth and rust; and these Vats—their very silence held us spellbound, as were the Isles before the Sirens sang.

But how, it may be asked. No sound? No spectral tread? No faintest summons? And not the minutest iota of a superscription? None. I sunk my very being into nothingness, so that I seemed to become but a shell receptive of the least of whispers. But the multitudinous life that was here was utterly silent. No sigh, no ripple, no pining chime of rilling drop within. Waters of life; but infinitely still.

I may seem to have used extravagant terms. My friend and I used none. We merely stood in dumb survey of these crusted, butt-like domes of stone, wherein slept *Elixir Vitae*, whose last echo had been the Choragium of the morning stars.

God knows there are potent explosives in these latter days. My friend and I had merely the nails upon our fingers, a penknife and a broken pair of scissors in our pockets. We might have scraped seven and seventy score growths of a Nebuchadnezzar's talons down to the quick, and yet have left all but unmarked and unscarred those mossed and monstrous laminæ. But we had tasted the untastable, and were refreshed in spirit at least a little more endurably than are the camel-riders of the Sahara dream-ridden by mirage.

We knew now and for ever that Time-pure *is*; that here—somewhere awaiting us and all forlorn mankind—lay hid the solace of our mortal longing; that doubtless the Seraph whose charge is the living waters will in the divine hour fetch down his iron key in his arms, and—well, Dives, rich man and crumb-waster that he was, pleaded out of the flames for but one drop of them. Neither my friend nor I was a Dives then, nor was ever likely to be. And now only I remain.

We were Children of Lazarus, ageing, footsore, dusty and athirst. We smiled openly and with an extraordinary gentle felicity at one another—his eyes and mine—as we turned away from the Vats.